Books by Laurie Alice Eakes

THE MIDWIVES

Lady in the Mist
Heart's Safe Passage

THE DAUGHTERS OF BAINBRIDGE HOUSE

A Necessary Deception
A Flight of Fancy

THE DAUGHTERS *of* BAINBRIDGE HOUSE, BOOK 2

A FLIGHT *of* FANCY

LAURIE ALICE EAKES

A Novel

Revell

a division of Baker Publishing Group
Grand Rapids, Michigan

Published by Revell
a division of Baker Publishing Group
P.O. Box 6287, Grand Rapids, MI 49516-6287
www.revellbooks.com

Printed in the United States of America

Library of Congress Cataloging-in-Publication Data
Eakes, Laurie Alice.
    A flight of fancy : a novel / Laurie Alice Eakes.
       p.   cm. — (The daughters of Bainbridge House ; bk. 2)
    ISBN 978-0-8007-3467-1 (pbk.)
    1. Young women—England—Fiction. 2. Families—England—Fiction.
3. Luddites—Fiction. 4. Riots—England—History—19th century—Fiction.
5. England—Social life and customs—19th century—Fiction. 6. Love stories.
7. Christian fiction. 8. Historical fiction. I. Title.
PS3605.A377F55 2012
813'.6—dc22   2012018539

Scripture quotations are from the King James Version of the Bible.

The internet addresses, email addresses, and phone numbers in this book are accurate
at the time of publication. They are provided as a resource. Baker Publishing Group
does not endorse them or vouch for their content or permanence.

Published in association with the Hartline Literary Agency, LLC.

12   13   14   15   16   17   18   7   6   5   4   3   2   1

To my husband,
who deserves to have every one
of my books dedicated to him,
but especially this one.

The Lord is nigh unto them that are of a broken heart; and saveth such as be of a contrite spirit.

Psalm 34:18

1

August 1812

Crowds swarmed around and jostled against the Whittaker carriage, slowing its progress from a trot to a crawl. Thick, oily smoke from torches penetrated the interior. Velvet curtains and cushions reeking of pitch felt ready to smother Miss Cassandra Bainbridge, who was already hot on this August night.

"I think we would be better off walking in the crowd than riding in here." She clutched her rose satin reticule in one hand and gripped her fiancé's arm with the other, as though ready to spring from the vehicle at any moment, which she was. "Perhaps we could take refuge in someone's drawing room until these bacchanalians go home."

Beside her, Lord Geoffrey Giles, Earl of Whittaker, chuckled and covered her hand with his. "Only you would use a word like *bacchanalian* to describe a crowd of drunken debauchery."

"It is the proper word for those who have celebrated too freely with drink." She glared at him down her long Bainbridge nose, though she could see little of his face in the gloom inside the carriage. "What should I call them?"

"The right word, of course." Whittaker shrugged, then moved

his hand from her gloved fingers to her nose, to the place where her mirror warned her a crease was already forming between her eyes.

Not that what her mirror said mattered much to Cassandra. That crease came from hours of honest study.

She gripped her reticule more tightly, as it held the efforts of her latest project—the design of a balloon—and leaned toward Whittaker's hand. Since the renewal of their engagement in June, the slightest brush of his fingertips came close to distracting her from thoughts of ballooning and Greek translations, and most definitely from wild, celebratory crowds worked to a fever pitch over Wellington finally winning a decisive battle against Napoleon's troops in Spain. If Whittaker moved his hand to her cheek—

A throng of young men slammed against the side of the carriage, tilting it onto two wheels. The horses whinnied and the coachman shouted. Cassandra screamed, a short burst of a cry, and Whittaker wrapped his arms around her, upsetting her elaborate coiffeur and sending her hair tumbling around her shoulders. Her hair and Whittaker's shoulder shielded her face against his coat lapel.

"Le's 'ave a ride," the drunken youths shouted in speech so slurred as to be scarcely comprehensible. "Don' be shelfish, arishtocrat."

"Lord Mayor's already stingy with t'luminations."

"More light. More light." The chant grew deafening.

Cassandra shivered now despite the heat. The men sounded angry, not celebratory. "They're angry over too few illuminations to celebrate the victory?"

"C'mon, Whittaker, open up." The rattle of the door handle accompanied the command. "We 'eard yer lady."

10

"They know your carriage." Cassandra raised her head. "But why would they assault you over too few lanterns and torches and such?"

"It's not me personally. The celebration seems to have gotten a bit rough, is all." Whittaker stroked her hair. "Hush now. The doors are locked, the coachman and footman are armed, and I have a brace of pistols here in the carriage."

Shots rang out at that moment, the crack of a pistol, the boom of a blunderbuss fired into the air. Whinnying again, the horses lurched forward. Without Whittaker's arms around her, Cassandra would have slid to the floor. She grasped his shoulder with one hand and twisted her fingers through her reticule strings with the other.

The jostling and demands ceased, though the crowd did not disperse.

"Perhaps we should have gone home with Christien and Lydia," Cassandra said, maintaining her hold on her fiancé and folded plans. "Christien is a trained soldier, after all."

"But this was the first opportunity we've had to be alone together for a week." Whittaker flashed her a smile, then kissed the crease between her brows. "This wedding is keeping you from me so much I think we should have eloped like your sister."

"They did not elope." Cassandra rubbed her head against Whittaker's shoulder. "They simply got married by special license. But this is my first marriage and Mama wants everything just so." She shuddered. "I hate every dress fitting and shopping excursion as much as I dislike this crowd."

Her ears strained for signs of the rough youths returning. She could distinguish nothing of them over the general din of the throng.

"Where will I wear all those gowns in Lancashire?" she added.

"You will need them when Parliament is in session and we are in town."

"But that's not until spring."

"With the Americans declaring war, it is going to be this autumn."

"But you promised." She started to pull away.

"I did not declare war." Whittaker tightened his hold and kissed her cheek.

"And all spring the Luddites kept you away."

"I did not go smashing up looms either." He kissed her lips.

She decided to stop arguing with him for the moment. She forgot about the rowdy revelers outside the carriage. This, after all, was why Cassandra had taken Whittaker's equipage instead of sharing one with her elder sister and her new husband—to be alone with her fiancé for a few minutes of tenderness, for some time of forgetting that Mama wanted her to buy one more fan or pair of gloves, that Whittaker's mama needed to introduce her to half a dozen more relatives, that Cassandra herself wanted to talk to her fellow aeronaut enthusiasts about her design. She simply wanted to remember this man whose glance, whose smile, whose touch, turned her heart to tallow. She needed moments like this like she needed nourishment for strength and air for breath.

Except he robbed her of breath.

Gasping, laughing, she drew back from his embrace—and began to cough. Nearby, something larger than torches blazed, the smoke heavy and sharp, thick inside the carriage. Around them, laughter and cheers had turned to bellows and protests, commands and threats.

Cold perspiration broke out beneath the sleeves of her pelisse and trickled down her spine. "Whittaker . . . what's wrong?"

"I cannot be certain." He leaned forward and lifted a corner of the window curtain. "A fire. That is obvious." He sounded calm.

Cassandra moved to the other side of the carriage so she could peek out the curtains too. Fire indeed. A carriage blazed in a side street. Men and women swirled around it, roaring incomprehensible but angry-sounding words, as though about to burn a body in effigy—or worse.

"This was a celebration for Salamanca," Cassandra protested. "Why the anger?"

"Too many people and too much spirits combined can cause trouble." He knelt before her and took her hands in his, letting the curtains fall over the window, leaving them in darkness—a private, sheltered cocoon despite the smoke. "We will be out of it soon and safely back to Bainbridge House."

"I was hoping we could go to the Chapter House. It's perfectly respectable, and I have my plans to give—"

"I am not taking you to a coffeehouse tonight. Your friends will have to wait for their balloon plans." Beneath the tumult around the carriage, Cassandra thought he muttered, "Forever."

They had enjoyed such a pleasant evening with Lydia and her husband, she did not want to argue with Whittaker. He did not like her ballooning enthusiasm, but she would change his mind once they were married. Then she would have more freedom to move about, not constantly under her mother's eye. Whittaker, not Father, would dictate her movements, and Whittaker was no dictator.

Unless he did intend to stop her from pursuing aeronautics.

She pursed her lips and squeezed his gloved fingers with her own, then released one of his hands to clutch at her precious reticule. "I think Lancashire will be perfect for ballooning once the harvest is in. All that flat land and the sea breezes."

"I think," Whittaker said, "you will have no time for balloons once we are wed. Mother intends to leave the running of the house to you. She wants to travel, visit friends, but with the trouble with the Luddites, she has been afraid to do so."

"But—" Cassandra released his other hand. "I know little of household management. I thought she would be there, help me. Geoffrey, when were you going to tell me this?"

"Mama was going to when she takes you to Gunter's tomorrow."

"Oh, that." Cassandra did not admit she had forgotten the engagement. "One of my ballooning friends—"

"Enough about balloons. It is as much a passing fancy as was your translation of Homer."

"Homer was not a passing fancy at all." Cassandra raised her chin. "I finished it. Then I saw the balloon and aeronautics—"

He silenced her with another kiss.

"What was that for?" she asked when she could catch her breath.

"To ensure I am no passing fancy."

"You know you are not." Because she had broken off their betrothal in the spring, she leaned forward this time and pressed her cheek to his, slipped her arms around his shoulders.

He drew her off the seat so they squeezed into the footwell between the two benches. The cacophony of the crowd, the oiliness of smoke, and the jostling of the carriage ceased to matter, may as well have ceased to exist. Always he won her attention this way, sending the world packing, even her scholarly interests and now her enthusiasm for flight. If he was in the same room, she could not bear to be more than inches from him and felt as though a piece of her were missing every time he left.

"I love you so much it scares me sometimes," she murmured into his ear.

A shudder ran through him. She understood why. He felt the same. Their profound attraction had gotten them reprimanded more than once, mostly by Cassandra's sister Lydia. But now seven endless days stood between them and their wedding. She wished it were seven hours, or, better yet, seven minutes.

They would reach Cavendish Square in little more than seven minutes unless more crowds stopped them. Chaperonage and separation. Annoying, dull dressmakers would crowd between them. Tea and cakes with his mother and embarrassing conversations with her own . . .

Cassandra dropped her reticule so she could bury her fingers into Whittaker's thick, dark hair. "Only a week," she whispered.

"Too long." He drew her closer.

Her hair tumbled over his hands. His cravat and her gown would be hopelessly crushed. Mama and her companion, Barbara, would lecture about proper conduct for a young lady. Her younger sister, Honore, would give her sly glances and giggle. Father would scowl at Whittaker and draw him aside for a "manly" conversation about propriety and dishonor. Cassandra did not care. Whittaker loved her despite her need to wear spectacles most of the time, despite her eccentric interest in Greek poets and flying machines. Surely once they were wed, he would understand she would die of boredom overseeing the household and stillroom and all those country housewife things, or, worse, being the London hostess for a member of the House of Lords. She accepted his proposal when he was plain Mr. Giles, a younger son. His becoming the earl due to an unfortunate accident to his elder brother did not change her. It certainly did not change his feelings for her. Alone in the carriage, every time they were alone, he made that amply clear. Marriage would be even better. So much—

The carriage rocked again. More drunken voices shouted through the panels. The door handles rattled.

Cassandra gasped. "Geoffrey."

"Stay down. I'll fetch my pistols." He started to rise. A strand of her hair caught on his cravat pin, halting him for a second.

And in that moment, the window glass shattered.

Cassandra screamed and ducked. Whittaker grabbed for his pistols. His feet tangled in Cassandra's skirt, and they fell against the door—the door at which several revelers tugged. With their combined weight pushing and the bacchanalians pulling, the latch gave way. The door burst open.

And Cassandra tumbled into the arms of a torchbearer.

2

The ruffian dropped his torch and ran. Blazing pitch landed against Cassandra's skirt. Delicate muslin smoked, flared. She screamed, leaped back, fanning the fire.

"Don't move!" Whittaker grabbed her arm to hold her fast with one hand, tore at the buttons of his coat with the other. No use. Too slow. Coat too tight to remove without help. No choice. He flung her to the street, thick with mud, droppings, nameless detritus. He rolled her in it, smothered the flames with his own body and then a horse blanket someone tossed over them.

And the screaming continued—women from the crowd and terrified horses. Crowd and horses bolted.

Cassandra lay in the street silent and still. Too silent. Too still. Gorge rising in his throat, his eyes burning from smoke and moisture, Whittaker knelt over her. He touched her cheek, so smooth beneath the soot of tar fire. Despite the heat of the night and the fire, the smoothness felt as cold as shaded marble. Too cold. Too—

"No! God, You would not do this to me." His voice emerged in a hoarse whisper yet sounded loud in the hush that had fallen over the remaining onlookers.

"God does what He wills," someone murmured a yard away.

Others hushed the woman.

Whittaker slid his fingers from Cassandra's cheek to her neck, that silky skin he forever thought of kissing. A pulse, faint, irregular, fluttered beneath his fingers. "Thank You, God." He glanced up and saw the footman and coachman glancing back from the carriage, now a hundred feet away, as they fought with the team lunging and flailing their hooves, making the vehicle rock. Even with the distance, their faces shone ashen in the carriage lamps.

"Samuel, come down here," he shouted to the footman. "We need to get her into the carriage and get her home. Then you can run for the apothecary."

"Best let 'er die," a man in the throng said. "She gonna wish she were dead if you bring her 'round."

Whittaker gritted his teeth against the cruel truth of the man's words. Charred shreds were all that remained of Cassandra's gown and pelisse. Little more of the blanket held together, along with the blackened remains of a man's coat. His coat. He did not recall finally removing it from his shoulders. He did not want to remove it from Cassandra's legs. He did not want to see what lay beneath. Blistered, reddened flesh, burns serious enough, painful enough for her to have lost consciousness. He prayed she would stay that way.

She did not. The moment he tried to lift her, her face contorted. She moaned and struggled in his arms.

"I am so very sorry, my dearest." The moisture in his eyes scalded, threatened to spill down his cheeks. He blinked to remove it. He tried to speak. A fist seemed to have lodged in his throat, robbing him of speech.

"Le' me 'elp you, milord." A wizened little man with breath reeking of spirits took hold of Cassandra's ankles. "She be better off iffin we carries 'er 'ome and not to t'carriage. 'Ow far?"

"I do not know." Whittaker glanced around, disoriented. The once overly bright and crowded street now appeared dark and deserted.

"It's a block or two, milord." The footman had leaped from the rocking carriage and reached their side. "Better to carry her with the nags so restless."

"Less jostling," the old man agreed. "Iffin she ain't too 'eavy for you."

Cassandra too heavy for him to carry a block or two? He could carry her a mile or two, a league or two, however far necessary to get her help.

"My dearest," he murmured. Aloud, he said, "I can carry her. Samuel—"

But the footman had slipped into the crowd, and the coachman had charged off with the horses and vehicle. Surely gone for help, not fleeing in fear.

"'Tweren't their fault, milord," the old man said. "'Tweren't nobody's fault."

"No."

Except his, for taking liberties he knew better than to allow, going home alone with her with the full intent of taking those liberties.

His gut wrenched and twisted as though between the blazing tongs of a blacksmith. He loved her so much, adored her so intensely, he could not stop himself from touching her. And with the marriage a week away, surely a few touches weren't unacceptable. And if they were, why would God punish her? Whittaker should be the one burned, groaning and gasping in agony as Cassandra was. She should have remained unconscious, oblivious to the pain.

"She should not be hurt at all, God," Whittaker cried aloud.

"God ain't got nothin' t' do with it," the old man said, puffing between each word.

Like her elder sister, Cassandra was not a small female, slender but tall and broad in shoulders and hips, blessed with womanly curves. The more they jostled her over the rough cobbles of the street, the more she cried out and struggled in their hold.

"We need a third man." Whittaker glanced around for someone to recruit. Other than a few shadows hidden in the darkness of areaway steps, no one showed himself. Torches had gone. Houses and shops lay in darkness. Only the remnants of the burned carriage lent illumination to the scene. No one wanted to be blamed for injuring a lady.

"Where is Cavendish Square?" Whittaker asked. "I do not know London."

He'd spent too much time in the wilds of the north of late, too much time away from Cassandra. If she died . . .

"This-a-way." The old man released Cassandra for a moment to gesture to the right.

She cried out and began to struggle. "It hurts. Make it stop. Make it stop." She was sobbing now, gulping wails that echoed off the tall, deserted houses.

Whittaker could not stop the moisture from forming in his eyes again, a few droplets from trickling down his cheeks. He saw little of the path before him, heard Cassandra's whimpers and wails in turn, felt the ripples of chills racing through her body, her fading efforts to push away from him.

"Go to sleep, my love," he said in a soothing tone, as though speaking to a child. "Sleep."

"She needs a good dose o' gin," the old man said. "Kills t' pain every time."

"I would never give her gin." Whittaker realized how haughty he sounded, condemning the man who stank of the spirit, and added more gently, "Her mother will have laudanum at hand."

"What's the difference?" The man shrugged, making Cassandra shriek in pain. "Gin or opium? Both'll kill ye."

So could burns. Gangrene. Sepsis. Amputation.

Cassandra without one or both of her legs?

Whittaker choked on something suspiciously like a sob. His hands shook. His body shook. He feared he might be sick like a drunkard. He stumbled along like a drunkard, gut churning, heart racing, conscience . . . Oh, his conscience stabbed him like a rapier in a duel he had lost. He'd come too close to dishonoring Cassandra, justifying it with the closeness of the wedding.

"Lord, please do not let her die, suffer, be scarred because I was careless," he mouthed to the night. "Dear God, please."

He feared his words reached no higher than the mostly blank chimney stacks of the houses. Then the buildings parted to reveal the round, grassy area of Cavendish Square and Number Sixteen close at hand, brightly lit in front, unlike most of its neighbors. Scarcely anyone was in town right now, but Lady Bainbridge wanted at least one of her daughters married in St. George's Hanover Square. Lydia had avoided that twice. Cassandra would not be so fortunate.

"If she had gotten herself married at her parish church in Devon," Whittaker cried aloud, "this would not have happened."

But other things may have. The countryside afforded so many opportunities for privacy.

His conscience twisted in his chest, and he gasped as though he were the injured party. Cassandra seemed to have lost consciousness again—a blessing.

They reached the bottom step of Bainbridge House. The door flew open and what seemed like a dozen people swarmed out of the opening—porter, housekeeper, butler, Lady Bainbridge, and her companion, Barbara Bainbridge. They knew. The apothecary was on his way. A bed had been prepared. Someone had sent for Lydia and Christien . . .

Information, instructions, and people swirled around Whittaker and Cassandra. Then suddenly she no longer lay in his arms and the little man had disappeared. Coatless, his shirt and waistcoat dotted with scorch marks and burn holes, Whittaker stood in the center of the entryway like a beggar seeking a favor from Lord Bainbridge. They had removed his lady from him, leaving him feeling as though the most precious part of his life had been wrenched away.

"Come into the library." Lord Bainbridge spoke from the depths of the hall behind the staircase. "Let the apothecary do his work while you tell me what happened."

Whittaker's ears heated beneath his hair, which was too neglected and shaggy for fashion. He intended to have it barbered before the wedding, though Cassandra loved to bury her fingers in it—

His whole face grew hot. The dimly lit entryway might disguise his blush. No matter. Bainbridge was no fool, and Whittaker had learned this past spring that he himself wasn't the best of liars. He had honesty too instilled in him to play the role requested of him. How Christien had kept up his work for a decade, Whittaker could not imagine.

"You will not help her standing there catching cold." Bainbridge strode toward the entryway. "And the womenfolk will never let you near her." In the candlelight now, the older man's face appeared gray, haggard, the lines on either side of his mouth more deeply etched than earlier that day. "We need a coherent explanation of what happened. The coachman arrived babbling like a lunatic."

"The unruly crowd." Whittaker's voice was hoarse and tight from the smoke he breathed and the tears he would not shed in front of another man. "May I have some tea, my lord?"

"Already ordered." Bainbridge gripped Whittaker's shoulder and steered him toward the library.

"I am all over mud and soot. I'll ruin the furniture."

"One of the maids is bringing down a sheet. We can place it—ah, here she is. That's a good child." Bainbridge took the sheet from the pale maid and continued into the library. With a firmness that suggested no one should open it without his permission, he closed the door, then flung the sheet over a chair. "Now sit before you fall. Are you in need of the apothecary?"

"No, my—Lord Bainbridge." Whittaker's right arm began to throb, blaze with the raw pain of a burn. He ignored it. It was nothing compared to Cassandra's hurts. "Sir, I must know . . . It looked so bad . . ."

"All in good time." Bainbridge pushed Whittaker into the chair. "Start from the beginning. Why did you not leave the party with Lydia and Christien?"

Whittaker met his future father-in-law's dark gaze without flinching—much. "We have not been alone together in weeks."

"No, and with good reason." Bainbridge smiled, but tightly. "The two of you seem to exercise little self-control when you are alone together."

"No, my lord." Whittaker wanted to close his eyes and avoid the hard, dark eyes with their gaze that probably set the new prime minister, Lord Liverpool, quaking in his Hessian boots.

"Have you dishonored my daughter?" Bainbridge inquired in a deceptively quiet voice. He still stood, his fists clenched against his thighs.

23

"No, my lord. That is—" Whittaker's face heated again, a flush that spread down his torso. "Not as I think you mean."

"I see." Bainbridge stalked across the room and stood at the curtained window without parting the draperies. He clasped his hands at the small of his back, and the knuckles gleamed white in the lamplight.

"We were ignoring the roughness of the crowd," Whittaker began. "Then someone threw something through one of the windows and Cassandra fell out of the door. She collided with one of the rioters with a torch, and he dropped it against her skirt."

"An accident?"

"What?" Whittaker shot to his feet. "What are you suggesting?"

"That you have enemies, Geoffrey Giles of Whittaker. You did not make friends in the north this past spring."

"But they would never attack Cassandra."

Yet they had pushed on the carriage, had mentioned his lady inside, had thrown the missile through the window, knowing she was there. And all the while, he thought of nothing but having his hands on her.

Bainbridge turned on him so swiftly Whittaker had to clench his own fists against his thighs to stop himself from jumping back. "I should call you out for this, if what you are implying is true. I should have called you out last spring when you and Cassandra were too close in this very room. But you are less than half my age and, I think, not skilled with weaponry."

"No—no, sir. I was the scholarly one of the family."

The reason Cassandra said she had first taken an interest in a younger son rather than his dashing older brother, John.

"I never thought I'd become the earl. Though," he added with a need to defend himself a bit, "the Luddite rebellion taught me a bit more about the use of firearms and blades. Still, I am not in your class."

"And if my daughter so much as loses a toe, let alone dies from her burns, I will be sorely tempted to forget that fact." Despite the harshness of his tone and words, Bainbridge's eyes glistened with unshed tears.

He was a harsh and often dictatorial father, but no one, not even the daughters who complained of his strict rules, doubted that he loved them, especially after the events of the spring.

Whittaker held the obsidian gaze. "It would be nothing less than I deserve, my lord. I fully confess that I am in the wrong."

Not that Cassandra had protested against his advances. On the contrary. She read things in Greek and Latin her family would never approve of. Probably things a Christian lady, let alone a single one, should not read at all. Things no lady should read, perhaps. She was curious, something he loved about her and despaired over at times.

If she died, he would have worse things over which to despair—guilt, the hole her absence would leave in his life . . .

He suddenly had the urge to run out of Bainbridge House and seek the quiet shelter of his house in Grosvenor Square, where he could send out his valet on a trumped-up errand to give himself the privacy to release his fear and pain in unmanly tears.

He swallowed down the impulse and held his ground. "I love Cassandra and will marry her no matter what happens, so long as she lives."

And she would live. Whittaker vowed to get on his knees and pray for a day, a week, however long it took to ensure Cassandra did not succumb to any of the ways people died from serious burns.

"The wedding," Bainbridge pronounced like a judge giving

a prisoner his sentence, "will of course be postponed yet again. You may leave now. We will keep you informed as to her condition and progress."

Whittaker stared at the older man. "I cannot stay to see what the apothecary says? I would like to see her."

"I expect she has been dosed with laudanum." Bainbridge's mouth twisted and his jutting chin grew more firm. "For the pain."

"Of course." Whittaker's arm began to pulse with pain too. It was one blister the size of the pad of his thumb, big enough it would leave a scar but nothing serious, nothing debilitating. But Cassandra's entire skirt . . .

Unable to hold back the lump rising in his throat, he swung toward the door. "Send someone for me with news, please."

"Of course." Bainbridge was as cold as the torched gown had been hot.

Whittaker hurried to the front door. He did not wait for the footman to open the portal but flung the latch up himself and raced into the night, to the cooler, if not fresher air of the city. Not until he reached his house in Grosvenor Square did he realize he had forgotten that his coachman and footman had vanished into the night. No matter. They would come home, and he could send them for news.

But when they arrived in the mews, shame-faced and contrite, having missed him at Bainbridge House, they did not have any information other than the apothecary calling in a physician. Other than them arguing between the use of ice or oil on the burns. Other than both agreeing Miss Bainbridge should be kept sedated, for she cried out in pain when awake.

26

The wedding was postponed too late to stop half a dozen of Whittaker's relatives from arriving in town. Whittaker sent his mother to Bainbridge House to make enquiries. Five days had passed since the celebrations that ended in riots and burnings in protest over too few illuminations to honor Wellington's victory. Five days since the torch caught Cassandra's skirt on fire. Five days since Whittaker's conversation with Lord Bainbridge in the library. No one had sent him word of any kind, and his own enquiries had gone unanswered. When he called at Cavendish Square, the porter told him the family was not at home, which was too absurd a lie for response. But surely they would allow Lady Whittaker into the house, if not the sickroom.

They did. An hour after departure, Mother returned home, her beautiful face blotchy, her eyes puffy as though she had been weeping.

"I am so sorry, my son." She pressed a damp cheek against Whittaker's. "Lady Bainbridge's companion and Miss Honore received me. Miss Honore gave me this." She handed him a folded but unsealed piece of foolscap. "And yes, I did read it." She dabbed at the corners of her eyes.

Whittaker sat down at his desk, the strength having left his bones. Mother would not be crying if Miss Honore had conveyed something good.

She hadn't. The note was short and scrawling, as though penned in a hurry.

Cass wants me to tell you, W, that she never wishes to see you again. HB.

3

"The last place I want to go right now," Cassandra declared from the chaise longue in the corner of her bedchamber, "is Lancashire."

The last place she wanted to go was anywhere near people, not two floors below her bedchamber, let alone be more than two hundred miles north of London and mere yards from Geoffrey Giles, Earl of Whittaker and his dear, dear mama.

"Just take me home to Devonshire," she continued.

"But we cannot." Mama perched on the stool to the dressing table, her thin white hands clasping and unclasping on the lap of her blue cambric dress. "We will not be there."

"His lordship is hiding us in Scotland until this new scandal dies down," Barbara Bainbridge added.

Cassandra's younger sister, Honore, flopped inelegantly onto the bed, sending her golden curls tumbling from their ribbons. "*Bainbridge* is going to become a byword for *scandal* if this continues. First Lydia takes up with a French spy—"

"Honore Elizabeth, that is enough," Mama scolded.

Cassandra shifted on the chaise, a welcome change after four weeks in bed, but nothing truly lent comfort to the legs with streaks and whirls of smooth or puckered flesh pulling taut on undamaged skin and muscle. That would improve with mild exercise, the physician had assured her. Some of the scars would even fade. Some would be there forever as a reminder of her folly. Of her sinful nature.

She leaned her head into the corner of the chaise and closed her eyes. "Take me to Scotland with you then."

Hundreds of miles from anyone she knew and from Geoffrey Giles, Lord Whittaker.

Honore sighed. "Because we have not been invited. This is for old people."

"Honore Elizabeth, that is not true and you know it." Mama's scold sounded as effective as a whack with a handkerchief.

The icy glare Barbara shot from behind Lady Bainbridge slammed into Cassandra as well as Honore. "Your mother has suffered enough distress over the past few months because of her daughters. Children are to be a delight, not a burden, and the three of you have caused nothing but trouble."

"Yes, Honore," Cassandra drawled like a bored young Corinthian at a gaming table, "we mustn't forget your *tendre* for—"

"Do not mention that name around me!" With a shriek, Honore bounded off the bed. "I made a fool of myself, I know, but it will not happen again, which is why I am going to Lancashire with you. I will meet respectable men in Lancashire, if any men at all."

"You may have Whittaker." Cassandra managed the pronouncement with a smile and a flippant tone in full force. "I expect he is honorable to a lady who isn't a freak."

"A freak?" Honore stared at Cassandra. "You're not a freak. I mean, it is not like anyone will see your . . . um . . . legs."

"A husband will." Cassandra swallowed the lump rising in

her throat and willed back the tears threatening to spill from her lashes.

"For shame, the two of you." Barbara's face turned as red as a costermonger's apples.

"It isn't proper talk for unmarried young ladies," Mama agreed.

If only Mama knew . . . But everyone protected Mama from the truth of her middle daughter's wantonness. Father knew. He'd almost called Whittaker out for nearly dishonoring Cassandra, as though it were all Whittaker's fault, as if she weren't complicit in, or even responsible for, their behavior the night of the fire. She had played the frightened maiden when she hadn't been frightened at all. She simply wanted to be held, reassured that he loved her in spite of her interest in ballooning. And once she had him enamored with his attraction to her, she would ask him not to forbid her ballooning once they were wed.

Oh, but she was a wicked, wicked girl. Surely her burns, the pain she had suffered these past four weeks—pain so intense she wanted to down the entire bottle of laudanum to deaden the agony forever—were God's punishment for her iniquities. She had been right in the spring—she and Whittaker should not be together.

The dam broke and tears spilled down her cheeks. "Leave me, everyone. I am not going to Whittaker Hall this week, this month, or this year. I will not r-risk seeing him." Her voice broke on a sob to go with the tears. She wanted to crawl under the chaise and hide until they all left her alone. "I am one and twenty now. I do not need your permission to go anywhere."

"But you need money," Honore sang out.

That was a bit of an inconvenience. If she did not do what

her parents wanted, they could cut off her pin money and she would have no means of support. No one would hire a governess or companion who needed a cane to hobble around.

"The sea air will do you good at Whittaker Hall," Mama said.

Neither she nor Honore nor Barbara seemed to notice Cassandra blowing her nose and mopping at her eyes. They had all seen her, the quiet, stoic one, weep too much in the past month to pay it any attention. It was the laudanum, the doctor said, and now the effects of taking less each day until she no longer depended on it to dull her pain. It wasn't working anyway now, not dampening the ache in her soul.

She could go to Lydia and Christien if they were home in Shropshire. But they were taking a delayed wedding journey to a location they had not disclosed, quite possibly so Cassandra could not run to them.

"Lady Whittaker wants you there," Mama persisted. "And the Hall will be easier for you to manage than that drafty castle in Sutherland your father wishes to visit for—what is it, Barbara? Pheasant shooting? As if England doesn't have enough pheasants of its own."

"I believe it is salmon fishing," Barbara said. "And England doesn't seem to have those."

"Ugh." Honore shuddered, then turned her huge, deep-blue eyes on Cassandra. "Whittaker isn't even home right now. His mama has assured us of that, and she has promised us some entertain—" She gulped.

"Dancing, perchance?" Cassandra asked dryly.

Honore charged across the room and hugged Cassandra gently, as though she were a woman-shaped egg and would break if handled with anything other than the utmost care. "Oh, Cassie, you'll dance beautifully again. The physician said so."

"Peculiar, that." Cassandra offered her sister a twisted, damp smile. "I could not dance before."

"Levity at a time like this." Barbara sniffed.

At least not going to Scotland would keep Cassandra from her mother's companion. How Lydia had managed to live with their increasingly bitter spinster cousin for seven years went beyond Cassandra's ken.

She could become just as dried up, as sharp-tongued and disapproving, now that she would never marry. Though her scholarly interests might save her. Especially her interest in flight. If she could fly, float through the heavens like one of the clouds, forget the world below . . . If she could do something important like create a balloon that could be steered, make a living giving expeditions, as did Sophie Blanchard in France . . .

Or perhaps she could learn a new language. Study Hebrew and translate the Old Testament of the Bible just for the entertainment of it. Or Sanskrit. Or Arabic. Yes, Arabic was closer.

The laudanum was talking in her head again, fogging her brain without dulling the pain.

"May I please have some coffee?" Cassandra asked. "I can make a better decision then."

"There is no decision to be made." Barbara gave out another one of her sniffs.

"You may have some coffee," Mama said. "Honore, will you—that's a good girl. We all head north day after tomorrow."

Honore pulled the bell rope by the bed, two quick tugs, a pause, and two more—a signal Cassandra had devised so she could get what she needed quickly while completely bedridden the first weeks after her accident.

At least everyone called it an accident. Cassandra called it an act of God, a divine spanking.

"Barbara shall go arrange the packing." Mama rose, one hand braced on the dressing table, suggesting she felt weak that day despite the sunshine and mild temperatures. Not consumption, the physicians assured the family, but she never had recovered from a lung fever the previous winter. Perhaps Barbara was right and the antics of her daughters drained Mama of her vitality.

One more whack to Cassandra's conscience.

She glared at her sister, wanting Honore to go away too. But as Mama, holding onto Barbara's arm, departed from the bedchamber, Honore sank onto the vacated stool and began to remove pins from her hair and scatter them about the table and floor.

"I shall keep you company."

"I do not want any company."

"Which is precisely why you shall have it. We will strategize our time at Whittaker Hall."

"I'd prefer to strategize a way of eluding time at Whittaker Hall." Cassandra shifted to a sitting position, her slippered feet on the floor. Although her right ankle bore a burn that would surely leave a scar forever, her feet had been spared. She would not be permanently lame. She needed to walk, and walking in the city was impossible, if not outright unpleasant, what with a few people being in town and giving her pitying looks. Lancashire would give her more than enough space for walking, especially with the hunting season not opening until after Christmas. At least, not fox hunting. And all that open land for ballooning.

All that house belonging to her former fiancé.

"How do you know he will not be there?" she asked Honore.

"His mother told me." Honore picked up a silver-backed brush and began to draw it through her shimmering hair. "She said he charged into the house a week after the fire, told a manservant to pack his things, then departed in the traveling coach. It returned several days later, but he did not."

Cassandra's heart stopped. "Are you saying they do not know where he is?"

"They know he is well." Honore leaned forward to brush the underside of her hair. It fell to the carpet in a waterfall of golden silk. "They receive messages from him, but he says nothing of his whereabouts."

"Hiding, the coward."

Anger mixed with envy clutched at Cassandra's belly. He, as a man of independent means, even though those means were limited due to his father's and brother's excesses, could hide from the scandal they had caused. She, however, had to go stay at Whittaker Hall, where his mother seemed prepared to pretend all was well, that all Cassandra needed to do was recover fully and the wedding would take place. Perhaps she should walk—hobble—into the Hall and pull up her skirt to show them her legs. No one would want her for his wife then, after he fainted, as Mama had the first time she saw Cassandra's burns. Even Lydia, strong and competent, had been sick after seeing the blisters. She too easily could have looked like that—or, worse, both Lydia and Honore—after the fire they had barely escaped in June.

But Honore was a spoiled child taken in by a wrong yet charming man. Cassandra should have known better. Cassandra did know better. She had lectured Lydia about faith in God. Now she knew what happened to hypocrites.

"I cannot face them, Hon." Cassandra started to grab her cane and rise, but a knock sounded on the door, and she flopped back into the corner of the chaise.

Honore bounded to her dainty feet and scampered across

the room with a fluid grace that sent her flounced skirt floating around her ankles and her hair swirling around her shoulders. She was so lovely no one at Whittaker Hall would notice Cassandra. She could take to wearing her spectacles all the time, those octagons of magnifying glass that distorted her eyes into something grotesque. Lady Whittaker would be writing to her son to find a bride who was not quite so flawed.

At the door, Honore spoke to someone, then returned with a tray. Fragrant steam wafted from the silver coffeepot and milk pitcher. Cups and a bowl of freshly grated sugar nestled around a plate of coconut macaroons. Cook, a stolid Englishwoman who had arrived after two French chefs had left their post without notice, tried to fatten Cassandra up at every opportunity. Food cured everything from broken hearts to broken bones, according to her.

"She sent five macaroons," Honore announced. "I believe I am to have two."

"We will not be having any if you do not keep your hair out of them. Why did you take it down?"

"It was giving me a headache pinned up and we are staying in tonight, so I see no reason for suffering. Cream and sugar? I shall do the honors." She giggled. "Mama says I need practice. I dropped a lump of sugar in some duchess's lap the other day."

"Better than spilling the tea in it." Cassandra grasped the cane propped against the arm of the chaise and hoisted herself to her feet. With care, noting from the corner of her eye how Honore avoided looking at her, Cassandra crossed the room to her desk, dragging her right leg behind her. Putting her full weight on it still caused her to grit her teeth to stop herself from crying out.

"Will you bring my coffee to me here?" She lowered herself onto the chair. And stared at the blank parquetry surface before her. She should have designs spread out there, not a coffee cup and plate of biscuits. But her balloon design had disappeared. She had dropped her reticule the night of the fire and lost her plans. Now she must re-create them.

"I cannot work at Whittaker Hall," she protested aloud. "Lady Whittaker expects me to embroider and knit or do something useful and boring like that."

"Or read to her with that lovely voice of yours." Honore set the coffee before Cassandra, then remained beside her chair, one hand on her elder sister's shoulder. "But I think you can work on your silly Greeks or balloons or whatever you like. I've been thinking about it."

Cassandra glanced up sharply. "You have?"

"I do think of things besides ball gowns and new parasols, you know." Honore's lower lip puffed out. "Especially when there are not any balls to attend or sunshine to keep away."

They both glanced out at the bright September day and laughed.

"All right, no one to go out walking with," Honore amended.

"You do not have any gentlemen callers? I cannot believe that." Cassandra picked up her coffee cup but looked at her sister rather than drinking.

Honore shook her head, a strand of her hair narrowly missing Cassandra's coffee. "No gentlemen. I've gone off gentlemen for now. After thinking I was in love with a scoundrel. I mean, I did not think he was a scoundrel. I thought I was in love. But it was just his looks, and he was not like the country lads I'd met before and thus fascinating."

"So you want to go to Lancashire to find a country lad after all?"

Honore grimaced. "I want to go to Lancashire to avoid Scotland, where it is truly cold this time of year, and . . . well, I am going to write a novel."

Cassandra stifled her laugh of disbelief behind a too large gulp of coffee, followed by a coughing fit.

Honore flounced away. "I know you are laughing at me, but I mean it quite seriously. I am going to write something far better than—than Miss Burney or—or Mrs. Radcliffe."

"Or Henry Fielding?" Cassandra asked dryly.

Honore frowned. "Who is Henry Fielding?"

"Never you mind. How do you propose to avoid Lady Whittaker to write?"

"The same way you will avoid her—I confided to Lady Whittaker that you will need a ground-floor room because steps are just too much for you, so she is converting the parlor right off of the orangery for your exclusive use."

"Indeed?" A flicker of excitement surged through Cassandra's veins.

Orangeries had doors to the outside. She could slip outside whenever she liked, walk with others not knowing. And perhaps even find a way to get her balloon up to Lancashire.

That would be difficult without funds. Of course, Cassandra had spent nothing of her quarterly pin money, and Father being Father, he would ensure they were given extra so as not to shame him with the impression that he was either too poor or too miserly to be generous with his daughters while they visited at the home of one daughter's fiancé.

Former fiancé. She had called off the wedding permanently, even if no one else acknowledged the fact. Whittaker knew it or he would not have made himself least in sight. So she could write to her ballooning friends and ask if they could manage to get the machine to Lancashire. She was part owner, after all, and hadn't yet been able to fly in it . . .

"You can pretend to rest all you like and have easy access to the library," Honore prattled on. "And I will keep you company and write my book. And I'll never tell Lady Whittaker that you are slipping out at night."

"You do not know if I will."

Honore sniffed most delicately.

"All right, Honore, I'll go without a struggle, but if you do not help me, I'll—I'll—"

"Yes?" Honore shot Cassandra a mischievous grin from across the room.

"I'll get her to matchmake you with Whittaker."

Honore shrieked, threw her hands over her head, and fled from the room.

Cassandra turned to her balloon plans. She must get them to Mr. Kent and Mr. Sorrells at once so they could begin the work needed for modifications to the current design they had worked on all summer. As gentlemen of independent means, surely they would help. Otherwise, she must start from the beginning, and that would take too long. She would never manage to fly across the Irish Sea or travel from the Dale to York by air if she did not have her balloon built to her specifications. If she could make one or the other journey work, others might wish to travel that way, soaring through the heavens . . .

When Barbara and two housemaids entered an hour later, Cassandra ignored their presence, Barbara barking out orders, the maids mutely obeying, armoire doors and drawers slamming, trunk lids snapping down. Cassandra calculated and drew and pretended none of them were there. She had gotten good at pretending no one was there during the worst of her illness. If she so much as opened her eyes, people asked about her pain, which immediately brought her focus to it. She kept it at bay by thinking of balloon dimensions and a way to keep the silk of the inflatable from leaking air, finding something that would not catch fire.

She was going to have the best balloon in England, win a race, and prove that females could be more than wives—they could be scholars and inventors too. She could avoid Lady Whittaker's machinations to maintain the engagement. Renew it, rather. Yes, renew. Cassandra had made it clear to Whittaker that this time was permanent. He could not stride into her life and take her into his arms, declaring undying devotion as he had in June, and have her melt like gold in a crucible. If she managed things well enough, she might persuade Father to give her dowry into her care eventually, or at least give her an allowance. As a male, he would surely understand why no man would want her now. She wasn't a beauty, terribly charming, or an heiress.

If only her insides did not feel so hollow—hollow yet not desirous of food. Like the pain, like her love for Geoffrey Giles, Earl of Whittaker, like the annoying interruptions of packing and preparing for the trip north, the hollowness would pass.

So would the seemingly endless journey in an entourage of carriages and outriders and taken in slow stages for Mama's sake. Wearing the spectacles Mama despised, Cassandra stuck her nose in a book no one would want her to read aloud to them along the way, and avoided conversation as much as possible. When they reached the Carlisle Inn, where Cassandra and Honore's roads would diverge from the rest of the family the next morning, their brother Beau joined them from where he had been visiting friends. A year younger than Cassandra, he bore the same golden good looks as Honore, but in a well set-up, manly way even at twenty. He was wearing the sober garb of a blue coat and fawn buckskin breeches, not something fanciful and dandyish as too many young men sported even in the country. He swept Honore into an enthusiastic embrace but touched the ends of his fingertips to Cassandra's proffered hands.

"Your face is still as pretty as ever, Sis," he greeted her.

"You are too kind to say so." Cassandra wrinkled her nose at him. "And I am not contagious like the chicken pox, you know."

"Well . . . uh . . . no." Beau reddened. "I did not want to . . . uh . . . hurt you or anything."

"You're such a ninnyhammer," Honore cried. "You'll hurt her feelings if you do not hug her too."

"No, he will not." Cassandra retreated to the inn bedchamber she would share with Honore and Barbara for the night.

But of course he had hurt her feelings. Beau had been her childhood friend. Close to her in age, he had been happy to catch frogs and caterpillars with her to examine them under a magnifying lens. Bugs and other creeping and crawling insects never frightened Cassandra off as they did Lydia or Honore. If Beau would come to Whittaker Hall instead of fishing with Father in Scotland, they could have a grand time of it. He would go up in a balloon with her without a fuss.

At least, she might be able to persuade him to after a while.

She laughed at herself as she removed her pelisse and began to repair some travel damage to her hair before a scrap of dim mirror affixed to the wall. She hadn't even been up in a balloon yet. She might discover that she hated being a thousand feet off the ground. But she doubted it. In the basket, she would be weightless, or feel like it. She would be moving without her cane or pain or—

A rap on the outer door of the Bainbridge rooms in the inn yanked her from her floating imagination, and she jammed a pin too hard into her scalp. Likely the new arrival was a servant with tea or some bit of luggage Mama had left in the carriage, or with word of a lame horse or loose wheel.

"Cassandra?" Honore's voice rang through the door. "Are you—"

The door flew open hard enough to smack against the wall, and Whittaker strode across the space between them and reached out his arms. "I did not think they could persuade you to come."

4

Cassandra stared at Whittaker, her mouth too dry for her tongue to form words, her limbs too stiff for movement. Not that she could go anywhere. The room was a trap. Whittaker stood between her and the door. Honore stood in the doorway. A host of people ranged behind her, and the window offered a twenty-foot drop to a cobblestone yard.

The yard sounded like a good prospect. Broken, her legs would not look much worse. But then she had thought her broken heart could not feel much worse either.

She found her voice. "You lied to me." No expression, just a flat statement. "I was told you weren't going to be at Whittaker Hall."

"I am not. I am staying in Manchester to learn more of spinning machines and things until . . . until . . ." He took a step closer to her, his eyes nearly black, not deep brown in the dimly lit room—dark and bleak. "Cassandra," he said in a murmur meant for her ears alone, "did you think I could stay away from you?"

She gripped the edge of the stand that served as a dressing table and set her jaw. "You have managed to for a month. You've managed to stay away from your family for a month. I should not think I would be any more difficult to dismiss. Probably less, considering I am now—" She could not bring herself to say it, admit aloud that she was now grotesque and lame. She looked down at the cane propped against the stand.

His gaze followed hers. Behind him, the others watched in silence as though expecting a climactic ending to some Elizabethan drama.

"I gave my pledge to you, Cassandra," Whittaker began. "Love is not love which alters when it alteration finds."

The Shakespeare quote broke her paralysis. She picked up the nearest object at hand and threw it. Unfortunately, it was her cane. Unfortunately, she never was good at throwing anything in a straight line. Unfortunately, the stick with its silver handle sailed right past Whittaker and smacked against the door frame a fraction of an inch from Honore's head. She shrieked and jumped back, bumping into Beau, who dropped a cup of coffee that splattered Barbara's gown. She began to scold.

In the tumult, Cassandra swung around, lunged for the bed and its sturdy posts, and wrapped her arms around one as though someone were trying to haul her away. "Out." She whispered the word, certain no one could hear above the hubbub.

Whittaker ignored her. He took advantage of the chaos in the parlor to draw closer to her, close enough to rest one hand on her shoulder and the other against her cheek. She caught his scent of outdoor freshness like an herb garden after a light rain—thyme, rosemary, perhaps a hint of mint. Her nostrils flared, wanting more of that familiar aroma. Her insides frothed up like syllabub. She closed her eyes and willed herself not to turn her head and kiss his palm, not to look at him up close and in daylight. Not much light came through the drawn curtain, but it was bright enough with him facing the window for her to pick out every detail of his face—the hint of gold in his brown eyes, the hint of a dimple in his right cheek as he smiled, the miniscule gap between his front teeth. Details that haunted her dreams.

She dug her nails into the bedpost to stop herself from brushing an errant wave of hair off his brow, bit her tongue to stop herself from telling him he needed to have his hair cut. She sought for the courage to drive him away with the repulsiveness of her scars. She could lift up her skirt and unfasten a garter to let her stocking fall, and he would run as fast as he had the night of the accident when everyone thought she would die. But she could not even glance at the marks herself, had a maid rub the salves from the physicians into them so she did not have to see what had happened to her once smooth, white skin.

She turned her face away from Whittaker, drew back from his touch. "God doesn't want us together. He—we—I am going to your home because your mother invited me and I was promised you would not be there. It means nothing. The engagement is over."

"Because you were injured? Don't be silly, my dear. I promised to stay with you forever—"

"Not before God, you did not. You are under no obligation. My father will not sue you for breach of promise. I will not declare you are not a gentleman. Everyone will understand."

"Everyone except for me." He moved so he could look into her face. "Cassandra, do you not understand—"

"Yes, I understand." She enunciated each word through clenched teeth. "I understand that you are a gentleman and your word is your word regardless of what you'll have for a wife."

"Cassandra." Father had come into the parlor. "This is most improper for Whittaker to be in your chamber."

"I did not invite him in here. Honore let him in, and we are

44

well chaperoned." She gestured toward her sister, Beau, and Barbara. Mama was somewhere in the parlor.

Whittaker turned toward Father, though he held his ground. "I needed to talk to her and she has been refusing me for a month."

"No," Father said, nudging Honore out of the doorway, "I have had you refused."

Whittaker paled. "But sir, why?"

"Cassandra is correct." Father stepped into the bedchamber and out of the doorway, leaving a clear path to the parlor door and the exit of the inn. "The fire that scarred my daughter was your fault, and I'd rather she not wed you."

"I never said—" Cassandra broke off. She could not contradict her father in front of Whittaker, or at all. Disobeying God had brought bad enough consequences, and He was merciful.

"You are allowing her to come to my home, though." Whittaker sounded and looked a bit like a small boy confused about a promised treat being denied him despite his good behavior. "Surely you knew I might be there."

"I knew no such thing. I was assured you would not be." Father glanced toward Beau. "Lady Bainbridge, Lady Whittaker, and I have other interests, and Cassandra needed a healthful place to fully recover. Whittaker Hall is precisely that place." Father crossed his arms over his chest. "Now go about the business I know you have."

Whittaker jerked back as though he had been caught stealing trinkets from the batter for a Christmas pudding. "Sir, I'd rather not—" He stopped at a hard glance from Father.

Cassandra stared from Father to Whittaker and back again. What business could Whittaker have that Father would know about? Other than the usual business attached to an estate and the mills Whittaker had inherited from an uncle—horror of horrors, an uncle in trade when one was the earl of Whittaker. She had liked the title Mr. Geoffrey Giles better until the Luddite disturbances in the past year. Those had made her glad Whittaker was the earl, removed from the danger other than ensuring his own looms remained safe—though they hadn't.

Whittaker did not look in danger at that moment either, except for the danger of being embarrassed by Father in front of her and the others once again encircling the doorway, Mama included this time. Whittaker was, after all, no more than three and twenty, a younger son never intended for the role his brother's premature death had landed upon his shoulders. He looked as though more than the mantle of title, rank, and those responsibilities lay over him. He was too well-bred for his shoulders to slump, but they twitched as though beneath a lash, and his chin lacked its usual firm line.

"I had to know for myself," he murmured. "If this is what Cassandra wants, I will be on my way."

"It is," Cassandra said.

She managed to look him straight in the eye as she said it. She managed to give him a half-smile. She did not manage a curtsy, nor to stop a single tear from slipping out of the corner of her eye.

Whittaker seemed not to notice the tear. He focused his attention on Father. "Sir—"

"Whether she wants it or not," Father said, "I will not have you wed her for her dowry, and if you go against my will, I will withhold it as I did with Lydia when she married Charles Gale."

Everyone except for Beau gasped.

Whittaker glared at Father. "So you have broken your word to me?"

"For my daughter's sake, yes."

"I do not see how—" Honore began.

Mama pressed a finger to her lips to silence her youngest daughter.

Cassandra thought she would be sick. Guilt and shame already shredded her heart. She suffered because of her behavior but had engaged in the behavior because she believed this man loved her. Yet there he stood quibbling with Father over his word and dowry agreements. She may as well be a haunch of venison at the butcher's stall.

She turned away from the men, away from the man she thought loved her despite her penchant for Greek poets and aeronautics, her spectacles and her tendency to forget to pin up her hair properly. She believed she served him well in letting him go, not making him obligated to wed a disfigured bride. And he argued with Father about her seven-thousand-pound dowry, a respectable but not exceptional sum. The damage to his mills must have been worse than he told her. Or Whittaker Hall wasn't prospering. Or her dowry had been the attraction all along for a younger son, as he was when they met. The physical attraction and dowry outweighed her shortcomings—shortcomings he had been trying to change for months.

She was going to be sick, but not in front of Whittaker. She watched him in the tiny mirror over the dressing table. He glanced her way, appeared as though he might take a step in her direction, then spun on his heel and strode from the room, pausing only long enough for the others to step aside and to give the ladies a brief, slight bow and Beau a nod. Then the outer door closed with an exaggeratedly soft click, and he was gone.

"Well then." Cassandra forced a broad smile across her lips. "Do you all have any more surprises in store for me?"

"He wanted to see you again," Honore burst out. "He asked

me to let him know our plans, if you were going to go up to Whittaker Hall, so I wrote to him."

"You wrote a gentleman?" Mama pressed one hand to her bosom. "Honore, did I not raise you better than that?"

"He is"—Honore glanced around—"was nearly family. I see nothing improper . . ." She sighed. "I thought I was helping."

"We do not need your interference, Honore," Father said. "Cassandra needs time to heal and regain her strength, not be importuned by a money-grubbing, immor—"

Father could not condemn Whittaker as being immoral without condemning his daughter too. Cassandra knew she deserved the accusation. She had gone against far too much of what she had been taught.

"Where is our supper?" Father demanded.

Barbara hastened to hunt down the inn servants and food. Mama retreated to a chair by the fire while Beau fetched a shawl, a book, and her needlework basket for her. Honore stood in the bedchamber doorway with her lower lip protruding and her eyes downcast.

Father turned to Cassandra. "Until the accident, I did not realize how easily you could be led into temptation, nor that Whittaker would do so. Apparently a few things were kept from me in the past."

"Father, he did not lead me—"

"Therefore, I think under the circumstances," he plunged on as though she hadn't spoken, "you are better off finding someone of a less . . . volatile temperament for your husband."

"No man," Cassandra said in a voice whose steadiness surprised even her, "of any temperament will want me now. I would prefer to concentrate on my studies and perhaps find a genteel teaching post one day."

"None of my daughters will earn their living." Father's dark whiskers stood out against his pale skin at such a notion. "That Lydia earned money by selling her pictures was disgraceful enough. But at least she was a soldier's widow and no one knew it was her paintings. But for you to teach? Out of the question. You might end up with a daughter of another peer for a student and my colleagues will believe I cast you out. Unthinkable. We will find you a husband of a less . . . passionate and more spiritual nature."

"Father." Cassandra looked down at the forget-me-not sprig muslin skirt over a petticoat of the softest white, over a chemise of delicate lawn and knitted silk stockings, too expensive and fine for travel wear, but the sole material that did not irritate her still-tender scars. "Be honest with yourself and me, please, sir. You know no man will want me now. Whittaker came because he felt obligated and, of course, because of the dowry."

She got out the words without a hint of a quiver in her voice.

"And breach of contract," Honore added.

"I'd never make such a public spectacle of my daughter," Father gave forth with all the pompousness of which he was capable—a great deal. Then he deflated like a balloon that had lost its air and touched Cassandra's cheek with a rare moment of tender affection. "I am afraid you are right, my dear. I hold him in high regard for keeping his word under the circumstances, as your dowry is not exceptional. But if not for him, the circumstances would not exist; therefore, I have given him his marching orders. He wasn't to have come here tonight." He glanced at Honore. "You stop interfering, missy."

"But I think he loves her," Honore protested. "And I know she loves him. If they will—"

"He was happy enough to leave once he knew Father did

not approve of the match anymore." For fear she might sound unattractively bitter, Cassandra kept her tone even. "After all, the Luddite riots have surely hurt him financially, and my dowry must come in quite convenient right now with the one factory of his smashed to bits."

"Quite," Father said. "And not one of you will be wed for your dowry alone. I expect your husbands to treat you with love and honor regardless of income. Whittaker has shown you neither by his own admission. I've already informed him if the two of you marry without my permission, as you are certainly old enough to do, I am under no obligation to pay him a farthing."

But she was just as guilty, or more so. Except Whittaker had walked out fast enough when he learned no money would be forthcoming. So he found her physically attractive—or had before her accident—and now with the scars and no money, he was happy to go on his way. Well, she had been schooling herself for this moment, planning for it. She was free for the most part. Father would come around soon enough, perhaps give her the dowry. She could do a great deal of good for the science of aeronautics with seven thousand pounds.

But first she must prove to him and everyone else that she was not wife material. Surely God had called her to something different, something without passion but using her intellect. Intellect was surely a gift. The other . . . well, that had led her into nothing but pain and suffering.

5

When he was nothing more than the Honorable Mr. Geoffrey Giles, Lord Whittaker wanted nothing more than to spend the rest of his life with Cassandra Bainbridge. Newly graduated from Cambridge, he had learned that his mother's brother, embarrassingly having been in trade, had died and left his silk stocking and cotton cloth weaving business to Geoffrey. "The only member of the family with good sense enough to run them into profit instead of the ground," Uncle Hern had written into his last will and testament.

Whittaker knew nothing about mills. He was supposed to go into the church or perhaps the military, as the younger son of a family with more history than prosperity, certainly nothing in the way of property or money to spare for the younger son. What he did know, however, was how to learn. He'd been an excellent student at university, enjoying his studies for the most part, and felt himself more suited to the church than soldiery or the diplomatic corps. But he was two and twenty at the time and could not be ordained for another two years, so he decided to see if he could make a go of the mills until then.

With this in mind, he plunged out of a spring rain and into an Oxford Street bookshop in search of something to explain ledgers and something talking about looms. Instead, he ran straight into a young woman with her arms loaded down with a stack of volumes that surely weighed as much as she. The books scattered. Her heavy, dark hair tumbled from beneath her hat and onto her shoulders, and thus the Honorable Mr. Geoffrey Giles met and began his courtship of Miss Cassandra Bainbridge. Three months later, he asked her to marry him. A week after that, his older brother went riding after a heavy rain, tried to jump a stream with a muddy bank, and landed head down in the water, his neck broken against a rock.

Mere the Honorable Mr. Geoffrey Giles became the ninth earl of Whittaker at two and twenty, and the wedding to Cassandra was postponed for a year, then called off, then set for the end of August, and now . . .

Much to his dislike for the pall of pipe and cheroot smoke and yeasty stench of ale surrounding him, Whittaker sat in the inn's taproom, trying to relax on a hard wooden banquette beside Lord Bainbridge and two men in scarlet regimentals with officer insignia on their shoulders.

"You are in a unique position to help us, my lord," said Major Gabriel Crawford, a man of perhaps thirty with an Etonian accent, probably a scion of one of England's "great" families. "You were most helpful last spring when the uprisings were at their worst. You can be even more helpful now."

"I have an estate to run." Whittaker tried to use logic on the men.

"You have a capable steward," Bainbridge pointed out. "I saw to that."

"Yes, my lord, you were quite helpful." Whittaker sighed, now suspecting his lordship had been a bit too helpful in that area. The steward rarely consulted Whittaker regarding anything, yet the land prospered. At least it brought in more income than it had under his father and then his brother's management. So he let the man do his job. "I would, however, like to be home now."

"That is out of the question." A white line formed around Bainbridge's mouth.

He did not, he would not, say it in front of the officers, but Whittaker knew why—Cassandra was there. Mama had sent the invitation, knowing that Whittaker Hall was a day's travel from the new home of Cassandra's sister, before she learned from him that Cassandra insisted she could no longer marry him.

The memory sent a jolt of pain through him. Did she think a scar or two would stop him from wanting her? No, the problem lay in the wantonness of his wanting.

With an effort, he resisted the urge to hang his head in shame and grind the heels of his hands into his eyes until the ache behind them turned into pain so great it would blot out all thought and feeling.

Instead, he looked each officer in the eye. "I will not again go into the kind of danger I endured last spring." He turned so he could look Lord Bainbridge in the eye the longest and hardest. "Until I set up my nursery. I as yet have no heirs."

A tic pulsed at the corner of Bainbridge's jaw, and a light flashed through his dark eyes, eyes so like Cassandra's that looking at them hurt, but he said nothing.

"You have an uncle and cousins," the other officer pointed out. "An heir and a spare."

Whittaker stared at the man as though he had suddenly started foaming at the mouth. "My uncle has expressed no liking for the title and estate, and my cousins are only twelve and ten."

"But they are heirs in the direct family line," the officer persisted.

"We would not even suggest you help us again," Crawford finished. "We value the continuation of our best families as much as you seem to do."

"Which is why I intend to marry," Whittaker began.

"You will have protection," Crawford added.

Bainbridge snorted.

Whittaker realized the older man had wedged him between himself and the wall, making escape impossible. He could not even vault over the back of the banquette, something he might have considered regardless of how foolish he would look, had it not abutted a wall as well. Outmaneuvered. Outsmarted. He was no match for experienced officers and a wily politician like Bainbridge. At the same time, in the social sense he outranked two military officers and a baron, even if he was younger than all three. They could force him to do nothing.

In the spring, they had asked. With Cassandra having doubts about their marriage, he had agreed. He needed an outlet for his frustration and pain. Now, however, he feared being away from her. Being away from her in May had carried her into friendship with those two men who led her into the lunacy of aeronautics.

Flight, indeed! Whittaker could tolerate, even understand, her interest in Homer and Virgil, and even some of the less respectable Greeks and Romans. But wanting to leave the ground? He did not like looking out windows more than three floors up, let alone thinking of nothing beneath him but air. She was going to get herself killed if he did not go back to Whittaker Hall to watch over her movements and stop her from trying to fly with nothing more substantial than a gas-filled bag of silk and an oversized basket. Not to mention the fire. One would think the chit would be afraid of the fire needed to keep the balloon filled

54

with hot air. But not Cassandra. In the name of science, she would overcome her fear.

Which was one reason he loved her so much.

He set his shoulders back and his chin firmly. "If you gentlemen will excuse me for being vulgar enough to say so, you cannot force a peer of the realm to take on a role he does not wish to shoulder."

Silence. At least at the table. The rest of the taproom had grown crowded and noisy with farmers and carters, stable hands and herders, who had carried the sweat of their toil to mingle with the smoke and ale.

As he watched the three men exchange glances, the stench of the room added its discomfort to the pain of Cassandra's rejection, and his guts roiled. He'd rarely been ill a day in his life and never been jug-bit from intoxication, so this discomfort sat on him with the force of a roof beam. He feared he would disgrace himself in front of these older, wiser men and the hard-working country folk, when he needed to behave like the member of the House of Lords he was, like the leader he was supposed to be.

But his love, his lady, had sent him away, and that took the stuffing right out of the middle of a man.

He took a deep breath to fill himself with something other than anguish. "In the event you are forgetting, I do outrank all of you, and you are not in a position to force me to do anything."

"Oh yes, but we are." Bainbridge spoke in an undertone barely audible amidst the hubbub of the room, a murmur that sent a chill racing up Whittaker's spine.

He kept his face blank and arched his brows. "Indeed, my lord."

"Indeed." Bainbridge's face also was expressionless. "We have information regarding your mother."

Whittaker's breath snagged in his throat. His hands balled into fists on his thighs. He said nothing for fear he would give away a trace of emotion. But they had to be lying. His mother was a Christian lady, devout in her faith, if a bit too involved with dissenters for the liking of the local gentry. Even so, that was nothing anyone did not already know, and Mama did not care that they either knew or disapproved. He should not fear knowledge these men might have.

"Regarding the paternity of your brother," said one of the officers, the younger of the two, with a salacious glint in his eye. "It could not have been your father."

"You are accusing my mother of being unfaithful to my father?" Whittaker managed a credibly scoffing laugh. "What a faradiddle."

"We know," Bainbridge said, "we have witnesses to the fact that your father, the seventh earl, was not home for eleven months, at the end of which your brother was born."

"Even if I believed you—" Whittaker had to pause to swallow against a dry mouth. "Which I do not, the law says that a child born in wedlock is presumed that of the husband. So you would have a difficult time making anyone believe such a tale about my mother."

"Not particularly." Crawford drew a cheroot from an inside pocket of his scarlet coat and lit it from the candle.

"The child is presumed legitimate unless the father is out of the country—or, as in this case, away from the estate, which the wife did not leave—for more than ten months." Bainbridge waved a hand in front of his face. "And put that thing out."

"I beg your pardon." The officer stubbed out the cheroot at once.

Though smoke still swirled around the low ceiling beams of the taproom, the cloud over their table dissipated.

"You cannot possibly know that thirty years later." The calmness of his tone pleased Whittaker.

"But we can." Bainbridge's complacence wasn't feigned. No one could be that good an actor. "Your father was on a diplomatic mission with France thirty years ago."

"But my brother and I look—" Whittaker stopped, but the damage was done.

He and his brother looked alike because they took after their dark-haired, brown-eyed mother, not their blond-haired, blue-eyed father. They possessed her curved brows and solitary dimple when they smiled. John's height and breadth of shoulders could have come from anywhere, anyone.

Mama an adulterer, though? It wasn't possible.

"But you do not dare test whether or not we are bluffing," Bainbridge said.

"You know I do not." Whittaker did not care how it appeared. He scrubbed his hands over his face, wishing he could scrub his entire body with harsh soap to eliminate the filth about his mother they had just poured over him. She was a new creature in Christ. God had forgiven her sins.

But Society would not, however old they were. They did not like being duped, and they would feel so. It would spill over into her present life. Even some church friends would shun her.

And Cassandra by being there.

So that was why the Bainbridges insisted Cassandra accept Mama's invitation, even though they now objected to the marriage. No wonder they objected to the marriage.

Whittaker managed to hold his head up and keep his voice steady as he asked, "What do you want me to do this time?"

They spent an hour telling him. By the time the taproom began to quiet as the patrons drifted out in ones and twos or groups, Whittaker learned what role they needed him to play in the game to stop, or at least damage, the Luddite rebellion in the northern counties. He was young enough to appear genuinely involved with men who had already demonstrated they would not hesitate to kill. And if he got in the way of a pistol ball or a knife, his uncle would inherit title and lands.

"Have you not considered that people will recognize me in Lancashire?" He tried to dissuade them at one point with utter logic.

"How often have you been there since you were eight years old?" Bainbridge returned.

A direct hit. He had been sent to school at eight years, then went to university, then was either in London or in the Dale or, for a few weeks before he learned of his brother's death, in Devonshire. Yes, he resembled his mother, but that could be disguised easily for men who were not necessarily Lancashire men, or even locals who saw what they expected to see.

What they would expect to see would be the earl dressed like a gentleman, clean-shaven and young. A dusting of powder in the hair, a few days' growth of beard, and rough garments, and even he admitted it was unlikely for anyone to know him.

Once the men finished giving him his instructions, they too slipped out of the taproom—the two soldiers, then Lord Bainbridge. Whittaker remained staring into the untouched glass before him until the candle guttered on its chipped saucer of a holder and the barkeep began to give him glances of annoyance. Then he rose and walked into the damp and chilly September night and paused beneath the gallery, allowing the mist to wash away some of the smoke stench from his clothes and hair. Nothing would wash the stain of family dishonor from his heart.

Above him, someone paced along the boards, a hesitant,

dragging step accompanied by a thud. An old person with rheumatic joints keeping them awake, or someone with an injured—

His head jerked back. "Cassandra?"

He headed for the steps. She was outside. She was alone. If he could talk to her when she was by herself, look into her beautiful eyes—

A hand landed on his arm, an elegantly gloved hand with a firm grip. "You are not going up there," Lord Bainbridge said.

"Unhand me." Whittaker pulled his arm free but held his ground. "I should call you out for what you said about my mother, but you are more than twice my age."

And it was most certainly not the Christian action to take.

Bainbridge chuckled. "I would not take the challenge."

Above, the footfalls had ceased. Because Cassandra had gone into her room at the sound of voices, or because she was listening? He prayed for the latter. To know she still cared enough to listen helped ease the pain of losing her.

"I will be rather good with pistol and rapier if I continue to practice," Whittaker pointed out. "Father saw me well-taught in the event I chose the military life."

Above, a footfall dragged. A door opened and closed. Cassandra gone inside beyond earshot.

Whittaker turned on the older man. Though his voice remained low, his tone held savagery. "How dare you blackmail me into risking my life? If I thought I did any good in the spring, I'd have gone willingly without you fouling my mother's good name."

"Not such a good name, is it? And you have done worse than that to my daughter. She is practically a cripple and in constant pain because of your actions."

She hadn't been protesting his advances in the carriage. On

the contrary. But he would not blame her. He would take full responsibility.

"I am still willing—" He stopped, realizing how bad that sounded. "I still want to marry her."

"And a fine dowry your estate and mills will need if you do not stop the Luddites from assaulting your property and destroying it further."

"Keep the dowry if that's what it takes to prove to both of you I want her beyond anything else." Whittaker swallowed. "Or is it my mother's past that stops you from wanting the marriage now?"

"Not at all. I've always known. I was with your father on that mission as an extremely junior attaché about your age. I know how long he was gone. But he pretended a journey home so as not to dishonor her, and I assume the bloodline wasn't corrupted all that much."

The bloodline, the first mention of the identity. Whittaker should have wondered. He'd been too stunned to consider the identity of his brother's true father. He did not want to know but now suspected the man might have been his uncle. Mama had been with her brother-in-law and his wife around that time, and they were close in age. But surely Whittaker's uncle would not cuckold his own brother.

No wonder Mama encouraged him to marry young. She must have seen how he felt about Cassandra, that irresistible pull to be close and closer still.

His eyes burned. His throat closed. He stood like a mute beneath the gallery, the mist swirling around him like his sins creeping through his bones to conquer his very soul.

"Then why?" he managed to choke out. "Why do you come between us now?"

"You both blame yourselves for her injuries. That's no way to start a marriage. If I do not keep you apart, you will never grow beyond that blame and your marriage will be poisoned from the start." Bainbridge's tone softened. "I let my first daughter marry unwisely the first time and had to watch her suffer for years. I will not allow that to happen to Cassandra." He touched Whittaker's shoulder, a comforting, fatherly gesture this time. "You both need to find someone with whom your passions do not run so high. And if I keep you apart, you will."

"Cassandra may, but I never will." As he spun on his heel and strode off for the stable to awaken a sleepy hostler to saddle his horse, he heard Lord Bainbridge laughing like a man with a secret he enjoyed keeping to himself.

6

Though Cassandra closed the door loudly enough for the men below to hear the latch click, she opened it again with a gentleness only someone close at hand would recognize as being other than the normal night sounds of a settling wooden building or the whisper of a cat slipping through the night. Behind her, everyone slept. Below her, Father and Whittaker talked in low voices that nonetheless drifted upward on the swirling mist, taut with anger on Whittaker's part, scornful on Father's. She missed a few words here and there, but not enough to miss the gist of the dialogue.

Father believed she and Whittaker could never be happy together because their passions ran too high. They were both quiet people, comfortable with silences between them, yet never lacking in conversation when they chose. But always that fire blazed between them, a rope of fire insisting they touch a hand or a cheek, a look that promised so much more. More and more they succumbed to temptation until a fire in fact stopped them from committing the ultimate act of betrayal to their upbringing and faith. Now she bore the scars of her folly. Father was right, and Whittaker must have agreed or he would not have walked away with such determination.

He strode out of her life like he could not wait to get away, ultimate proof that he was glad to be rid of her without a fight about promises broken. She was now free of him and his disapproval of her aeronautics.

So why did her chest ache like someone had removed her heart by force?

She slumped onto a chair. It bore no cushion, and one of her not yet wholly healed burns rubbed the edge. She sucked in her breath to stifle a cry of pain that would awaken everyone. They'd spent enough sleepless nights because of her, certain for the first week that she would have to have both legs amputated. "Let me die if you must," she had pleaded with the physicians. "I'd be better off dead."

They hadn't amputated, though the pain and wounds grew worse. She figured they agreed with her—she would be better off dead than a lady without legs. She could not imagine life spent in a bath chair or being carried when the chair would not fit through doorways or go up steps.

She had healed, though, thanks to a young physician Father called in, who insisted on cleansing tinctures that burned with their high content of spirits, then the burning soothed with applications of cold compresses. Ice compresses. The apothecary and other physicians told him he was beyond his reason and her death would be on his head. But she lived. The burns healed. Her life returned.

But not to normal. Normal would be marriage and children. Not for Cassandra now. She would have books and balloons. Those gave her a reason to live—the prospect of flying especially now that walking was painful still.

"I will fly from the Dale to York," she vowed in a murmur. "I will view York Cathedral from above."

If the wind wasn't fickle and sent her across the Irish Sea to Belfast instead.

She smiled at the notion and made her way to bed. She would think of aeronautics instead of Whittaker. In time, as Father predicted, he would forget her in favor of another girl, a pretty, vapid girl who would make him an excellent countess and a mother to his heir and a spare.

Her mind drifted like a balloon on a summer breeze, but sleep eluded her. Her legs itched and burned. Barbara snored. Honore kept murmuring an incomprehensible name in her sleep, probably the name of the man who had come too close to ruining her in the spring. Poor child. To think she had loved a man with a pretty face and some charm, who used her for his own ends and—

The outer door closed, then the one into the room Father shared with Mama. Cassandra endured the need to lie still in the broad bed for another quarter hour, according to the chiming of a distant church tower clock, and then rose, donned her dressing gown, and entered the parlor. One candle still guttered in the candelabra on the table. Hearing nothing from her parents' room, Cassandra lit the other candles and carried the branch of lights to a small desk in the corner, where pens, ink, and paper lay for the convenience of the best guests who could afford to purchase a set of rooms for the night.

She drew one sheet to her, checked the trim of a pen, and opened the bottle of ink. She did not have Lydia's skill with drawing likenesses of people or even the scenery around her. Cassandra drew machinery, things that coiled through her brain like those electricity machines. Or her brain worked through formulas like recipes poured out of that pretty little cook who had graced Bainbridge House for several weeks in the spring. She was an artist. Cassandra was a chemist. They'd once discussed how the two weren't all that different. Only the ingredients changed.

"Vitriol versus vinegar," Cassandra murmured.

Deciding the paper was too small for a good detailed design, she began to work on one of her formulas, a way to make the silk of a balloon more airtight. She knew many used a mixture of birdlime, turpentine, and linseed oil, but that could prove highly flammable and needed more than one coat on either side of the silk. Doing so would take days, and how would she manage to find a place where she could boil a pot of something so odorous, let alone dangerous? Not to mention stretch the silk for the balloon. Surely it would make the fabric too stiff to properly inflate and deflate as needed. Elastic gum, perhaps? No, heavier still than the birdlime. She would adjust the amounts of the birdlime concoction first, since it was so common. Perhaps no linseed oil? Birdlime was oily enough. Yes, that might work. She still encountered the difficulty of where to melt it . . .

Her musings and calculations kept her awake through the night so that she slept in the coach, annoying Honore, who wanted to chatter about how much she would enjoy autumn in the country.

"Lies," Cassandra managed to mutter at one time. "You will despise it."

She would too, if she ended up confined to afternoon calls from dull neighbors or evening parties or, worse, that favorite country house party activity of acting out a play.

"I will not hate it in the least. London over the summer was quite, quite dull." Honore launched into a list of things Lady Whittaker had promised they would do.

Cassandra went back to sleep, and Honore woke her when the Hall was but a mile or two off so she could tidy herself.

"You have creases on your face," Honore announced. "And your hair is a disaster." She smoothed a hand through her own perfectly coiffed golden locks. Even her traveling gown seemed to have remained wrinkle-free.

Cassandra's looked like jacquard, so many lumps and ridges had it formed without her moving. And her hair was a disaster, slipping from its pins. Good. The worse she looked, the less likely her ladyship would be to want Cassandra for a daughter-in-law.

"I am certain she'll understand." Honore set her beribboned straw hat at a jaunty angle. "Lady Whittaker, I mean, as to why you look so crumpled. You have been ill, after all. I'd say you are still very much an invalid."

Cassandra yawned. "Do, please, say so."

Except how could an invalid go for the long walks she would need in order to find a place for the balloon? And how would her aeronautic friends write to her without everyone knowing? So many details. She would rather be back in Devonshire or, better yet, at Lydia's little cottage in Tavistock. Except Lydia had sold the cottage, saying it reminded her of painful times after her husband left for the war.

The carriage slowed. For the first time since climbing into the vehicle, Cassandra glanced out of the window. On the other side of the outriders, a high wall ran along the road. Behind it, trees towered in autumnal profusion of heavy, dark green and touches of gold where the leaves began to turn. Iron gates stood open in welcome, and a drive stretched long and straight ahead in a dim tunnel between the oaks and pines. A rather smooth and well-maintained drive for a family allegedly pinched for funds. Beneath the trees, though, lay telltale signs of neglect—piles of last year's moldering leaves and a tangle of brambles that would make walking through the parkland uncomfortable at best. The lawn, curving beyond the tree line, also demonstrated a lack of consistent care with irregular mowing and several bare patches.

In contrast, the house gleamed in a blend of gray stone and red brick, mullioned windows, and shining squares of glass in creamy frames. Clean glass caught the sun like gemstones.

"It looks old." Honore spoke in a whisper as though the occupants could hear her. "I do hope it isn't drafty."

"It's bound to be." Cassandra clutched her reticule containing new balloon plans, ones she had made while lying in bed for weeks.

She stroked her reticule, this one blue velvet to match her pelisse and slippers. In the wee hours of the morning, she thought perhaps she had solved her coating problem. That left finding a place to purchase a quantity of birdlime and a cauldron and build a fire . . .

One difficulty at a time. The current one lay before her in the form of a tall, middle-aged footman lowering the steps of the carriage and holding out his hand to her. Of course he reached out to her first. She was the elder. As far as most people knew, his future mistress of the manor. But if Honore went down first, she could distract everyone from Cassandra's awkward descent.

"Honore, you first," Cassandra directed. "I do believe I've dropped my . . ."

Because she could not think of anything she might have dropped, she simply bent forward as though searching. A lie. Shame on her. Lying to preserve her dignity, or what dignity remained to her.

But not a lie. She had dropped a tear. Out of nowhere, her eyes burned and the droplet splashed onto her knee.

"You are so slow," Honore said brightly. Affectionately. Too brightly. Never too affectionately. For all her foolishness, she was the kindest of sisters.

More burning, another tear.

Cassandra dashed her sleeve across her eyes as the footman lent his support to Honore, who began to chatter as though he were a friend long missed instead of a servant. Cassandra swallowed, blinked, and picked up her cane. By the time the footman extricated himself from Honore, Cassandra was on the ground with three steps to climb up to the front door. Only three. She could manage three, especially if a groom or footman came to her aid.

She started for the house in Honore's wake. Her cane sank into the soft earth that formed the carriageway, and she teetered, her weight coming down on her worst leg. She gasped in pain.

A hand slid beneath her elbow. "Miss Bainbridge, allow me."

She froze at the unfamiliar voice, so cool, so clipped, so obviously the product of a fine school upbringing. Eton or Harrow, perhaps. The hand was strong, holding her upright with a palm beneath her elbow. Slowly she glanced up to eyes the color of the English Channel after a storm—gray-green and cool. He wore no hat, and his hair gleamed honey-blond in the sunlight, a bit darker than Honore's golden locks. And he was in uniform. The red coat did not suit him, draining his naturally pale complexion of color. But for that flaw, his fine bones made for an attractive countenance.

"We have not been introduced." A bit rude, perhaps, but he was being familiar for a stranger. "I beg your pardon, but you appeared in instant need." He smiled.

She forgave his uninvited contact.

"Gabriel Crawford." He removed his hand from her elbow so

he could bow. "Major Gabriel Crawford at your service, Miss Bainbridge. And I suspect you need that service up these steps."

"For a few more weeks only, I am assured."

A nonsensical thing to respond, true though it was. But ahead of her, Honore had mounted the short flight with her long-legged grace. The doors opened to receive her like gleaming arms, and her laughter drifted back into the afternoon.

Cassandra should have been the first one over that threshold—as a bride.

Her throat closed up again. Honore had done her a favor in going first. Cassandra would not enter first like a new bride.

Eyes fixed straight ahead, she dug her cane into the ground and started forward. Major Crawford's hand remained beneath her elbow without invitation, without rejection, without providing her the jolt of longing that the most proper of touches from Whittaker never failed—

She drew her thoughts up short and pulled herself up the first step, then the second, then the third. With her lips set, she managed not to gasp or even whimper in pain. Then she stood on solid flagstones worn smooth from hundreds of years and thousands of feet and crossed the threshold without Geoffrey Giles, Lord Whittaker, at her side. No line of servants greeted her. She wasn't their master's wife. They would serve her as a guest and nothing more. Instead, a lady in black gauze over a pale gray silk glided forward and reached out her hands, noticed that Cassandra's held a cane and a reticule, and rested them on her shoulders instead. "Welcome to Whittaker Hall at last, Cassandra."

Lady Whittaker, the earl's mother, kissed Cassandra's cheek. Though touched with silver strands, her hair shone the same brown as her son's—so dark it appeared black in most lights—and she had the same brown eyes. She smiled and a dimple appeared in one cheek.

Cassandra bowed her head to hide more foolish tears. "Thank you for the invitation, my lady."

"Oh, please, you should call me—" Lady Whittaker broke off. "We'll discuss that later. Major, will you be so kind as to see to the unloading of their luggage. I am taking this young lady to her room. She looks in need of refreshment and a rest."

"Of course." The major bowed and turned toward the front door, adding, "Until later, Miss Bainbridge."

"Cassandra slept most of the way in the carriage." Honore appeared from the shadows of the great hall with its suits of armor standing in two corners like headless warriors, niches set with some sort of statuary, and one area set up with a fire and chairs to make the cavernous space welcoming. "But I am certain she'll do well to lie down flat."

Bless Honore. Indeed, the backs of Cassandra's legs itched and burned. She needed soothing ginger lotion rubbed into them. She also needed a show of protest.

"I am truly quite all right, my lady."

"Nonsense, you are too recently an invalid." Lady Whittaker herself bustled toward one end of the hall, leading the way down a corridor off the main hall, past a grand staircase so old a somewhat rusty dog gate hovered over it like the blade of a guillotine, and around another bend. "Watch your step here—the floor changes, as this is the newer wing of the house."

The floor turned from stone to wood. The dull *tap*, *tap* of Cassandra's cane turned into an echoing *thud*, *thud*. She winced with each contact. So loud. She would wake anyone nearby. Except no one would be nearby. All the rooms opening off the corridor appeared to be small, cozy parlors, a breakfast room that would receive the morning light, and—hurrah! She smelled it before she saw the long table, globe, and shelves through the half-closed door—the library.

Without any books.

She could not resist stopping to push the door wide and look inside. Though two of the walls bore row upon row of shelves, not a one held a book. The only book in the room was an enormous Bible open on the table. The rest of the shelves were either empty or laden with decades of periodicals. *The Gentleman's Magazine*, *La Belle Assemblée*, *The Ladies' Monthly Museum*.

"But Whittaker reads." The words burst unbidden from Cassandra's lips. She clapped her hand to her mouth, smacking herself in the chin with her reticule.

"But of course he does." Lady Whittaker paused a yard away and turned back. "He has his own library in the master suite on the other side of the house."

And up a floor, no doubt.

"This is the ladies' library," Lady Whittaker continued. "My husband, God rest his soul, gave me a few copies of *The Gentleman's Magazine* when it held articles he thought I would find of interest and not objectionable to a lady's sensibilities, and I have simply scores of sermon pamphlets I do intend to have bound soon."

"I am certain those will do us a great deal of good," Cassandra managed past a strangled throat.

The truth. They would be a tremendous help getting her to sleep should she have difficulty—if she did not fret about all Whittaker's lovely books out of her reach unless she got herself well enough to climb steps.

Realizing Lady Whittaker was smiling at her as though she

had granted Cassandra a great gift, she smiled back. "It's a lovely room."

Which was the truth.

"Whittaker may have told you that I am interested in a bit of engineering, so that table will come in quite conveniently."

"It does." The proud mama nodded and simply glowed. "He uses it himself for his drawings."

His drawings? What drawings? Surely she hadn't been betrothed to the man for a year and more without knowing he drew . . . anything.

"You will find all the paper and pens you need in there."

"And I can read to her while she calculates." Honore winked at Cassandra behind Lady Whittaker's back. "We may make her a fashion plate yet."

"She is very pretty as she is." Nothing but sincerity shone in Lady Whittaker's glance from Cassandra's crooked hat to her crumpled hem. "Rich colors suit you better than pastels, do they not?"

"So Honore tells me." Cassandra looked down, too conscious that what lay beneath that hem was anything but pretty—as opposite as it could get.

"But we are embarrassing you, are we not?" Lady Whittaker turned abruptly and bustled ahead.

Cassandra hastened to follow, afraid in the dimly lit corridor that her ladyship would turn yet another corner and she would be too far behind to see her and perhaps fall down the steps as she had that one night in the theater.

Whittaker hadn't been offended by her looks in the spectacles that made her eyes appear like something from the ocean that fishermen would toss back for sheer ugliness. He'd kissed her in the library to prove it. And kissed her, and . . .

A hand clamped on her arm. "Stop," Honore hissed between her teeth.

She stood on the near side of a doorway Cassandra had been about to pass. Now that she had stopped and light streamed through the open doorway, Cassandra noted a short flight of steps down to another door. The faint aroma of oranges and lemons wafted through the air.

"Is that the orangery?" Honore asked a little too loudly, as though that were her intent in stopping Cassandra.

"Yes." Lady Whittaker came back to the doorway. "We have oranges and lemons in there, so it is kept quite warm, a pleasant place in the winter, rather hot in the summer."

And a convenient exit without traversing the entire house.

"The gardens are beyond." Lady Whittaker sighed. "Not what they once were, I am sure, but still lovely in the spring. Everything is dying now." Her face grew wistful. "One day we'll repair the other glass house and I'll have strawberries all year round too. Now I settle for them in June and bottle as many as we can. But you can see all that tomorrow. We keep country hours here, so I am afraid you missed dinner, but I'll send in some refreshment and you can rest until supper. Miss Honore, your room is right next door here. You see, it was no trouble to turn these into a lovely little suite of rooms, as we still prefer to use the old part of the house for entertaining. Larger rooms. My father-in-law built these for warmth, not large gatherings, so the family uses them in the winter, though they are a bit far from the kitchens and—"

She broke off and laughed. "Now listen to my tongue running on wheels. I've been so looking forward to your visit, though the circumstances . . ." Again that melancholy droop to her lips, the lower one full yet firm like her son's, though she had to be at least Mama's age, as Whittaker's brother had been several years his senior. "I'll send in Betsy to serve you right away." With a swish of her skirts, she spun on her heel and hastened down yet one more corridor.

"I am going to get lost," Cassandra said.

"Just sniff for the oranges, though you might want to wear your spectacles."

"You may be right in that." Cassandra entered her chamber. Soft carpet deadened her cane and footfalls. The scent of lavender hinted at sachets set around to keep the moths from velvet curtains and bed hangings. Everything was blue or green or a blend of both—Cassandra could not tell in the fading evening light. She would ask the maid for candles to be lit. No, she would simply lie down.

"I am so weary." She stumbled toward the bed.

Honore sighed. "But then you will not sleep tonight. And a maid is bringing refreshment."

"I am not hungry."

"Cassandra, you know what the physician said. You must eat well and get plenty of exercise as much as you can . . ."

Her sister's lecture, sounding more like managing Lydia than frivolous Honore, faded to a buzzing in Cassandra's ears, a higher-pitched echo of the blood suddenly roaring through her skull.

She reached for the edge of the quilted counterpane to turn it back and felt something crackle beneath her fingers. Embroidered satin coverlets did not crackle. But paper did.

Someone had left a letter inside Cassandra's bedclothes.

7

Darkness crept across the room where the last rays of dusk grew too weak to penetrate the grimy windows and the proprietor proved too cautious to light candles. Nonetheless, Whittaker knew the faces of the men around the table sticky with spilled ale. As he knew they had with him, he had made certain to see them each in enough light to identify them later. Their likenesses, poor an artist as he was, lay in papers he had managed to sneak into his rooms at Whittaker Hall one night while the household slept.

He had tried to sneak farther into the Hall but had failed to reach Cassandra's rooms. Too many servants scurried about, even with Mama's economies. But his rooms were sacrosanct, out of reach of the maids and safe for him to enter with no one the wiser, including his keeper, Major Gabriel Crawford.

Whittaker's fingers balled into fists on his thighs at the idea of that man staying in the home Whittaker had inherited. His rightful home, his inheritance, his legacy, the home in which his future wife resided. At least the lady he still intended to be his wife, God willing.

Which He did not seem to be.

His hands tightened until the muscles in his arms bulged

against the coarse linen shirt he wore under a leather jerkin. Cassandra was the woman Whittaker had prayed for all his life. He knew it mere days after meeting her. So why, a week before their wedding, would God destroy that intended union?

And place him amongst men who stank of sweat and ale and worse? He would not allow any of them near his looms and cotton and silk fabrics. No one would buy such befouled fabrics. Whittaker felt unclean in the same room with their vulgar tongues and murderous spirits. He prayed for nothing more than to get out of this house and back to Whittaker Hall, try to figure out a way to see Cassandra, talk to her, convince her—

"So are you with us or not, Geoff?" The tone of the man was sharp, impatient. Hugh, with an accent more that of East Anglia than Lancashire or any of the other northern counties. A suspiciously long way from home. But then, they raised sheep in East Anglia, so perhaps the crisis with the loss of work amongst the weavers did affect him, as he claimed—affected him enough to drive him to leave his work and join the Luddite rebellion.

"Are you going to help us make sure it doesn't die out?" Hugh persisted.

"I am here, ar—ain't I?" Whittaker tried to hide his educated accent.

Rob, a broad-faced Yorkshire weaver out of work now, snorted. "You haven't listened to a word we've said."

"Woolgathering." Whittaker chuckled at his own joke.

"It's a woman," said the last man in the group, Jimmy, a silk stocking weaver from Nottingham who'd helped destroy his master's looms back in the spring.

Whittaker, needing an ally, had stopped Jimmy from getting caught and jailed, if not outright hanged.

"Always a woman when a man woolgathers." Jimmy chuckled.

Whittaker laughed too. "Aye, it is a woman. Can't help but think about the silk of her hair when we're talking about silk weaving. It's so—" He stopped himself from describing Cassandra's midnight tresses. "Like you could spin it into gold."

"Well, ain't you the poet." Hugh's tone held a sneer. "Let's get our work done and you can go have yourself another look at it."

"If you pay attention," Rob added, "we can get it done faster."

"Beg pardon." Whittaker picked up the tankard one of the men had set before him earlier and pretended to drain it. In fact, the contents went down the sleeve of his shirt, a maneuver he had practiced for hours with glasses of water. The reek of ale left behind revolted him. It seemed to seep into his pores and taint his blood.

"Don't you think it a bit risky going after the Hern mills?" he continued. "They're not just two or three looms in a cottage. They're a whole factory with guards."

He'd made sure of the guards as soon as the trouble began a year earlier. Not enough at first, and one shop fell to the axes of the rebels.

"Someone is likely to get shot," he concluded.

"Worth the risk." Jimmy picked up the pitcher on the table and filled each mug as easily as though a branch of candles stood in the center of the table, instead of it being cloaked in darkness. "If we can bring the Hern mills to a halt, the owners will pay attention to our need for fair wages and stop fixing the costs of renting looms."

Whittaker bit down on his tongue until it hurt to stop himself from protesting. He thought he paid a fair wage, but he wasn't running a charity. The men had to work hard, but then, so did he between running the mills and the estate.

"You'll get the owner's attention, all right," Whittaker said. "The attention of a blunderbuss round in the head."

"Gotta take the risk for the cause." Hugh sounded cheerful, excited. "But if you are too much of a coward . . ."

Silence fell around the room like the deep twilight outside the window. Nearby an owl hooted, signaling nightfall indeed. Below, the taproom grew louder, boisterous with men arguing over the merits, the dangers, the necessity of rebelling against factory owners of cloth and stocking.

"Let them send more soldiers." One drunken voice rose above the tumult loud enough to penetrate the floorboards. "They do not scare me."

"They should," Whittaker muttered before he could stop himself.

"Coward for truth," Hugh taunted.

Whittaker shrugged even if the man could not see the movement. "Gotta stay pretty for my lady, is all."

That made the men laugh. The tension left.

A chair scraped across the bare floor. "Tomorrow night," Rob said. "We've got twenty men. We'll torch the place."

Over Whittaker's dead body. Which, sadly, might be the truth.

He had to get the information to Crawford, who was due at the cottage sometime this night. But Whittaker wanted to see Cassandra first, had to see her, tell her—what? That he still loved her no matter what, in the event he died saving his mills or helping the rebels? He'd already told her and she hadn't wanted to know. Still—

"Tomorrow night," the other men chorused, Whittaker included.

They slipped out of the inn via the window, grabbing ahold of a tree and descending into the blackness beneath the spreading branches. Whittaker waited until all the men should have been gone. He wanted none of them to see him heading toward Whittaker land, the woods of the parkland, instead of the laborer's cottage he now had to call home.

The leaves rustled, dry in the early autumn night. From practice, his feet found purchase without flaw. In seconds he touched the ground, then stood waiting, listening, chilly in the air from the ale-wet sleeve. He could hear nothing of his surroundings over the raucous singing from inside the taproom. He moved away from the tree onto the path leading past the inn, then onto the road. He headed toward his cottage, striding with purpose until the tumult of the men fell behind and the night grew silent save for the wind, light and damp, portending rain, swirling through the hedgerows. In moments, he would reach a gap in that hedge, one he had made himself. Across a ditch and over a field would see him to his own wall. His entire being ached with the need to see Cassandra, talk to her. Surely matters would be different without family present, so he could learn . . .

That she truly wanted rid of him? That it was her idea and not her father's? Or, worse, her belief that God did not, after all, want them together?

"Surely not, Lord. Surely she is the right woman for my helpmeet, my—" Talking aloud would not keep his movements unobtrusive when the cut in the shrubbery arrived. He had so little time to reach the Hall and return to his temporary home before Crawford's call.

He found the cut, the hint of a dimple in the even line of branches. He turned sideways to slip through—

And an arm snaked around his neck, a hand clamped over his mouth, another hand stuck the point of a blade at the base of his spine. "Where are you going, my friend?"

Major Gabriel Crawford, servant of the Crown, lackey of Lord Bainbridge, blackmailer, and, worst of all, barrier between Whittaker and Cassandra. Oh, he had seen how the major had greeted her at the carriage, had watched from an attic window as another man was solicitous, guiding the lady who should have been Whittaker's wife over the threshold.

But she was not his wife because he had failed to protect her. Because, like his mother, he was unable to control his passions. Whittaker knew it, accepted that Bainbridge was probably right in thinking him not good enough for Cassandra, leading her in the wrong direction as his mother had gone in the wrong direction. And yet he loved her still. He still wanted her as his wife, and no blackguard of a soldier, officer or not, was going to stop him.

"I am going to inspect my estate," Whittaker said.

"No, you are not." The blade jabbed without piercing, probably a rapier with a duello practice button on the end, not dangerous at the moment but too easily so. "You're being followed and will lead the men right to the Hall."

"Then why not right to you here and now?"

"I was able to detain them before stopping you."

"But—" Whittaker closed his eyes and counted to ten, ten images of Cassandra—her nose literally between the pages of a book because she refused to wear her spectacles in front of him, Cassandra turning her face up so sweet and pretty in sunlight or candlelight, Cassandra clinging to that bedpost and as pale as the sheets on the bed behind her . . .

He was no good at this game.

"You need someone else," Whittaker said. "I'll get caught and killed if I cannot tell if someone is following me."

"There is no one else we can . . . ahem . . ."

Blackmail into risking being killed. No one they trusted.

"One of the rebels for a price?" Whittaker suggested.

"Family loyalty amongst our better families works much better." Crawford laughed with the same dry rustle as the wind through the hedge. "Family, country, God, in that order of loyalty. Do you not agree?"

"God first," Whittaker said.

The words were reflex, though. He hadn't put God first since Cassandra broke off their betrothal the first time. Or perhaps not before that, or she would not have felt the break was necessary.

He felt as though he deflated like one of those balloons of which she was so inexplicably, dangerously fond.

Again, the autumn-leaf laugh. "If family did not come first, my lord, you would not be here now." Crawford's voice hardened. "But you are staying here. You will not be sneaking back to your house under any circumstances. You are being watched and will be stopped."

"By whom?"

The major did not answer him.

"I have information for you." Whittaker hoped the abrupt change of subject would disconcert Crawford.

"I thought you might. That's why I was on my way to your cottage. I will meet you there in five minutes." Then the major was gone, slipping beyond the hedge and into the ditch with barely a whisper.

Whittaker stumbled back onto the road as though he had stepped into the shrubbery due to illness brought on by an excess of ale. If anyone came close enough, the stench of it would lend credence to the ploy. But no one came close. He thought he heard voices far behind—drunken, singing voices from the inn.

He arrived at his cottage, little more than a hut with one room downstairs and two bedchambers above with ceilings so slanted from the roof that he could stand upright on only one side. The cottage was on his land. During the day, he tended his own sheep. His shepherd had mysteriously disappeared. Everyone presumed he had gone to Nottingham or Yorkshire to join the rebels there—what was left of them after the military had come in. Lancashire was relatively quiet, the leaders of the Luddite movement against the owners of the mills mostly caught, jailed, and either awaiting trial or hanged already. But pockets of resistance continued. Whittaker was supposed to ferret them out, find the leader, and bring him to justice, while trying to stay alive himself.

Inside his cottage, despite knowing Crawford would slip in at any moment, Whittaker set the fire flaming high enough to boil a pot of water for cleansing his ale-stained shirt, as well as a kettle for tea. Crawford loved tea, requested it with unwonted courtesy on his other visits. Perhaps he would be in a better humor, more willing to let Whittaker see Cassandra just once, if tea preparations were already under way upon his arrival.

When the major strode into the cottage without knocking, Whittaker was spooning bohea into a chipped china pot.

"Very good." Crawford arranged himself on the room's sole seat, a settee without cushions. He, like Whittaker, was dressed in a laborer's garb of rough wool, linen, and leather. "You should not be so clean, though, Geoffrey." Crawford's familiarity set Whittaker's teeth on edge. "Shepherds stink of sheep."

"Not this one." Whittaker ladled steaming water into the teapot. The tannic fragrance of black tea wafted from the spout. "You'll have to bring me more sugar if you want it."

"I do not." Crawford grinned, too relaxed, too pleased with

himself. "Your betrothed—or should I say your former be-trothed—is rather a pretty girl, isn't she?"

Whittaker said nothing. He poured the tea into an earth-enware mug and managed to hand it to the major, not dump it into the man's lap. Whittaker had done too many things of which the Lord would not approve. He did not need to add to his piles of sins. Especially not now.

"But the younger sister is a stunner," Crawford continued, raising the cup to his lips. "All that yellow hair and lively spirit. She and her ladyship are planning a dinner party for your neighbors."

"Miss Honore is a charming young lady." Whittaker took his own mug of tea and propped one shoulder against the man-tel shelf so he could look down on the major, his only advan-tage—height while the other man sat. "A bit of a featherbrain compared to her sister."

"Bluestocking." Crawford curled his upper lip. "All Miss Bain-bridge talks about is aeronautics. I made the mistake of telling her I flew in one of those contraptions once."

Whittaker stiffened. "You did not."

"But I did." Crawford laughed and even colored slightly. "Admit I unmanned myself by being sick over the side. Good thing I chose the Army over the Navy, eh? No high places for me. She is so determined to go up in one herself."

"She will not. I mean, she cannot up here. Her friends are back in London."

"Ah, but they are not. Now, what news do you have for—"

"What did you say?" Whittaker leaned over Crawford, his cup of scalding tea tipping the liquid precariously close to the lip. "Her London ballooning friends are here?"

"They called on Miss Bainbridge this afternoon. I had to

assist Miss Honore with arranging the blue drawing room for dancing and met the gentlemen."

Gentlemen indeed. Barely.

Whittaker set his cup aside before he broke it. "About the news I have for you."

"Of course." Crawford sipped at his tea with a delicacy that would have been effeminate on a less well set-up man. Miss Honore was probably forming a *tendre* for the major already. "But I thought you'd want to know that these gentlemen with the balloon plan to take it up tomorrow."

"Tomorrow." Whittaker's jaw hardened. "They cannot."

"Of course they can. Now, about that information?"

"From where are they launching it?" Whittaker demanded.

Crawford shrugged.

"Do you want your news?"

"Your south pasture." Crawford smiled. "With her ladyship's permission, of course."

"We shall see about that." Whittaker spoke between clenched teeth.

"You cannot go there, you know." Crawford yawned. "Now, do please get on with things. I am ready for my bed."

"News." For a moment, thinking about how he could stop a balloon launch that very well might include Cassandra, Whittaker could not remember what he needed to tell the major. The single room of the cottage ground floor spun out of focus, the fire turning into a conflagration tumbling from the sky, his lady smashing to her death. It had happened to others.

Surely, after her experience, the fire needed to make the air for the balloon would stop her from going up. Then again, Cassandra would think of them separately, the fire of a thrown torch, the coals in a brazier for her latest passion.

"News," Crawford snapped.

Whittaker jumped, speared his fingers through his now overly long hair. "The Hern cotton mill is their next target. Tomorrow night. Twenty men intending to torch it."

The mill, whose income was saving Whittaker Hall from ruin and from rebuilding the destroyed mill, now that he did not have Cassandra's dowry. As Major Crawford gazed at him, green eyes wide and mildly amused, Whittaker felt like someone had run his guts through a spinning machine.

He could stop Cassandra from a balloon launch, or he could save his mill and the livelihoods of two dozen families.

8

Cassandra sat at the desk in the sitting room she shared with Honore and smiled down at the note she had found beneath her counterpane her first night. Somehow, seeing those words lessened the pain in her legs and renewed hope to her soul. Somehow, somehow, Roger Kent and Philip Sorrells had bribed a servant to slip her the message.

In the event you've been forbidden to see us or something, Mr. Sorrells had written.

No one had forbidden her. Whittaker wasn't there and could not forbid her even if he were. She could see the men openly. They were educated gentlemen from good, if not noble, families. Their birth kept them on the fringes of Society but not out of it. Lady Whittaker would not object to their calling on Cassandra in the open. So she wrote them at their lodgings in the Dale and awaited their visit.

It came immediately, though their visit had to wait until the Hall was not crowded with other guests so Cassandra and her friends could discuss ballooning freely. Those were weeks of so many calls from neighbors wanting to meet the Bainbridge ladies that Cassandra did not have to feign the fatigue that kept her to her room in the between times, even taking a few of her meals on a tray. They were days in which Lady Whittaker never found the opportunity to speak with Cassandra alone.

Could she manage that until Christmastide? Doubtful. Her legs would be healed by then, the physicians assured her. Healed except for the scars that would never leave.

But Mr. Kent and Mr. Sorrells had managed to have a few private words with Cassandra while she showed them the orangery and Honore entertained the major with asking his advice on room arrangement for a party the following week.

"Tomorrow night in the south field," Mr. Sorrells said. "Lady Whittaker said she sees no reason why we should not use it, as it is fallow right now."

"Of course," Mr. Kent added, "I doubt she would have agreed if she knew you were going to come watch."

Only watch, alas. Cassandra wanted to join them, but even they refused.

"We do not know how things will go with it." Mr. Sorrells's long, pale face grew longer with concern. "Your design for the basket appears sound, but we have our concerns about the wings working."

Mr. Kent, as round as his friend was long, nodded. "Your calculations appear right, but everyone else so far has used paddles for steering."

"Which makes no sense to me." Cassandra drew a lemon branch down to inhale the sharp tang of the fruit. "Paddles are for the water, those American boats they call canoes. But what do ships use? Sails to catch the wind. If one is sailing with the wind, doesn't the use of sails make more sense?"

"They look more like parasols," Mr. Kent grumbled.

"You convinced us enough to attempt it this once." Mr.

Sorrells smiled at her, softening his angular features. "But we will not risk you even for your own design."

"You've suffered enough, Miss Bainbridge." Mr. Kent blushed. "If you do not mind me saying so."

She did, but she would not say so. If she let them dwell on her infirmity, they might turn all protective like Whittaker and refuse to let her go up at all. But she would, if she had to fly the balloon on her own in the middle of the night.

As matters stood now, the aeronauts had chosen to go up after dark so as to draw as little attention to themselves as possible. She would participate by keeping torches lit in the field to guide them back, if they could maneuver the balloon and not get swept out to sea by an offshore wind—always a risk. Inland, one could always find a place to land that was safe, if inconvenient. But if swept out to sea at night . . .

Well, she had agreed perhaps she should remain on the ground for the time being. She had caused her family enough anxiety over the past several weeks. But torches?

She bit her lower lip as she slipped the note from the aeronauts back into her drawer. Thus far, fires in fireplaces and grates did not frighten her. Nor had she backed away from the braziers that kept the orangery warm. Candles certainly did not distress her. But the thought of keeping torches lit for an hour or more sent a shiver racing up her arms and burning down her legs. She might grow weary and drop one onto her skirt or, worse, her shawl. A bit of hot tar might land on her sleeve. Perhaps if she simply stuck them in the ground she would be all right. But then she might brush the flame with her shawl or skirt while lighting a fresh one if the men stayed up too long. And if they did not maneuver back to the field, she would not know when she could leave.

No matter. She must overcome even the thought of what could happen if she wanted to see the launch, actually help with the launch, unlike the ascents she had witnessed outside London. Those had been as a spectator from afar. This time she would loose the tether ropes herself.

Her heart began to race. Maddeningly, the clock told her the time was half past six of the clock. Soon the bell would ring calling them to the light supper Lady Whittaker served in the evening—bread and soup, fruit, and perhaps a jelly or ice.

Cassandra braced her hands on the edge of the desk and rose. With short, aching steps, she crossed the sitting room to where she had purposefully propped her cane beside the door. She would not depend on it forever. By Christmas, she would walk on her own even up stairs. She must do so if she wanted to show Father by the time he and Mama returned from Scotland that she could be independent so they would not attempt to find her a husband or toss her onto the marriage market again. With a bigger dowry, some men would ignore the scars.

Like Whittaker?

His house certainly needed repairs and refurbishments. His grounds needed tending. Eventually she would have Lady Whittaker drive her around in the little pony cart she liked so she could see how the tenants fared, though that was no longer any of her business.

For now, she tapped her way to the parlor Lady Whittaker used for family suppers. With its red-velvet draperies at the windows and red Turkey carpet on the floor, it offered warmth on a chilly autumn evening. So did her ladyship's smile at Cassandra's entrance.

"Tonight we dine alone, my dear." She nodded to the footman who pulled out her chair, then he moved to pull out one for Cassandra adjacent to her ladyship's place setting. "Honore has been invited to the Luvells'."

Cassandra paused in the act of lowering herself onto the chair. "She said nothing to me about it."

"Well, you see—no, Jennings, leave everything here on the table. We'll serve ourselves." Her ladyship said no more as the footman transferred a soup tureen and other dishes from the sideboard to the table and left the room, closing the door with barely a click of the latch. Then she turned her lovely dark brown eyes on Cassandra, and the pity in them made her ill. "It's all young people, and quite a romp they'll have, knowing the Luvells, so Honore and I thought you might not like it above half, being a scholar and all."

"No, no, I would have made my excuses, of course." She could not go to the balloon ascension if she had gone. "But—"

No, saying Lady Whittaker had made an error in deciding for her was rude. Still, she would have liked to have been able to choose for herself. They might call her a scholar, but making a decision for her was treating her like her brain had been burned along with her legs.

She stared at her glass of lemonade, the candlelight reflected in the pale yellow liquid like miniature dancing flames. "I'll appreciate a quiet evening. Honore does chatter a bit too much when the major is here."

Which was too often.

"I find her chatter delightful. And so does the major." Lady Whittaker ladled soup, thick with chunks of meat and vegetables, into Cassandra's bowl. "He would be an excellent match for her, you know. A very good family and respectable prospects in his future."

"He does seem to be an improvement above her last beau. But

after Lydia's experience, Father isn't fond of the idea of one of us marrying another military man."

"With the right lady, most men will sell out. Oh dear." Lady Whittaker colored beneath her dusting of rice powder.

Lydia's first husband hadn't sold his officer's commission to stay in England with his bride.

"Lydia is happy with her new husband," Cassandra said. "I doubt she even thinks about Captain Gale anymore."

"No, no, of course not. But still . . ." Lady Whittaker picked up her spoon, set it down again, spread her serviette over her lap, then raised it to dab at her lips, though she had neither eaten nor drunk anything.

Cassandra curled her fingers around the edge of the table. The aromatic soup was making her stomach ache and even give out an embarrassing little growl. "My lady, is something amiss?"

"No, no, do please eat." She broke off a dainty morsel of bread, buttered it, and popped it into her mouth.

Cassandra followed suit, though with a larger chunk. She needed nourishment if she was to walk nearly a mile.

"But now that we are alone for once," Lady Whittaker said as soon as Cassandra's mouth was full, "we can have a comfortable cose about my son."

Cassandra swallowed too soon. She would have seen the danger signs of this supper *à deux* if she hadn't been thinking so much about the balloon ascension. The bread stuck in her throat, and she consumed half of her lemonade washing it down before she could respond, "There is truly little to say about your son, my lady. God has shown me quite clearly that we should not marry. I thought as much last spring, but then Whittaker persuaded me most . . . um . . . fervently. But this time . . . I am sorry, but it is quite, quite clear to me."

"Not to him. He loves you dearly, you know."

Cassandra selected a chunk of meat from her bowl, something that would keep her chewing awhile and negate the need to speak. She could not say she did not love him. She could only say she no longer *knew* if she loved him. She could not say that perhaps her aeronautic interests overshadowed her desire to be his wife.

"He did not want to be away while you were recovering here," her ladyship continued, still nibbling on her food. "But he is so preoccupied with this Luddite rebellion and the danger to the mills. Not that a nobleman should involve himself with something so vulgar as trade, but that, alas, comes from my family. We were completely bourgeois, you know, we Herns. Quite beyond the social pale for an earl's wife was I, except we met by accident and . . ." She sighed and blinked her luxuriant eyelashes. "My father offered him a dowry of twenty thousand pounds."

Cassandra choked on a morsel of Cheshire cheese. Nearly three times her own dowry, which was considered quite handsome.

"It wasn't in the least a love match." Her ladyship spoke as though Cassandra hadn't reacted to the amount of the dowry. "Love for me came later. Almost too much later." Color tinged her cheeks. "But it would not in the least be that way for you and Whittaker. He is not interested in marrying you for your dowry, you know. He has offered to forego it to prove that to you, draw up some sort of marriage agreement that will give you control, if that can be done, which I am certain it can. Solicitors can make anything happen with their contracts. So if that is your apprehension, especially seeing that Whittaker Hall is in need of funds, please put it from your head." She huffed out a quick breath of relief. "There. It's said. I've been wanting to say that since you arrived, but we have not had a moment."

"Thank you." Cassandra did not know what else to say.

"So you agree with me?" Her ladyship leaned forward, reaching one slender hand toward Cassandra. "When he is able to return, you will agree to the wedding? It would have to be between Advent and Lent, of course, which is the middle of winter and harsh up here, but—"

"My lady." As gently as she could, Cassandra interrupted the excited flow of chatter. "I merely thanked you for telling me about the dowry. I did not say I would agree to the wedding."

"But why not?" The question was practically a wail. "My son is handsome and kind and intelligent and responsible. He's nothing like his—well, he does favor my brother more than the Gileses."

"If your brother had your beauty, my lady," Cassandra said diplomatically, "then in looks, Whittaker certainly must."

She had seen a portrait of Geoffrey's father, the seventh earl of Whittaker. He was sandy-haired and florid, handsome as an overblown rose is beautiful. Geoffrey and his brother were as beautiful as their mother, except with the square jaw that gave their faces a masculine cast. Perhaps too beautiful for Cassandra's good. Too tempting with those walnut-brown eyes and almost black hair, chiseled features, and a gentleness, a tenderness of spirit . . .

"He got my brother's intellect too. Not that the late earl, my husband, and my first son weren't intelligent," Lady Whittaker hastened to say. "They simply lacked his curiosity."

Cassandra's own curiosity reared its head long enough to wonder how a mother could speak so calmly and with so little emotion about a son she had lost a little less than two years earlier. Mama cried when Beau left for university each semester. Whittaker had come close to weeping over the loss of his older brother, though part of his grief stemmed from having to take on the role of the earl, the head of the family, when he preferred the mechanics of the weaving machinery.

Cassandra tamped down the interest. Curiosity had gotten her into too much trouble already. Now she must pretend she did not particularly care about Whittaker's background, his interests, or even where he was. Guarding his mills, of course, as he had in the spring. She understood why, now that she'd seen firsthand his need for their prosperity.

She also saw the time racing toward the hour for her to leave, if she was to make her way to the field on time to be of use, to see her balloon fly. If it flew and did not catch fire or crash or remain stuck on the ground. But she could not rise from the table until after the countess, who had barely touched her food.

Cassandra hadn't eaten much of hers either. Her stomach ached, but not with hunger. Her legs throbbed from sitting on the hard, wooden chair, where the edge scraped against a particularly tender scar behind her knee, despite gauze padding wrapped around her thigh and beneath her garter. If she sat much longer, she would not be able to make the walk in the half hour she estimated it would take to go the distance.

Two months ago, she could have made the trek in fifteen minutes.

She rubbed the pulling skin on her right leg, realized what she was doing, and jerked her hand up to take a slice of apple from the plate before her.

"I am keeping you sitting too long, am I not?" Her ladyship's gaze dropped from Cassandra's face to her lap. "Are you still in much pain?"

"Not a great deal."

At least not in her legs.

"But the scars pull on the skin and muscles, the physicians told me. I have to walk quite a bit to pull everything back and regain my strength."

"Then we shall continue our talk tomorrow in the garden if the weather is fine, and in the long gallery if it isn't." Her ladyship rose. "Would you like that fruit sent to your room? I worry so about Whittaker that I scarcely eat these days."

Cassandra pulled herself to her feet. "But surely you do not think he is in danger at the mills. I mean, have not the Luddites been subdued?"

"Subdued but not defeated. And he—" Lady Whittaker turned away with an abruptness verging on rude. "Good night, my dear. I look forward to our talk tomorrow."

She left before Cassandra needed to speak a response, leaving her wondering if Geoffrey's mother was a bit touched in her upper works. Perhaps losing her husband and eldest son had unhinged her mind, which maybe even added to her younger son's betrothal ending, denying her the daughter-in-law she obviously wanted. Or perhaps the dowry that she denied them wanting. Sometimes Cassandra's own head felt crazed. She acted so foolishly around Whittaker, denying the solidity of her training and principles.

"And if thy right eye offend thee, pluck it out, and cast it from thee: for it is profitable for thee that one of thy members should perish, and not that thy whole body should be cast into hell," Cassandra quoted from the fifth chapter of Matthew.

Her eyes were fine, other than not seeing more than half a dozen feet in front of her with clarity, but she had plucked out part of her heart, the part that loved Whittaker to distraction.

Most of her heart.

No, no, now she had more time to work on improving travel.

Surely floating through the sky would be more pleasurable than riding on jouncing horses or in carriages. Faster too, if the wind obliged. Perhaps she had a higher purpose.

God had gifted Cassandra with intellect, not beauty; an aptitude for language and mechanics, not for needlework and household management; an aptitude for solitude, not joining her life to another. She failed when she tried. God had taken drastic steps to show her the error of her ways, but she was willing to comply now.

The upcoming mile-long walk seemed daunting at the end of the day and in the dark. Somehow she must find a lantern. A lantern with the flame enclosed in glass and metal would be far better than a torch as Mr. Sorrell suggested. Next time she would confiscate a lantern from somewhere. For now she must rely on a quarter moon and starlight to guide her through the garden and out a narrow gate into the parkland. She had found the route earlier in the day when sunshine drove everyone outside for some exercise after the rain and mists of the previous day. Tonight the sky was so clear the surprisingly smooth and well-trodden path gleamed like a pale ribbon across a dark skirt. A glance upward told her branches had been cut back to allow light to shine through even at night. A lovely notion.

A notion that brought her up short, shivering.

She clutched her shawl around herself and stared at the sparkling sky. An odd place to have a path clear when the paths in the front of the house remained untended and overgrown. One would think a lord would want his guests to have fine paths to walk on, not the passages out to the fields.

Trembling from more than the chilly autumn night, she continued, ignoring the pain in her legs when she could, stopping to rest when she could not. She wished she owned a watch so she knew the time passing. It felt like an hour and a half, not half an hour, before the trees ended with a stone wall and another gate. This one was bolted, but from the inside. If some gamekeeper or gardener inspected the gates and locked the gate before she returned, she would be in serious trouble, but she had yet to see any servant moving outside at night. And Honore would find her. Honore encouraged her ballooning interests, bless the dear girl.

On the far side of the second gate, light flickered in the distance. It still looked a mile off, and the ground grew rough over the stubble that sheep had left behind. Yet the light shone as a beacon, a lighthouse guiding her to safe harbor. She forgot pain and apprehension. Her heart lifted as if it were full of the hot air that sent the balloons soaring into the heavens. In moments she would see . . .

Ah, yes, she did see it, the thirty feet of colorful silk bag bobbing over the brazier that produced the fire needed for the hot air. The basket strained at its moorings while one man stood beside a torch planted in the ground and another man stood—

Cassandra stopped so fast she teetered. Air trapped in her lungs.

Two men stood in the basket. Three men in all tended the balloon launching. The one still on terra firma lit a second torch. The flaming pine pitch shone yellowish-white full on his face.

Geoffrey Giles, the ninth earl of Whittaker, stood not a dozen yards away.

9

At least the man bore Geoffrey's features—the sharply defined cheekbones and jaw, the thick, dark hair, the broad shoulders. But the hair was more unkempt than usual and dusted with gray, and those shoulders wore a leather jerkin like a laborer. Slight differences and enough to stop her from calling out his name and demanding to know what he was doing there. He looked at her as though she too were a stranger, a quick scan from head to toe, perhaps his gaze lingering a little too long where it shouldn't have, like that of an insolent youth. She had encountered that often enough in London and Devonshire fairs and treated him as she did those young men.

She turned her back on him as though he did not exist and addressed her friends. "You found another assistant?"

"He said Lady Whittaker sent him to help, as she wanted no accidents in her fields but didn't want to stop the flow of progress." Philip Sorrell grinned like a schoolboy let out on an early holiday.

"Don't expect she'd like us here if she knew you were," Roger Kent added.

The laborer who looked like Whittaker snorted.

"Well, I am here, so we can send this fellow away." Cassandra turned toward the man and reached out her hand. "I can take the torch."

"Aye, miss." He started to hand it to her, then swung away with an abruptness that sent sparks swirling behind him like dancing stars, and stuck the torch in the ground near the first one. Cassandra remained where she was, frozen, her hand still outstretched and shaking. Her mouth felt like someone had rolled a ball of lint over her tongue, and she could not breathe. The stench of pine pitch made her stomach burn. For a moment, sickness rose in her throat. She swallowed and returned her attention to the balloon.

"It is—" The words emerged as a croak. She swallowed again. "The balloon looks filled now." That was better, strong and steady. "Shall I untie the lines?"

"If you can." Mr. Sorrells leaned over the side of the basket. "Or that fellow can help you."

"Balloon's filling too slowly." Mr. Kent bounced up and down, making the basket sway. "Let us be on our way before the night is gone."

Both men looked so excited, their faces glowing in the firelight, that Cassandra ached to clamber over the edge of the basket and join them. Going up would make her life complete. She would not feel the slightest twinge of regret over Whittaker if she could sail into the heavens. But the men would not let her this time, not on this balloon's maiden voyage. They thought it too dangerous in the event of a mechanical failure. But at least they said only this time and not never. Whittaker had persisted in saying, "When we're married, you will never . . ." as though she would lose interest because she bore his name and wore a ring on her finger.

The man who looked too much like him for her comfort

stepped to one of the lines and began to untie the knot. Heart pounding, Cassandra followed suit.

"Is the tubing tight?" Mr. Kent said above her. "We want to ensure the tube doesn't come out so we keep the balloon inflated properly."

Mr. Sorrells's sigh sounded loud enough to be air escaping from the silk bag. "For the tenth time, Roger, yes, the tube is tight."

Of course it would be. It must be. The tube ran high enough into the inflated balloon that no one could reach it from the basket. A design flaw. Yet the balloon had to be far enough above the brazier and bottle of acid to keep it from catching fire. That had happened and men had died in other flights. Surely a compromise could be worked out, or another method . . .

"Miss Bainbridge, please." Mr. Kent leaned down right above her. "Are you going to untie that knot or leave us tilting like a seesaw?"

Cassandra glanced up. Indeed, with the other ropes untied, the basket tilted dangerously from the tug of the balloon. Coals could spill from the brazier, and vitriol-coated iron shavings could spill from the beaker that, with the heat, created the necessary light hot air for the balloon to work. Her inattention might have caused a disaster.

In her haste to untie the knot, her fingers fumbled, making amok of the lines.

"Let me." The man nudged her fingers away and loosed the rope.

Cassandra jumped as though splashed with the acid bath. The man's hands were rough, dry, and cracked, not a gentleman's hands. Yet their touch sent a jolt through her, heat, a breathless longing. She glanced at him to see his reaction, but he stood motionless, his hands clasped behind his back, his head tilted up to the ascending balloon.

The ascending balloon! She was not even watching after waiting for this moment for so long, wanton that she was. Her cheeks burned as she gazed toward the heavens. The silhouette of bulbous silk and oval basket was etched against the stars, blurring as the distance went beyond her range of sight, since she had not thought to wear her spectacles. Whoops of joy from Sorrells and Kent floated through the air like a shower of gold rain. Pure joy. And she forgot the man nearby, that mortifying flash of wanting to be touched. Her longing focused on the diminishing sight of something she had helped design.

She pounded her cane on the sheep-shorn grass. "I should be up there too."

"No, my dear, you should not be." Whittaker's voice came from the laborer with rough garb and hands.

She spun toward him. Her cane stuck in the ground, soft from the rain of the day before, and she twisted her right ankle, the one most badly burned. A cry spilled from her lips and tears stung her eyes.

"Cassandra." Whittaker caught her. Strong arms, stronger than she remembered, folded around her. "Are you in pain? Stupid question. Of course you are. Shall I carry you back to the house?"

Ah, the temptation to say yes, to let those strong arms enfold her and hold her against him, to rest her head on his broad shoulder. Yet he had said she shouldn't be in that balloon, had denied her the greatest desire of her heart.

She wrenched herself free. "What are you doing here?"

"This is my field."

"You are supposed to be in the Dale protecting your looms."

His face twisted. "More than you know. But when I heard you were helping with this balloon launch, I came to ensure you did not go up with them."

"You have no right."

"You are staying in my house. You are under my protection."

"You have odd ways of protecting your guests." Cassandra curled her upper lip. "You have not once made an appearance. And speaking of appearances, what are you doing dressed like that and—" She wrinkled her nose, aware now that she was close to him. "You reek like sheep and ale."

"And you smell like apples. A little sweet. A little sour. So refreshing." His voice dropped to the low timbre, the smooth pitch, that never failed to send a shiver racing through her.

It did not fail this time. She clutched her cane like a weapon. If he came near her again, she would . . . she would . . .

"I am protecting my looms, as you said I am." He took that step nearer to her.

She did nothing.

"And as you see, I am ensuring your safety, my dear."

"I am not your dear."

"You made a promise you always would be." He stepped close enough to touch her again but did not reach out.

She was tall for a female, not like Lydia, but more than Honore and Mama. Yet he was still a full head taller. To look into his face rather than at the top button of his jacket, she had to tilt her head back, as she had done so often when she was his dear, his darling, his love, and he hers, when her face turned up to his meant an invitation almost from their first meeting. Certainly from the first time they found themselves alone together in one of the walkways at Vauxhall. Music and fireworks in the distance. Darkness and quiet around them. The lightest brush of his lips on hers felt like the explosions coloring the skies above the trees. She should have known then that he was not right for her, should have confessed to Mama or Lydia—though neither had been around—that she could not sort out whether she loved him or lusted for him. The trouble caused by the latter had surely suppressed the former.

"I lied," she whispered through a constricted throat.

She should be revolted by the odors of sheep and ale. Yet beneath, she caught his familiar scents, the clean earthiness of leather, the fresh, exotic tang of sandalwood.

She forced air into her lungs to make her voice stronger. "I mean, I was mistaken. I only—"

He kissed her lightly, tenderly, so sweetly her eyes burned. Then he turned away from her. "I cannot stay. Without the mills, as you have most likely noticed, Whittaker Hall will fall into rack and ruin, and the scores of men and women and their children who rely on me for a living will be penniless at best, thanks to my wastrel father and gamester brother."

A difficulty her seven thousand pounds in dowry would have solved without him having to rely on the income from the mills.

The mills. Luddites. Danger.

"Whittaker," she called after him.

He kept going, his long legs eating up the ground to create distance between them.

"Geoffrey?" She stumbled after him. "You are not truly in danger. Wait! You cannot—"

He could not what? Save his livelihood and that of all those who worked in the mills and on the estate? But surely not. An earl hired people to do what needed to be done. He did not go himself. But if he did go himself, the choice belonged to him. She had no more right to stop him than he had to stop her from going up in a balloon. They meant nothing to one another. They were nothing to one another. Nothing. Nothing.

She rubbed her right thigh. Even through her petticoat and shift and skirt, she felt the ridge of a scar forming where once a row of blisters had lined her leg, blisters that had almost cost her that leg. Mama had warned her. Lydia had warned her. Lydia had married for the infatuation of passion the first time and regretted it for years. Now she had found her love, the man God wanted for her. But then, Lydia was beautiful, perfect, not hideously marked. Cassandra would devote herself to science as much as Father and Society allowed. Whittaker would find another lady, another dowry.

Cassandra pressed her lips together and turned to the torches. Both threatened to die. She needed to light fresh ones to help guide the men back, if they could get back. They could raise and lower their elevation to find different currents. The sails and paddles might enable them to steer.

With Whittaker gone, the pitch burned her nose. The night wind roared in her ears like that angry crowd pushing at the carriage, brandishing their torches, demanding more light from the nobleman inside. They were mad. She had been mad, shamed at her behavior. The torches brought memory of pain rushing back so she couldn't move. In seconds, her friends could die. The field would be dark. The men might not know where to land or even if they landed in the right place.

Shaking, she lifted one of the sticks with its end dipped in pitch. Holding it at arm's length and bending from the waist to keep herself as far from the flame as possible, she touched the new brand to the old. It flared at once, a white-hot light shooting into the night. Now she either needed to hold onto it or plant it in the ground like the others. She could not hold it.

Her arm ached from the effort of holding it straight out from her body. She could not kneel to set it into the ground. If she did, she might not get up again. She must hold it until she needed to light a new one—another difficulty. She could never hold two.

Her hand trembled and sparks flew. One dropped onto her sleeve. She screamed, slapped it out with her other hand. The torch dropped from her fingers. It lay on the fortunately damp grass and smoldered, more smoke now than flame, invisible in the dark.

"This will never work," she cried aloud.

She. Must. Get. Ahold. Of herself. Must. Must. Must.

Teeth clenched, she picked up another torch. Just enough fire burned on the one Whittaker had lit for her to ignite the pitch of the new brand. Before the flame flared high, she shoved the end into the soft ground as she had seen Whittaker do. There, she had accomplished something on her own, overcome one fear. But the wind had changed, stiffened. First the torch flared higher from a gust in one direction, then another. She glanced up, sniffing for rain, straining her eyes for signs of clouds on the horizon or, more importantly, a sight of the balloon with its tongue of fire licking against the night.

The rain, the tang of salt from the sea, drifted on the wind. Dampness moistened her face, but no clouds showed. The torchlight blinded her from what sailed across the heavens, whether God- or man-created. Rain could prove disastrous. Besides getting poor Mr. Sorrells and Mr. Kent soaked, it could put out the brazier that produced the hot air and make them crash.

She laughed aloud, more a snort than a true expression of mirth. Of course it would rain. This was England. Yet men ballooned in the Lake District, the lands with the most rain she had ever heard of in England or the continent. They would have to learn to manage if they wanted to make ballooning a practical form of travel.

Out of breath, her legs burning, she paused to light another torch and felt a drop of rain on her cheek. She couldn't stay. She couldn't wait for them. The physicians told her to have a care for her health until she had fully regained her strength. She had a mile to walk back to the house. If she didn't start back now, she would be drenched. The torches wouldn't stay lit in the rain anyway.

Muscles so tense she could barely place one foot in front of the other, Cassandra retraced her steps across the field to the parkland gate.

"Don't do it!" Despite being breathless from running across his fields to a horse, followed by a mad gallop to town and then a race through the streets on foot, Whittaker tried to make his voice heard. Above the roar of twenty men bellowing destruction of the greedy mill owners, he doubted anyone heard him. "Destruction isn't the answer."

If they heard him, they ignored him. Hugh had worked the followers of so-called Captain Lud into a frenzy of anger and hatred for anyone who owned, rented, or even worked one of the looms before Whittaker managed to reach the outskirts of the Dale, where his uncle had predicted the future of the weaving industry would lie and thus had built his mills.

"The days of the small one or two looms in a man's cottage are done, lad," Uncle Hern had said before he died.

And therein lay the trouble. Men working the stocking and cloth looms at home couldn't make enough money now with the competition of the larger mills that could keep men hired for production all day and all night, where the looms were owned instead of rented. Mills that could afford the latest designs in machinery. Progress was not fair to the men who had done the same work as their fathers and their fathers before them. Whittaker had not created the change, though, and he needed the money too badly to let his uncle's hard work and sacrifices go up in flames or fall to the axes many of the men carried.

"If you destroy the mills," he tried again, "you'll have no place to work. At the least—"

"Stubble it, Geoff." Hugh grabbed his shoulder with a hand like an iron shackle.

Whittaker stubbled it—for the moment.

"We gotta teach these mill owners a lesson so's they pay us a fair wage." Hugh dropped his hand. "Ain't nothin' gonna stop these men outside an army."

Which they just might get, and Whittaker was on the wrong side. If only he could tell them he paid a fair wage, took less in profits so the men could support their families. He was not responsible for the numbers of them who drank half their week's wages before they got home.

Except that had not been so much of a problem when the men worked at home with their wives and children around them, helping, collecting the fees.

Whittaker tried another tack. "But surely the Hern mills have guards. These men aren't armed."

"The Hern mills don't got enough guards." Rob had come up on Whittaker's other side.

Probably not, but Major Crawford knew about the imminent attack. He might send soldiers. Guards with muskets could do more damage than men with axes and cudgels. Unfortunately, they flourished firebrands too. A touch of flame to a bale of cotton fresh off the ship from America, a bundle of flax recently harvested in Ireland, or, worst of all, oily wool from his very own sheep, and the conflagration would destroy his livelihood.

As fire had destroyed his marriage plans.

"They'll hang you if you're caught," was all Whittaker could think to say.

But surprisingly few men had been caught, fewer hanged for their destruction of looms and workshops in Nottingham and Yorkshire. The men around him knew it. They remained too anonymous or too dedicated to the same cause as everyone else to betray one another. The three he could identify for the authorities were not enough, were too unimportant. The authorities wanted leaders, men whose capture, trial, and execution would matter enough to the others to stop future revolts. No revolutions by the mobs would happen in England.

He charged forward with the others, seeking faces, listening for names. The men wore caps pulled low to shield their eyes, beards to conceal their facial features, even scarves as makeshift masks on this cold and increasingly damp night.

Whittaker prayed for rain. A deluge might dampen their enthusiasm for destruction. But the clouds only loosed their water in an occasional shower, leaving enough dry spells for the torches to be relighted and burn brightly, and leaving his prayer as unanswered as had been every one since Cassandra's accident. Like his father, God punished him by ignoring him or taking away something he dearly wanted.

"Oh, Cassandra." He murmured her name like a groan of pain, then skidded to a halt.

What was he thinking to pray for rain? It might save his mill, but Cassandra's health was not good enough for her to be out in the rain, soaked to the skin. If she caught a chill after fighting the fever brought on by her burns, she might succumb to a lung fever.

No, no, God would not hurt Cassandra to punish him. He knew that in his head. His heart ached so badly he could not breathe.

"Going pudding-hearted?" Hugh called back. He and Rob spun away from the mob and flanked Whittaker again.

Whittaker pressed a hand to his side. "Stitch in my side is all."

"Uh-huh." Hugh prodded Whittaker forward with something harder than a fist to the spine.

Rob grabbed his upper arm in sausage-like fingers. "You wouldn't be wanting to slip off and rouse the authorities, would you?"

"Not at all." The absolute truth. He had already warned the authorities. The stitch was real too. He should not have gone to see Cassandra. Yet he could not have risked her going up in a balloon. Recently two men had died when their balloon caught fire and crashed. Cassandra must have nothing more happen to her. He did not know if her friends would protect her. But even if they did, those friends should not be alone with her, two men and one female in the middle of the night. She was not thinking clearly. Or at all.

And neither was he. He had to keep going, yield to these men's shoves forward into the middle of the crowd. Shouting, cursing, threatening men roared their way toward one of the Hern mills with the owner in their midst, at the front of the pack. He was with them now, a part of the rebellion. Who cared that he had been blackmailed into it? If Bainbridge, Crawford, and his companion denied the blackmail, Whittaker was a dead man. Worse than a dead man—part of the nobility turned against his country.

A traitor.

The crowd trapped him at the front of the throng, a good place to be to win men's trust. A bad place to be to stay alive if the guards were prepared.

They were prepared. The first volley of gunfire boomed over the heads of the charging men, a warning shot over the bows. No one heeded it. No one stopped. Enough of them knew the time needed for men to reload or exchange one musket for another. And the missiles began to fly—cudgels, stones from the street, and flaming torches from one end.

"Take 'em down, lads," someone shouted. Whittaker could not tell from which side.

Guns fired, fists and harder implements struck flesh. Men groaned or screamed in pain, bellowed outrage, fought in silence. All became a melee of surging, struggling bodies—arms and legs, flying fists, and tumbling forms lit by a fire at one end of the mill.

Flames danced off the silver gorget of a military man. Crawford had sent reinforcements, bless him. Whittaker ducked away from the man, remaining behind others, avoiding blows and shots on his way to the fire. He had to put out the fire, stop the devastation—

Another scarlet-coated man materialized in front of him. He held a horse pistol in both hands and took aim from less than a yard away.

"No," Whittaker called out. "I'm not—"

A flash flared brighter than the distant fire. Whittaker lunged aside—too late. Other blasts and a strange roaring blotted out the boom of exploding gunpowder, and the hit slammed into him like a blacksmith's hammer. He staggered back, caught his foot on rough cobbles, and fell, his head striking the iron gatepost to his own mill and knocking him unconscious.

10

Swallowing to keep herself from sobbing, Cassandra flung open the door to her bedchamber so hard it banged against the wall. A shriek pierced the door to the adjacent room and Honore flew from her bedchamber to grab Cassandra and drag her into a chair. "Where have you been? Oh, never you mind. I know. You are soaked quite through and you must get into your bed at once. Here." She thrust a nightcap at Cassandra. "Put this over your wet hair. Did you not think to put up your hood?"

"I do not like hoods. They keep me from—"

"Never you mind that either. Hurry. One of the maids just warned me. Lady Whittaker is coming down here any moment now. Something about how she wants to deliver the bad news herself."

At that moment, footfalls clattered down the hall and someone pounded on the sitting room door. "Cassandra? Honore?" Lady Whittaker called.

Cassandra and Honore exchanged a glance, mouths open, eyes wide.

"I'll delay her." Honore dashed for the sitting room.

Cassandra dragged herself to her feet with the aid of the chair's sturdy arm and kicked her muddy boots under the bed as she yanked her dressing gown on over her soaked dress.

111

"Is Cassandra awake?" Lady Whittaker was saying in the next room. "I must speak to her."

Cassandra's gaze flew to the clock. Half past one of the clock. Her stomach turned somersaults, twisting itself into knots. Her heart had surely ceased beating. She couldn't feel it beating over the nausea from knowing something was wrong.

"Would you like me to go awaken her?" Honore asked. "I am awake because I'm writing a book, you know, and that keeps me up until all hours, but Cassandra is still—"

"I am sorry, child. I will wake her myself if necessary."

It was not necessary. Things just must appear so.

With shaking hands, Cassandra shoved the nightcap over her wet hair and stumbled to the door. She tugged it open as Lady Whittaker was reaching for the latch. "What's amiss?"

"Oh, my dear." Her ladyship clasped Cassandra's hands. Hers felt as cold as Cassandra's. Tears brightened her deep brown eyes. "It is Geoffrey. He—I do not know how to say this except for straight-out. He has been shot."

Honore gasped. Her face paled.

Cassandra's head spun. Images of Whittaker in his laborer's garb flashed through her mind. "He cannot have been shot. I just saw—" She pressed the back of her hand to her lips. "I mean, who would shoot him? Where? When? All seemed well enough—" She stopped her babbling a second time—too late.

Lady Whittaker's eyes narrowed and her lips compressed for a moment.

Cassandra took a step backward. "I, um, did see him for a few minutes this evening. He—he came to see me, but we were never alone, I assure—"

"You are soaked. We shall concern ourselves later as to why you've been out in the rain. You had best get out of those wet clothes, child," Lady Whittaker said. "We do not need you catching a chill when you have been so recently ill."

"You do not need two invalids if—if—" Cassandra's voice broke. She could not ask the question burning bile in her throat.

Lady Whittaker took Cassandra's hand and drew her to the fireplace. "He is still alive. I know little more. The major sent a messenger. They are bringing him home—Geoffrey, that is, not the major, though I expect he will be coming too. Something at the mills, I expect, the awful Luddites destroying men's livelihood, and now my son after—but that's neither here nor there." She picked up the poker and thrust it into the coals as though stabbing an enemy's heart.

Her heart? The notion crossed Cassandra's thoughts. After what Whittaker had endured as her fiancé, he didn't deserve to be wounded for any reason. If he died, Cassandra would have her freedom without effort, but the cost was not worth the end result.

Lord, please do not answer my prayer this way.

"Honore, will you ring for some tea?" Lady Whittaker requested. "Gallons of it. And coffee. I must have coffee if I am to be up all the night." She turned her attention back to Cassandra.

"I did not go out to meet him," Cassandra said. "I would never behave so dishonorably as to meet a gentleman at night, I assure you. That I saw him was purely—"

"I wish you had gone to meet him." Lady Whittaker's tone held a sharp edge in her interruption. "He likely would be all right now if you had. Get yourself into your nightclothes and into bed. I will return later when I know more." With a swish of her black twill skirt, she swept from the room. Not until the door had clicked shut behind her did a sob escape from her lips.

The soft cry may as well have been a gunshot wound to Cassandra's conscience.

"But I am not responsible," she said.

It did not help. Her throat closed too hard for so much as a sigh, let alone a sob, to escape.

Honore's face glowed ghastly pale in the firelight. "Did you argue with him and make him do something awful that got him shot?"

"No. Yes. No, I simply told him again that there is no longer any future for us, and then we helped the balloon launch and—I wonder if they landed safely in the rain. I couldn't stay to help. I'm sure the torches must have gone out because of the rain, and I was so cold. I am so cold. Will you help me with these hooks? I do not wish to call a maid."

Honore began to unfasten Cassandra's gown. "I cannot believe Whittaker was shot. We were enjoying ourselves so much at the Luvells' party. They have four offspring between eighteen and twenty—two are twins—and do not mind in the least if we have a romp. I believe Major Crawford was a bit shocked at our pace of dancing, but he took it in good stride. He is so stiff most of the time, he's as dull as a stick."

"Who cares about romps and stiff Army majors when my friends were up in the balloon when the rain blew in, and—and Whittaker—" Cassandra hugged her arms so covered in gooseflesh she felt the bumps through her sleeves.

Honore paused. "I am a beast to prattle on so, but I wanted to distract you. You truly look ill."

"I am going to be truly ill if I do not get dry." Tears spilled from Cassandra's eyes. "And being a watering pot won't help that, will it?" She dashed at the drops. "I do not even love him anymore."

"Lying is neither becoming nor Christian." Honore finished

with the hooks and tugged on the shoulders of the gown. "You love him to distraction. I saw it in your face the last time you saw him."

Cassandra yanked her arms out of the sleeves of her gown and began to untie the tapes holding up her petticoat. "I do not love him."

Lust. The feelings were nothing more than pure desire creating impure actions.

"But that does not mean I want anything awful to happen to him."

"How did you see him tonight?"

A knock prevented Cassandra from answering.

"Come to my room," Honore called through the panels. She scampered into the other bedchamber, closing the doors to the sitting room between them.

Cassandra finished removing her damp clothes. Once she stood in her shift before the fire, heat reached her skin and the chills began to subside. She wrapped her dressing gown around her and perched on the edge of a chaise to remove her stockings, then, hearing the maid leaving Honore's room, she stopped. Honore had screamed the first and only time she had seen Cassandra's burns. They were more smooth, white flesh now rather than the angry red they had been then, but the skin was shiny and ridged. Inhuman.

Cassandra left on her stockings and located her slippers beneath the chaise. Lined with lamb's wool and trimmed in swansdown like her dressing gown, they would have her toes thawed in minutes. The tea would help too. But what of Mr. Sorrells and Mr. Kent? They must be freezing up in that balloon, if they were still up there and not broken bodies crashed on the unforgiving ground.

Cassandra shook off the thought. She and Whittaker had believed themselves safe inside a carriage from Grosvenor to Cavendish Square. Life was dangerous. People had to take risks. Look at Whittaker, wounded.

Dying?

She bit the inside of her lower lip to keep it from trembling. She had rejected him. For his own good, of course. She didn't want him to wed her out of obligation, out of guilt, out of his need for her dowry, which would make him feel more guilty.

If the mill had been destroyed, he would need that money even more.

Cassandra shook off the thoughts of her ability to help with a single word, and rose. She wanted that tea.

Honore had set it up in the sitting room between their bed-chambers. The room was too large for such a cozy phrase, but it was made more intimate with the use of oriental screens whose faded yet still lovely silk-on-silk embroidered scenes of fantastic birds suggested some ancestor had brought them back from China in an earlier century. Cassandra and Honore marked out a seating area close to the fire. Whatever other economies Lady Whittaker practiced in her household man-agement, she did not stint on coal. Perhaps because coal was inexpensive in Lancashire, with mines close at hand. Perhaps the Giles family owned a coal mine too. Or had at one time. Whittaker never mentioned it; the mills held his interest. He loved their mechanics, the potential for greater production and work.

"Cloth—fine cloth—could be afforded by more people," he had once told her. "Stockings too, though I shouldn't admit that to a lady, I suppose."

Now Cassandra flopped inelegantly into a chair and held her

hands out to the blaze. "Did the maid tell you anything of his lordship's condition?"

"His lordship?" Honore set a cup of steaming tea and milk in Cassandra's hands. "You're calling Whittaker *his lordship* like you are barely acquainted?"

"We are no longer betrothed. Now, please, any word?"

Honore fluttered down onto the adjacent chair with her usual grace and poise. "They've brought him in and taken him to his rooms on the other side of the house is all I know. The maid said everyone is at sixes and sevens over something he keeps muttering."

"Muttering?" Cassandra straightened. "He's awake then?"

"A bit, but rather out of his head." Honore sipped at her tea and gazed past Cassandra, her bright blue eyes distant as though she were in deep thought.

Cassandra set her cup on the table before her and grasped her sister's arm. "You know more. You talked to the maid for quite a while."

"I did, but he's out of his head, as I—" Honore broke off and sighed. "It is just servants' gossip, Cassie." She looked at Cassandra. "They're saying he claims he was shot deliberately."

11

Cassandra. Whittaker wanted to see Cassandra. It was the one coherent thought he possessed for what felt like ten years of his life but which was, in truth, no more than three days. He knew he lay in his own bed and that Mama barely left his side, and when she did, the housekeeper or a maid tucked herself away in a corner in the event he called for anyone. He did. Often. He called for Cassandra. She never arrived.

On the third day since a British soldier had shot him despite Whittaker's protest that he was not one of the rioters, he woke with a clearer head, less throbbing in the rather minor wound in his arm, and a raging hunger for more than the broth and weak tea Mama had been spooning down him since two of his weavers had carried him to the Hall. But when he opened his mouth to ask for nourishment, what emerged was, "Cassandra?"

"Geoffrey." Mama rushed to his bedside. Her eyes showed new creases at the corners and lines of red shot through the whites. Her skin was paler than ever, her gown wrinkled. But her smile glowed like the fire behind her. "My dear boy, you are awake."

He managed a smile, though the stretching cracked his lips and hurt his head. "Yes, and hungry. But Cassandra? May I see her?"

"I will fetch you some porridge."

He wanted ham and eggs.

He wanted to see Cassandra.

"Will you send in one of the footmen to help me make myself presentable and bring her to me?" he asked—pleaded, really.

Mama's response was to close the door quietly behind her.

Perhaps the time was too early or too late. But the curtains had been drawn back from the window. A patch of pale blue sky shimmered through the glass. No clouds, so the sun shone, but not into his chamber, which meant the hour ranged sometime between dawn and noon. Perhaps she had gone out driving if the weather was fine. As much as he wanted to think it, he could not expect her to be hovering outside his door, anxious for word of his condition. More than once she had told him they were through, their betrothal and marriage wrong.

Yet after he kissed her the other night, she looked dazed, dreamy, nearly as happy as she had appeared while gazing up at the ascending balloon.

So he was competing for her affections with a balloon.

Whittaker raised his arm and raked his fingers through his hair. It felt lank and unkempt. Beard stubble itched along his jaw. No wonder Mama ignored his requests to see Cassandra. He did not look respectable enough to receive a male caller, let alone a female one. He supposed a proper young lady should not visit him in his bedchamber anyway. All the more reason to get up, wash, shave, dress.

Could a body dress with one arm in a sling?

"A flesh wound," he recalled the apothecary saying. "He

119

should be all right if it doesn't take an infection. The head is more serious."

It was. The pistol ball that slammed into his arm and went straight through had knocked him off balance enough that he struck his head. Everything grew hazy after that, a muddle of voices and pain and someone kicking him in the side. He recalled not making a sound, playing at being dead, though he did not know why instinct told him to do so.

He tried to think of that now, but his brain refused to cooperate. His stomach growled, insisting on being filled. Even porridge sounded good. Mama would make it full of butter and sugar with a hint of cinnamon. She had always treated him special, whereas his brother—his half brother—

No, no, Mama would never be unfaithful, would never have broken her marriage vows. The very notion turned his hunger pang to a pain. The shooting had warned him he played too dangerous a game, yet to imperil Mama's reputation seemed even riskier.

The door opened and Mama returned, one of the footmen in tow. "Your porridge will be here soon, and here is Gareth to help you look respectable, as several persons wish to speak to you as long as you can manage visitors."

"Cass—"

"Major Crawford, of course, and I've sent for the apothecary to tell him you are in your right mind again."

"Was I in my wrong mind?" Whittaker tried another smile. Easier this time.

Mama shook her head, flicking a glance toward the middle-aged footman. All of their footmen were middle-aged, or was it both of their footmen? Most houses went for young men, well set-up youths. Theirs were fine-looking men, just older for the position and thus less costly. They did not have a butler in the country, just the housekeeper and several maids.

"I will return in a quarter hour or so," Mama said, then left.

"Shall I shave you, milord?" Gareth asked.

Whittaker assented to that and more. Mama returned in half an hour, and though fatigued, Whittaker felt more himself—clean and smooth-faced, his hair unmatted, but still hanging over his ears and the collar of his dressing gown as though he were trying to create his own periwig from an earlier age. She bore a tray she laid across his knees, then stuck the spoon into the bowl of fragrant oatmeal porridge.

He took the handle from her. "I can feed myself, thank you."

"But slowly. The apothecary said for you to eat slowly. He is here and will come in to see you as soon as you have finished your breakfast. If this agrees with you, you may have a coddled egg and some toast later."

It agreed with him. Amazing what some solid food, even cooked grain, could do for a man's well-being.

"No wonder the weavers riot." He stared into his empty bowl. "They are not making enough money to feed themselves and their families."

"But surely your weavers do." Mama looked puzzled. "I know my brother was not always fair in his wages, he so wished to profit, and your father and brother left the estate—but I should not speak ill of the dead."

"Truth is truth, Mama. Father and John left matters here in a shambles. But I will not correct their errors on the backs of my workers. My weavers were not amongst the rioters. At least none that I saw."

"Then why attack your mills? Do they not understand that is ruining work, not making matters better?"

"Logic flees when mobs rule." He tried to lift the tray from his lap but could not manage with one hand. "Now may I see this apothecary and get that beyond me so I may receive callers?" He made Mama look him in the eye. "I want to see Cassandra. Please? Just for a moment? I know it is improper, but surely with you here, and her sister may join her too. But—what is amiss?"

Mama blinked hard and shook her head. "I am so sorry, my dear, but Cassandra is quite ill. She seems to have taken a chill, and one of her burn wounds—what are you doing?"

"Getting out of bed." Heedless of the coverlet, Whittaker shoved the tray onto the mattress beside him and swung his legs over the side of the bed. "You should have told me straightaway."

"You cannot go down there. You are not well enough yourself." Mama grasped his arm.

He extricated himself from her hold and grabbed at the bedpost until the dizziness left his head. "I can. I shall." Thinking of the rain that had brought him around from the blow to his head, made him conscious enough to get help, he knew how Cassandra had gotten her chill—standing in the rain awaiting her aeronaut friends.

The other men in her life.

He released the bedpost and headed for the door. "This is all my fault."

"No, Geoffrey, you must not." Mama grasped his arm to stop him. "She—well, the apothecary is considering bringing in a surgeon to—to—she somehow caused an inflammation in one of her . . . burns, which he fears may grow gangrenous if not tended to at once."

A smooth, dry hand brushed the hair away from Cassandra's face. A palm lingered against her cheek, too broad for Honore's or Lady Whittaker's. Too hard for the apothecary's doughy flesh. Too familiar for an apothecary's too, but definitely belonging to a male.

A male in her sickroom. Perhaps they had brought in a physician. The apothecary said something about one of her burns not quite healed—

A surgeon. Oh no, they had sent for a surgeon to remove her leg.

"No, no. You cannot." The protest emerged in a croak. Her eyes flew open, tried to focus in a room lit by firelight.

"Cannot what, my dear?" the man responded.

If ears could blink in surprise, hers did. She must be mistaken. The congestion in her head had caused a roaring in her ears for days, muffling all sound around her from voices to clinking china. He would not dare come to her bedchamber in what must be the night. Her fevered imagination had created his voice out of the surgeon's.

She peered up at the face above her, shadowed by a fall of sleek, dark hair and light behind him. "Please, do not amputate my—my leg. It got well before. It will get well again. Please. It was the rain, the wet—"

"Hush. No one is going to perform surgery on you."

The touch on her lips brought clarity. Not her imagination.

"What are you doing in here?" She whispered because that did not hurt. "You are half-dead."

"Nothing of the kind." Brazenly, he perched on the edge of the bed. She opened her mouth to protest, but he smiled. "Mama is right here too, playing chaperone. Has been for two days."

"Still improper," Cassandra murmured. "We are not betrothed."

"And so I told him," Lady Whittaker said from somewhere near the hearth. "And he should be resting himself. But I cannot get him to leave here without having the footmen carry him away, for which he threatened to dismiss them, which would be unkind and not worth the trouble."

"But you would never do that. Dismiss them," Cassandra said.

Whittaker's hand returned to her cheek. "You still think enough of me to know that."

"Of course." She closed her eyes, too weary to say more, weary enough to fall into the first restful sleep she had enjoyed since the night Whittaker had been wounded. The night of the ascension.

She still knew nothing of her friends. She had awakened the next morning with a raging fever and the realization that one of her burns, the worst one on her right ankle, had rubbed raw against her boot. Through a haze of fever and pain, she recalled the apothecary saying the word *sepsis*. Infection. The danger of burns. He exclaimed over her scars. Lady Whittaker wept, murmuring about not realizing they were so extensive.

"You poor child . . . the pain . . . no wonder . . ." were all phrases Cassandra recalled her ladyship saying.

The final one stuck the most. No wonder what? She had broken off the betrothal? Of course she would. The bride of the ninth earl of Whittaker must not be repulsive to her husband. And she was repulsive, to hear the apothecary speak, and he was a man. A pudge of a man with face and hands like rising bread dough, but still male.

Yet apparently Whittaker, with his mother's cooperation if not approval, had spent the day beside her bed. He arrived the next day too, this time dressed save for a coat, but with a banyan over shirt and breeches.

"Not drawing room wear," he greeted her, "but all I can manage with this sling. Can you manage some breakfast?"

"Where is Lady Whittaker?"

"I have no idea," her son admitted.

"But I am here." Honore leaned over the bed and kissed Cassandra's brow. "I shall play chaperone."

"But it is bright in here. He can see how hideous I am." Cassandra turned toward the half-open curtains and window through which sunshine streamed like melted butter from a pitcher.

"You are not hideous." Whittaker lifted a handful of her hair off the pillow and let it slide through his fingers. "A little pale, perhaps, but not hideous."

"You do not know the whole of it." Cassandra closed her mouth and her eyes.

She must make him go away. In another minute she might grasp the hand beside her face and hold on as though she did not want to let it go. Having him close, hearing his voice, felt too good, too right, to her heart.

Her intellect gained strength over her heart, and she managed to push him away. "How are my friends? Did you hear of what became of Mr. Sorrells and Mr. Kent?"

Whittaker jerked away so quickly she felt the movement.

"They are quite all right." Honore seemed oblivious to Whittaker's reaction, so cheerful did she sound. "They called the next day, but you were sleeping."

"And no one told me?" Cassandra attempted to sit up with the coverlet clutched beneath her chin. "Honore, you surely realize I would want to know at once how they fared."

"They are not dead." The coldness of Whittaker's tone, the sudden hardness of his jaw, suggested perhaps he wished they were.

"Did it work? Did my sails—" Realizing that she croaked rather than talked, Cassandra shut her mouth again.

Honore, golden and cheerful like the sunshine, approached the bed, a cup in her hands. "Drink this. Hot tea with some honey and lemon."

"Thank you," Cassandra said, not moving.

She could not take the cup without sitting up and could not sit up with Whittaker standing there. She flicked a glance at him, willing him to leave.

He took the cup from Honore instead. "Help her to get settled against the headboard, Miss Honore. Miss Bainbridge wishes to remain modest."

His gaze connected and locked with Cassandra's. Her cheeks burned as though her fever had not broken. "Swine," she mouthed, fighting a rush of tears.

"Cassandra." Honore's eyes widened in shock. "You didn't just call Whittaker a swine, did you?"

"Yes, I believe she did, and with reason." After setting the tea on the table beside the bed, he turned his back on them and strode across the room.

Cassandra held her breath, expecting him to walk out of the room. But he simply strode to the window and faced the garden beyond, one hand braced against the frame. Sunshine glinted off mahogany highlights in his dark hair and limned the breadth of his shoulders. Somewhere in the year and a half she had known him, Geoffrey Giles had grown from a gangly youth into a well set-up man. Her middle quivered despite her illness, and she turned away in time to notice Honore staring at him, her eyes bright with reflected daylight, her lips parted in a secret little half-smile. Cassandra stared at her for a moment, then understood.

Honore, who had treated him like an older brother at best since he began to court Cassandra, now stared at Whittaker with the kind of admiration she had heretofore reserved for men like Gerald Frobisher in the spring and now Captain Crawford—as though he were a potential beau.

12

He was a swine.

Whittaker listened to the silence behind him and decided he would be better off banging his head against the window until darkness claimed him than opening his mouth and teasing Cassandra with reminders of their behavior. In truth, shame, not fright, had driven her from the carriage and into the crowd with its flaming torches. Shame had driven her from him. Yet when she showed more concern toward those two ne'er-do-well gentlemen aeronauts than she had demonstrated toward him as her host, let alone the man who had so recently been her fiancé—who still wanted to be her betrothed, her husband—he could not stop his tongue.

God, I am a fool, he cried inside his head. *I believe she is wrong in her thinking, but I will not win her back this way. Please show me how.*

His soul felt as bleak as the autumn garden beyond the glass—shriveled like the leaves on the rosebushes. His words remained as silent as the Bainbridge sisters behind him. He should leave, apologize to Cassandra for disturbing her, and return to his chamber. Mama had said something about guests. He had paid little attention, but if visitors were expected at the Hall, he needed to get well. He needed to talk to Crawford and get out of being his spy if the major's own men could not recognize him enough to keep their pistols aimed elsewhere—preferably not at any of the men at all. The rioters might need to be stopped, but not by lead balls.

He turned from the window in time to catch Miss Honore Bainbridge staring at him as though—his face heated—she liked what she saw. She caught his eye and smiled. He felt a clout to the middle, not a pleasant one. More like his gut, not his arm, had been pistol-shot. He did not need Honore Bainbridge complicating his life any further.

She likely has the same dowry as her sister, a voice whispered in the corner of his head.

But he loved Cassandra, not her dowry. Cassandra, who had pulled the coverlet over her head like a child hiding from bogles in the night.

"I believe," he said, "I will return when Miss Bainbridge is more prepared to receive visitors." Without another glance at Honore or her elder sister, he left the room, able to breathe again once he stepped into the chilly dimness of the hallway.

But his own injuries had taken their toll on his strength, and he could simply walk, not dash off, as he wished to do. Too soon he caught the patter of soft slippers on the floorboards and caught a whiff of a scent he recognized, though if he had been asked a quarter hour earlier, he would not have been able to say he recognized it, nor what the scent consisted of. Something of sweet flowers, rather than the fresh tang of citrus that seemed to hover around his Cassandra.

No, she was not his Cassandra now. Nor did she follow him. Seconds before he reached the door into the great hall, she caught up with him—Miss Honore Bainbridge, all shimmering golden beauty even in the poorly lit passage.

"My lord." She smiled up at him, touching his arm for the briefest of moments. "Whittaker, a moment of your time?"

"I think not, Miss Honore." He tried to sound stiff, cold, like her father.

She laughed. "Oh, very good, my lord. Cassie says you never thought to be the earl, but I think you will make a very good one if you can talk like that. But it never works with me when Father cuts up stiff like that—well, not most of the time—and it will not work with me when you do either. Remember, I knew you when you were plain Mr. Giles."

"I believe I was never quite plain Mr. Giles." He tried hard not to smile at her brazenness and failed. "I believe there was an 'Honorable' in there somewhere."

"Yes, of course, the Honorable Mr. Geoffrey Giles, whenever someone wrote you a letter." Miss Honore's laugh tinkled off the plaster walls.

She was so bright, so energetic and lovely, and with her fragrance she reminded him of spring. He had thought everything was going his way in the spring. The mills were prospering, the rioters had not yet reached Lancashire, and the sheep had given plentiful wool from the winter's growth. Best of all, he and Cassandra would be wed in June.

Then she saw the balloon ascension and rioters destroyed one of his mills . . .

"We cannot stand here talking, Miss Honore," he said with more curtness than he intended. "It is improper for us to be alone here like this without a chaperone, and I am ashamed to say I need a chair."

"Of course you do. So thoughtless of me. Here." As though she were a gentleman, she rushed forward to open the door to the great hall.

It too was cold, colder than the passage, but a fire burned on the hearth at the far end, where a carpet and chairs made a comfortable place for visitors to wait without freezing on cold days. Despite the sunlight, this was a cold day, and yes, Mama had said something about visitors. She wanted to tell him more, but he had insisted on sitting vigil over Cassandra, ensuring no one amputated her leg unless the wound did go gangrenous. She fretted about it so much she whimpered and muttered in her sleep, crying out in fear. The apothecary insisted. The surgeon insisted. No physician of any repute resided near enough for an opinion, so Whittaker had been using his authority as the head of this household to say no.

But if he was wrong, she could die.

He trudged to the nearest chair and barely managed to wait to sit until Miss Honore had found her own seat closer to the fire. "I will not change my mind about surgery for Cass—Miss Bainbridge," he began. "She—"

"No, no." Miss Honore waved her hand as though erasing his words from a slate. "I am so grateful to you for that. I was going to tell her or suggest you tell her, but then I saw you two in there, and . . . well, do not tell her, or she will marry you out of gratitude."

Whittaker raised a hand and shoved his unkempt hair behind his right ear. "I beg your pardon? Miss Honore, I do apologize, but you are making little sense to me."

"Oh no, and I must start learning to put words together to make sense if I am to write a Gothic novel."

"Y-yes, I expect you will."

About that moment seemed like a good time for the visitors to arrive.

"So I shall start over by saying that I think the two of you are quite, quite in love with one another."

"Indeed."

Not a crunch of wheels on gravel or the beat of horses' hooves, alas.

Miss Honore giggled. "There you go acting like an old earl again. But look me in the eye and tell me you are not quite, quite in love with Cassandra."

He glanced at the door, willing the knocker to sound.

"I knew it." Miss Honore clapped her hands. "When she called you a swine, I knew she still loved you too."

"Then I give up hope of ever understanding her."

"Perhaps, but I can help." Miss Honore leaned toward him so far her knees practically touched his.

They appeared to be having an intimate cose together, and he barely resisted the urge to push his chair back a few inches, because it would then scrape on the floor and make an obvious racket. Besides, if she could help him understand Cassandra, he should give her a listen.

"If she learns you saved her . . . um . . . from surgery, then you ask her again to marry you, she will say yes out of gratitude, not because she thinks it is right," Miss Honore continued. "I am not certain why she thinks the two of you should not wed—well, that is not quite true. I do know of one reason." She pressed her hand to her lips as though to stem her flow of words, and her bright eyes clouded.

Whittaker resisted the urge to squirm like a schoolboy before a headmaster after some infraction of school rules. Not that he had ever broken school rules. He had been one of those most revolting of youths—at least to his peers—one who rarely stepped out of the straight and narrow. Then he met Cassandra . . .

Heaviness settled in his middle like a load of lead shot. "What is it, Miss Honore?"

"It matters not." She shook her head. "At least it does not if you love her, and she you. And besides, something troubles her. I truly do not know what all is wrong, but I want to help fix it. She is so unhappy, unlike when she was about to marry you."

He could not, would not dare to hope. Miss Honore was a silly romantic child, for all her eighteen or nineteen years.

"She has been ill. That makes anyone unhappy," he said.

"Yes, but—oh, just trust what I say." She moved back in her chair. "She thinks all she wants is to work on balloons and Greek and such nonsense, and that Father will let her take her dowry and live on that if she doesn't marry you or anyone else. So you must convince her that is not what she wants. At least, that it is not *all* she wants."

At last he caught the crunch of wheels on the gravel drive, and he prepared to rise, realizing he was not dressed for callers and should exit the hall at once. "I believe my failure at that is why we are having this tête-à-tête—my failure to convince her she wants more than balloons and Greek. And now I should—"

"Wait a moment." Miss Honore gave him a pleading glance. "I have taken too long to say what I wish to say, like Mr. Richardson does in his novels. Lady Whittaker gave me one to read, and it was dreadfully dull. But about Cassandra . . ." She worried her lower lip, deepening its already natural pink.

Full and ripe like Cassandra's.

He compressed his own lips and rose. "I am not ready to receive callers, Miss Honore, and I believe some have arrived. Shall we continue this later?"

"One more moment." She grasped his right arm and followed him toward his wing of the house. "You see, I was thinking you should pretend you do not wish to wed her. I mean, it does seem like it might be true after she called you a swine."

Especially when he deserved it.

"I cannot pretend what I do not feel, Miss Honore. Now, if you please . . ."

Someone began to pound the knocker with more vigor than necessary.

"I think we should make her jealous," Miss Honore announced.

"We?" That stopped Whittaker in his tracks. He halted with his hand outstretched toward the door handle and stared down at the lovely young lady clinging to his arm. "Are you saying you and me?"

She stuck out her lower lip in a pout so exaggerated it had to be pretense. "I should be put off by your shock, my lord. Why ever not me? I have a fine dowry. I am passably pretty—"

"You are beautiful, and you know it too well, I think."

"And Cassandra thinks she is ugly."

"Which is why she needs her spectacles." His heart twisted, and he extricated his arm from Miss Honore's hold. "Perhaps that would work. Cassandra loves nothing more than a challenge. But it won't work if she doesn't want matters to change between us."

"But I think they would change if she thinks someone else—oh, that knocker."

It had pounded again. Whittaker feared he would have to answer, but a parlor maid in a neat chintz gown and frilled cap all but ran from the servants' door tucked beneath the great staircase and raced for the front door.

"It will have the opposite effect, I am certain." Whittaker opened the portal to his wing. "And even if it were worth the risk, I will not, as I believe you imply, set sister against sister, even to win Cassandra back."

"But if we could find—Lady Whittaker." Miss Honore stepped back to allow Mama to bustle through the opening.

"Geoffrey, do go don a coat if you are going to be down here," she said. "You look positively undressed."

"I believe I will stay in my room while you entertain guests. The notion of donning a coat does not appeal to me."

"But they will be here for days," Mama protested.

The front door opened to allow the entrance of a blast of frosty wind, on which was borne two children, a pale young man, and a lady with hair the color of garnets beneath the brim of her yellow straw hat. She flashed Whittaker a brilliant smile from a lush mouth and a glance from eyes that appeared dark in the shadowing brim and poorly lit hall. Beside him, Miss Honore caught her breath, then giggled.

Whittaker's jaw hardened and he gazed down at his mother. "Who are these people?"

"Your cousins, my dear." She flicked a glare at the lady. "I am afraid I do not know who she is." Which did not stop her from gliding forward, holding out her hands to the newcomers. "Welcome to Whittaker Hall. You must excuse his lordship. He suffered an accident the other night, and one of our other guests is unwell. Nothing serious that you must fear catching, but we have been a bit at sixes and sevens."

"And it will not stop," Miss Honore murmured.

Whittaker wondered if he might be safer going back to spying for Crawford. Between Miss Honore's preposterous plan to flirt with him to make Cassandra jealous, his wish to return to Cassandra's side and at the least apologize for his unkind remark earlier, and his head, which had decided to throb and swim, he thought life amidst the odorous sheep suddenly sounded peaceful, calm, undemanding.

He could at least retreat to his room until he could arrange a chaperone for another visit to Cassandra.

For the second time, he opened the door to the family wing.

"So you must forgive his state of dishabille," Mama was saying. "Do be polite, Geoffrey, and bid good day to your guests."

But they were not his guests. He should have listened when Mama explained about why his young cousins had come to call. No, to stay for a visit.

Slowly he removed his hand from the latch and strode forward with as much vigor as he could manage, though his arm added an ache to his head's difficulties, and the nearest chair looked far more inviting to him than the red-haired beauty poised with one gloved hand resting on the shoulder of the younger of the two boys. A gloved hand above which shimmered a bracelet heavy with small but brilliant sapphires.

Beautiful and possessed of fine jewels she could afford to wear while traveling.

"This is your cousin Laurence," Mama said, indicating the elder boy, a pasty, gangly youth of about twelve years. "And this is William." The younger boy bowed, then opened his mouth and started to speak, but the female's hand visibly tightened and he shut his lips again. "Their tutor, Mr. Caldwell, and—" Mama faced the young female. "I am sorry that I do not know you."

"I am Regina Irving." The woman—definitely not a girl—spoke in a low, throaty voice. "Cousin to the boys on their mother's side. She has decided to stay and help nurse Mr. Giles and sent me along to help with the boys, as I have been living with them since my own parents returned to India last year."

"Oh, of course." Mama's smile grew natural, bright, and her eyes sparkled. "You are most, most welcome."

Of course she was. Even Whittaker now knew who this female

was, the unmarried daughter of his uncle's brother-in-law, who had made a fortune with the East India Company. Unmarried and the only child of a wealthy man. No wonder Mama grew happy when she learned the lady's identity. If matters did not work themselves out between him and Cassandra, he could make a suit for Miss Irving, though she was at the least five and twenty. Between Miss Honore's and Mama's schemes, he would never manage to restore his betrothal to Cassandra.

And then Major Crawford sauntered into the Hall behind the newcomers, a scarlet-coated reminder of Whittaker's other obligations to spare the family honor.

13

For the second time in an hour, Cassandra tugged at the bell rope. For the second time, no one responded. While the sound of children's voices rang across the barren garden and light faded from the sky, she awaited someone to help her dress and bring her supper. Yet not even Honore returned to their rooms. Heavy doors and thick stone walls masked any noise from the rest of the house. Short-staffed or not, guests or not, someone should have come.

Someone should have come if something were not terribly wrong. Suddenly she found herself on her feet and at the bedchamber door without giving a thought to her cane. Then she realized she could not go out to the great hall or to the family wing in her dressing gown. They might have guests.

Of course. They did have guests. Those two boys in the garden must be the offspring of some callers who had distracted everyone from remembering Cassandra. That was all. Nothing was wrong with Whittaker.

Relief left her weak and leaning against the wall for support. She could think about her empty stomach now. If she wanted food, she would have to find it herself.

Unable to dress unaided, she drew a shawl on over her dressing gown for a bit more modesty and headed for the orangery. An orange or two would do for the moment, and if she set the pot of tea left for her close to the fire, she could heat it. Someone would come eventually, Honore if no one else. Still, leaving her alone for so long after such vigilance over the past few days seemed rather peculiar.

Her soft slippers whispering on the flagstones, she descended the steps to the orangery door and lifted the latch. The door swung inward without a sound, the hinges well-oiled. The sharp tang of lemon and orange and the freshness of wet earth greeted her nose.

And the rumble of male voices greeted her ears.

They sounded like two dogs growling at one another, the volume low, the words indistinct, but the feelings clear. These were two men not in the least happy with one another, perhaps ready to snap and lash out. She should return to her room, but the scent of the oranges increased her hunger. She eased the door open farther and edged her head around the frame to see if perhaps she could reach one of the trees, snatch an orange, and retreat without the men noticing her presence.

No such good fortune. The instant she stepped into the glasshouse, she caught the flash of a red coat and the glint of brazier light on pale hair, as Major Crawford stood with his back to her. Facing her, looking straight at her, his uninjured arm bent a bit at the elbow with the hand fisted against his upper thigh, was her erstwhile fiancé.

"I am not mistaken," Whittaker told the major in a low, hard voice so as not to be overheard by the boys and their tutor on the other end of the orangery. "One of your men shot me."

"An accident, I assure you." Major Crawford kept his voice low also, but his stance was relaxed, one shoulder propped against a decorative screen. "The fellow didn't recognize you until it was too late, I'm afraid. He has been reprimanded, I assure you of that too."

"And I still have a hole in my arm and a concussion in my head," Whittaker shot back. "I will not risk this again. Do you understand what I am saying? I will not be your emissary with the Luddites any longer. I would be unmasked right now if one of them instead of one of my loyal men had found me lying on the road. As it is, my weavers wonder why I was dressed like one of the laborers. It cannot continue, and I have responsibilities here at home."

"All seems to run quite smoothly from my perspective." Crawford smiled. "And I have been here to notice."

"We have more guests now. And I need to oversee repairs at the mill."

And watch over Cassandra. He had left her on her own, and she got herself ill and one of her wounds had gone septic again. Miss Honore and Mama could never control Cassandra's willfulness, and now with the distraction of Miss Regina Irving—the considerable distraction—the household was going to be in an uproar.

"My uncle has sent my cousins here so he can have some peace and quiet to recover from some illness," Whittaker continued, "and—never you mind my family business. You can find someone else to blackmail into performing your dirty work."

"But is that not the difficulty, my lord?" Crawford asked. "Your family business?"

A shout rang through the orangery, one of the cousins, a family responsibility Whittaker felt unprepared to manage at the moment. Later, with his own sons . . .

140

"Preserving her ladyship's reputation," Crawford added, "so your family isn't socially ruined and you can marry an heiress."

Whittaker sighed. "I do not wish to marry an heiress."

"Not even Miss Irving?"

"Not even Miss Irving."

Miss Honore had whisked her off to an upper-floor bedchamber to refresh herself, and Whittaker had not seen the beauty for hours. But a man did not forget looks like hers. She smoldered like a fire about to burst into a conflagration. Cassandra would not stand up well to the heiress in looks or dowry, yet he held not a hint of interest for Miss Irving and spoke with sincerity. Cassandra would care nothing about a scandal involving his mother. Discretion was not one of her qualities.

Nor his, to his shame.

The major's lips tightened at the corners. "But neither would you wish to see her ladyship's name dragged through the mud over a scandal thirty years old."

"It was not a scandal then; it will not be one now."

"You did not think that three weeks ago."

Nor did he think it now. Whittaker knew Society too well to believe that so much as a whisper that his elder brother may not have been the legitimate earl, even for the short time he had carried the title, would make Mama a pariah amongst her friends. It could damage business for the mills, as many believed taint spread through the blood and would believe her younger son of too passionate a nature for their delicate daughters.

He pictured Cassandra's pretty lips mouthing the word *swine* because of his pain-spawned reminder of her own passionate nature, and curled his hand into a fist against his thigh. "I need another week at the least. How can I explain my absence?"

"You will." Crawford shrugged. "You'll have to. If you don't, you'll get a worse blow over your head the next time, probably with some blacksmith's hammer that will turn your skull into a crumpet."

"Charming description." Whittaker's fist tightened. "Now if you will excuse me, I have guests."

"Not until you give me a date when you will return. Your mills were spared the other night, but another one was destroyed last night."

"Whose?" Whittaker felt the blow as though it had been his looms destroyed.

"Featherstone's."

"He is a decent fellow. I am sorry to hear that."

"It could have been prevented if you were working with us."

"I could have been working with you if one of your men had not shot me."

"It won't happen again. England needs you, Whittaker, and you are the only person young enough whom we can . . . compel to help."

"There will be an end to this, Crawford. I will not—"

A rush of air signaled the opening door, and he stopped, expecting either Miss Honore or Miss Irving, but not the two of them. The new arrival was not talking, as would be the case if both ladies arrived in tandem.

A solitary lady stood half behind the door, peering around it like a rabbit poking its nose out of its warren to sniff for danger. Her gaze met his, and she took a step backward, catching the wide sleeve of her robe on the door latch. It clanged like a gong, and her pallid face turned the color of Mama's summer roses.

Crawford spun around, his hand dropping to where his sword would hang when he was on duty. "Miss Bainbridge. Good—good evening."

"Who is she?" Laurence's booted feet thudded up one of the aisles between the trees.

William thudded right behind him. "Cousin Whittaker, why is there a half-dressed lady in here?"

"I am not half—I mean, I will not be . . . I thought the orangery would be empty." Cassandra spun around, lost her balance, and caught herself on the door frame.

"Allow me, Miss Bainbridge." Crawford strode forward.

"What is wrong with her?" William persisted.

Indeed, what was wrong? Or more accurately, how badly was she injured? Whittaker knew Cassandra was using a cane to walk more than a few feet, but he thought it weakness. Now he realized her legs might be damaged worse than he'd thought.

The realization held him immobile, silent, until Major Crawford reached out as though intending to curve his hand around her arm. Whittaker all but charged forward and shouldered the officer aside—with his bad arm, unfortunately, shooting pain from elbow to shoulder—and curved his arm around her waist.

"You should not be out of your sickroom, Miss Bainbridge." He spoke a little too loudly for the sake of his cousins. "If you wanted oranges, you should have rung for them."

"I did, but no one answered. Now if you please, I can return to my room alone." She grasped his hand as though to remove it from her waist with as much force as necessary.

A waist too narrow and a hip bone too lacking in flesh, apparent with only a layer of velvet and cambric between his fingers and her flesh, instead of stays that changed the natural form of a lady. He stepped behind her to shield her from the other man's view and murmured, "Do not make a scene, Cassandra. I am taking you back to your room."

"Perhaps you should be discovering why your household is so poorly run."

"Not poor management. Too few staff and too many people in it to take care of."

She flinched and her hand dropped. She said nothing as he led her from the orangery door and back toward her room. She need not have spoken. He had gained no points with her in whatever game of wills they played. She did not want his reminders of the state of his finances. He suspected he had lost ground by obliging her to leave the room as he had.

She did not move away from the support of his arm, though. Not because she wanted to be close to him, he suspected— because she needed it. Her steps felt uneven.

"Does your ankle pain you?" he could not stop himself from asking.

"I do not discuss my ankles with men, my lord."

He almost laughed at her frosty haughtiness.

"Cassandra, do not be a widgeon. I am not a stranger."

"We would be better off if you were." She braced her hand on the wall and stared at the door to her bedchamber. "Thank you for your assistance. When there is some available, I would like some supper."

"I will bring it to you myself, if necessary." He raised his hand, aching to brush her hair back, touch her cheek, tilt her face toward his. He reached past her and opened her door. "Good evening, Miss Bainbridge."

"Good evening, my lord." She entered her room without so much as a glance at him. "Thank you."

He leaned against the wall and watched her enter her chamber. The ache to touch her felt like a pinch compared to the pounding emptiness of loss deep inside him. She might fear the amputation of her leg; he felt as though she had already excised his heart, mangled it, and then tried to hand it back. More than her shame over their behavior had driven her away from him. She knew God forgave one with a repentant heart. They had discussed that in the summer.

And had succumbed to temptation again.

Still, something more distressed her. He saw it in her skittishness around him. Miss Honore admitted to noticing it. If only Cassandra would talk to him.

But she would not, so he may as well make himself useful. Hearing his young cousins' voices piercing through the orangery door, Whittaker headed in that direction again to head them off from disturbing Cassandra. And he would find Major Crawford to tell him that with or without the threat against Mama, he would go willingly back to the Luddites as soon as his arm healed enough.

14

Thoroughly weary of her bedchamber after nearly two weeks of confinement, Cassandra carried a copy of *Gulliver's Travels* into the great hall and seated herself by the fire for an hour or two of entertaining reading and analysis of Jonathan Swift's satirical prose. She had yet to find all the historical details to which he referred in the story and was determined to do so. She had occupied herself so much with the ancient world of the Greeks and Romans, she had not read much in more recent history, if a hundred years was recent. While at Whittaker Hall with its limitations in reading materials, and Father having restricted what books she could bring with her, she decided to remedy that lack in her knowledge, while the rest of the party, including the young cousins, took a ride on another gloriously sunny and cold October day.

Whittaker had gone too.

Cassandra had seen little of him since the night she stumbled upon him and the major in the orangery. He had, however, sent a stack of books to her chamber with a politely worded note:

> *My family is not usually of a scholarly bent; therefore, you will find little to your taste in the library. These are from my personal collection. Partake at your leisure and send for more as need arises.*

Once folded, the sheet of fine paper, embossed with the Whittaker family crest at the top, made a fine marker for her place in the book. She opened to it now and drew it out to tuck against the back cover until she had need to close the book. For the first time, she noticed his signature at the bottom of the brief missive. It was his formal signature. The signature of a nobleman, an earl of the realm. Every other letter he had sent to her, at least two score, held an informal double G at the bottom for Geoffrey Giles. Then he had switched to a simple W when his brother's death elevated him to the title. But this signature could have been used to frank a letter or conclude a letter of concern to the regent on behalf of Parliament.

Her chest felt suddenly tight, as it had during her fever. She took a deep breath to loosen it and coughed. That was all it was—the need to release some lingering congestion. Under no circumstances did the formality from her former fiancé distress her. He belonged to her past. If she must be good so she could go her own way, she must leave him behind.

With spectacles Miss Irving would no doubt outright sneer at perched on her nose, Cassandra bent over *Gulliver's Travels* and began to read. What an odd age that had been when ladies invited gentlemen into their boudoirs so they could advise the female on her attire. No wonder Swift made such fun of it when his adventurer traveled in the land of the giants—the revolting-ness of a woman's flaws he could see from the advantage of their dressing tables and with his eyesight tuned to view much smaller objects. Pimples and moles normally covered by a gown or at least a fichu were monstrous from his perspective.

Cassandra's own scars began to tingle, and she removed her spectacles to dab at her eyes with the edge of her shawl. Silly that a book intended as entertainment, as well as a political commentary on society of the time, should make her weepy. She needed a distraction. If only she knew where Mr. Sorrells and Mr. Kent were staying so she could send word that she was now able to receive callers. Talking of aeronautics would certainly distract her. She had a dozen or two questions to ask them.

Instead of the friends she wanted to see, she heard the patter of light, quick footfalls coming down the staircase and glanced up to see Lady Whittaker approaching. She wore a bright paisley shawl that contrasted with her black dress in a rather striking fashion. Though she must have been in her late forties or perhaps even early fifties, Lady Whittaker was still a beautiful woman with warm brown eyes, slim and energetic, her hair barely touched with such a bright silver it looked ornamental. Her sons had certainly inherited their looks from her, though not their height and breadth.

She smiled at Cassandra and quickened her steps. "Good, you have come out. I am so glad you are well." Her gaze dropped to the slippers.

"Nearly." Unlike with Miss Irving's scorn, Cassandra blushed over her footwear in front of Whittaker's mother. "The apothecary suggested I not wear stockings for a few more days. Perhaps I should not be out here—"

"No, no, I was actually envying you." Lady Whittaker laughed. "Would you like some tea?"

"Yes, thank you."

She had wanted some earlier, but no one responded to her ringing of the bell from her room, a regular occurrence these days.

"You must only ask for what you need." Lady Whittaker rang a handbell on a low table, since the hall bore no pull. "We perhaps need another maid or two, and we have enough to ensure our guests want for nothing. Thanks to the mills, we do not live in abject poverty, which might be the situation if my brother had not left his business to Whittaker."

Cassandra squirmed a bit. One did not discuss money with people outside the family unless it regarded a business arrangement.

"So," Lady Whittaker continued, "I do not understand why no one responds to your bell. No one here has taken a dislike to you. On the contrary. We like you quite as much as we have in the past, or even more so. Though I do wish . . ." She dropped onto a chair across from Cassandra. "I do wish you and Whittaker would not have broken your betrothal. And it has nothing to do with your dowry, I assure you."

Cassandra stared down at her book with the note from Whittaker peeking out the top. "I will never do as a countess, and we . . . I think God has other plans for your son and for me. And those plans do not mean the two of us together."

"Why are you so certain of this, my dear? Geoffrey was so happy—ah, the tea."

The door beneath the staircase swung open on a draft that sent sparks flying up the chimney with a roar as a maid appeared with a tray. China clinked against silver, and a billow of steam from the spout of the teapot promised a hot refreshment.

"Just set the tray here, Molly." Lady Whittaker indicated a table beside her chair.

The maid did so, then stepped back, her small, plump hands twisting in her snowy apron. "Milady, begging your pardon, but Tims said I ought to be telling you straightaway about the bell in Miss Bainbridge's room."

"What about the bell? And why was Tims in the house?" Her ladyship's gaze focused on the maid.

"I know as how he's naught but a groom, milady, but he's

right handy with mechanics things like the bellpulls, and when we in the kitchen noticed how it weren't working when we pulled it, we had him come in to have a look."

"If he is good at mechanical things, I can understand that." Lady Whittaker nodded. "Go on then. What did he say?"

"He says—" The maid shot Cassandra a troubled glance, then returned her focus on her mistress. "He says as how the one in Miss Bainbridge's room has been disconnected like—"

"Like what?" Cassandra posed the question on a sudden chill running up her spine.

"Well, um, I don't like to say it."

"Say it," Lady Bainbridge commanded, her gentle voice suddenly hard. "How was it disconnected?"

"It were cut, milady." The maid looked as though she were about to burst into tears. "I didn't want to say aught, but you asked for the tea and someone had to say and—it weren't none of us, milady. I'll promise before the vicar or anyone I speak the truth. We all will."

"Molly, you dear child." Lady Bainbridge reached out and patted the girl's hand. "Of course none of you did this to Miss Bainbridge. The question is, who did?" Lady Whittaker mused aloud. "If you hear of anything, even what you might think is simply gossip, do come tell me, all right?"

"Yes, milady." Molly dipped into a curtsy, a silent plea to be dismissed puckering her face.

Lady Whittaker nodded and the girl fled, no messenger killed this time.

"I expect it was one of Geoffrey's cousins playing a prank." Lady Whittaker bent over the tea tray and poured a cup of fragrant bohea. "Milk or lemon?"

"Lemon, thank you." Cassandra tucked Whittaker's letter

into her book and set it aside so she could accept the cup her ladyship handed over. She cradled the warmth between her hands, not realizing how cold they had become until she touched the tea-warmed china. She inhaled the sharp citrus tang of the lemon wedge floating in the dark brew, hoping it would clear her head, exchange the dark thoughts in her mind for sensible ones.

One sensible notion was that her bellpull had not been working since before the cousins arrived. Neither of them could have found the line to the attics and severed it so quickly. Likely only one person in the house other than the servants even knew how the lines ran. Yet why would he play such a mean trick on her?

For the same reason he had reminded her, with one word, how her holding the coverlet up to her chin while he was in her bedchamber was false modesty around him, had reminded her of her shame. She had hurt him—his pride, if nothing else. Wounded people, like wounded animals, lashed out when hurt. He'd regretted his words even before she called him a swine for saying such a thing to her. She had read it on his face. Now the two acts of unkindness, of ungodly behavior, lay between them, hidden and festering like the sore on her ankle.

That, however, was far different than cutting her bellpull. Not letting her contact a servant for assistance when she needed it was too low. He simply would not do such a thing no matter how wounded his pride or even his heart. But who else in the house cared to discommode her?

"You look troubled, my dear." Lady Bainbridge broke into Cassandra's thoughts. "Surely you do not think this was anything beyond a prank."

"It is just such an odd prank." Cassandra sipped at her tea.

"But easily repaired." Lady Bainbridge sighed. "Perhaps Tims can repair it, though Geoffrey can likely fix it himself once his arm is better. But I have been wondering what would happen next and hope this is all it is."

"My lady?" Her ladyship's words made no sense to Cassandra.

Lady Bainbridge laughed, albeit without much humor in the sound. "The saying that troubles come in threes? First your accident happens, then Geoffrey is shot by someone on the side of right while he is trying to defend his mill, and now someone is playing tricks on you. Far better this than something worse."

"Indeed."

And her ladyship did not count the broken betrothal in the troubles.

"Of course," Lady Whittaker continued, "Geoffrey would say that calling off the wedding again is a serious trouble. I do believe he shed a tear or a few over that, you know."

Cassandra managed to refrain from a derisive snort—barely. The pounding of the door knocker saved her from having to say anything.

Though she shifted as though prepared to leap up and answer it herself, Lady Whittaker awaited one of the maids to emerge from the servants' quarters to open the wide portal. Molly did so, dragging the thick, varnished wood back to a blast of chilly, hay-scented air and a sight that nearly brought Cassandra leaping to her feet.

She managed to stay in her chair yet could not suppress her smile or spontaneous reaction. "Mr. Sorrells. Mr. Kent."

"Ah, Miss Bainbridge." Philip Sorrells strode forward and clasped her outstretched hand. "So good to see you up and about again."

"I trust we are not intruding?" Roger Kent addressed Lady Whittaker, bowing in more formal and proper greeting.

Blushing, Mr. Sorrells turned and bowed likewise. "Do forgive my ill manners, my lady. I was overcome by joy to see our dear Miss Bainbridge looking so much better."

"I understand." She might understand, but a crease had formed between Lady Whittaker's brows, and she did not smile. "I thought you said you were returning to—where are you from? Bristol men, are you?"

"Brighton, my lady." Mr. Sorrells's normally warm voice had turned as cold as a pond with ice rimming the edges, as he was apparently quite aware of the insult Lady Whittaker had dealt the two young men. "And Roger here is from Gloucester."

"We met at the University of Glasgow," Mr. Kent said, either unaware of or not heeding the tension in the room. "Both quite failing to become physicians."

"But learning enough science to know balloon flight is possible and that Miss Bainbridge is the most intelligent female we have ever known."

"More so than half the students at university," Mr. Kent added.

Cassandra glowed under such praise. Her insides jumped and bounced with the urge to ask them questions about their flight, the effect the rain had upon them, how well the sails had steered them back. She compressed her lips to hold in the spate of enquiries until the gentlemen were seated, more cups and fresh tea produced along with a plate of Shrewsbury biscuits and seedcake, and comments about the bright but fine weather exchanged.

Finally, she burst out, "Tell me all about it. Did you get drenched in the rain? Did it harm the fire? Where did you—"

"Wait, wait." Laughing, Mr. Sorrells lifted a hand holding a sweet. "One at a time."

"The sails aren't particularly useful yet," Mr. Kent pronounced.

153

"But we did manage to land back in the field by changing our elevation to catch different wind shears."

"Landing was a bit difficult," Mr. Sorrells said, "without any torches."

"The rain was a difficulty with that," Cassandra began, then caught Lady Whittaker's gaze upon her and shut her mouth before she admitted she had been lighting torches in the middle of the night for the gentlemen.

Mr. Sorrells finished his biscuit. "Never you mind that, Miss Bainbridge. It all went well. We were able to fill the balloon with enough air to rise above the rain and stayed almost perfectly dry."

"More than did those on the ground." Lady Whittaker looked directly at Cassandra.

"So sorry you got a chill from getting soaked," Mr. Kent said.

Mr. Sorrells shot him a murderous glare.

"No matter, my friends." Cassandra set her cold and barely touched tea aside. "I believe her ladyship knows I was out there. Lord Whittaker did already."

His mother started. "He did? Is that how you saw him that night, Cassandra?"

"Yes, he was kind enough to assist us in our ascent," Mr. Kent said before Cassandra found a proper response. "Most kind of him."

"His intention was not to be kind," Cassandra pointed out. "It was to ensure I did not go with you."

"I suspected as much." Mr. Sorrells glanced at Lady Whittaker. "Next time we will ensure nothing stops you from going up, Miss Bainbridge."

Innards quivering like a bowl of jellied eels, Cassandra leaned forward. "Will you? I mean, you know I want this above anything. When will it be?"

"We are not certain." Mr. Kent turned his attention on Lady Whittaker, who was stiff and scowling in her chair. "We need to improve the way we seal the balloon to keep it from leaking air. Our current formula isn't working all that well."

"Of course." Cassandra leaned back in her chair, pretending to be relaxed, a little indifferent. She had understood her friends' message—they would not give details in front of someone else who so clearly disapproved of balloon ascensions for Miss Bainbridge.

She nodded. "I have been working on a new formula for sealing the silk. Where are you staying? I will send over my new receipt."

They gave her the name of their inn along the road to the Dale, then changed the topic to the mundane again and departed after a proper half hour.

Cassandra hated to see them depart. She wanted to talk more of balloons and formulas, but she understood that doing so in front of Whittaker's mother was not wise. She could make arrangements to meet them with no one else the wiser, especially now that even Honore had people to entertain and keep her entertained. First, however, she would have to get through more conversation with Lady Whittaker.

Except she did not stay to continue their earlier dialogue. Murmuring something about seeing if Tims could assist Whittaker in repairing the bellpull, she left the hall soon after Mr. Sorrells and Mr. Kent, gathered up the tea things herself, and disappeared through the baize-covered door to the servants' quarters.

Hearing the riding party returning, Cassandra beat a hasty retreat to her bedchamber. The sight of her bed brought on a wave of fatigue, and she lay down for a brief rest before supper.

It turned into a sleep so deep she did not even hear Honore go into her room to change from her riding dress, and supper arrived by way of a tray in her room because the hour of the meal had passed. *Gulliver's Travels*, which she had left in the hall, lay on the tray. Beneath her notes on satirical points in the tale, a familiar hand had scrawled, *You are a bit harsh to our ancestors.*

Whittaker, of course. Next time she saw him, she would ask him why her observations were harsh and not reasonable. They could have one of their good arguments, one of their—

She shook her head against a wave of emptiness at realizing those arguments would probably never happen again, and shook out her napkin.

Another note fluttered to the floor. This handwriting was far different, less legible. She picked it up with some difficulty and held it close enough to her nose to read it without her spectacles.

Next Monday. Three of the clock. Dunstans' east meadow. Will try new sealant day after tomorrow. Dunstans' west meadow. Yours, PS.

As cryptic as the words were, Cassandra understood Philip Sorrells's note perfectly. The next ascension would be in five days. If she was there, she could go up.

She was going to fly.

15

"Miss Irving would be an excellent catch, do you not think so, my lord?"

Whittaker halted on his way across the garden and spun around to face Miss Honore Bainbridge. Her cheeks glowed pink in the brisk wind from the sea, and she breathed hard from racing after him. He had heard her footfalls but hoped he could outwalk her. If he stopped now, he might not catch up with Cassandra, who had left thirty minutes earlier but moved far more slowly. But he was too well-bred to not respond to a lady speaking directly to him.

"Yes, I expect she will be . . . for someone else." He began walking again, though more slowly. "Now, if you will please excuse me, I need to catch up with Cassandra, as I do not know where she is going."

Miss Honore fell into step beside him. "She is at the Dunstan home farm, or will be soon. Something about painting silk with some chemical process so the balloon stops leaking air."

Whittaker closed his eyes for a moment, envisioned Cassandra catching herself on fire with a chemical explosion, and increased his pace. "Has she no sense?"

"Have you no sense?" Miss Honore grabbed his arm. His wounded arm, out of the sling sooner than the apothecary advised but healing well just the same. Still, the yank on it felt like a blow, and he glared at her.

She scowled right back. "If you stop her from this, you will never win her back."

"And if I do not, I may not have her to win back."

Miss Honore frowned, bit her lower lip, then released his arm. "All right, we shall join her so we can ensure her safety. Will that do as a compromise?"

"I suppose it must, if you can keep up with me."

"I caught up with you, did I not?"

"You are rather impertinent to your elders, are you not, Miss Honore?"

She giggled. "You are barely four years older than I am, Whittaker."

"Right now, child, I feel forty years older. Now speak your peace so we may be done with it before we catch up with Cassandra."

"It is quite simple, my lord." She bobbed a curtsy on the formal address. "You should court Miss Irving. I know she is little more than a cit."

"Miss Honore, such language."

"It is merely cant for a city merchant's daughter, is it not? It is not a curse. She is not quite gentry, but she is very pretty and—"

"My mother," Whittaker interrupted in repressive accents, "was the sister of a mill owner, and now I own mills. The days of making money from the land alone are falling behind us, Miss Snobbery."

"Well, of course." Miss Honore trotted beside him in silence for several moments, her face flushed and pinched beneath her deeply brimmed bonnet.

Whittaker relented. "More than one gentleman or lady has wed beneath his or her social order to procure a fortune."

"Some would say Cassandra is beneath you." Miss Honore sounded subdued. "Now that you have the title, you could aim much higher than a baron's daughter."

"Or much wealthier, if that was my aim, yes. Neither is."

Cassandra was his aim, and he saw her across the meadow, moving at a far slower pace than they were going but employing her cane less than he had seen her do earlier.

"Sometimes I think Cassandra—" He remembered who his companion was and refrained from the rest of his observation.

Miss Honore clasped his hand. "It's true. She does think herself beneath you now that you are the earl. And she—well, the silly chit thinks she is ugly."

"I know. The spectacles."

And she must have a scar if her ankle suffered a bad enough burn that the medical men considered amputation. A minor thing to him. But Cassandra, with her two beautiful sisters, would feel uneasy about her attractiveness to him. As if he had not shown her often and too well how he felt about her.

He speared his hand through his ragged hair and picked up his pace again. If she was meeting Sorrells and Kent in someone's meadow, Whittaker would rather catch her and stop her before she had reinforcements for whatever she was doing. He should write to her father and tell him to somehow curtail Cassandra's actions before they got her hurt or killed. But a letter would take weeks, and Whittaker wasn't supposed to be around her enough to know with whom she met. He was supposed to stay away from the Bainbridge ladies even in his own home.

"It is because she thinks she is not pretty that you should court Miss Irving," Miss Honore was saying beside him.

Whittaker glanced down at her. "I thought you said Miss Irving is beautiful, and she seems to me a young lady who knows it."

"She is not in the least young. She is at least five and twenty."

"Heaven forfend such an age. Almost in her dotage."

"Do not tease me, Whittaker. It is not nice. You know very well I was thinking about Cassandra."

"Yes, of course you were. I apologize. But surely you do not think I should try to court a lady two years my senior."

"If a man will marry a lady of inferior social class for her looks and money, he will marry one of superior age for the same."

"But I want her for neither."

"No, you do not, but you want Cassandra to think you do."

"I want no such thing."

Ahead of them, Cassandra had stopped. She cocked her head as though she heard their voices but could not make out who they were, or perhaps she could not see them.

"It is just pretend," Miss Honore protested.

"In another four days, I will be gone again. By the time I return, Miss Irving and my cousins will have completed their visit."

"Oh no, no, you must not leave." Miss Honore still gripped his hand, squeezed it hard. "Not if you want Cassandra back. Do not leave her to more calls from Mr. Sorrells and Mr. Kent. They will lead her astray."

Whittaker had led her astray. He could not guarantee that he would not do so again, as much as he knew he should not. If she could love him again, he would get a special license or carry her over the border to Scotland so they could marry immediately and not have to wait the three weeks required under the English Marriage Act. But he had never endangered her life like these aeronauts—until the night of the riots.

And he needed to spend time with her if he was to win her. She was too adroit at avoiding him.

"Tomorrow night," Miss Honore prattled on, "when we all go to the assembly at the Golden Fleece, you must flirt outrageously with Miss Irving."

"Miss Irving has shown no interest in me, child."

Ahead of them, Cassandra began to climb a stile. She held her skirt up with one hand and balanced herself on her cane with the other. The wind caught the edge of a flounce, flipping it up to reveal she wore no stockings, but slippers too flimsy for walking across the fields in late October.

"Does the girl not even know how to dress to take care of herself?"

"Stockings hurt her, um, ankle," Miss Honore answered.

Stupid. He should have realized that.

"Then she cannot come to the assembly."

Alas, another opportunity gone unless he too found reason to stay home from the public assembly, which was held at one of the neighborhood's finer inns for the local gentry or anyone with the price of a ticket. It would be a respectable and mildly entertaining evening with good food and often better music, some dancing, and a great deal of flirting amongst the young people. It would be an excellent time to meet up with Cassandra, get her alone to talk at last. But if she refused to go . . .

"She will go," Miss Honore said. "Your mama and I have made her promise because she simply cannot stay home alone with the servants until the bellpull in her room is repaired."

"Yes, the cut bellpull." Whittaker squinted through the fence to see if Cassandra had succeeded in making a safe landing on the other side of the stile. "Very odd, that. It is not as though she constantly demanded attention."

"She tries to avoid attention. Oh dear, I think she has—"

Whittaker was already running, sprinting the last twenty yards to the stile. He bound up and over the steps to find Cassandra sitting on the bottom one on the far side, rubbing her knee through a now muddy gown.

She glanced up, squinted a moment, then sighed. "I should have known it was you. And Honore too? May a lady have no peace?"

"Even in the country, perhaps especially in the country where you do not know your way," Whittaker pronounced, "a lady should not be walking about on her own."

"I am still on your land, am I not?" She stood, wobbled a moment, then regained her balance and her poise. Without another glance at him, she set off.

Whittaker leaped to the ground. A groan escaped his lips as the landing shot pain through his arm, but he caught up with Cassandra. "Your conduct in traipsing about the land, mine or not, without escort is appalling and imp—"

Miss Honore kicked him on the back of the leg. Unlike her sister, she wore stout little boots, and the blow nearly knocked his knee out from supporting him. He staggered to catch his balance and she grabbed his arm—the injured one again, the minx.

"You sound like Father," Miss Honore said. "Such a tyrant."

He did, bless her for pointing it out.

"I am responsible for your safety, is all," he concluded—a lame excuse.

"Thank you for your concern." Cassandra sounded anything but thankful. "Now, if you will excuse me, I am meeting friends here. That is, somewhere. Ah." Her nostrils flared, and she turned toward the smell.

Whittaker sniffed and his nose burned. Someone was burning pungent oils. Pungent oils were flammable.

And there they were. Beyond a low-lying hedge, he caught the flicker of a fire with a pot suspended above it. Steam or smoke or both roiled above the cauldron.

"That is horrible." Miss Honore held her handkerchief to her face. "I want to go home."

"You are welcome to." Whittaker gave her a cursory glance. "You are perfectly safe between here and the house in the daylight."

"But Cassandra should not be here with three men," Miss Honore protested.

"It will not be the first time." Cassandra grasped a handful of the hedge and lifted it to make an opening. "They are honorable." She glanced at Whittaker. "Most of them." She slipped between the shrubs.

He deserved that one, and it hurt like a rapier thrust.

"Miss Bainbridge." Sorrells and Kent greeted her with too much warmth.

"The birdlime is ready for the mixing," Sorrells added.

"What, pray tell," Miss Honore asked Whittaker, "is birdlime?"

"It is a white, sticky compound made of holly and various other oils to make birds stick to tree branches. Quite unsportsmanlike for hunting, in my opinion. But I doubt that is what your sister wants with it."

Whittaker had made a point of learning that birdlime could be spread on cloth to keep water from going through it. Or air, apparently. But it burned all too easily, consisting mainly of oil mixed with turpentine. And Cassandra walked right up to the fire and took a long-handled ladle from Mr. Sorrells.

Leaving Miss Honore to either follow him into the clearing or go home on her own, Whittaker shoved his way through the hedge, heedless of breaking branches, and snatched the spoon out of her hand. "You are far too close to the fire. If any of this spills, it will make the fire flare up and likely catch your gown ablaze."

"We didn't think of that." Kent reached out his hand for the ladle. "And we have to throw some onto the fire to test that it has cooked enough before we measure in the turpentine."

Cassandra said nothing. Nor did she move. Silence circled the fire, the bubbling, oily cauldron, the meadow. In the distance, a sheep baaed and someone rang a bell. But no one moved or spoke for a full minute that felt like a full day to Whittaker, as his tone, his words, his actions played through his head like a drama, with one scene enacted again and again and again.

He stepped back and inclined his head as a demonstration of humility. "I am sorry, Miss Bainbridge. I am being overbearing again, am I not?"

"Considering that this formula is mine," she responded with a bit of chill but not coldness, "you are."

"He's only considering your safety," Kent said, beginning to stir vigorously, sending billows of noxious steam into the air.

"We all are concerned for it." Sorrells was gentler, his look at Cassandra tender. Loving?

If he had not intercepted that glance, Whittaker might have left Cassandra with her friends. They fully intended to look out for her safety in the mixing of this brew. But if one of them felt more for Cassandra than friendship born from the mutual interest of aeronautics, Whittaker could not afford to leave her to their care alone.

He could, however, afford to take an interest in her knowledge of chemistry.

"I did not know you were interested in chemistry," he admitted to Cassandra.

"I never thought about it before." Her face lit up. "I mean, I never could have experimented with more than a few herbs and cordials at Bainbridge House. But when I was . . . ill, I got some books and began to read about how to keep air from escaping from the balloon and about the problems with what had been tried thus far."

"What about oil of turpentine? No cooking," Whittaker suggested.

"Burns too quick," Sorrells said.

"And doesn't work," Kent added.

"I decided we needed something thicker, stiffer when it dries, but not too stiff and heavy, of course."

And there was Cassandra as he knew her—beautiful in her animated speech of something that interested her, that used her considerable intellect. Whittaker watched her face, the brightness of her eyes, the mobility of her lips. He drank in her words like nectar, as though she spoke of love to him, fool that he was.

She did not speak to him alone; she spoke to all of them, explaining the process, the texture the birdlime must be, how despite being an oil, it had to be of a dryness to burn when dropped onto the fire before one poured in the turpentine, or it would not work.

"If it works," she concluded her lecture, "one can have a lower fire beneath the balloon and have less risk when in the air."

"If it works," Whittaker mused aloud, "one could make a lining of it for cloaks and keep people dry in the rain."

"You are right, Whittaker, you could." She smiled at him. Their eyes met across the fire and steaming pot of sealant, and for that moment, their old camaraderie restored itself.

Heart feeling as though it had fallen into that boiling pot and melted with the birdlime, he swallowed, looked at the balloon instead of Cassandra, and asked, "May I help or at least watch?"

"Not until tomorrow." Kent spoke first. "It's laid out now because it got sorely wet the other night and we needed to dry it out."

"Fortunately," Cassandra added, "the weather has cooperated." Her gaze shot to the horizon, where a line of darkness portended imminent rain.

They could not work on the balloon in the rain. Cassandra could not use smelling of turpentine and birdlime to keep her from the assembly. Then again, she might keep to her room and out of his reach for the day.

"You may use my shearing shed tomorrow. It is not being used this time of year."

The expression of gratitude on Cassandra's face lent the offer more value to Whittaker than to the aeronauts.

"I'm still wondering if we should use elastic gum instead of birdlime." Sorrells bent over the cauldron. "It wouldn't smell quite so bad and surely works as well."

"I think it is too stiff and heavy for the silk." Holding her skirt tightly against her legs with one hand, Cassandra took the ladle with the other and lifted up a bit of the mixture, then let it trickle back into the pot. "Douse the fire and cover this from rain. It need set for only a day and we can use it." She handed the ladle to Mr. Sorrells with a smile, then stepped away from the fire.

Whittaker released his breath, not realizing he had been holding it until he did. "May I escort you home, C—Miss Bainbridge?"

"We have a cart," Mr. Sorrells announced. "She won't have to walk."

"But we need it for the vat of oil," Kent pointed out.

Sorrells's long face grew longer. "I forgot. Well, tomorrow then. Where's the shed? Is it big enough?"

Whittaker gave him directions, then rounded the fire to offer Cassandra his arm. The way he intended to show her home, along well-trodden paths with no stiles to climb, she would be in his sole company for a quarter hour. He must use it wisely. He must not say anything that would prevent him from finding more time with her alone, a quarter hour, a half an hour, a lifetime.

He thought of nothing to say. No letters formed words in his brain for sentences to come out of his mouth. She held his arm, gripped it, actually, and seemed to lean her weight upon it, slight though that was. Too slight. She was too thin, her gown too loose.

"You should not have come out so soon after your illness." The comment spilled out unbidden, unwise.

She glared up at him. "I do a great number of things I should not do, but you have no place telling me so."

"You were going to be my wife."

"Yes, I was. Past tense, my lord."

The use of the formal address cut deeply into his middle, it slid so easily off her tongue.

"Cassandra—"

"Miss Bainbridge."

"No." He stopped in the middle of the lane and faced her. "You have been Cassandra to me for nearly two years. You will be Cassandra to me forever."

"I can be nothing to you forever, Lord Whittaker."

"Why?"

"Because . . . because . . ." Her lower lip quivered. Her eyes grew bright with moisture. "If you wish to help tomorrow, you will not press me."

Blackmail seemed to run in the family.

He inclined his head. "I will desist for now if you intend to come to the assembly tomorrow night."

"I already promised Honore I would."

A bit lighter in spirit, he resumed walking, her hand tucked into the crook of his elbow, his other hand twitching with the desire to cover her slender fingers. He had promised not to press his questions today. The following evening was another matter. Meanwhile, he changed the topic back to her chemical compound for sealing air inside the balloon. He had learned more than a little about chemistry while learning the work of the mills, mainly for dyes. A method of keeping water out of or even inside cloth could prove valuable. Weave the cloth, then treat it for water tightness and sell it for the making of cloaks and greatcoats.

"The rather unpleasant smell is the trouble," Cassandra was explaining as they entered the house. "One has to be careful when selecting birdlime. That from Spain—oh, I am sorry."

They had walked into the hall and a sea of faces—at least a dozen people milled about with refreshments and polite smiles. All of a sudden, Whittaker recalled their odorous, smoke-stained, and dusty clothes. From her reddened cheeks, so did Cassandra, and her hair was not even pinned up. She had tied it back with a ribbon and pushed it inside the collar of her cloak.

"I must wash," she muttered, and fled as fast as a lady with a decided limp could.

Whittaker caught his mother's eye from across the hall, shook his head, and skirted the room to the door to his wing. A few neighbors greeted him. He paused long enough to nod or make his excuses and then vanished. Mama would make his excuses for not returning to her gathering. Even if she did not, he cared little. He and Cassandra had enjoyed the best dialogue between them since the night of the riots and fire. And she had promised she would see him tomorrow—twice.

That made getting through the evening long and tedious. The bulk of the visiting neighbors left before Whittaker changed his clothes with the help of one of the footmen, as he did not waste money on a valet in the country, but Mama, the major, Miss Irving, Miss Honore, and the cousins awaited him in the hall.

"Cassandra is resting," Miss Honore greeted him. "She seemed rather weary."

"I can see why." Miss Irving's finely etched nostrils flared as though smelling something unpleasant. "I should think that long a walk was more than a cripple could manage."

"What was Miss Bainbridge doing this afternoon?" William asked.

"Ask her," Laurence said.

Everyone followed his gaze to the opposite end of the hall, where Cassandra now hesitated in the doorway, her face a pale blur beneath the pile of her dark hair.

She looked at the younger of the cousins. "We were cooking birdlime and turpentine for a balloon, Master William. It is a messy, smelly business and must be done outside and away from a house."

"What's birdlime?" William asked. "Is it the same as bird drop—"

"No," the adults chorused.

Cassandra laughed and came forward, her limp a bit more pronounced than earlier, but her cane not in view. "It is a sticky, messy substance made of holly in this case, but sometimes other things, and it works to keep the air from leaking from a balloon."

"A dangerous business." Miss Irving yawned. "And tedious."

Whittaker joined Cassandra with the boys, conscious that Major Crawford, seated on a sofa beside Miss Honore, went so far as to turn his head and watch him move, keeping his lips firmly set as though Lord Bainbridge had asked him to chaperone Whittaker and Cassandra. And perhaps he had. His lordship did, after all, blame Whittaker for Cassandra's accident, a blame he no doubt deserved.

He could make up for it, though, show her the depth of his love—somehow. For now, he settled for being interested in her project, which did interest him.

She stood before the boys, her face soft in the candlelight. "Warm air goes up higher than cold air, so we have to keep the warm air inside the balloon and the cold air out so the balloon will float and carry us up and up and up." She raised her arms to demonstrate. "But cloth isn't perfectly woven—"

"Even cousin Whittaker's cloth?" William interjected. "My papa says the Hern mills are some of the finest, for all they are small."

"I expect they are fine, as Lord Whittaker works hard to make them so," Cassandra said.

Feeling like she had handed him a precious gift, Whittaker

added, "But we make cotton and wool, which is too heavy. I expect Miss Bainbridge's balloon is made of Spitalfield silk."

"Or something smuggled from France?" Laurence giggled.

Cassandra laughed too, and Whittaker wanted to hug her close with the joy of the sound. "I only helped pay for the balloon. I did not order the fabric, so I have no idea where it was woven."

William's and Laurence's faces shone with delight. They both began to speak at once, asking to fly in the balloon, to see the sealant being applied, how the balloon knew to go up.

Appearing bombarded, Cassandra glanced to Whittaker, a plea in the look.

"Not now, lads." He rested a hand on each of their thin shoulders. "Another time if Miss Bainbridge's friends do not disapprove."

"Her very good friends," Crawford said from behind Whittaker. "Are they not rather good friends for a lady to have, even if they are gentlemen?"

"They are scarcely gentlemen," Mama broke in, "and we have had enough talk of balloons for one night. Off to the schoolroom, boys. Whittaker, do lead Miss Bainbridge into the dining room. I am certain supper is ready and see no need for her to sit and then have to get right up again."

"With so much difficulty." Miss Irving rose without the assistance of even a hand on the arm of her chair—all tall, fluid grace like a cat—reached out her hand as though expecting a gentleman to appear for an escort, then scowled as Major Crawford, the only other gentleman present, offered his arm to Mama.

"You may take her in if you prefer," Cassandra whispered. "I do not mind walking in with Honore."

"You are the highest-ranked lady here after Mama. Miss Irving is the lowest."

"Whittaker." Miss Honore shot him a frown.

Apparently Miss Irving had heard the exchange despite their hushed tones, and her glare should have frozen him into a pillar of ice right then and there. So much for Miss Honore's scheme to have him pretend to court Miss Irving to make Cassandra jealous. It would not work where Cassandra was concerned, and Miss Irving appeared to have no liking for him either.

He grinned and tucked Cassandra's hand into the crook of his elbow. This was good. This was right. He should be taking her in to supper in his dining room every night. And afterward—

He focused on being a good host, offering a blessing over the meal, keeping conversation from flagging. With six of them to table, talking solely to one's immediate neighbor was not necessary. Cassandra talked and ate too little, but when he started to admonish her, Miss Honore kicked him under the table, reminding him to stop being autocratic like their father.

It was not his intent; he simply wanted to keep her safe, make her well, protect her from ever being hurt again.

That, of course, meant keeping her out of the balloon and away from flammable birdlime and turpentine. With the former, he might succeed. With the latter, he had promised his assistance, despite Major Crawford's presence to ensure he stayed away from Cassandra. Messages would take so long to reach Lord Bainbridge, Whittaker might have a chance to win Cassandra without her father's wrath coming down upon him.

Before he could no longer avoid returning to the shepherd's cottage.

On the following day, for the sake of spending more time with Cassandra and rebuilding her trust in him, Whittaker fended off his cousins to keep them from coming along, and he and Cassandra headed across the garden toward the farthest outbuilding, where the sheep were shorn of their wool in the spring. Not that he had ever seen the shearing. First he had been too young, then he had been away at school or university, causing a bit of a difficulty in playing his current role.

The role of Cassandra's suitor came much easier to him. Having her beside him felt so good, so right. He smiled down at her. "Your ankle seems to pain you less."

"It is doing well, almost as though the fresh air is good for it. If the surgeon were not such an ugly little man, I would kiss him for deciding not to cut off my—to amputate." She laughed. "That sounds mean, since he must have lost a good fee on that."

"Better his fee than your ankle, my dear."

In truth, Whittaker had paid the man anyway, mostly to make him leave. Agreeing with Miss Honore that Cassandra might be grateful enough to Whittaker to wed him should he ask her again, he said nothing of the fee or who had made the decision.

He said nothing else of a personal nature. A dozen questions crowded onto his tongue, but he bit them back and talked of the weather—no rain yet, but more threatening than the night before—the music they would hear at the assembly that night, the time Miss Honore was spending with the major.

"Father does not want any of us marrying a military man," Cassandra said. "But Honore is a natural flirt, and he is the only eligible male present other than you."

"She would not flirt with me."

"Ha!" Cassandra's snort was derisive. "She was clinging to you like a limpet yesterday, and she kicked you under the table last night."

"She is not flirting, and it would not matter if she were." He smiled down at Cassandra. "Would it?"

"She is as much a Bainbridge as I and has the same size dowry." An edge biting like the north wind sweeping toward them had crept into her voice.

For a moment, Whittaker stared at her, uncertain what was wrong. Before he worked it out or asked, he caught the whiff of birdlime and turpentine and heard Kent calling to them from beneath the shelter of the shearing shed roof.

It was not a proper shed, having only a floor, a roof, and low walls on two sides, but it was a good shelter for their purposes. Already the balloon lay spread out on the floor and a fire burned in the pit over which the water was heated for cleaning the wool. The cauldron rested above the flames, kept low until they needed to heat the vat of sealing substance.

"We waited for you," Sorrells greeted them. "Weren't sure how much to heat your receipt."

"Just enough to make it spread." Cassandra paused to peer into the vat of the sticky, oily stuff and wrinkled her nose. "It smells rather more peculiar than I thought it would."

Kent picked up the container and headed to the cauldron. "Maybe it's the fermenting for a day that does that."

As Kent walked past, Whittaker's nostrils flared. *Peculiar* was a mild word for the reek of the sealer. He caught the pungency of birdlime and turpentine, and beneath those aromas—

"Do not!"

He dove after Kent in an attempt to stop him from pouring

the formula into the already hot pot. He struck the man from
the side and Kent staggered under the impact. The vat tipped.
Cassandra screamed and threw herself against Whittaker and
Kent, shoving them backward with all her insignificant weight,
as the slimy sealant splashed onto the fire and exploded like
Guy Fawkes fireworks.

16

"What did I do? What did I do?" Roger Kent's voice rang out in shrieks of horror. "Oh, oh, oh, my arm! What did I—"

A crack like a whip cut off his hysterics.

"Get control of yourself, man," Whittaker said in calm, dispassionate accents. "Cassandra? Sorrells?"

"Yes, quite all right, if a bit shaken," Sorrells said.

Cassandra opened her eyes and pushed herself upright. Mr. Sorrells and Whittaker stood over her, their faces tense. Mr. Kent squatted a few feet away, nursing the imprint of someone's hand stark against the paleness of his cheek.

"I believe I am all right," she said. "A bit winded."

And her heart galloped like a runaway mare. If she could catch her breath, she might have hysterics like Mr. Kent. The fire—the flare of exploding oil and an ingredient none of them had added to her sealer—came too close to her gown. A scorch mark ran along the edge and the heat seared through her, igniting awareness of every burn scar on her legs.

She drew her knees up and wrapped her arms around her legs to hide them more than her petticoat and gown already did. "I am all right."

"Trying to convince us or yourself?" Whittaker crouched beside her and cupped his hand beneath her chin, tilting her face toward his. "Your formula seems a bit dangerous."

She ground her teeth. "It was not my formula. You know it was not."

"What was it then?" Mr. Kent demanded. "We all nearly blew up like a powder magazine."

"I believe," Mr. Sorrells drawled, "that this is about what was in that vat, no, Miss Bainbridge? Lord Whittaker?"

"Yes." Whittaker continued to gaze into Cassandra's eyes. "I smelled it a second too late."

"As did I." To break eye contact with Whittaker, Cassandra looked around for her cane to help her rise. It lay a dozen feet away, thrown by her or the explosion, or just left behind when she dove to push Whittaker back from the fire. She did not remember. She simply recalled catching a whiff of saltpeter amidst the turpentine and birdlime and throwing herself at Whittaker.

Sorrells must have caught her glancing about and guessed the reason, clever man that he was, for he headed for the cane. "I'll get this for you, Miss Bainbridge."

"I will help you up." Whittaker slipped his hands beneath her elbows and lifted her as though she weighed nothing.

He stood too close to her now. The frog clasps on her cloak brushed the round buttons on his greatcoat. His hands burned through the fabric over her elbows, and he would not stop looking at her, embracing her with his eyes, his lips curved in just enough of a smile to imprint the dimple on his cheek. Her hand twitched, wanting to lay a finger on that dimple as she had so often—

She jerked away, landed on her right foot, and gasped at the pain in her ankle.

"Shall I fetch a litter to carry you—ah, we are about to have company." Whittaker finally stepped away from her and turned toward the track leading from the house.

A crowd of people approached, including Miss Irving, with her rich hair and bright green feathers on her hat, gliding like a swan upon the surface of a lake. And Honore, also graceful but in a more athletic way—a colt.

"We heard a loud bang," Honore called out. "Is everyone all right? Cassandra?"

"I am well." Cassandra reached out for the cane Mr. Sorrells provided for her. Their fingers brushed and she felt nothing. Gloriously, no blazing spark.

At least she was not a wanton with every man, just the one still too close to her.

She moved away from him, but he followed. They arrived at the group of guests and servants together.

Miss Irving looked Cassandra up and down as she seemed in the habit of doing whenever they met. "Your gown is spoiled. Unless you want to sew a ruffle there."

"Thank you for an excellent idea." Cassandra nodded to the older lady. "It would save the cost of a new gown."

"Cassandra," Honore hissed.

"What happened up here?" Major Crawford asked. "We saw the flash from the orangery."

"It was like Guy Fawkes Day," Laurence cried.

"Can you do it again?" William wanted to know.

"Please, no." Mr. Kent scrambled to his feet but still emitted a tremor every few minutes. "I came half an inch from going up like fireworks too."

"What did happen?" Miss Irving asked.

"Someone put—" Cassandra and Whittaker began together.

They glanced at one another, back toward Mr. Sorrells and Mr. Kent, then shrugged.

"I have no idea," Whittaker said. "Someone must have mixed the formula incorrectly."

"That is what happens when a female plays at alchemist." Major Crawford gave Cassandra a condescending look. "Perhaps if you like mixing things together, the cook will let you make us biscuits."

"You would never wish to eat them," Honore interjected. "Cassandra tried that once with our former chef Lisette. She woolgathers and forgets to add something or adds it twice."

"It was grand. As bright as the sun," William declared.

"Was not." Laurence bestowed a scornful glance upon his younger brother. "Perhaps the moon, but the sun—"

"Enough." Whittaker broke into the potential argument with his quiet firmness. "It was bright and hot and dangerous, and everyone needs to leave here until we are certain all is well. Ca— Miss Bainbridge, do please return to the house with the other guests. I am certain Major Crawford will lend you his arm."

"Most definitely." The major removed his arm from Miss Irving's hold, though his other arm was free, and held out his hand to Cassandra.

Cassandra glared at his white glove, then at Whittaker. "This is my project. I am not leaving you to it. But thank you, Major."

"You should not be up here," Whittaker insisted. "This is—" He broke off and grinned. "If you insist. The rest of you, assure Mama and the household that all is well and we will be back in time to dress for the assembly."

"The assembly!" Honore and Miss Irving grabbed at their hair, which Cassandra thought looked perfectly coiffed, especially compared to her tangled locks.

She resisted the urge to shove a tumbled hank of hair behind her ear. Unlike Miss Irving, she was not wearing sapphire earrings, and her lobes suddenly felt naked. She did not even know if she had earrings for that evening. She did not recall packing any jewelry. Honore would have thought of that, though. She thought of everything. But Cassandra did not care.

Except at that moment, gazing at her lovely sister and the heiress, she did care that, in the company of four gentlemen, she must look like more of a ragamuffin than the grubby schoolboys did.

Schoolboys. Pranks. Harmless intent gone wrong.

As the party from the Hall returned at a leisurely stroll, save for the cousins, who chased one another like a couple of puppies, Cassandra watched them through narrowed eyes until their images blurred into shadows, then blended into the surroundings. Still, the childish, piping voices rang back along the lane, faint, but a few snatches distinct. "I dare you!"

"What are you thinking?" Whittaker asked from too close behind her again.

"Dares." She headed toward the vat of sealant. "Schoolboy pranks unknowingly dangerous."

"You are right, Miss Bainbridge," Mr. Kent said. "With two lads that age about, one can never be too careful."

"Where would two lads that age get gunpowder?" Mr. Sorrells asked.

"From the cellars at the Hall." Whittaker sounded pensive.

Cassandra glanced up from the concoction in the vat she was now heedlessly stirring with the tip of her walking stick. "You keep gunpowder in your cellar?"

"My father did. I have not thought about it in ages, as I have been too busy to go shooting since my brother died. What are you doing, Cassandra?"

"Seeing how much is in here." She lifted her stick out and allowed the sticky, oily substance to slide off the end. "Probably enough to blow us all up if we had spilled any onto the fire after the rest was poured into the pot. And certainly after we started heating it. Your clumsiness did us all a favor, Mr. Kent."

"Not my eyebrows." He rubbed at his face, and his eyebrows all but vanished, charred from the flash.

A chill ran up Cassandra's spine, and she backed away from the vat, the fire probably still too close at hand. "A-are you all ri-right?" She clenched her teeth to stop them from clacking.

"Of course, my dear. They'll grow back." Mr. Kent stared at her with a wrinkle on his denuded forehead, the only indication now that he wanted to raise his eyebrows.

"I think," Whittaker said, "that you are the one who is not all right."

"Of c-course I am." Cassandra intended to bark out the words. A remnant of a quiver ruined the effect.

"Why don't we walk her back to the house?" Mr. Sorrells suggested. "We can clean up this mess and mix another batch later and keep it under lock and key somewhere."

"Against ill-informed and mischievous schoolboys," Mr. Kent added.

"I will walk Miss Bainbridge back to the Hall." Whittaker grasped her left hand and tucked it into the crook of his elbow. "If you gentlemen will please dowse the fire completely and get rid of this muck." He toed the vat. "Burying it in the middle of a field seems like the safest thing."

"It will poison the ground." Cassandra had stopped shivering. Her voice returned to calm and steady. "The woods might be better, not someplace the sheep graze. Beneath an already dead tree."

Whittaker audibly exhaled. "The Lord knows we have enough of those in the park. I can send up one of the groundskeepers to assist you."

"Thank you, my lord." Mr. Sorrells was as calm as ever, a man with a dispassionate nature.

Father would approve. Philip Sorrells owned little property, but he had a comfortable income and a good enough family name, and he saw nothing wrong with her aeronautics interest. If Father insisted she wed, perhaps an unflappable man like Mr. Sorrells would make a good catch. He would likely not care any more about her scars than he seemed ruffled by the near disaster this afternoon.

She flashed him a warm smile. "Before you mix a new batch, let me think about the formula a bit more. Now that it has sat a day, it seems too thick. I am wondering if some linseed oil might thin it down while doing the job well."

"Or your objection to using elastic gum might not be valid," Whittaker suggested.

"I am considering that," Cassandra admitted. "Gum is harder to get and harder to melt, though, especially in this cold. But perhaps if we . . ." She stopped talking to think, only then realizing that Whittaker had started down the lane to the house and she had followed meekly along.

She did woolgather. Now she did not know what to say. Discuss the accident that was no accident? Pretend nothing happened so Whittaker would not find one more thing to count as too dangerous for her? Say nothing at all?

She chose to say nothing at all. He had been kind. She did not want to argue with him.

He remained silent too, until they drew close enough for Cassandra to be able to see the trees beyond the steamy glass of the orangery. "Are you well enough to attend the assembly? If you are not, I can stay—"

"Of course I am well enough. Do you think I am some fragile flower?"

"Not usually, but these past two and a half months have been difficult for you."

"And I cannot sit about and think the world is unkind to me and so intend to avoid it."

Even though she would prefer to do just that—the avoiding part anyway. But not if Whittaker intended to remain home if she did.

"Honore and our maid have helped me take in one of my gowns so I will not shame your household by appearing like I have gone to the assembly in a sack."

Whittaker stopped at the door to the orangery and faced her. "You would be beautiful if you did appear in a sack."

"You are absurd, my lord."

"Honest. Your hair is glorious." He lifted a handful and let it trickle from his fingers like a waterfall. "Your eyes are so dark and wide." He touched the tip of his finger to the corner of her lid.

She blinked and turned away. "Only so I can see where I am going more than a yard ahead of me."

"Your spectacles are useful in that."

"And hideous."

"They are charming."

"You are addlepated."

"Possibly." He smiled and stroked his thumb down her cheek. "You have the most beautiful skin. If the Spitalfield looms could produce satin like your skin, they would have no competition from smuggled French goods."

She swallowed and stood rigid, trying not to melt against him at his smile, his words, his touch. This aching need to be close to him was wrong. She had learned her lesson, relearned it every time she felt one of her scars.

Which were far from the creamy perfection he expected—more like the product of a weaver gone mad and mixing silk with raw wool, cotton, and nettle fibers.

She pressed her hand to her middle. "I must go," she croaked.

"Cassandra, not yet. I want to—"

"No." She shoved open the door of the glasshouse and slammed it behind her, then turned the latch so he could not enter that way. By the time he went around, she would be in her bedchamber and beyond his reach.

He rapped on the glass. "I have not thanked you yet."

"For what?" she mouthed back so no one inside the house could hear her.

"For saving my life."

There, it was out, the words neither of them had wanted to say aloud.

Cassandra spun the latch and opened the door. "It was nothing, an accident I managed to prevent this time."

"No, Cassandra, that was no accident. You are too intelligent to believe that was a schoolboy prank any more than I do."

She sighed and dug her cane into the muddy earth outside the orangery door. "I know, but who would someone want to injure or—or kill? Mr. Kent or Mr. Sorrells? I cannot see either of them having enemies. They are too congenial. Or could it be me?"

"Or me?"

"You?" Her head shot up.

Whittaker's mouth compressed into a thin, hard line for a moment. "I can think of a dozen people who knew I was going to be working with you today."

Stomach roiling, Cassandra asked, "So which one of us was a target, and why?"

17

Whittaker backed Cassandra into a corner, and now he could not answer her question with the answer he considered. To his knowledge, only the Luddites would want him dead if they had found him out, or else the one man who had shown enmity to him.

Cassandra's father.

In no way could he tell her that. She did not always get on well with her autocratic parent, but she did love him and respect him as her father, if nothing else. In turn, Lord Bainbridge loved his daughters. He exercised his full right to control their lives, and all of them managed to elude that control in some way, Cassandra most of all. She might believe Lord Bainbridge capable of plotting against his daughter's former fiancé, but he would not have had one of his minions tamper with the balloon coating. He would not risk Cassandra's safety or her life itself in such a way.

"I have no idea," Whittaker said. "Perhaps I am starting at shadows."

"Then we both are." Cassandra looked at him, her eyes wide and clear, so dark brown they were nearly black, a startling and lovely contrast to her flawless complexion.

He shoved his hands into the pockets of his coat to stop himself from touching her again. "I will see you this evening. We are taking two carriages, so I may not see you until we reach the assembly, as I may end up in the other vehicle."

"That is probably best." She closed the door. Through the misted glass, he watched her walk away, leaning on her cane as though she bore a heavy burden, not putting her weight on her right foot.

How terrible that burn on her ankle must have been to still cause her such trouble.

His own shoulders threatening to slump beneath a dozen burdens, the last of which being guilt, he trudged around the house and entered through the front door. For once no one sat in the hall. The fire burned low on the hearth, neglected with no one warming beside it. He should have at least two hours to have some refreshment and go over his accounts or read. Both had been neglected over the past two and a half months, as he joined the men reconstructing his mill destroyed in the spring in an effort to use physical exertion to work off the pain of Cassandra's rejection. It had not worked, and he had sought her out. He would keep seeking her out despite Miss Honore's advice.

He must also seek out his comrades amongst the Luddites and try to discover if any or all of them had learned his identity through his too-thin disguise. Together they played their roles of conspirators too well. But if he could meet with them separately, meet with each man on his own ground, perhaps he could learn all he needed to know and bring an end to the masquerade and to drawing Cassandra into danger.

Drawing Cassandra into danger.

He halted halfway up the steps and leaned on the banister. If the explosion was aimed at him, then being close to him proved dangerous to Cassandra. Yet whoever had done it must have known she would be with him; therefore, the person did not care if she were hurt. But where would the rebels have obtained such a quantity of gunpowder? It was expensive.

He spun on his heel and retreated down the steps to the kitchen, where he found the housekeeper and maids sipping tea. At his entrance, they sprang to their feet with a clatter of earthenware crockery.

"Milor'?" Mrs. Tims wrung her hands. "Is aught amiss?"

"Nothing to concern you. I simply need the key to the cellar."

She blinked but was too good a servant to question why. She simply removed a key from the ring hanging from her chatelaine and gave it to him.

Whittaker thanked her and crossed the room to the cellar door, unlocked it, and then turned back. "Is this always locked?"

"Yes, milor'." Mrs. Tims nodded. "And I have t'only key I know about."

Whittaker frowned and turned back to the steps descending into blackness.

"Milor'." A maid spoke close behind him. "You'll be wanting a candle." Feeling foolish for not having thought of that, he turned back, thanked her, took a candle, and headed downstairs to the dank cellar smelling of mold and mice. Little used for storage now and even less frequently cleaned, the cellar bore the marks of recent passage. Behind a stout door, the room lay empty save for more dust, with a clean circle in the center of the floor where a barrel had stood. Someone had made an effort to brush out footprints in the dust and had been unsuccessful. Imprints of two different shoes stood out against the stone, one large and one smaller, recent enough to show up in clear outline.

He climbed to his room, pausing long enough to return the

key to the housekeeper. His head whirled with questions, notions, everything but answers save for one—someone had taken the gunpowder from the cellar. Someone had gotten into the house, through the locked door, and then back out again. Not impossible with so few servants about. Anyone from one of those servants to a perfect stranger could have gotten in.

But they would have had to know about the gunpowder to take such a risk.

A servant then, someone who had been in the Hall long enough to know his father and brother. A man who did not like Geoffrey Giles as the earl, or a man in sympathy with the Luddites who knew of Whittaker's activities?

Nauseated, his arm throbbing, he entered his rooms, which were isolated and quiet and forever smelling like the cheroot smoke that had seeped into the carpet and paneling from his predecessors. He would tear it all out and replace rugs and walls when the estate could afford it.

If anything happened to him, the estate would never be repaired. His uncle was not well and his cousins were too young to manage it and the mills. Mama could never cope. She had no head for numbers.

Cassandra could manage. No doubt she could manage better than he. But Cassandra must go. She was not safe with him.

"Lord, I do not know what to do." He stood staring out the window at the overgrown parkland and barren fields. "I have truly made amok of everything."

No answers came to him. He closed his eyes and could not even think of an appropriate Bible verse to give him guidance and wisdom. He had set himself too far away from the Lord to have a consequential relationship with his Savior. Once upon a time, he would have discussed this feeling of distance from

God with Cassandra. She would have said something wise. They would even have prayed together. Somewhere along their path, they had pushed God aside in favor of their own wants.

Guilt plucked at his spirit. He needed to change his relationship with the Lord but did not know how. Mama would know. She was a wise and godly woman and his best chance at a spiritual adviser. Perhaps even an adviser about Cassandra.

He went to the bellpull to ask a footman where he might find his mother and remembered Cassandra's cut bellpull. He had not yet repaired it. Tomorrow—no, that was Sunday. The day after, before he slipped away, he would ensure she was not left without the means of getting attention quickly if she needed it.

And why would someone rob her of that means of communication? The idea that she was the target of someone's malice sent him to the door, ready to sweep her up and take her immediately away from Whittaker Hall. But he could not do that and risk Major Crawford thinking he had abandoned his mission and revealing Mama's indiscretion of the past.

Cassandra's safety or Mama's reputation. Neither option sounded good. A thought began to form in his mind, then someone knocked on the door. He opened it to see Gareth.

"Lady Whittaker sent me here to help you dress, milord."

"Of course. The assembly."

He donned his evening dress, too elegant for a country inn assembly, as it was made for London. The tightness of the coat pinched at his still-healing arm. If Cassandra were not so insistent that she was attending, he would stay home. For some reason, she chose to go to the sort of entertainment she normally despised. So he bore the discomfort with the hope that the wool would stretch a bit with wear and took to tying his own cravat until it fell in snowy folds over the placket of his white shirt. In the center, he affixed his best pin, a sapphire Mama had given him for the previous Christmas, created from a ring she never wore. Black knee breeches, white silk stockings, and black shoes with silver buckles completed the austere ensemble.

"You would look quite elegant," Mama said when she met him in the corridor, "if you had gotten your hair cut. It quite ruins the effect of a man about town."

"I never was much of a man about town." He offered her his arm. "But I was out enough to know you are prettier than any of the London mamas."

"Do not speak falsehoods." Mama laughed and rapped his knuckles with her fan. "But thank you for the attempt to flatter this aged lady."

"Not at all flattery, and should ladies half your age be so lovely."

She did indeed look lovely in muted violet satin and foaming lace over her shoulders.

"I expect Miss Irving will outshine us all," Mama said.

Miss Irving was indeed a vision in green silk spangled with gold and accented with emerald jewelry. Miss Honore shimmered in blue the color of her eyes and a pale gauze overskirt.

And Cassandra!

She wore a gown the color of pink roses with creamy lace and pearls. His pearls. Or the ones he had given her for a betrothal gift. Not family heirlooms, so she had been under no obligation to give them back. That she had not, that she wore them now, sent his heart singing with hope.

Instinct drew him forward to go to her, but he hesitated and Miss Irving stepped into his path. "You will be so kind as to escort me, will you not, my lord? I know no one here but will soon if you take me in."

She was a bold piece but absolutely right. To deny her would be churlish and rude.

He offered Miss Irving his arm. "Certainly. This is a small country affair. Everyone will be friendly."

"I have actually spent most of my life in the country," she prattled. "Each year I beg for a Season, but with no one to sponsor me, it has been difficult to manage."

They reached the carriage. Mama was inside. On the other side of the drive, Major Crawford handed Miss Honore in with a bit too long a hold on her gloved hand and an exchange of flirtatious smiles. Cassandra must have entered that vehicle first, for she stood nowhere in sight.

Resigned, Whittaker turned to Miss Irving and gave her his hand to steady her ascent into the vehicle. "Country folk can sometimes be as exacting in their acceptance of strangers as London."

"Worse," Mama said. "London is so large they expect that strangers and even those on the fringes of social acceptability can get a place in the finest houses with the right manipulations. But here, if one's reputation is tarnished, judgments are harsh, as one stands out more."

"And I cannot hide that my inheritance comes from trade." Miss Irving sighed. "Thus here I am, five and twenty and unwed. Quite a shame to my mama, which I believe is why she has taken herself off to India with my father." She emitted a trill of mirth.

"Perhaps," Whittaker suggested as he settled on the backward-facing seat across from the ladies, "you should go to India. I should think a host of younger sons would be more than happy to meet you."

"Geoffrey," Mama snapped as though he were a schoolboy. "That is rude of you."

"Not at all." Miss Irving met and held his gaze, her lips curved into a half-smile. "Younger sons from the right family can often be an excellent prospect."

He was a younger son. Or had been one. But if she were indicating that she intended to chase after him, she would catch cold.

"You will not find any eligible titles tonight," Whittaker said by way of warning her off.

Her smile simply broadened.

Mama let out a delicate cough. "I simply think this will be excellent entertainment, and the food is always very good. Some dancing for the young people. Some young ladies singing."

"You mean caterwauling?" Whittaker grinned at her. "Remember the last assembly and Miss Dunstan?"

"Do not remind me." Mama clapped her hands to her ears as though the young lady produced her tuneless shrieking in the confines of the carriage.

"Dear me." Miss Irving's smile faded. "Will she be there tonight, do you think?"

"I expect she will. She is seventeen and her parents want to launch her next spring." Mama sighed. "She is quite pretty. They simply need to teach her to keep her mouth shut more often. Nothing worse than a chattering—" She stopped and laughed. "A chattering female like me."

"You do not chatter, Mama."

"I have done a bit of singing at soirées," Miss Irving announced. "It is one way to endure them—participate in the entertainment. But I assure you I neither screech nor caterwaul, and I can hold a tune. Singing is actually a great pleasure of mine."

"Perhaps Miss Honore could accompany you one evening." Mama sounded anything but enthusiastic, but the remark was expected of her.

"I thought the harpsichord was broken," Whittaker said without thinking.

Mama shook her head. "I did not mean accompany on the harpsichord. We have a pianoforte. Your brother bought one shortly before . . . Well, it is a good instrument I have kept in fine repair. Much more modern than a harpsichord."

His brother had purchased a pianoforte shortly before he died? Whittaker did not even know John played. No one in the Giles family was musical, or had taken the time to find out if they were, in at least two generations, thus the ill repair of the only instrument that had been in the never-opened music room—the ancient harpsichord.

"Where is this pianoforte?" Whittaker asked.

"In the music room, of course." Mama laughed. "If you would come home to Lancashire for the house instead of the mills, you would know this. I had the harpsichord moved into a bedchamber, and now the pianoforte sits for me to play quite badly upon, until recently when Miss Honore went in there and played quite delightfully."

"Major Crawford also plays—" Miss Irving pressed a gloved hand to her lips as though she had spoken out of turn.

Perhaps she had. She and the major barely seemed to know one another.

"I thought I heard him tell Miss Honore something of the sort," Miss Irving continued too quickly. "Oh, look, here we are. What a charming little inn."

The inn was not precisely little, since it contained a common room large enough to accommodate the gentry within a twenty-mile radius, which trended toward fifty or sixty people in attendance during the months when the hunt did not bring a hundred more along and the gatherings grew more exclusive. For

Miss Irving, however, Whittaker Hall was probably a charming little house, since it possessed only thirty bedchambers to her two hundred in the home her father had purchased from a noble family that had fallen on hard times. Or, more accurately, bad luck at the gaming tables.

Where the Hall had come too close to going out of the family.

He should consider creating an entail for the estate. What did it take? The current owner plus two heirs in succession who had reached their majority? That meant waiting nine years until Laurence reached his. No worries there. Neither he nor his uncle was a gamester, and Laurence was too young if something happened to his father or Whittaker. But if something happened to the mills and the income dried up—

"Geoffrey." Mama tapped him on the arm with her fan. "You are woolgathering again."

"I am so sorry." He started up and leaped to the ground to assist the ladies down. From the corner of his eye, he watched Major Crawford laughing up at one of the ladies in the other carriage. Whittaker gritted his teeth and proffered his hand to Miss Irving.

She took it, clung to it for a moment too long as she flowed out of the carriage and set rather dainty feet for a lady so tall onto the freshly raked gravel of the inn yard. She remained at his side, waiting for Mama to descend, but the instant Miss Honore and then Cassandra emerged from their carriage, Miss Irving grasped Whittaker's arm and all but shoved him toward the brilliantly lit rectangle of the inn's front door.

It stood open to spill chatter, laughter, and the strains of a violin onto the yard, along with the aromas of roast chicken, baked apples, and a blend of perfumes. The Whittaker Hall party appeared to be amidst the last to arrive, judging from the crush already inside.

"So provincial." Miss Irving spoke directly into Whittaker's ear, close enough to stir his overly long hair. "I do wish to go to London."

He moved his arm away from his side to place some distance between them. "It is not much different, Miss Irving. The entertainments are much the same. The crowds are just ten times larger."

"But so much more elegant, and one never sees someone one suspects is nothing more than a freehold farmer playing at being a gentleman." She sighed and used the excuse of stepping over the inn's threshold to tuck herself closer against him.

"Some of those freehold farmers," Whittaker pointed out with no thought to the propriety of his remark, "have a larger income than do I."

"And so, no doubt, do I." Miss Irving let out a trill of laughter that rose above the strains of the quartet of string instruments in one corner.

Several people swung around. Their eyes flicked from Whittaker to Miss Irving and back to Whittaker. Eyebrows raised. A few smiled. Some frowned and turned away. Most began to press forward, greetings already on their lips.

Those were the highest ranked of the local Society. They wanted to know what beauty his lordship escorted into the assembly. Most knew Cassandra from her four London Seasons. All knew of the broken betrothal. All had heard of guests at Whittaker Hall, and the speculation as to what Whittaker's intentions toward Miss Irving might be shone in their glances, rang in their questions.

"How long will you stay here in Lancashire, Miss Irving?"

"We are certainly seeing more of you here in the country than we ever have before, my lord. Do you plan to make a habit of it?"

"Can we count on you for the hunt?"

"Do you ride, Miss Irving? Not to hounds, of course, but some of the ladies like to play at following the fox."

Whittaker squirmed and tried to see where Cassandra had settled herself. Miss Irving preened and dissembled and continued to cling to Whittaker's arm until a set began to form for the first of the country dances. Spying Cassandra perched on the edge of a chair across the room, Whittaker extricated himself from Miss Irving's clutches, introduced her to a gentleman he remembered from school, and slipped through the crowd to Cassandra's side.

"May I fetch you some refreshment?" he asked.

She started, then glanced up at him. "You should be dancing, my lord. I believe there is an uneven number of ladies to gentlemen tonight and they need you."

"Not me." He touched his injured arm, tender inside the form-fitting sleeve of his coat. "The jostling would likely unman me in less than a set."

She laughed her low chuckle. "I doubt anything could unman you, Geoff—" Her teeth flashed down on her lower lip.

He touched her shoulder where the satin of her skin met the silk of her gown. "You may always call me Geoffrey, Cassandra. We were friends long before I acceded to the title."

"It is quite improper now." She turned her face away from him and said something else, but he did not catch it in the tumult of six musicians accompanying the thud of feet stamping and skipping across the wooden floor, and shouts of correction or laughter when someone made a misstep.

Speech had grown impossible. He remained at Cassandra's side nonetheless, watching the dancers and her in turn. She sat motionless, her face impassive, save for the telltale tapping of her right foot in time to the tune. Not much more than a yard away, Miss Irving and Miss Honore spun and glided and pranced with the fluidity of soaring birds, as though gravity meant nothing to them.

Cassandra had never been such a fine dancer. Nor had she shamed her partner in the movements. They had laughed together over her missteps and kept going, enjoying the music, enjoying one another.

Losing that camaraderie suddenly felt like a beam crushing down on his shoulders, and he dropped into a crouch beside her so he could speak into her ear right above the pearl drop he had selected himself at Rundell, Bridge, and Rundell. "Will you go into the coffee room with me for some refreshment and less noise?"

She tensed, her hand flying to the ear he had spoken into. Her lips rounded in refusal. Then the dance ended and Miss Sylvia Dunstan stepped up to the harpsichord.

Cassandra glanced at the would-be singer, then nodded her assent to accompany Whittaker.

Feeling as though gravity meant nothing to him, Whittaker took Cassandra's hand in his and rose. He continued to hold her hand after he tucked her fingers against his forearm and led her from the common room. The door swung shut behind them as Miss Dunstan began to wail out "Nature to Woman Still So Kind" from *La Tour Enchantée*.

"Such a pretty song to be so—" Whittaker caught sight of Lord Dunstan and refrained from finishing his sentence.

A slight pressure of Cassandra's hand on his arm told him she understood. Camaraderie between them. They had always enjoyed music together if it was well performed.

Then Cassandra and he had argued during the interval at

the opera because she had ignored him in favor of discussing aeronautics with Sorrells and Kent, and nothing had been the same between them since. She forever wanted to discuss ballooning. Not tonight. Tonight he would steer the conversation to something else.

"Would you like food or something to drink?" he asked.

"Some mulled cider, perhaps?" She began to pull off her gloves. "And one of those cheesecakes will go so well with it."

"And a few other things?" He refrained from mentioning that she was far too thin.

He settled her on a chair in the corner and headed to the refreshment table seconds before the door to the common room flew open and a dozen males charged through on a wave of flat high notes. Amongst them were Philip Sorrells and Roger Kent. Both headed straight for Cassandra's table.

18

A glass of mulled cider spicy with ginger and nutmeg and a plate of delicacies slid onto the table in front of Cassandra. She flashed Whittaker a smile of thanks without breaking her flow of dialogue with Mr. Sorrells and Mr. Kent.

"So what happened when you added the linseed oil? I do wish you had waited for me before you tried it. And now it will set for two days before we can use it, and I will not be able to—" She stopped before she mentioned going up in the balloon. Whittaker, drawing out the last chair at the table for four, would most certainly interfere if he found out about her plans.

"It smells even worse," Mr. Kent said.

"But isn't as thick," Mr. Sorrells added. "Good evening, my lord. Is that arm of yours giving you pepper?"

"A bit." Whittaker fixed his gaze on Cassandra with such intensity she felt as though he touched her across the table. "It gives me an excellent excuse to keep Miss Bainbridge company."

"I should think she would have plenty of company." Mr. Kent shot a glance and a wink at Mr. Sorrells, who turned red.

Cassandra blinked. Across from her, Whittaker's jaw tightened. She could not think why. Mr. Sorrells was her colleague in aeronautics, nothing more. Yet that glance, that wink . . . No, it was nonsense.

"We had to escape the caterwauling," Kent continued. "Whoever told that female she could sing?"

"Her doting mama." Cassandra wrapped her suddenly cold hands around the hot cider. "I heard her in London a time or two also. Dreadful. My sister Madame de Meuse always said the child will never catch a husband that way."

"Or someone will wed her so he can make her stop." Whittaker grinned at Cassandra.

Her toes curled inside her slippers. Her hands tightened on her cup. She lifted it and took a deep draught to wet her dry mouth and hide her face. Surely he should not still have this effect on her. From two feet away, that broad smile and flash of dimple in his right cheek should not melt her insides like elastic gum in a hot cauldron. Oh, she must stay away from him the rest of the evening. Yet with neither of them able to dance, avoiding him looked impossible.

It was impossible. Miss Dunstan finished her song and everyone else began to pour into the coffee room for refreshments. The din of voices and clink of utensils against crockery limited dialogue. Gentlemen and ladies paused by their table to greet them before moving on to an empty place.

Cassandra sought Honore. She sat on the opposite side of the room, with Major Crawford dancing attendance and a young man who could barely be out of school trying to gain her attention, much to the frustration of the younger Dunstan daughter, also barely out of the schoolroom. Good. Honore was safe. Father would not like a military man courting one of his daughters again, but Honore might bring him around if the flirtation grew into something more. The major was stationed there in the north, at least until all the rebels were ferreted out and either jailed or scared into behaving. With a wife possessing a fine dowry, he might sell out altogether, unlike her sister Lydia's first husband. Lydia was happy now, though, and the major seemed urbane enough to keep Honore under control without boring her.

Certain she need not concern herself with her sister, she resumed her discussion of the balloon coating. "May we continue to use the shearing shed, my lord?"

"Of course. I said you could." He glanced from Mr. Sorrells to Mr. Kent. "Did you keep the formula in a safe place this time, away from tampering?"

"Yes, my lord, we most certainly did," Mr. Kent said.

"Can't have anything happening to our best aeronaut, now can we?" Mr. Sorrells smiled at Cassandra.

Much better. Mr. Sorrells's smile did nothing to her insides, just like his touch did not turn her knees to syllabub. She was not lost to all propriety and Christian ladylike behavior with other men. Whittaker alone. She must avoid him.

Difficult when he sat across from her and remained at her side in the common room, sent shivers up her spine when he spoke into her ear and she felt his warm breath . . .

The cider had made her too warm. She needed air, space. She sat in a corner, unable to move without disturbing the three men at their meal.

Then she spied Miss Irving, beautiful, elegant, and nearly as tall as most of the men in the room. She flirted with a gentleman farmer, no one she would ever wed due to his social rank barely above a yeoman, and caught Cassandra's eye. From a dozen feet away, Miss Irving arched her delicate brows in question. Cassandra scanned her gaze across her three companions.

Miss Irving received the message. After bestowing a brilliant smile upon her interlocutor, she sauntered to Cassandra's table.

"So the little invalid manages to be grip-fisted with the best gentlemen in the party." Miss Irving flashed her emeralds as she reached a hand to Cassandra.

She took it with too much gratitude to care about the "little invalid" remark. "Do you know Mr. Sorrells and Mr. Kent?"

She presented Miss Irving to the gentlemen, all of whom had risen at the other lady's approach, then slid out of her chair. "Do take my seat, my dear Miss Irving. I am quite finished here and really must speak to my sister." Too slowly, each step painful without the support of her cane, she tucked herself into the thickest point of the crowd and headed for Honore's table.

She did not need to glance back to know that no one followed her. They were all too polite and well-schooled in manners to do so. She was too polite to interrupt Honore's reign over a group of mostly young people, so she merely nodded to her sister as she passed and slipped out the nearest door.

It took her into a dim passageway with the clatter of pots and pans and the stronger aromas of baking pies pouring from one end, and the blessed coolness of the autumn evening at the other. She selected the latter, not wanting to intrude upon the kitchen, which must be in a hubbub with all the guests. Fortunately, she found herself in an herb garden, sweetly fragrant even with the plants mostly dormant for the winter. A chill nipped the air, but the wind was calm and the sky clear. Two lanterns hung on either side of the door, shedding some light to the narrow path between the herb beds, and she carefully made her way outside the pool of light to a low, stone wall. Only a few minutes. She would remain for a few minutes, breathe air not tainted with clothes that could have been better washed or aired, too many perfumes, and that sultry heaviness she experienced whenever she found herself in the company of Geoffrey Giles, Earl of Whittaker.

Earl indeed. He would make a better vicar. Or would have once. Now neither of them had taken much time for the Lord. She thanked God for her legs healing enough not to need to be amputated, but other than that, He was nothing but one more autocratic parent telling her what to do and punishing her when she did wrong.

"But I will not be good if it means sitting around doing nothing more than needlework and gossip."

All right, Lady Whittaker did many charitable things like taking food to the poor and even some nursing. Admirable, but not something Cassandra managed well. She had tried with her own mother. It was expected of the lady of the manor. It was expected of a countess.

"I am no countess, God, so why would You make me one if I wed Geoffrey?"

Miss Irving would make a far better countess. She was not the sort to make calls of mercy and would dispatch someone who was with the appropriate largess. Perhaps Cassandra should promote an alliance between Regina Irving and Whittaker.

The notion made her smile, a smile that froze on her lips as the door to the inn opened and Geoffrey Giles, Earl of Whittaker, stepped into the arc of lantern light.

He could not see her in the darkness beyond the light, but a servant had said he saw her slip out the herb garden door, and he heard a sharp intake of breath not a dozen feet away.

"Cassandra?" He spoke her name softly, not wanting to disturb the peace of the garden after the din inside.

"I am here." She sounded resigned.

He strode forward and dropped onto the wall beside her. "You should not be out here alone."

"I most certainly should not be out here alone with you." Despite her words, she did not rise. She crossed her arms over her chest and stared straight ahead. "What do you want?"

You, my love. Only you.

"When you slipped out a back door," he said aloud, "I thought you might have found an outside exit and did not want you in the night alone."

"I am perfectly safe alone."

"No female is safer alone. Except . . . I have to tell you myself. You are safer alone than with me."

Her eyes grew wide. "Surely not."

"Have you ever been harmed when in anyone else's company?"

"No, but . . ."

He pressed on. "My carriage was attacked in London. I was shot deliberately by someone who should have known not to fire on me, and someone tainted your balloon formula with gunpowder when I was with you and had announced I would be."

Her hands dropped to her lap, and she half-turned to face him, her face a pale blur in the radius of lantern light beams and starlight. "No one told me you were shot deliberately."

"I was concussed and you were ill. I have scarcely had the opportunity since." He laid a hand against her cheek in the hope she would continue to look up at him with her beautiful dark eyes. "I told one of the soldiers who I was during the assault on my mill, but he still fired at me. The blow to my head did more damage than his pistol, but he aimed at me. At me."

"Why?" The single word emerged as a croaking whisper. "You need your hair cut, but even with it so long you scarcely resemble one of the—" She stopped and drew back. "You were dressed like one of them at the balloon launching. The rioters, that is, not a gentleman. Surely the soldier just did not believe you."

"That is what Major Crawford says. Perhaps I would believe that without the gunpowder in your formula."

"And now you think the attack on your carriage"—her right hand dropped to her thigh, and she began to rub the silk of the gown flowing over her knees—"was deliberate?"

The faint strains of music drifted from the inn. Dancing had resumed. Cassandra could take her time absorbing what he had told her. No one would miss her and probably not him either. "Why, Geoffrey? Why would someone want to harm you?"

"That depends on who."

The urge to tell her about the blackmail, the Luddites, the dangerous game he played, burned on his tongue. He could talk through his suspicions with her, gain advice, another view. But the more she knew, the more he placed her in danger. He should not even be at the assembly amongst people who might recognize him later. He should leave now, slip away into the dark, and stay away from Whittaker Hall and Cassandra and any chance of bringing her further harm.

"I can't say, but I must go." He slid his fingers beneath her chin and tilted her face up. "I should not have come, but I had to take a moment alone with you to say goodbye."

Her lower lip quivered. "Where are you going?"

"I cannot say."

But that quivering lip, so full, so soft, so kissable, lightened his heart despite what potentially faced him.

"So—" She swallowed. "So you finally accept the ending of our betrothal?"

"Only until this matter is done with."

She drew away from him, composed, stiff. "Even afterward, my lord."

"I was Geoffrey moments ago."

"A slip of the tongue. Go now."

"Cassandra." His chest ached. "The ending of our betrothal was not my choice. You know that. Before all this happened, with a word from you I would have carried you over the border for a Scottish wedding. When this is over, I still wish to do so."

She shook her head. "I cannot. It was wrong. We were wrong. We made promises, and we broke them every time we were alone together. We pushed God out of our lives because He was an inconvenient reminder of our bad behavior."

"I know." He could scarcely speak from a chest too tight for breath. "I am still trying to work out how we can repair that damage."

"We cannot." She stood, glowering down at him, her hands on her hips. "I am scarred for life. Do you understand that? Hideously scarred. My legs are so ugly now, my mother and sisters fainted when they first saw them. Even Lydia was sick."

She may as well have punched him in the solar plexus or worse. Physical blows would have held less pain than her words.

Inadequate though it was, he said, "I knew about the ankle."

"Yes, and my left calf and right thigh and both knees." She rubbed at her thigh again as though it pained her, and her voice grew husky and thick. "I am a monster no man will ever want in his bed. And you talk about putting the past behind us? You are a fool." A sob escaped her. "A fool if you think I can ever forget and believe I am forgiven for my sins of wanting you too much, when the reminder haunts me every day."

19

Whittaker's face paled so fast the color change showed in the dimness of starlight. He swallowed audibly and reached his hands out to Cassandra. "My dear, I did not know . . . I did not realize . . . I am so sorry for your pain and—and—" He sighed as though bearing a heavy burden.

Cassandra strove to lighten it for him. "You need say nothing. I sent word the betrothal was off the instant I was conscious enough to realize what I would look like in the future—a freak. A monster."

"Cassandra, no."

"No? You have no idea what my legs look like and you will never find out. I could not bear it if you—" Her voice broke on a sob. She swallowed it down and pressed on. "If you turned from me in disgust. A man with your passion will want a wife you—you want to look upon. Like in Song of Sol—"

She clapped her hand to her mouth. She was not supposed to have read that book of the Bible. It had been carefully removed from every volume of Scripture in the house. But she had simply bought her own Bible to find out what had been so neatly excised from the holy Word of God.

Whittaker flashed a grin at her. "Of course you found a way to read it. It is beautiful."

"And I am not." Cassandra blinked back tears. "Not even my dowry is worth a wife who will disgust you and likely lead you into the sin of adultery because you cannot bear to look at me, let alone touch me. And you need a legitimate heir."

"In what low esteem you hold me." His tone held a note of bitterness. "But I suppose I deserve that. I took advantage of your sweetness."

"No advantage taken. I was always willing. Too willing." She pressed her hands to her face to stop the tears trying to course down her cheeks. "I invited your advances. We were to be wed. I justified it as all right. But now, since the accident, I feel shame and guilt like I will never be clean, and those scars are a constant reminder of our sin."

"But Cassandra, my dear one, do you not understand? The fire could have happened regardless." An ache cracked in his voice. "Others were burned that night too. The crowd was mad, crazed over too few lights for celebration and full of too much free spirits. It had nothing to do with our behavior."

"Which still does not justify it."

"No, but—"

"When I am near you, I do not think with my head. I think of things I should not as an unmarried lady, as a lady who professes to be a Christian."

"Then marry me when I'm done with my . . . work."

"Whenever you are done with whatever work you are risking your life over, I will still be scarred."

"That matters not a whit to me. I love you."

"Easy to say now when you have not seen anything so grotesque." She pushed the palms of her hands toward him to ward him off, though he had not taken a step or so much as raised his hand to reach out to her. "I am not willing to take the risk. Now if you will excuse me, I should look in on the dancing to ensure that my sister is conducting herself with proper decorum." She turned away with more a stagger than a graceful whirl of her flounced skirt and headed back toward the inn.

"Cassandra," he called after her, "wait."

She kept going.

He fell into step behind her on the narrow and mercifully short path to the door. "You still love me, do you not?"

She stiffened and did not answer. Alas, he already knew it. Her words, her actions, had given it away.

Of course she still loved him. If she did not, she would seize the opportunity to be a countess and the lady of the manor with a man she had also considered her friend for nearly two years. If she did not love him, him turning from her with revulsion would not matter. But she was worth nothing to him. He would not only get a wife he could not bear to make the mother of his heirs, he would not, according to his own claim of Father's words, receive the dowry his estate needed.

She opened the door and, without glancing back at him, said, "Miss Irving is beautiful, rich, and charming when she needs to be."

"I have no interest in Miss Irving." He sounded as though he spoke between gritted teeth. "I have no interest in riches or another estate to manage—"

"But think of the fine Indian cotton her father could provide for you. So much softer than the American stuff."

"And no interest in muslin cotton. Cassandra—" He did stop her in the middle of the passageway then, his hand gentle but firm on her shoulder. "What must I do to prove I speak the truth about my love for you?"

Had they been at Whittaker Hall, she might have acted boldly

210

and lifted up her gown, petticoat, and shift to show him the shiny, puckered flesh of her legs. That was all she needed to do to prove she spoke the truth—that he would run for comfort elsewhere. Rather now, before they wed, than after.

But since they were at a public inn in a servant passageway, she simply shrugged and dislodged his hand from her shoulder. "You should never buy a pig in a poke, my lord," she admonished him, then slipped through the nearest doorway. It led her through a coffee room, where two elderly gentlemen discussed the local member of Parliament in disparaging accents. Hastily she continued through to the assembly room and out to the inn yard. A line of trees across the road promised shelter and darkness. She tucked herself into the shadows and buried her face in her shawl to muffle her sobs and smother her exclamations.

"God, how could You let this happen to me? What happened to forgiveness?"

"Miss Bainbridge?" Someone spoke her name in soft, tentative accents.

She caught her breath in mid-sob. Her head shot up. "Mr. Sorrells?"

"Yes, I was leaving and saw you come here and was afraid you might be ill. Forgive me for the intrusion." The barrier of the hedgerow she had hidden behind rustled. "May I do anything to help?"

"No, but thank you." She held her breath, waiting for him to go away.

He did not. He pushed through the hedge and joined her in the tiny clearing beyond. "I thought you might be able to use this." He pressed a white linen square into her hand.

"Thank you." She lifted it to her nose. The smell of linseed tickled her nostrils, and she managed a small chuckle. "Interesting cologne, sir."

"Not pleasant compared to your scent of lemons."

"Mr. Sorrells?" Cassandra blinked at the shadowy figure before her. "You are surely not flirting with me."

"A little to make you laugh." He patted her hand. "The pain goes away, you know. At least, I know. I lost someone I loved once too."

"You did? I mean, that is, I am so sorry."

She shriveled with embarrassment. She called him friend and never talked of anything with him but matters pertaining to ballooning, rather like he was nothing more than a master of hounds, rounding up balloons instead of dogs. But he was no servant. He was a gentleman of modest but independent means, welcome enough in Society.

"She ran off to Canada with a soldier. Their ship sank on the crossing."

"How horrible for you."

At least she bore the comfort of knowing Whittaker lived and was well . . . for the moment. He played some dangerous game he would not discuss, a game that might get him killed.

Her dislike of herself in that moment had nothing to do with her scars and everything to do with the ugliness in her heart.

20

Whittaker returned to the shepherd's hut, to the major waiting for him.

"You have been overly long." Crawford had helped himself to tea.

"I am here now." Whittaker would not make excuses to the major of first going home to repair Cassandra's bellpull. The man might hold the upper hand in what he knew of Mama's past, but Whittaker outranked him socially and preserved that petty power as his sole defense—for now.

"What do you want?" he demanded.

"I should think you would be grateful to me having your work here save your mill."

"It also got me shot. Now what do you want with me?"

For a moment so brief Whittaker would have missed it had he not been staring hard at the man, the major's eyes flashed and his jaw hardened. Then he became the languid gentleman again. "I want to know who the leaders are—quickly. I have been mucking about here in the north long enough. My regiment is in London and I wish to enjoy the fleshpots there rather than the strict morals here."

"Strict morals?" Whittaker took a step closer to Crawford. "What about your attentions to Miss Honore?"

"Purely honorable." Crawford laughed as though he had made a great jest. "She is a charming creature with a good dowry, and though her father is nothing more than a baron, he holds considerable political power and is a step higher than my own father."

"Ah, so you are the son of a baronet. You have done well to have purchased a major's commission."

Crawford shot to his feet, the tightness returning to his face. "I earned this commission. My father could only afford a captaincy for me, but I was promoted for my work here in the north. And I will be a lieutenant colonel at the least if you do your work without getting yourself killed." He strode to the door and yanked it open. "And do not think you are my only spy. You are being watched." He slammed the door behind himself so hard it shook the house frame.

Whittaker slumped onto the vacated settee and dropped his face into his hands. He did not like lording his rank over others. The Lord of all knew he did not like even having the rank. And if the major was going to force his hand to take actions Whittaker found dangerous and unpleasant—spying on men whose families had depended on the Gileses' and Herns' employment for generations and felt ill-used—Whittaker needed to maintain some of his power. The Lord knew too well how much he had lost everywhere else.

But his snobbishness had played in his favor for once. He had angered the major enough for him to definitively admit that someone watched his noble spy.

"So you do not trust me, Major," Whittaker murmured to the plain, whitewashed walls of his cottage.

He rose and began to make his simple meal of cheese and bread and an apple. He wanted hot soup. To get it meant going to a tavern, and he did not wish to encounter any of the rebels he knew right then. He needed a day or two to plan his next steps, work out how to discover the information the major wanted and who wanted an earl dead badly enough to risk hanging for it.

"Make friends," Whittaker said to himself. "Make friends."

Thus far he had avoided any more contact with the rebels than necessary. They were men with whom he held nothing in common, uneducated men save for their skill at weaving. They were traitors to their country and disloyal to their employers.

And they were taking him away from his purpose—winning Cassandra back.

That thinking kept him awake most of the night as he pondered how to extricate himself from the blackmail, from the risk of being shot again or taken up as a traitor and hanged, of being away from Cassandra too much while Philip Sorrells spent too much time with her.

So he set aside his repulsion and headed out the next night.

Near the hedge tavern where he had seen Rob and Hugh taking their supper, he hesitated in the shadow of a pine tree. He intended to join them for a bowl of the owner's tasty stew. Perhaps if he befriended them, pretended wholehearted interest in their cause, talked assault outside of their meetings, they would trust him enough to give something vital away such as the name of the man who gave them—or at least one of them—orders. He would have to find a different way to befriend Jimmy, for he had a family with whom he took his meals.

Risking his family's future with his rebellion against factory owners and the Crown.

Whittaker curled his upper lip and stepped out of the shadow of the tree. The sourness of ale fumes replaced the tang of the pine. He grimaced but forced himself forward.

From the corner of his eye, he caught a glimpse of another shadow, a flicker of movement. He pivoted on one heel. "Is someone—" He stopped. He was forgetting to roughen his accent.

He saw no one anyway. Starting at chimeras, at nothing substantial.

He headed for the door again, bracing himself for the smells of unwashed men, spilled spirits, and rough talk he would find inside. He must not show his distaste, his dislike. He was supposed to be one of them, quiet, solitary, but agreeing with their cause in a cautious way.

He reached for the door handle.

"You don't want to go in there." Jimmy spoke from the darkness behind Whittaker.

He jerked his hand from the latch, dropped it to the knife hilt at his waistband. "I do if I want my supper."

"If that's all you want, then come to my house. It'll be naught but bread and dripping, but the bread's good."

And likely Whittaker would be taking tomorrow's breakfast from someone like Jimmy himself.

"Why?" Whittaker asked, turning slowly.

Jimmy shrugged. "You're too young to be cozying up to the likes of Rob and Hugh. If you're tired of your own company, then you'll find plenty in my house."

"That's, um, very kind of you." Despite the melding of his words together, Whittaker still sounded too educated for the role he attempted to play. Not knowing what else to say, he shrugged and stepped away from the tavern door. "Let's be off then."

Off to a possible trap?

One hand on the hilt of his knife, he fell into step beside Jimmy. "Will your wife care about an extra to table?"

"My wife?" Jimmy snorted. "I don't have a wife." His tone was decidedly bitter.

"I'm sorry. I thought . . . You mentioned making enough to support a family once, and I thought . . ."

"Aye, I have a family. Four children, but my wife left me after the baby was born. I came home from the mill one day, and she was gone with every spare penny in t'house."

"I'm sorry." Whittaker recalled Miss Honore's brief missive expressing Cassandra's wishes. In two and a half months, she insisted she had not changed her mind, and her father had agreed and sent Whittaker packing too.

"I lost my la—woman too," he murmured. "We weren't married yet."

"Best for you 'til you can support her and any little ones proper."

And not need Cassandra's dowry.

But that was years into the future. Her father would find her a husband before then—a nice, quiet, and dispassionate man like Philip Sorrells.

"Maybe you're right." Whittaker sighed. "But the nights are lonely."

"Aye, that they are. Here we go." Abruptly, Jimmy turned down a track invisible to Whittaker, though after a few dozen yards, he began to recognize the terrain even in the dark.

Beyond the mills, beyond the fence surrounding his own weaving houses, lay hovels no larger than his own bedchamber. They smelled of rotting vegetables, coal smoke, and night soil.

His stomach churned. His feet dragged like those of a schoolboy not wanting to take his punishment.

Going into Jimmy's cottage was punishment. From what a solitary tallow dip on a plain deal table showed, the single room forming the lower floor appeared spotlessly clean. So did the old woman and three children seated around that table, though a whimpering baby, lying in a wooden box for a cradle beside the grate that gave off more smoke than warmth, smelled as though he or she needed to be changed.

A very young baby. So Jimmy's loss of his wife must have been recent.

Whittaker's heart wrenched. He stood on the threshold, his head ducked to keep from banging his brow on the lintel.

Jimmy went straight to the cradle and lifted up the baby, murmuring something that made the whimpering cease. The others scrambled from their stools, the three children swarming around him and chattering like a flock of sparrows. The old woman crossed to the dresser in a corner and removed the remnants of a loaf from the shelf. A knife flashed. What wasn't enough food for one man was divided in two.

How to repay the man's kindness without insulting him?

Watching Jimmy embrace and talk to each of his children in turn, then carry the baby into a dim corner to take care of the dirty napkin, Whittaker could not believe the same man engaged in wholesale destruction of property and sometimes lives.

No, Jimmy would avoid taking lives. Surely a man who played nursery maid to his child instead of leaving that for the old woman—surely his grandmother, judging from her lined and wrinkled skin and white hair—was too good to harm a human being. And yet, perhaps mill owners and those workers who would not join the Luddite cause were fair game.

Pondering these thoughts, Whittaker did not realize that

everyone was staring at him until Jimmy gave him a playful punch on the shoulder.

"Come in, man. We aren't warming the outside."

They were not doing much to warm the inside either.

With a muttered apology, Whittaker stepped into the single room and pulled the door closed behind him.

"Let me introduce the children," Jimmy said. "Sally, Little Jimmy, Timothy, and Susan is the baby there." Tenderness filled his voice as he spoke each name.

An emptiness opened inside Whittaker, a longing for children of his own, a family to greet him when he returned from the mills or Parliament. Not that most children in his class were allowed to greet their fathers at the door. Their wives did not go up in balloons either. But his family would greet him at the door. All of them—wife, children, perhaps a dog or two . . .

He bowed to the children, making them laugh.

"Is he a prince, Papa?" Sally asked.

Jimmy chuckled. "Aye, to you, no doubt, he is just that. But right now we're havin' our bread and dripping. Ma, come meet my new friend, Geoff."

His mother? Surely his mother should not look seventy instead of forty-five or fifty, the same age as his own mother. Jimmy was not all that old, especially not for a man with four children.

Four children and a mother to support on his meager wages. When this was over, Whittaker would find work for the man in the Hern mills.

Jimmy led the way to the table. His mother brought wooden plates with the bread smeared with a glaze of meat fat probably procured for a pittance at the nearest chophouse or tavern. It smelled vile, perhaps a little rancid. Whittaker ate it anyway, washed it down with water, and longed for a chair with a back he could lean against, beside a fire that warmed him.

Jimmy worked a whole lot harder and had neither. Yet he had a mother and children who loved him. They came to him in turn to receive what appeared to be a silent blessing, with his hand resting momentarily on their heads, then they vanished up a stairway little more than a ladder, and the room grew quiet save for the baby's snuffling noises beside the hearth and the patter of fresh rain outside. The residents of the nearby houses must have been asleep or away.

"Thank you for joining me," Jimmy said into the stillness. "Ma don't talk much 'cause I won't let her say aught ill of my wife in front of the children, and she says that's all there is to talk about. And the nights are long."

Whittaker nodded. Long nights alone he understood.

"Maybe one day," Jimmy continued, "I can learn to read to fill the time before I can sleep. I'd love to read my Bible."

Something Whittaker had not been doing much of lately, and he bore no such excuse as being unable to read. Guilt prompted him to blurt out, "I could read it to you if you like."

Too late he realized he should not admit to any kind of education.

"I'd like that, but not now." Jimmy did not appear in the least surprised that Whittaker could read.

His skin chilled beneath his woolen shirt and coat. If Jimmy was not surprised, it might mean he knew more than was safe for Whittaker.

He dropped his hand to the hilt of his knife.

Jimmy curled his fingers around Whittaker's wrist gently but firmly. "You don't need to be pulling that out. I'm not your enemy."

Whittaker did not move except to raise his eyebrows. "I have an enemy?"

"Aye, at least one." Jimmy laughed and released Whittaker's wrist. "That's what I wanted to tell you. I don't know if it's Rob or Hugh, or maybe it's a friend of theirs, but I followed them one night and overheard them talking."

"Did you, now?" Whittaker pretended nonchalance. "Seems an odd risk to take when you have a mother and four children depending on you."

"They're why I do this. Until we make more money, I cannot support them. They won't have a future if the machines take over our jobs."

"But neither will they have a future if you get yourself hanged."

"I won't."

Whittaker wanted to call him a fool. No man should be so cavalier about his mortality, especially when others depended on him remaining alive.

"You," Jimmy continued, "are the one who will die."

Gunshots and gunpowder!

Whittaker gripped the edge of his stool and tried to control the bunching of his jaw muscles as he strove for a disinterested mien.

"Rob and Hugh know who you are," Jimmy announced.

Whittaker's stomach felt as though the pork dripping had turned back into a boar and commenced galloping around his innards. "Truly? And who is that?"

"The ninth earl of Whittaker, with a death sentence hanging over him."

"Hmm. And what would his lordship be doing consorting with those wishing to steal his livelihood?"

Jimmy laughed, a great guffaw. "You can't talk like us no matter how hard you try. You can get the accent right, but you still talk like a nobleman."

"Indeed?" Whittaker's ears went hot beneath his hair.

Jimmy laughed harder. "And you're too cool and calm. You should've knocked me flat for laughing at you."

"I would never—" Whittaker's lips curled into a reluctant grin. Still, not admitting anything, he said, "So if someone knows me, why don't they stick a knife in my back?"

"Gotta look like an accident, milor'. You can't just go around killing peers. They'd hang everybody they could think was in the area at the time." Jimmy leaned forward. "But you watch yourself and your mills. They're going to kill you and burn the mills." He shoved back his stool with a screech of wood against wood. "Now I'll walk you home before anyone notices you're gone."

"How would they know that?" Whittaker asked, rising also.

"You're watched." Jimmy strode to the door and opened it.

Slightly colder air rushed into the room, along with the noisome smells of the lane. The shepherd's hut would feel like a palace when Whittaker returned.

He wished it were a fortress.

If someone wanted him dead, he could not go back to Whittaker Hall and risk the lives of the inhabitants. Yet staying alone in the cottage sounded just as foolish.

Except that entailed risking only his own life. His own life and the mills.

If Jimmy was telling the truth.

"Why are you telling me this?" Whittaker asked as they reached the road.

"I don't know why you joined us, and sometimes I think what

you say makes sense. And I hear you're a fair employer. Your workers won't rebel."

"I know what it's like to have—"

What was he saying? That he knew what not having money was like? What a lie. He had no idea what being poor felt like. Cassandra had not walked away from their betrothal because he was poor by noblemen's standards. He never worried how he would eat or whether or not he would be evicted from his house without warning. His mother didn't look twenty years older than her age because of a lifetime of hard work and too little joy.

Jimmy knew all those things too well. And apparently he knew a great deal more.

Whittaker took a deep breath and did something he never before thought he would have—ask advice of a man who ranked amongst the lowest of classes. "What do you propose I do? Leave the gang?"

"Not unless you plan to go to London and out of their reach. If you're staying here, they'll get you for knowing as much as you do."

"Which is why I'm not sure I believe you."

But he did, of course. Seeing the shepherd's cottage a hundred yards up the lane, Whittaker suppressed the instinct to dash inside and lock the doors until morning.

"Why would they keep giving me information and letting me come along with them?" he pressed.

Jimmy shrugged. "Easier to find an accident to kill you." He rested a hand on Whittaker's shoulder, halting him. "You don't have the power to stop this rebellion even if you take down their leader—whoever gives Rob and Hugh orders—so watch your back and your mills. I want to work there one day." Speech delivered, he slipped away into the darkness like a shadow, like a chimera.

Whittaker did not return to the cottage. He turned his steps toward the Dales and the Hern mills. Hiding in the cottage looked like cowardice. If these men or someone higher than them in the rebellion wanted him dead, he would remain out in the open and give them a fight.

And he would die protecting the future for his heirs and for men like Jimmy, who deserved to be able to support their families on the twelve hours a day they worked.

21

Cassandra could not sleep. Every puff of wind, every creak of the house, every rustle of bare branches, brought her startling awake for fear that rain had begun to fall, a gale had blown in, someone was coming to stop her. Added to the fear of sleeping too late, she found herself pacing the floor at four o'clock in the morning, rubbing her legs where the scars pulled on her skin, wondering if she would be too tense and clumsy to climb into the balloon basket.

If only females could wear pantaloons and Hessian boots like men, then getting about would prove so much easier. Skirts hampered one dreadfully. But she dressed in a proper gown, an old and warm one of heavy linen with one woolen petticoat beneath and a velvet pelisse on top. For extra warmth, she draped a shawl around her shoulders and rounded up a pair of knitted mittens, then put them back. She needed as much use of her fingers as possible to open and close the valves on the balloon, to ensure the fire burned consistently as needed, to hold on if the basket rocked. She settled for soft leather gloves and slipped out of the house before first light. Honore would tell everyone she would not be coming out for breakfast, and no one would expect her for the morning rides that Miss Irving insisted everyone but Cassandra enjoy each day.

"Miss Irving." Cassandra ground her teeth on the name. "Mushroom."

Unfortunately, the nabob's daughter may have been produced in the obscurity of the bourgeoisie, but her father's fortune certainly helped her spread out at the highest echelons of Society, at least in Lancashire Society. Everyone included her in the parties to which they invited the Whittaker Hall guests because of her connection with the family, however remote, through the two boys. The table in the great hall, where the mail waited for Lady Whittaker to collect and sort and deliver, always held more cards for Miss Irving than for Cassandra.

No matter. In less than an hour, she was going to fly.

She stepped through the gate on the other side of the parkland and into the field. In the distance, light flickered through tendrils of morning mist. Rain might stop her from going up. Mist would not. It would burn off before she landed. Even though October had slid into cold and wet November, morning fog did not last the whole day.

As best she could, she hastened her steps. Her leather-soled slippers slid on the damp grass stubble. She should have chalked the bottoms of her shoes like dancers did. Too late now. Her cane helped her keep her balance, and nothing rubbed against her still-healing ankle.

And she was going to fly.

If possible, she would have leaped her way across the field, cavorting and shouting with glee. Instead, she approached at a quick but sedate pace and lifted a hand in greeting to her comrades in aeronautics. Her friends for certain, for all they were gentlemen.

They lifted hands in response, and Mr. Kent shouted something unintelligible, for he munched on an apple.

"It's all ready for you," Mr. Sorrells announced as Cassandra drew within earshot. "Are you ready to go up?"

"Beyond ready, I think." She smiled when she wanted to laugh.

He smiled too. "Very good. Are you certain you wish to go up alone? One of us can go with you, you know."

"I think one of us should." Mr. Kent lowered his apple. "We haven't yet gone up alone ourselves and aren't certain one man—er, woman—can manage on her own."

"I have thought something about it." Cassandra gazed at the balloon, the silk bag coated with the new mixture of birdlime, turpentine, and linseed oil, expanding as the fire pushed the gas into the tube leading into the silk. It was a sight far more beautiful to her than all of Miss Irving's jewels. "I want to be alone my first time."

"But if something goes wrong and you need assistance," Mr. Sorrells pointed out, "such as you having to land in a field far away, you might be too far away to walk."

"Not that we think you're infirm," Mr. Kent hastened to add. "That is . . . um . . ."

"I am a bit lame." Cassandra grinned at him. "Let me climb into the basket and see what I think once there."

With the balloon nearly filled, the basket bobbed a foot or more off the ground, tugging at its mooring ropes. That made the top of the basket at her shoulders. She could climb up like mounting a horse. It was not even as high as a horse's back. But then, with a horse, her left foot would be in the stirrup to give her a bounce up. Perhaps she should add something to the sides, at least loops of rope into which one could slip one's foot. Until then . . .

Her cheeks a bit warm, she turned back to her friends. "I will need a bit of a leg up, if you please."

"Of course." Mr. Sorrells approached her.

"I thought perhaps we should bring a box or something," Mr. Kent said around another bite of apple, "but we couldn't find anything appropriate that was moveable."

Cassandra shrugged. "No matter. A strong hand will do."

Mr. Sorrells's hands looked strong enough to give her the boost she needed to clamber over the side of the basket. It would not look elegant. She did not care.

Heart racing, she rested her hand on the top edge of the basket and placed her left foot in Mr. Sorrells's cupped palms. "Ready?"

"I'm ready." He nodded. "One. Two. Threeee."

She gave the bounce one would for mounting a horse as he lifted. But she bounced off her right foot. Pain shot through her right ankle and up her thigh, and she staggered instead of lifted. She fell against the side of the basket. The balloon bounced, the basket swayed, and Cassandra and Mr. Sorrells landed in a heap on the ground.

"I say, are you all right?" Mr. Kent tossed his apple aside and ran to them. He clasped Cassandra's hands and hauled her to her feet. Not until she stood again, shaken but otherwise unharmed, did she notice that her skirts had caught up in her pelisse on one side, and the line of puckered red flesh from mid-thigh to knee shone in the misty gray light of morning.

Face as hot as the fires fueling the balloon, she yanked the fabric loose from the clasp on which it was caught and let her petticoats and skirt fall. "I should have realized getting into the basket would be difficult for me."

She thought she might be sick right then and there. They

were going to send her away, tell her it was unsafe for her to fly, as Whittaker did. A lame female could not be an aeronaut.

Philip Sorrells took her hands in his and gazed down at her from rather fine gray eyes. "Miss Bainbridge, we should have been the ones to think. Why do I not climb in first, then lift you in? Would that be amenable to you?"

"Yes. Yes, I think that will work fine."

"And I can catch you if you fall," Mr. Kent added.

"Thank you." Cassandra bit her lower lip. "I think perhaps, Mr. Sorrells, you should stay with me, if you are amenable to that."

"Gladly." He continued to hold her hands. "I'd be honored to escort you on your first flight."

He continued to gaze at her with a kind of awe and wonder, as though he found her . . . important, perhaps even pretty. And he had seen her scars.

"Will you find me lifting you in offensive, Miss Bainbridge?" Mr. Sorrells asked.

"No, I think not."

Offensive, no. Mortifying, yes. She wore stays beneath her gown, simple ones she could lace up the front herself, so she barely felt his hands on her waist, strong hands lifting her up and up until, with a flick of the hem of her skirt to get it and her right leg over the edge of the basket, she half-stepped, half-tumbled into the balloon gondola. It bucked and swayed. Like a tower, the balloon rose above her, just out of reach, bulbous and tall with its sack of hot air.

"The power of air," she murmured, gazing up and up at the colorful sphere against the grayness of the morning, its top lost in the mist. "Glorious."

"It is." Mr. Sorrells stood in the basket beside her.

"Shall we be off?" Cassandra peered over the edge. "Oh, you have added hooks to the lines instead of knots. How clever! So much easier to release them."

"Yes." Sorrells ducked his head. "It was my innovation. This way a body can go up all on one's own. See, you can reach the hooks from here." He leaned over the side and released one of the ropes mooring them to the earth.

Cassandra did the same on her side. They bounced and tilted a bit, then Mr. Kent released the other two hooks and the basket began to rise as silently and smoothly as smoke from a chimney on a windless day. Mist swirled past Cassandra's face, cold but soft fingers mingling with the heat of her tears. Happy, joyful tears. She wanted to shout, sing, perform a jig.

But she did not wish to disturb the silence, the peace. A world of gray fog surrounded her. Below her, the earth existed as no more than a layer of pale gauze. Above and around, wrapping her in its gentle embrace, clinging to her lips and lashes, the cloud sheltered her from the world. No matter that she could not ride now. No matter that she could not dance now. She could do something far better.

She could fly.

"Miss Bainbridge." Mr. Sorrells's voice broke the silence.

She jumped and turned. "Yes?"

"Look up."

She looked up. For several seconds, nothing happened. Mist continued to slide over her like damp fingers. Then a miracle occurred. One second they floated in a cloud. The next, sunshine washed over them like heat and light after a walk through darkness and rain, like the first flower of spring, like the gold separated from the dross.

Her throat closed, robbing her of speech, of breath. Her lips

230

parted in a silent exclamation of wonder. Below her, she left behind the clouds. Above her, the sun reigned.

"God is up here," she managed to say at last.

"And everywhere else," Mr. Sorrells added. "But I agree that one feels closer to Him here."

"I suppose we should turn down the fire." Cassandra turned to do so.

Mr. Sorrells did the same. They collided in the confined space of the basket, laughed, and both said, "Go ahead."

"You should practice," Mr. Sorrells said. "Not too much. We don't wish to lose altitude."

"No, not until the cloud burns off."

Cassandra adjusted the damper on the brazier so less hot air would flow into the balloon and they would climb no higher. Reports said people who went too high found breathing difficult and even suffered some peculiar disturbances of their minds. Too much she wanted to enjoy this sensation of floating, of being as graceful as Honore or Miss Irving. She liked feeling closer to God, a place she had not been since the night of the fire. He had given her this precious gift. She had lost the man she loved because of her sinful behavior, but she had been given something precious in return.

As well as two good friends, friends who had not gone pale at the mention of her scars, let alone the sight of them. They did not try to stop her from what was most precious to her.

She slanted a glance at Philip Sorrells. Not as good-looking as Whittaker, but far from unpleasant to set one's eyes upon. He was intelligent and kind and possessed a comfortable competence to live on. If Father insisted she wed, she could do far worse.

She smiled at the notion and peered over the side again. "Oh, look, the mist is burning off."

"Have a care." Mr. Sorrells touched her elbow.

Had that been Whittaker behind her, her body would have reacted in ways she knew were wrong, ways that led her into misbehavior. Mr. Sorrells's touch once again caused no tingling rushing up her spine, no hollow, yearning aching for more and more and—

"Some people get dizzy when they look at the ground so far below," he continued.

"Not me." Tendrils of mist clung to the pastureland now below them, parting like a gauzy curtain to reveal a flock of sheep munching what was left of the grass. They looked like a child's toys discarded on a nursery floor, so tiny did the distance make them. Although sheep were rarely quiet, their baas did not reach the balloon, nor did what should have been the *chunk, chunk, chunk* sound of a man splitting logs outside a dollhouse of a cottage with smoke curling up from its chimney. The smoke dissipated before it reached Cassandra's nostrils.

She smelled nothing but their own fire to heat the balloon's air, the hint of linseed oil and turpentine, and the damp wool from Mr. Sorrells's coat. She heard nothing but the faint hiss of flames and her own wildly beating heart. She saw the world slipping past her at a speed no horse could travel. Meadow, sheep, cottage flashed past in favor of the village, an armload of houses, a handful of shops, the spire of the church. Beyond, billowing dark smoke signaled the edge of the city and the mills.

Whittaker's mills lay there somewhere. No doubt he sat or walked about in one, inspecting damage, advising or even making repairs himself, getting men back to work as quickly as possible. If she saw the one damaged in the spring, she might know which small factories belonged to him. She leaned a bit further forward, scanning the larger buildings on the edges of the Dale.

"We should try to turn back," Mr. Sorrells suggested behind her. "The sails are imperfect for steering, and I think the wind is shifting a bit in our favor anyway."

Cassandra narrowed her eyes, peering through the tendrils of mist still clinging to the ground. "In a moment."

"What are you looking for?" Sorrells leaned over on his side.

"The Hern mills. I think they are here about."

"They are." Mr. Sorrells suddenly sounded as cold as the cloud that had surrounded them earlier. "I'll take us down a few hundred feet so we can see them more clearly."

He released the valve that allowed air to flow out of the balloon. The change was imperceptible to the eye, but suddenly they began to descend, dropping down with an abruptness that left Cassandra's stomach somewhere in her throat.

She caught her breath. "That I was not expecting."

"I should have been more careful and eased you down." Mr. Sorrells did not sound particularly apologetic despite his words. "But you wanted to see the mills, and there, to your right. I mean your left. Where that man is—" He stopped abruptly.

Cassandra glanced behind her to see him still leaning over the side of the basket, so she bent over her edge and peered down. The distance made details impossible to detect, but she recognized the man's easy gait, the breadth of his shoulders, the tilt of his head that set his overly long hair swinging and shining with touches of auburn in the first rays of sunshine reaching the earth.

Whittaker, dressed like a laborer rather than a nobleman, sauntered down the alleyway behind his mills. One hand rested on his hip as though about to draw something from his pocket. The other hand held a bulging canvas sack.

Another man slunk behind him, keeping to the long shadows still cast by the buildings that early in the morning. He too rested one hand on his hip. In the other, he held an object too small to detect, but he lifted his arm up and back. A single beam of sunlight flashed.

"Whittaker!" Cassandra screamed. "Geoffrey, down!"

22

The cry dropped from above, a shout sounding oddly like his name. He halted and glanced up. Above him, a balloon glided like some bird from another world. Though several hundred feet in the air, the long, dark hair lifting and drifting with the wind carrying the aeronauts past could belong to only one person.

"Cassandra Bainbridge, I declare I will—" He began to run forward in the path of the balloon, though it floated far faster than any man could run. Still he shouted after her as though she could see him. "Cassandra, I am going to—to—"

A flash snagged the light at the corner of his eye. He leaped back, pivoting on one heel in time to see a man slink between two weaving shops like a feral dog down an alley.

A knife lay at Whittaker's feet.

If Cassandra had not shouted to him from her infernal balloon, the knife would now stick out of his back and he would be lying on the street like discarded rubbish.

He dropped into a crouch and picked up the knife. More like a dagger—long, slender, lethal. Someone had been bold enough to throw it at him, if not during full daylight, at least during light bright enough that Cassandra had seen him from several hundred feet off the ground.

She was off the ground far enough for a fall to kill her.

She had seen someone throw a knife at his back.

Whittaker leaned against the wall of the weaving shop. Inside, the looms lay in silence, still too damaged to function. He had salvaged much of the cotton and woolen thread, but the rebels had taken axes to the looms.

As someone had wished to take a knife to him, a silent, swift way to do away with him. "Lord, I never made any man my enemy I can think of."

He stared at the knife. Throwing with deadly accuracy took a special skill. The would-be assassin might not even be someone who knew him. Numerous men from sailors to gypsies possessed the skill to hit a target with a knife from yards away, and too many of those would exchange a few guineas for slipping their dagger between the ribs of a man for whom they held no feelings.

So where was Major Crawford's spy now? He might have been of use if he were following Whittaker's movements. That was why Whittaker was still in town—he needed to draw the man out—though he should be long gone before the sun rose much higher. Whittaker had developed a plan for escaping the clutches of Bainbridge and Crawford's blackmail. To do it, he needed to find the man Crawford had said spied on him, to ensure he was not representative of the Crown.

As if Whittaker would tell the Luddites which of them worked for the Crown, even to help himself. He might as well take the dagger in his hand and slip it into his heart all by himself. The Luddites had killed before. They would kill again.

Whittaker held up the knife, allowing sunlight to dance along the steel blade. It was good steel but nothing exceptional. The hilt was well-worn, smooth and shiny from considerable handling, and made of hard but common enough ash wood. It was the sort of knife one could buy in any cutlery shop in a large city or from some tinker along the road. If he showed it to the constable, he would give away his mission, opening up Mama to the scandal of Crawford's condemnatory information, and the constable would be able to tell him nothing. If Cassandra had not warned him from the car of that infernal machine . . .

But she had. She had saved his life.

Shoving the dagger into his pocket with one hand, he rubbed his eyes with the other. All night he had kept vigil on his mills. First he had warned another weaver of a potential attack on his facility, then gone to his own. He could not afford to lose more looms. The ones damaged in the spring were just now becoming operational again. Another assault would suck dry the rest of his profits for the year, and the estate would suffer.

The Bainbridge sisters were right in one thing: he did need a wife with a good dowry. A pity he loved a woman whose father would not give him one unless something changed.

"If I deliver the leaders into your hands?"

He was spending too much time alone and talking to himself like a crazed man. He wanted to talk to Cassandra—after he gave her a scold—

What was he thinking? He had no business scolding Cassandra. He was not her father. He was not even her fiancé now.

The would-be assassin may as well have stuck the knife in his back and twisted. It would have hurt no worse than her walking away from him the previous Saturday night.

The light growing too bright for him to remain where many people knew him and would likely see through his disguise in a second, Whittaker ducked down the same passageway between two mills that the knife thrower had taken. No recesses in the walls allowed for places to hide despite the darkness still clinging to the opening between the brick walls rising up on either side of him. Beyond lay warehouses filled with linen and wool thread from the water-powered spinning mules. One day he would like to have his own spinning facilities. They would prove more profitable. Until the mill was destroyed in the spring, he had poured his profits into Whittaker Hall. It was beginning to support itself, but now all the profits went to protecting and repairing the mills.

No wonder Cassandra did not wish to marry him. Especially now that she had told him about her scars, she surely thought he wanted nothing more than her dowry. Her father must think he wanted nothing more, that only a desperate man, not a sensible one, would wish for financial recompense to marry a flawed wife.

But it is my fault! The cry rang so loudly inside his head he might have shouted it. If he had experienced the anguish of guilt before, it now left him so crushed inside he dared not look at his reflection. He could not like what looked back at him.

And now she had run off to fly. The idea of being that far off the ground in an open-air basket made him want to cast up his accounts. Yet Cassandra acted as though she might be on nothing higher up than a first-floor gallery.

He reached his own climb nearly as high as a balcony—the fence surrounding the mills for what had proven to be insubstantial protection. He had tucked a rope, knotted and looped, to the top of the barricade. He climbed it now, telling himself that he would not hurt himself if he fell. The fence rose no more than ten feet in the air, made of straight, wooden slats set vertically to discourage easy climbing. His own secret entrance into the yard had shown the fence's protection to be a farce, with the ease of the would-be assassin's entrance. Had he used a rope of his own?

No time to look. The bell had rung. Weavers would arrive through the front gates at any moment. Whittaker poised on the top of the fence, pointed boards digging into his hands and thighs, and drew the rope up to toss down the other side. He then lowered himself to hang from his hands and drop. The ground was soft. He remembered to bend his knees. Not so much as a twinge in ankles or knees. Hearing voices on the other side of the fence, he picked up his rope and began to wind his way through the other warehouses and smaller weaving shops, then some mean houses—little more than hovels—on the edges of the factory area, which gradually gave way to fields and trees and places to hide from curious passersby.

Few of the travelers on the road gave him a second glance. They were stolid farmers hauling their wares into town. Apples scented the air. Whittaker's stomach growled. He considered buying a bagful of fruit and a wheel of the cheeses he saw on one wagon, then recalled Cassandra warning him, the flash of the blade barely missing his back, Cassandra hundreds of feet off the ground—and his appetite fled.

"When I find you, my dear lady, I will . . . will . . ."

He would hold her tightly with her feet on the ground. And she would hate that. Perhaps not the holding part. But she wanted no one telling her what she could and could not do.

"Do not scold," he told himself as he reached his cottage in midmorning and made himself a bit of bread and cold sausage. He ate standing in the cottage doorway, staring up at the sky. He could not simply trot across the fields in the middle of the day, not Whittaker Hall fields, and wait for her to land—if she landed neatly and not in a heap of blazing wreckage.

When he climbed the narrow stairs to his bedchamber, little more than a dormer beneath the roof beams so low he could not stand upright, he could not sleep for seeing Cassandra caught beneath flaming silk. A single dose drove memories of the celebrations through his mind, the pounding on his carriage, the taunts directed at him, the torch dropped on her gown.

He jerked upright, sweating despite the chill away from the fire. He had slept, and in his sleep he had dreamed a memory. In waking he began to worry on a notion that sent him downstairs to heat water for shaving and washing, with the lightest application of his own soap rather than a spy's rough lye.

He donned a clean shirt, then, as the early autumn dusk began to fall, he set out through the meadow and woods to see Cassandra. After that, he would find Major Crawford and tell him about the knife too close to his back.

With the major staying at the Hall, not to mention Miss Irving, who had clung to him at the assembly like a limpet to a rock, Whittaker waited on the edge of the parkland until he saw everyone gather in the dining room for supper. Miss Irving clung to the arm of Roger Kent of all men, the major escorted both Mama and Miss Honore, and Cassandra tucked her hand into the crook of Philip Sorrells's elbow. Her face positively glowed in the candlelight as she gazed up at the man, and he bent his head over hers like a bird of prey over a mouse. Or perhaps merely possessively. Either way, Whittaker clutched a branch so hard it snapped off in his hand with a crack like a pistol shot.

At once, a footman appeared at the dining room window and drew the curtains.

Whittaker left his hiding place and skulked around the perimeter of his own home, his own house and lands, until he reached the orangery. He looked first to ensure his cousins and their tutor were not occupying the one indulgence that Mama insisted Whittaker keep going, then cut through it to Cassandra's sitting room. A maid might enter her bedchamber to turn down the bed, bring hot water, and refresh the fire, but she had no cause to be in the sitting room. Miss Honore might arrive first, but Whittaker could manage her. As for Cassandra? He had proven himself incapable of managing her at all. But they needed to talk. He needed a description of the man who had thrown the knife, if she had one. He needed to talk to her.

He needed her.

He waited beside the settee, ready to dive behind it if anyone else entered one of the ladies' chambers. No one did, not even a maid, though an open periodical and Cassandra's spectacles lay on a chair by the hearth as though she had been called away in haste.

Beyond the curtains, clouds gathered in the sky and rain began to patter against the windows. The fire died down to nothing more than winking red eyes on the hearth, and Whittaker left his post to shovel coal onto the sparks before they died altogether. He had just set the poker back in its stand when he heard her coming. No tap of her cane but deliberate footfalls, one slightly lagging behind the other. He pressed his hands against his thighs to stop himself from darting forward and flinging open the door. He could be mistaken. It might be a maid bearing a heavy load of water cans.

Cassandra opened the sitting room door first and headed straight to her chair. With a sigh that turned into a yawn, she slipped on her spectacles and began to settle on the chair.

"Cassandra?" He spoke her name in a murmur.

She gasped and spun around. The periodical sailed from her hand to land splayed open on the carpet. "What are you doing here?"

"I have come to talk to you." He gripped the mantel to stop

himself from closing the distance between them. "About this morning. But we cannot talk here. Miss Honore could come in."

"And the maid and perhaps your mother and—go away. This is not proper."

He held his tongue. The words "Your flying in a balloon is not proper either" burned on the tip of it, but he managed to hold them behind his teeth.

"Will the orangery be empty now?"

"Yes, the others are playing charades. I have had enough company for one evening and pled fatigue."

"You look weary."

Up close now, he saw the dark circles beneath her eyes, the puckering of her brow—signs of fatigue for her. A white line encircled her mouth too.

He took a half step toward her. "Are you in pain?"

"A little. I took a bit of a tumble this morning, and I—" She pushed her palms toward him. "This is none of your concern. Go change your dress and join the party. I am quite certain Miss Irving wished for your attendance this evening . . . again. She is looking better than fine in diamonds tonight."

But Cassandra wore his pearls.

"I have no interest in Miss Irving, Cassandra. We need to talk about this morning."

"Ah, that." She rose. "I suppose you are correct in that. I wanted to stay and see, but there was nowhere to land—if you chide me about flying, I will go back to the great hall and you can either follow me there and explain why you are looking like a ragamuffin, or—"

"Do not blackmail me. I have enough of that to manage without you adding to it."

She stared at him. "What did you say?"

"Too much." He sighed. "Not enough. But we cannot stay here. Besides being highly improper, Miss Honore or a maid may indeed arrive. Will you join me in the orangery?"

"I . . . may."

"No one will come looking for you?" He narrowed his gaze. "Mr. Sorrells will not expect a fond good night?"

"Not at all. We are not courting . . . yet." Her smile was tight, brittle.

Whittaker stopped before he said the man was not good enough for her. Despite the title that made him good enough for any lady in many people's eyes, Whittaker knew he himself was likely not good enough for her.

"But I believe that is in the near future," she continued. "We get on well together. He does not scold me about flying. On the contrary, he encourages me." She snatched off her spectacles to show her big, dark eyes. "And *he* treats me like a lady."

"Then he has heard of ladies who go up in balloons at dawn?" Whittaker could not stop himself from firing back this time. "I have not. And if you thought that was such ladylike behavior, you would go in the middle of the day and invite my mother and everyone else to watch the demonstration. Or perhaps I am mistaken and they all eschewed their morning ride in favor of watching your ascent?"

"That was unkind and unfair," she said in an undertone. "I thought better of you."

"No, you do not." He took a step toward the door. "You are angry with me because I have not always treated you like a lady, but I have yet to hear one word of protest from you. You were always more than complicit."

"And which one of us will bear the reminder of my shame forever?" Tears starred her lashes and she rubbed her right thigh.

His heart melted, leaving his chest tight and his own throat thick. "Both of us bear it if you can never again believe I love you."

"I cannot. It is lust. It is money." She wiped her eyes on a corner of her shawl. "It is anything but me as I am now."

"Why do you think that after a year and a half of believing me?"

"I was wrong. I saw differently today." She did not look at him.

He moved closer to her so he stood in her line of sight. "What about today? Just flying?"

"No." She shook her head hard, dislodging several hairpins. "I saw something different. When I tried to climb into the balloon, I fell and my skirt came up. Mr. Sorrells saw my scars and was not in the least repulsed, as you were with the mere mention of them."

"Cassandra, I was not repulsed."

"You turned pale. You cannot deny that."

"I may have. I was horrified, sickened, saddened." He dared touch his fingertips to her cheek. "And guilt does not go down well."

"So guilty you walked away?"

He strode to the door. "I am going to the orangery. If I promise not to scold you about the ballooning, will you please come?"

She pressed the back of her hand to her lips and her gaze darted back and forth, frightened prey seeking a bolt-hole. He left her alone to find it if she willed. The corridor stood empty and quiet. Fifty feet down the passageway, around a corner, and through a thick door, the great hall did not let sound into this wing of the house.

Whittaker turned toward the orangery. Its steamy, fragrant warmth greeted him in silence. No tutor or little boys sat about. The gardener had gone to his quarters. In the farthest corner from either door, a rustic bench nestled beneath a lemon tree with tangy, aromatic fruit dangling above. They smelled like Cassandra. No sweet, flowery perfumes for her.

He settled on the bench and prepared to wait in vain. Their brief but sharp exchange in Cassandra's sitting room did not bode well for this discussion taking place at all. If only they could talk as friends as they used to. Now their contact had turned to sparring, lashing out, as though they wanted to hurt one another.

"What am I doing wrong, Lord?" he cried aloud. "I want to protect her. Shelter her. Love her." He speared his fingers through his unkempt hair. "I want—"

The door opened and closed. Uneven footfalls sounded on the slate floor. "Lord Whittaker?"

He flinched. If anything she said had been calculated to hurt him, her use of his title wounded him the most. It placed such distance between them, made them mere acquaintances, not the friends and almost lovers they had been.

And therein lay much of the problem—the latter, the too much closeness. She placed social distance between them to protect herself from a lack of physical distance. Their behavior had been wrong, and she thought she was being punished while he could go off and court and wed beautiful, rich females like Miss Irving.

"I want no one but you."

If Cassandra heard him, she showed no indication of it. Her face was smooth, neutral in expression. She seated herself as far away from him as possible on the narrow bench and looked straight ahead. "When ballooning," she began as though lecturing his cousins, "you are greatly subject to the direction of the wind. Various methods have been employed to change this, to give one some directional ability. Paddles much like those employed on a canoe have been used to some good effect, and so have sails that are more like parasols so they can easily be raised and lowered to catch the wind in varying directions. Our balloon uses the latter in addition to raising and lowering our elevation to catch differing wind currents."

"But you were not employing those sails today."

"No, we were floating on the breeze, as it was good and strong and not going toward the sea."

Suppressing the urge to ask her about the "we" she referred to, Whittaker said, "I could see where that could be a hazard—going to the sea."

"Yes, though a few have flown to and from Ireland. Balloons have also come across the English Channel from France."

"Ah, an invasion fleet from the French via balloon. Do the Martello towers on the coast have cannons mounted on the roof to take down armed aeronauts?"

She glared at him. "You are mocking me."

"No, indeed, I am not. If Bonaparte had enough balloons, he would be difficult to stop, as they can fly so high, far out of gun range."

"They would encounter difficulties when coming down."

"Fortunate for England. And I suppose he could carry only one or two men per basket with equipment along."

"Yes, they are too small to hold more and remain aloft. Though if we are to make practical use of balloon travel, we must create one that is larger. We need to perfect the directional sails first, however. If the wind changes, one could find oneself over the water and then in Ireland or France before one could land, without intending to do so."

"You seem to toss about this 'we' a great deal." The words

burst from Whittaker heedlessly, a little too sharply. "With whom were you flying?"

"Mr. Sorrells, of course." She spoke too casually.

Whittaker attempted to match her tone. "So he knows someone tried to throw a knife into my back?"

"Yes, but he will say nothing to your mother. I made him promise."

"Kind of you." He took a deep breath to clear his next words of more sarcasm. "You two discussed me then?"

"Of course we did. You have had too many bad things happen to you in the past few weeks, and this morning you were in disguise and someone was again trying to harm you. We want to know why."

"Why?"

"Because—" She twisted her fingers together on her lap.

He moved closer and took one of her hands between both of his. Despite the heat of the orangery, her fingers felt like she had soaked them in icy water.

"You still care about me at least a little?" he dared ask.

She looked down. "Of course I do. And I care about your mother. You are all she has left."

"I know."

"Then why do you do it?" Her head shot up. Light from the braziers blazed in her eyes. "Why are you taking foolish risks?"

"I can't tell you."

"But it has something to do with the mills, with the Luddites."

"Yes, I'm quite certain now that they want me dead."

23

Cassandra slowly drew her hand free of Whittaker's to draw her shawl more tightly around her. She wished it was wool rather than the fashionable silk. Even in the steamy orangery, she needed more heat to stifle the chill racing through her.

"You have to stop whatever you are doing to anger them," she said in a croaking voice. "Give the weavers whatever they like, sell the mills. Or—" Her eyes widened. "The disguise. Your absences. You are up to something dangerous."

"I—Cassandra, I wish—" He sprang to his feet and paced half a dozen feet away from her, keeping his back to her. "I came to see you tonight to tell you that you need not worry about my suit any longer. I am needed elsewhere, and you—you—" He grasped a lemon tree branch, then released it, sending it swinging and swaying like a dancer, and shoved his hands into his pockets. "You are best off encouraging Philip Sorrells to court you."

"You are—you are finished with me?" Cassandra's lips felt stiff, her middle tight, her eyes hot. "You finally agree with me that we can never have anything between us again?"

"No, I do not agree with you." He faced her. "I am not finished with you, with us. I still love you as much as I ever did." His voice held a hard edge that belied his words, but his eyes had taken on an odd sheen. "But I cannot risk your safety." He sighed and shoved his hands through his hair. "And perhaps you are right. Perhaps God is saying we should not be together. I cannot say anymore what God wants for me. Once I thought it was the church and you for my wife. Then I inherited the title and you seemed so unhappy about that. And for the past six months, I have lost ground on everything I have set into my plans for Whittaker Hall, for my future." He cleared his throat and looked away. "For us. So, yes, I think perhaps God has other plans we do not yet understand."

"Then—then I should leave here." She could not leave the orangery right then, let alone the house. Though motionless, she felt as though she swooped and swayed like the lemon tree branch. "Honore and I can join our parents and Beau in Scotland. I would have to leave behind my balloon, and—oh, Geoffrey, the flying was even better than I hoped. We rose up through the mist and then the sunshine broke through and it was so glorious and—" She clapped a hand to her mouth. "What am I saying?"

He smiled at her broadly enough for the dimple to show in his cheek. "You sound like my Cassandra. But the idea of rising through the clouds even to reach sunshine makes me feel a bit ill, to be honest. I am not fond of heights, you know."

"No, I did not know."

Somehow she should have. How, in a year and a half, could she not have known he did not like heights?

"Is that why you are so against my interest in aeronautics?"

"No, my dear, it is because balloons are dangerous and I think you have suffered enough."

"But I saved your life today because of being in one." She tried to smile.

His jaw hardened. "I know. And until I can extricate myself from men who want me dead, I cannot stop you."

"You cannot stop me even if you were not—" She sounded like a petulant child and stopped, stared at him with her mouth open certainly unattractively wide for a moment before she managed to form coherent words. "What do you mean by extricate yourself? Is that an admission that you are up to something dangerous?"

"I've said too much." He turned toward the outside door. "I must be on my way. Please tell no one I was here."

"I think not, Geoffrey Giles." Cassandra pulled herself to her feet and limped after him. "You cannot leave now. Not after what you told me. Or, to be more precise, did not tell me."

"I cannot." But he stood motionless with his hand on the door latch, gazing at their mingled reflections in the glass on the door. "All that should concern you is that you need not be bothered with me for perhaps as long as you stay here. I thought that would please you—me not being around to importune you further." Though his tone had returned to its even keel, the dent in his right cheek—the dimple she had once loved to press her fingertip and her lips against—flashed in and out.

She understood that signal as well as a midshipman read flags on a masthead. Better, perhaps. Whittaker was trying not to grin. He was trying not to grin because he was teasing her, daring her.

"Oh, you." She ground her teeth. "You are a scurvy knave."

"Tut, tut. Such language." He faced her and gave her his full grin. "But I suppose that is a step higher than *swine*."

"I never—I mean, I never should have—I am sorry for calling you that. It was uncalled for."

"So was what I said." He raised his hand, then let it fall

250

without touching her. "Perhaps there is something to the notion that tainted blood is passed down to the children and your father is right in wanting us apart."

Cassandra stared at him. "What are you saying? What tainted blood could you possibly have? I mean, your father was a gamester. Perhaps it is rude of me to say so, but it is no secret amongst the haut ton. We—you and I—talked of it, but you have never shown any inclination to—"

"Shh." He laid his forefinger across her lips. "Not my father. My mother."

"Your—" Cassandra's eyes widened. "Your mother is—is . . . well, perfect."

"Yes, now." His gaze darted past her, flicked around the orangery. "We cannot talk here after all. Anyone outside can see us or walk in, and I would like to tell you something." He rested his eyes on her face. "I would like to tell you. We used to tell one another secrets."

"Like children."

"Like friends."

For a moment, as they stood within touching distance, their eyes locked. Her chest grew hollow with the loss of him, of everything that had been good between them—the conversation, the shared dreams, the friendly arguments about philosophies and politics. Given the slightest excuse, she feared she would throw herself into his arms and beg him to love her. But her leg had begun to ache, the healing flesh pulling on the old like a patch of new cloth on an old garment. A stab of pain sent a hiss rushing through her lips.

And Whittaker broke the eye contact. "For your safety," he said too quickly, "we should not be seen together."

"Then good night." She took a step backward.

"Wait. Can you get away without anyone noticing?" He laughed without humor. "I expect you did this morning to go flying."

"They go riding in the morning unless it is raining, in which case they stay abed."

"Then meet me at the gate from the garden to the parkland at eight o'clock. Do you know where I mean?"

"How do you think I get to the field to meet Mr. Sorrells and Mr. Kent with the balloon?" She inclined her head. "Ah. It is you who keeps the path clear."

"It is. Tomorrow then. I will show you the rest of the way."

"But Mr. Sorrells is taking me driving tomorrow if the weather is fine."

"It will be raining." As though he held the power to grant such a condition with a word, he opened the door and a gust of damp, cold wind scented with rain blasted into their faces. "Good night, Miss Bainbridge. I will have you returned home by eleven o'clock when civilized gentlemen call."

He knew—oh, he knew she had stretched the truth when she implied that Philip Sorrells would call for her at the same time Whittaker said he wanted her to meet him. No gentleman would take a lady driving so early at the beginning of November. Sunny day or not, eight o'clock was still early enough for fog to lie thick on the roads and fields.

"You are a swine," she ground out between her teeth. "I take back my apology."

He had long since vanished into the dark, wet night. She slammed the bolt home to keep him there, then turned toward the corridor door to her bedchamber, but not to sleep. Her mind raced like some ancient runner from Marathon. As though words memorized from a play, her dialogue with Whittaker ran through her head again and again, but jumbled and disjointed.

He was done with her. Someone wanted to harm him. He encouraged her suit with Philip Sorrells. His mother was not the model of ladylike and godly perfection everyone thought her?

Lost in her mangled memories of the past half hour, Cassandra did not notice Honore seated on the chaise until she flung herself against Cassandra. "Where have you been? Oh, never you mind. I must tell you." She drew back to show a glowing face and shining eyes. "He kissed me, Cassandra. Major Crawford kissed me. Miss Irving had asked Lady Whittaker if she could borrow something to read, though I cannot imagine that years-old copies of *La Belle Assemblée* interested her. So they were here in the library, and there we were quite alone in the hall. And he took my hand and told me I am beautiful and kissed me." She spun in a circle. "And now I feel like I am up in one of your silly balloons. Are you not happy for me?"

"I would like to be."

If she could stop the images, the sense of floating off the earth she had experienced after the first time plain Mr. Giles had kissed her.

"Father will not approve of another military man for one of his daughters." Cassandra sounded like a killjoy spinster and could not stop herself.

Honore just laughed and hugged her arms over her front. "He says after he finishes his work up here, he will sell out."

So had Lydia's first husband claimed—then he returned to his regiment a week after their wedding and she never saw him again.

"He is the younger son of a baronet," Honore continued, "but it is a very good family and they are not poor. He has a tiny income, I know, but with my dowry, and if he obtains a diplomatic post as he desires, we will be quite well enough."

Cassandra straightened. "He has asked you to marry him then?"

"Well, no." Some of the glow left Honore's face. "I suppose you will tell me I am terribly naughty to let him kiss me without a proposal first."

"I would not be that much of a hypocrite." Cassandra closed her eyes. They felt hot again, as they had in the orangery. She would not give in to tears here any more than she would have there. What was done was done. Whittaker had accepted that God did not want them together, that they were bad for one another's futures.

If only they did not share so much past.

Twin tears escaped her efforts and rolled down her cheeks before she could dash them away.

Honore gasped and dashed across the room. "Oh, Cassandra, I am such a selfish beast going on and on about how happy I am when you look so sad. Is it Lord Whittaker? Do you still love him?"

"It makes no difference if I do. He is done with me."

"I think not. He scarcely left your side the other night, and the two of you went off alone together."

"He followed me, yes." Cassandra dabbed at her eyes with her shawl. "He tried to make me think he still wants to marry me, so I told him how bad the—the scars are."

"If he loves you, that will not matter to him, surely."

"But it does. His face. You should have seen his face if you think it does not matter. And tonight—"

Honore grabbed her hand. "You saw him tonight? Where? How? I thought him in the Dale."

"He was here."

"Trying to press his suit again? See, he does still love you."

"No, to tell me I should allow Mr. Sorrells to court me."

Yet he wanted to see her again, but in secret.

The sympathy on Honore's face brought more tears to Cassandra's eyes. Had Lydia been there, Cassandra would have confided in her. Honore deserved her moments of bliss after receiving her first kiss. If Major Crawford did sell out, he would be a fine husband for Honore—handsome, charming, acceptable family.

"So I shall go out driving with Mr. Sorrells tomorrow if the weather is fine," Cassandra said. "He is a most suitable match, do you not think?"

"For you? Undoubtedly." Honore laughed. "He may have left university because he was not a good student, but I think that is because he wanted to study other things. Major Crawford did not go to university at all. He is more like me and has no interest at all in the ancients. But he does speak beautiful French. I suppose that is necessary if he wishes for a diplomatic career next."

"I expect it is. Shall we work to improve yours?" Cassandra decided she may as well assist Honore in her romantic endeavors.

"That would be so very kind of you. He murmured something to me in French when he left, but I understood a bit of it." Honore laughed. "I am afraid Miss Irving understood all of it, though I never would have guessed that she would know any more of French than what comes in smuggled fashion plates and silks, but she looked rather annoyed with him, which surprised me too. I thought after last Saturday night that she was dangling after—but of course it is nothing with Lord Whittaker, especially with him always at those mills of his."

"She would be a fine match for him," Cassandra said. "She is an heiress and beautiful, and not unkind. After all, she did travel here with her young cousins."

"To catch herself an earl." Honore rose. "Then again, she was in the paddock helping William improve his riding this morning."

"Perhaps we should get Lord Whittaker to stay here and press his suit with her." Cassandra managed to say the words with a credible smile.

Honore stared at her. "You would let him get betrothed to another lady right under your nose?"

"Why not? He encouraged me to do the same with another gentleman." She dropped her head into the corner of the chaise arm.

"Then he was right," Honore muttered and stalked to the sitting room door. "I should get to sleep if I can. We are riding bright and early."

"Honore?" Cassandra spoke her sister's name with a note of warning. "Do not go marching off without explaining that last remark."

"What? About not being able to sleep? I will be thinking of the major, of course—"

"Do not go all innocent on me. What did you mean by Whittaker being right?"

"Oh, that." Honore sighed. "He said that he would never make you jealous by flirting with another female. And I thought it was such a fine idea for him to win you back. But I will have to work out another plan."

"You, child, are incorrigible. But do not waste your energies on my romantic interests. Concentrate on your own."

"Happily." With a flutter of eyelashes and lace frills, Honore vanished into the next room.

Cassandra smiled, then rose and rang for the maid to come help her undress for the night. Once in night rail and dressing gown, however, she drew out the desk chair and pulled paper from the drawer and the stopper from the ink bottle. She intended to write down her impressions of flying. Perhaps one of the periodicals for ladies would enjoy a tale of a lady floating through the heavens in a balloon. She also wished to mark the changes she might make to create more useful rudders out of the parasol-like sails, to help maneuver the balloon more efficiently instead of being at the whim of the breezes depending on one's elevation. To be fair, she should consider using the paddles once or twice. They had worked for the men in France. But the sails were working a little for herself and her fellow aeronauts.

Though all these things ran through her head, she found herself writing down as much of her conversation with Whittaker as she could recall. Once on paper, once reviewed, she found all the gaps in what he had said. He was telling her only half-truths about the attempt on his life that morning, as well as the other incidents.

Including the assault on their carriage in London?

In the morning, he must tell her everything else. Rain or shine, she would not leave his side until he explained everything. If the sun came up, Mr. Sorrells would simply have to wait for her.

Rain began to fall before she wiped her quill clean and shoved the stopper back into the ink bottle. At first, drops pattered against the window like a handful of pebbles tossed against the glass. Then the wind picked up and drove a deluge down the window, a pounding cataract that did not cease even as Cassandra awoke, dressed with the assistance of Molly, and drank several cups of scalding tea.

"Best you dress warm-like," Molly said. "This stone house makes the chill go straight through a body. Shall I bring you some breakfast?"

Cassandra glanced at the mantel clock. Twenty minutes before eight o'clock. "No, thank you. The tea is enough. I have some reading I must get done today so I can return the book, and would prefer not to be disturbed."

"What if it's that nice Mr. Sorrells?" Molly glanced up from where she knelt on the floor to straighten Cassandra's hem and winked.

"Not even for him." Cassandra laughed at the girl's sauciness. "It is not a day for driving."

"Not a day even for ducks." Molly shivered. "Ring if you need one of us."

She departed in one direction, and a few minutes later, Cassandra departed in another. Molly, no doubt, joined the other servants in the large but always warm kitchen. Cassandra slipped through the orangery and into the rain, which soaked through her woolen cloak and hood in moments. Without her cane for extra support, she would have slipped on the muddy ground and fallen. But at least the torrents of water and the darkness from overhanging clouds would make her practically invisible from the house. It certainly kept everyone else inside. Only a crazed female would be stepping into the woods to meet a man who had said quite plainly that he no longer wanted her. She should turn back, leave him to wait and drown beneath the trees, and warm herself by the fire with the book she truly wanted to finish that day.

She slipped through the well-oiled gate and into the darkness of the trees beyond.

Even with most of their leaves gone, the trees formed a canopy of interlocking branches that created partial protection from the rain. It dwindled to a manageable drizzle, adding a sense of hush inside the parkland.

Too much of a hush. Too little movement. Too much stillness.

"Whittaker?" Cassandra called in a low voice. "My lord?"

Drip. Splash. Patter. Water running off her cloak made most of the sounds around her.

"Geoffrey?" she tried again.

More rain sluicing from the sky, the branches, her clothes. Otherwise, not one footfall, not one tall, broad figure, not the merest whisper of a voice disturbed the woodland.

Geoffrey Giles, Earl of Whittaker, had failed to make their rendezvous.

24

He was being followed.

Whittaker stood a dozen yards inside the parkland gate and knew he was not alone. Beneath the trees, the partial shelter from the rain offered enough quiet for him to hear the click of the gate latch behind him. The gate he had locked. He could not mistake the dull ping of iron against iron and a squeal of hinges no louder than a newborn kitten's mew.

Hairs rising on the back of his neck, he stepped into the shelter of an oak and spun toward the entrance.

So swift he would have missed it had he blinked, a shadow melted into the density of overgrown vines and tree limbs. A twig cracked, then silence reigned save for the ceaseless rush of water against the interlaced branches above.

And Cassandra was a quarter mile away waiting for him. At least she should be by now if she were coming. He needed to get to her quickly, warn her to get back to the house. Yet if he did, he could be leading the assassin right to her. Unless it was the major's watchdog.

Unless they were one and the same.

Madness. This game was giving him notions far beyond reason. Major Gabriel Crawford was a respected military man. Respected military men did not go around hiring assassins against peers of the realm. They especially did not when they worked with another peer. And whatever Lord Bainbridge thought of Whittaker, he would not condone his death.

If it was the same man who had thrown the knife near the mill the day before, Whittaker could not return to the field gate either. If the person following him meant him harm, he would walk right into a trap.

He stood motionless, waiting, listening, praying that Cassandra would grow too weary or cold to wait for him. Or perhaps he should be praying she had not come out in the rain at all. He should not have asked it of her. He should have thought of another way to talk to her, to tell her everything. Yet with her standing before him so pretty in her blue dress and ribbons twisted through her hair, he could scarcely think. Every word he spoke about leaving her to Philip Sorrells felt like a dose of poison. He was right, though. The third person in the parkland seemed like the final proof that he must remain separate from her, the one clear message he had received from the Lord in months.

Leave her. Leave her. Leave her.

His heart so heavy he felt as though each footfall would sound like a roll of thunder, Whittaker began to move through the trees. The rain would cover up the rustle of what foliage remained on low-hanging branches, as well as the sound of his rough workman's shoes on the bed of fallen leaves. He knew this parkland. Until he went to school himself at the age of twelve, he had spent the holidays when his older brother was home hiding from him amidst these trees so he could read without being disturbed. He knew the location of the other gates. Their latches and hinges would be rusted enough to screech like banshees, but he could be away and across the fields before whoever followed him found him.

And Cassandra would be back in the house, out of reach. She would be safe. That mattered more than anything.

"You had best respond to my messages today, Major Crawford," Whittaker muttered as he reached another gate and began to work the latch.

It had rusted shut. After several blows and a cut on the side of his hand, it broke apart and the gate popped open. Just one more repair—an inexpensive one—but dozens of them added up to a great deal of money for an estate that could not bear it and keep the farmers' homes in good repair, yet not raising the rents or lowering the wages of the mill workers.

Perhaps the Lord was telling him to marry the heiress.

He could not believe it. Surely God did not intend for a man and wife to have no attraction for one another. Miss Irving was beautiful, and her glances at him he recognized as appreciative. Their interest ran no further. They shared nothing except a relationship so distant the marriage laws would not prevent an alliance between them. If she answered to a suit from Whittaker, it would be for the title and nothing more. Nothing more than him answering to the siren call of her inheritance. He would rather live in a hovel like the shepherd's cottage with Cassandra than in a manor house with Regina Irving.

But if the Lord wanted something else from him, he should pursue it. He had pursued his own way for too long, and all that resulted was playing spy for the Crown by force, and disaster for Cassandra.

Soaked to the skin, Whittaker entered his cottage. Warmth from the banked fire filled the single ground-floor room. He built up the blaze, made tea, and sipped it while his clothes steamed dry. By the time both were finished, he had made up his mind about what he would do next. First step came with his meeting that night.

"This continual destruction gets us nowhere," Whittaker began.

"Aye, we've heard that from you before." Rob yawned as though bored with Whittaker's argument. "We're trying to teach the owners a lesson about cutting our wages."

"Which they're doing now to pay for the repairs," Whittaker shot back. "And you damaged the Hern mill. That owner hasn't lowered anybody's wages."

Hugh leaned forward, a looming shadow in the dim room. "We heard he was going to now that he ain't marrying money."

"Did you, now?" Whittaker made himself sit still and silent, afraid of what else he might let slip. A dozen questions crowded into his head. *From whom?* ranged at the top of the list.

"That's what we do to them who thinks they can rob a man of his honest pay," Jimmy said, his voice as soft as the silk he wove. "It's a warning like."

Whittaker shrugged. "I can understand that, but maybe we should look at the rumors and make sure they're true first. If they aren't, we could be the ones robbing men of their honest day's pay."

"Hern was a mistake," Rob conceded.

"No, it wasn't," Hugh and Jimmy chorused.

"Two of our men got shot," Rob persisted. "No one warned us the place would be guarded so heavily."

"Or maybe someone warned them." Hugh shoved back his chair with a rasp of wood against wood. "I'm wondering which one of you it were."

They all sat still and silent now. Even the taproom below seemed to hold its collective breath for half a minute. Whittaker fully expected the men to surround him and bind him, admit aloud they knew who he was, and hang him as so many of their own had been hanged for assaults on weaving shops and officers of the Crown. He braced himself, ready to bolt for the window. Slowly he lowered his right hand from his thigh in the hope that he could grab the knife shoved into his boot before they overwhelmed him.

Jimmy moved first. He shoved back his chair hard enough to topple it backward. Whittaker grabbed his knife hilt.

Before he drew the blade free, Jimmy turned on Hugh. "Maybe your informant ain't so good. Maybe you led us right into a trap."

Whittaker relaxed infinitesimally. Jimmy was indeed protecting him, drawing attention from him. Perhaps even trying to learn who the true enemy was?

"Are you accusing me of sommit?" Hugh surged to his feet as well. "'Cause if you are, just come out and say it."

"I'm saying you might not be gettin' such good information," Jimmy said.

"Who was it?" Rob demanded, standing also.

Whittaker lounged back in his chair as though entertained by a drama. The less attention on himself, the better.

Hugh took a step backward. "I ain't goin' to say who. It were good information. I mean, the rest he's given us has been. He must've made a mistake."

"That mistake got my cousin killed." Jimmy never raised

his voice, yet it slid across the room with the undertone of a threat. "More mistakes like that might get someone else killed."

Hugh leaned over the smaller man, his face inches from Jimmy's. "Are you threatening me?"

"Maybe." Jimmy did not back down.

"Then maybe I should—"

"This is getting us nowhere either." Whittaker rose and shot out an arm between the two men. "Back away, both of you. We gain nothing if we fight amongst ourselves."

"So what're your ideas for makin' things better for us weavers?" Rob jutted his chin at Whittaker. "Seein' as how you're so sure what won't work."

"I wish I could say work only for those who pay fair wages," Whittaker said with care, "but there's too few of those." His mill owner's heart rebelled against what he suggested next, yet it was better than the destruction and the death the uprising had caused thus far. "If you stop working altogether without destroying the looms, the owners will have to pay more to get you back. They don't make money if they have no weavers."

"And who will feed our families?" Rob asked.

"Who's feeding our families now?" Whittaker returned.

Hugh snorted. "Them who pays the tithe tax—the landowners and the churches."

"And the mill owners," Jimmy added.

"Why should I work twelve hours a day for naught," Hugh pressed on, "if someone else will take care of my wife and children?"

"Have you no pride?" Whittaker held back a sigh of frustration. "Because I do, and it tells me that what we're doing now is getting nothing but more men out of work and a lot dead."

"Then you ain't with us no more?" Rob took a step closer to Whittaker. "'Cause if you are . . ."

Whittaker held his ground. "I won't take part in any more senseless destruction like at the Hern mills."

How he wanted to say he would take part in no more destruction at all. But the major's threat still loomed.

Whittaker sat down and drew his chair back to the table and the sour stench of the ale before him. "Let's sit down and discuss what we do next."

"The Murdoch spinning mill." Hugh returned to his chair, and the others followed as he laid out a plan for destroying the water-driven spinning machines that produced finer, stronger, and more consistent thread than did the hand spinners but were dangerous. At the same time, they put hundreds of spinners out of work.

A touch of guilt stabbed Whittaker that he had thought of buying a spinning mill himself when the money became available. He felt guilty for how much his looms had put men out of work, though they had been there long before he expected to inherit. Yet if he sold the mills, a new owner might not be so generous, and Whittaker Hall would suffer, putting more men out of work on the farms.

Lost in his thoughts, he barely heard the plans the men made. He did not need to know them. In the melee of an assault, no one noticed his absence, or had not thus far. All he needed to tell Major Crawford was that an attack was imminent. The military was supposed to take care of the rest. Sometimes they did. Sometimes they failed to arrive on time. What mattered most about the night's meeting was that he had one more important sliver of information.

Hugh was the key to learning who insisted on continuing the

destruction, though the rebellion had died down in most other areas. If Whittaker could learn the identity of Hugh's informant—misinformant—then Whittaker would give the major what he wanted and be free to go about his life, rebuilding the mills and Whittaker Hall, building a family with a wife and sons and daughters.

The latter should look like Cassandra. But they would not. Could not. She did not want him for her husband, and he was beginning to accept that she might be right. Once upon a time, when he remembered to do so, he had prayed for God to provide the means to spare him from financial ruin and thus sparing the livelihoods of dozens of men and women. Then he met Cassandra, fell in love with her, and only later learned of the modest but so useful dowry. He would have her as his wife without it, and yet perhaps he would not after all, for too many would suffer without the infusion of money. Perhaps God was showing him another way to prosperity for those dependent upon his success to make their living.

Tomorrow he would go home to court the heiress. With the Irving fortune, he could buy mills from owners who could not rebuild and needed the funds as much as did the weavers. He could do more good with a fortune than without. It was the right choice, surely a godly choice.

As he made his way home through the night now free of rain, he wondered why, if this was all so right, he found himself praying that Regina Irving truly found him no more intriguing than he found her.

25

"Tomorrow?" Cassandra hugged her arms across her middle and smiled up at Philip Sorrells. "I can go up again tomorrow?"

"Provided no more rain comes today." Mr. Sorrells spoke in a hushed tone so as not to be overheard by the rest of the company, including the boys, their tutor, and Lady Whittaker, who were using the open end of the great hall to practice a badly performed version of *Richard III*, directed by Regina Irving.

Cassandra had been more than happy to admit she could not act and to remain near the fire. Mr. Sorrells had joined her in the adjacent chair, as he had the day before. She had still been chilled from her walk through the garden and her wait for Whittaker in the woods, not only from the drenching she had taken but also from apprehension for his safety. He was not the sort of man to make an assignation and not keep it. Considering she had seen someone try to kill him, she knew reason for her concern.

If she were not so excited about the potential to go ballooning the next day, she would have been praying he would get a message to her so she would know for certain he was safe. She had said a few prayers the day before and thanked the Lord no dead bodies had turned up along the way.

Now, however, all her focus lay in Mr. Sorrells's announcement that the balloon would once again be ready for going aloft if she was interested.

"May I go alone?" she asked, then held her breath, waiting for him to be as protective as a nursemaid with a newborn, as Whittaker tended to be. He would say no without hesitation.

Mr. Sorrells took several moments before he shrugged. "I don't see why you can't. Roger and I have gone up on our own, and it is a simple matter. Now that we know you need a little assistance, we can bring something you can use to climb up."

"Lovely. Lovely. Lovely." If she did not fear falling on her face, Cassandra would have sprung to her feet and danced around the great hall in excitement. As it was, her voice rang off the stone walls and spread across the vaulted ceiling. The players stopped their action to turn and stare at her.

And Whittaker walked through the door from the family wing. "Good afternoon, ladies, gentlemen." He bowed to the would-be actors at the far end of the room, then turned his attention on Cassandra. "What is so lovely, Miss Bainbridge?"

"Hmm, um, just some improvements to the balloon." She tried to avoid his gaze.

He would not let her. "Perhaps you can tell me about them sometime."

"Yes, if you—" Cassandra began.

Miss Irving glided forward as though she possessed wheels instead of legs. "No boring balloon talk now. Lord Whittaker, you are right in time to take the role of Henry Tudor."

Cassandra expected him to decline with the excuse of estate or some other business. Instead, he agreed without hesitation and followed the heiress back to the makeshift stage.

"A sturdy box will do." Cassandra turned back to Mr. Sorrells as though their dialogue had not been interrupted.

They continued talking about the flight. Cassandra even looked into Mr. Sorrells's eyes a few times, admiring their clear, gray irises and direct intelligence. Another time, she dared touch his arm while she made a point about how often they should apply the sealant to the balloon silk.

"It will evaporate, you know," she concluded.

Mr. Sorrells rose. "And now that you speak of evaporating, time seems to have done so. We have been invited for dinner and I must go change my attire."

"Yes, and my sister is determined there shall be music." Feeling a little queasy, Cassandra held out her hand and Mr. Sorrells helped her to her feet.

He continued to hold her hand. "But you won't dance."

"No, I still cannot." From the corner of her eye, she caught sight of Whittaker watching her, and she extricated her hand from Mr. Sorrells's—slowly. "Mrs. Dunstan is highly superstitious like the prince regent, and I would make thirteen to table so offered to not come."

"But Lord Whittaker is here now, which will make the table even," Mr. Sorrells pointed out.

"If he intends to remain home." Focusing on happier thoughts, Cassandra said, "But I will be at the balloon bright and early."

"And so will we." Philip Sorrells bowed, bade farewell to his host and hostess, and all but dragged Roger Kent from the house.

The boys and their tutor headed up the steps for the schoolroom, and Honore swept down the corridor to her room with an exclamation about the bird's nest of her hair needing repairs before she received guests for dinner. Miss Irving followed her young cousins upstairs with her own excuses of changing for the party.

"Must go don my uniform," said the major, who wore country garb of buckskin breeches and woolen coat. "Makes me stand out like a lighthouse beacon, but it is expected of me. Be seeing you shortly, ladies, Whittaker." And he too left the hall.

Cassandra stood beside her chair, irresolute. To get to her chamber, she must pass Whittaker and his mother. The former looked at her with sympathy, the latter with some confusion. Both would want to say something to her about the evening's entertainment. If she said she did not care about not being able to dance, as a small country dinner party held no interest for her, she doubted they would believe her. What single lady of one and twenty did not enjoy a party?

One like her, the bluestocking who disliked the vapid gossip.

She had waited too long to make her exit. The Gileses needed to walk past her to get to their wing. Both of them stopped by her chair.

"Do you not need to get yourself ready too?" Whittaker asked. "Not that you do not look charming."

"She does." Lady Whittaker spoke a bit too brightly. "That pink suits her, brings out the natural roses in her cheeks, which have returned since she has been here."

Returned and now bloomed. Cassandra's face heated. "You are too kind," she murmured. "I should go see that Honore has everything she needs and allow the two of you to get ready."

"You are not coming to my mother's party?" Whittaker asked.

"I offered to stay away so Mrs. Dunstan does not have palpitations over thirteen to table."

"Surely you did not agree to this, Mama." Whittaker narrowed his eyes.

"I did not agree." Lady Whittaker twisted her hands together. "But I had no idea if you would be home or not, and Mr. Danby could not come. And the Dunstans are our closest neighbors and we do not wish to insult them."

"Balderdash." Whittaker's jaw hardened. "I will not have one of my guests insulted in favor of a woman afraid of a number. I will be here for dinner." He turned on his heel and stalked into his wing of the house.

"I do believe," his mother said, "he is coming into his role quite nicely."

"Which may be the greatest reason it is best we are not going to be wed." With Whittaker had departed Cassandra's warmth, and her throat felt tight. "I would not make a good countess."

"I thought the same when my father told me I was to marry Geoffrey's father. You will learn the role."

Choosing to ignore the verb tense her ladyship used, Cassandra said, "I have no idea what to wear."

"Wear that gown with the silver netting you wore to dinner here the other evening," Lady Whittaker suggested. "I have rarely seen you look prettier." She laughed. "Oh dear, that sounded rude of me. I meant that you looked prettier than you always do."

Cassandra laughed. "I am not the beauty of the family, I know. But thank you. I will do my best."

Cassandra could not wear the pearls with the white silk gown, with its overskirt of silver gauze. They were too creamy. But Honore produced some silver earrings set with diamonds that their parents had given Cassandra upon her twenty-first birthday.

"Did you pack all my jewelry?" Cassandra could not help but laugh.

"I knew you would forget." Honore spun in front of Cassandra, sending her lace ruffles flying. "Will I do well enough? Do you think the major will wish to kiss me again?"

"I expect he will wish to, but whether or not he should is another matter. You know you should not be kissing or even holding hands without a declaration of intentions from him."

"Says Saint Cassandra." Honore pouted at her sister. "And I suppose Whittaker did not take you on the Lovers' Walk at Vauxhall Gardens and kiss you three weeks after you met?"

"Well, yes, but—" Cassandra turned away to hide her blush.

"And what about you and Mr. Sorrells today? That was as near to hand holding as not."

"I do not think that was holding hands."

"Ha. Everyone else did. I thought Whittaker was going to land him a facer."

"Honore!" Cassandra shook her head at her sister's use of cant. "Do not use such vulgar language in company, please."

Honore giggled. "You have gone so righteous of late. But you do not fool me. Your Bible has dust on it." Shot fired, Honore swept from the room and allowed the door to close a little too loudly behind her.

Cassandra glanced at the bedside table on which rested her Bible. A light coating of dust undisturbed by so much as a thumbprint marred the tooled leather cover. Other than a few quick prayers for Whittaker's safety the previous day, she had not read her Bible nor prayed since thanking God for the healing of the infection in her leg. Not six months ago, she was certain God had control of her life. She still believed that—He had made marriage to the man she loved unthinkable. He had also punished her for her bad behavior, and for that she had abandoned the Lord as a parent bent more on her good appearance to others than on anything she wanted, as with her own father. So she rebelled, as she had so often rebelled against her father. She did not wish to stop rebelling. That might mean no more flying, no more experiments, no more Greek translations. It might mean marriage to a suitable man.

Deliberately, she turned her back on the dusty Bible and left the bedchamber without her cane. She would manage without it. Someone would lend her his arm to lead her into dinner.

Miss Irving met her inside the great hall, as though she had been waiting to pounce before the guests arrived. "You are looking very fine this evening, Miss Bainbridge."

Cassandra smiled graciously. "Not as fine as you always do."

"How kind of you considering . . ." The older lady laid her hand on Cassandra's arm. Her face was earnest, perhaps even a bit tense. "Are you quite certain your betrothal is over?"

"Yes, of course I am." Cassandra looked Miss Irving in the eye. "If Lord Whittaker decides to court you, do not give me a moment's consideration."

"Thank you." Miss Irving bowed her head. "It would please my father so much if I married a title."

"But would it please you?" Cassandra asked, but Regina Irving had already turned toward the far side of the hall where Whittaker and his mother had arrived, and she either did not hear or ignored the query.

"And would it please Whittaker?" Cassandra asked no one at all.

Seeing him take Miss Irving's arm and lead her to a chair, Cassandra knew a courtship between them would not please her. She was such a dog in the manger there. Cassandra did not want him, but she did not want anyone else to have him either.

Except she did want him. She simply knew she could not have him. She offered him nothing that he needed—the right airs to be a countess, enough money to ease his financial straits, the beauty he deserved.

Not wanting to trail behind Whittaker and Miss Irving, Cassandra hesitated inside the hall and fiddled with a button on her glove. If she waited long enough, surely someone else would arrive.

Someone else did, in the form of Mr. Kent and Mr. Sorrells. They greeted her with enthusiasm and vied for which one of them would lead her to a chair. Amusement diminished her tension, and she could greet the other guests with her head high, if her walk still a bit unsteady.

Then dinnertime arrived. As she was the highest-ranked lady other than his mother, Lord Whittaker led her into the dining room and seated her on his right side. Lady Smithfield, the young and jolly wife of a knight, sat to his left. She commanded most of his attention, and the young man to Cassandra's right seemed more interested in the food than conversation, so she was spared the necessity of talking to Whittaker at any length. He did, however, manage to murmur before Lady Whittaker led the ladies back to the hall for cups of tea, "I will talk to you later."

Cassandra did not have the time to say she could not. She needed to follow her hostess and the other females.

"I have chalk for your slippers, since I have learned that my nephews' tutor plays the pianoforte rather well. He has moved it onto the gallery above us." Lady Whittaker removed a small wooden casket from the drawer of a Pembroke table and held it out to Miss Irving with an apologetic glance at Cassandra.

"Can you not dance at all?" Miss Irving asked.

"Perhaps something more sedate like a minuet." Cassandra stared down at her silk-covered legs. "But no one dances the minuet anymore."

"A pity. It is such a pretty dance."

It was a courting dance, with all the bowing and curtsying and partners moving toward and away from one another.

"If you change your mind," Miss Irving said, "I will help you chalk your slippers."

"Thank you."

Such kindness now that she seemed to be catching herself a title to please her father.

And Cassandra had rejected a title to please hers. To please both her earthly and heavenly fathers, both of whom now disapproved.

She had her flying. She must remember she had her flying.

Had she been at a larger party in London, she would have sought out the library once the dancing commenced. It would not have been the first time she had done so at a ball or party. The heat and smoke from the candles, added to numerous perfumes and pomades, made her head ache. She favored the company of a good book, preferably one she had not discovered before, to ballroom flirtations.

Even with only five couples dancing to the music drifting rather romantically from above them, the amount of laughter and couples staying for extra sets with one another suggested considerable flirtations, especially between Honore and the major, who, beneath Cassandra's watchful eye, seemed to cling gloved hands a little too long before the figure of the dance separated them.

No hand holding pressed the contact between Whittaker and Miss Irving, but they danced two sets in a row, and both seemed to smile a great deal. When Cassandra saw them lock eyes at the end of a reel, she murmured something about turning music for the tutor and skirted the hall to the staircase. Gripping the rail, she climbed with care until she reached the first floor, where she had not ventured in the weeks she had been at the Hall. The gallery stretched to the left, bright with candles. To her right ran a long corridor with two rooms brightly lit and awaiting the needs of the guests. She turned left and approached the pianoforte, then passed it to watch the hall from behind the screen of the carved balustrade.

"You have gone too far if you intended to turn music," Whittaker said behind her.

She spun around and caught her balance with a hand against the railing. "What are you doing up here? Do they not need you for the set?"

"Only four couples are needed for a quadrille. Miss Irving took herself off to repair her hem after Kent trod on it, and I asked Mama where I would find you." His smile was gentle, teasing.

Knee-melting.

"What do you want?"

"To apologize for not making our rendezvous yesterday morning." He stood in front of her, away from the balustrade but close enough for his sleeve to brush hers. "I was followed and did not wish to risk your safety by drawing him to you."

"Thank you." She inched away. "Do have more care for yourself."

"I am having a care for you, even if it means we cannot meet for me to tell you—"

"It is best we did not meet. I told Miss Irving she has my blessing on a courtship between the two of you. Or near as told her that."

"And you and Sorrells are practically in one another's pockets of late, I know, though he is paying a great deal of attention to Miss Dunstan right now." He held out his hand. "Do not hide up here, Cassandra. We want your company."

"No, Geoff—Whittaker, I am decidedly *de trop* down there."

"You could never be *de trop*." His voice was soft, his gaze softer. "I wish—no, I need to talk to you still."

A flutter of movement at the top of the steps drew Cassandra's attention to Miss Irving waiting, her lips set.

"Your lady is impatiently awaiting you," Cassandra said.

He glanced over his shoulder, nodded, then turned back to Cassandra. "I need your advice, your intellect."

Miss Irving started toward them. "The quadrille is ending, my lord."

She emphasized *my* a little too much.

Cassandra ground her teeth, though she knew she had no right to care. She had given the other lady permission.

"The orangery," Whittaker mouthed and turned to Miss Irving, his smile in place, his hand outstretched to her.

Cassandra waited until everyone was engrossed in the next set of dances, then descended the steps one tread at a time, trying to bear little weight on her right foot, until she reached the ground floor. Then she slipped along the wall to the door to her wing of the house. She was about to open it and escape to her bedchamber when she noticed four couples instead of five made up the formation of the quadrille.

Honore and Major Crawford were missing.

26

Whittaker's gaze followed Cassandra leaving the hall for her wing of the house, and he trod on Miss Irving's foot. She gasped, glared at him, and spun away to meet her next partner in the figure of the dance. Over the head of his next partner, plump and pretty Miss Dunstan, he tried to catch Mama's eye to signal for her to bring Cassandra back to the party and barely stopped himself from treading on Miss Dunstan's toes too.

The ever-changing pattern of the dance swept him to his next partner, then the next, and then he faced Miss Irving again and realized Miss Honore was not part of the group. Nor was Major Crawford.

"The little fool." Whittaker released Miss Irving's hands and stepped out of the line. "I know this is rude of me, ma'am, but I must find Miss Honore."

"She and the major slipped out that door while you were talking to her sister." Miss Irving indicated the door through which Cassandra had vanished.

Whittaker headed for it, Miss Irving at his heels.

"I expect they are in the orangery," she said.

"I expect so." He spoke through clenched teeth.

Miss Honore Bainbridge did not know the meaning of

discretion, let alone how to act it out. Of all the parties during which to disappear, she chose one so small she was missed in minutes. Whether he was an eligible suitor or not, slipping away to be in private with Major Crawford was not appropriate behavior for a young lady who had recently completed a disastrous first Season.

"Do go back and join the party," he told Miss Irving at the door. "I will manage this with her sister."

"But I am part of this . . . family, am I not?" Miss Irving smiled. "I have been encouraging her in her alliance with the major, as she has told me all about her misalliance last spring." She lowered her lashes. "Amongst other things."

Whittaker shoved open the door with more force than necessary. "What things?"

"Let me see." Miss Irving tapped her fan against her chin. "Miss Bainbridge falling down steps at the opera house. You and Miss Bainbridge being . . . indiscreet in the library . . ."

What was Miss Honore thinking in talking about such things?

Whittaker picked up his pace down the long passageway. "The past between Miss Bainbridge and me is . . . past."

"I wish it were." Miss Irving caught up with him again. "We did not know that the Bainbridge ladies would be here. After all, your betrothal was over, or so we heard."

"It was. It is." And the pain felt as raw as it had the day he'd received Cassandra's message.

He glanced back at the heiress looking every bit as wealthy as she was, beautiful enough to not need rich fabrics and jewels to enhance her looks into being a diamond of the first water. If she received introductions into Society, she would find herself another title in moments and all her money would go elsewhere.

Which it should if she and another man were that mercenary.

In that moment, chasing down Cassandra and Honore Bain-bridge, he knew he was not that mercenary. God might be plac-ing barriers between him and Cassandra marrying, but in no way did the Lord want him to wed a woman for whom he was gaining some liking yet for whom he felt no attraction beyond admiration of her appearance—as empty as admiration for a finely executed painting.

He stopped in the middle of the corridor and faced the heir-ess. "Miss Irving, you are one of the loveliest females I have ever had the privilege of meeting. In London, with the right introductions, you would make a splash in any circle."

"But I have made no splash with you." Her smile was tight, brittle. "I doubted this would work, but I had to tell Papa I tried."

"But you feel nothing for me either," Whittaker concluded.

"No." She shook her head. "I think I could quite happily marry you. You are, um, more than attractive to me, courteous, kind, intelligent, if somewhat inattentive to your guests, though I do understand you have the responsibilities of the mills right now. Of course those mills are one reason why my father and your uncle, who are great friends, thought this might be a grand alliance— you would not mind so much my father making his money in trade. But you are not even paying attention to me." Miss Irving pouted, but her eyes sparkled. "Thinking of Miss Bainbridge?"

"In truth I was not, but now that you say so, I need to retrieve those ladies."

Miss Irving laughed. "Perhaps I should learn from their rebel-lion and marry a wholly unsuitable man instead of the titled one my father craves."

"You should marry a man for whom you feel—" No, he could not say to this acquaintance that she should marry a man for whom she felt passion and respect and liking.

All those things he felt for Cassandra.

"We sometimes walk a fine line between being obedient to our earthly fathers and being obedient to our own hearts," he concluded.

"I would say the Bainbridge sisters have crossed the former in favor of the latter. Shall we go get them?" Miss Irving tucked her arm through his and headed toward the orangery.

They had reached the short flight of steps down to the glass-house when voices filled the corridor.

"I do believe," Whittaker said, "everyone is joining us."

He took the steps in a single bound and flung open the orangery door in time to hear Cassandra's voice in a low but harsh lecture.

"You may have more hair than wit, Honore Bainbridge, but surely last spring taught you to behave with a little more discretion than this. And as for you, Major Crawford, you should know better than to walk out of a party that small, where you would be missed in a minute. You are fortunate I found you first and not the entire party. I am ashamed of your behavior, the two of you, and will write Father in the morning. Now come with me before—"

"Too late." Whittaker strode forward to stand beside Cassandra. "The entire party is coming."

Indeed, voices and footfalls rang out from the corridor.

"And they will find nothing wrong." Crawford leaned languidly against one of the steamy windows, one booted foot propped on the edge of an orange tree planter. "Miss Honore was feeling faint and needed some—"

"Air in here?" Cassandra gestured to the burning braziers heating the air to unnatural warmth. "What fool will believe that?"

"Seems to me," Miss Honore said, her lower lip still managing to puff out in a pout, "that you two are the pot calling the kettle black."

"Yes, and look how I have paid for it." Tears filled Cassandra's eyes, making them appear bigger and darker than they already were. She held her hands out to her sister. "Honore, do not let yourself be led astray like this. If our earthly father does not punish you, God will. Or do you want to end up—" She stopped and pressed a hand to her lips.

But she had spoken into the unnatural stillness of a dozen people holding their breath in waiting silence.

"I do believe," Mama said from the doorway, "everyone here would enjoy the treat of an orange to refresh themselves after such rigorous activity. Geoffrey, will you assist me in finding the ripest ones?"

"Oh, may I look?" Miss Dunstan darted for the nearest tree. "The last oranges you gave us were wonderfully sweet."

The party scattered, everyone in search of his own ripe orange. Cassandra grabbed Honore's wrist and seemed to be dragging her to the door by force, all the while speaking in an undertone. Miss Honore's lower lip stuck out enough to make a fine bird perch.

Whittaker stood in front of Major Crawford, preventing him from going anywhere. "You, sir, will pack and leave this house at once."

"Can't. Have to stay in the neighborhood, as you know." He grinned.

Whittaker did not take the bait. "There are inns aplenty close at hand. I will not have you attempting to debauch an innocent like Miss Honore Bainbridge."

"Scarcely an innocent. Or did you think no one knew about

her scandalous activity last spring?" The major yawned. "Of course they do not, but they could."

Whittaker clasped his hands behind his back. Striking the man would not only be wrong, it would be pointless. He kept his voice calm. "You do not need to remind me of my duty. I will have your information for you shortly, and then, if you do not remove yourself from Miss Honore's presence, I will have a thing or two to write to your superior officers." Message delivered, Whittaker spun on his heel to join his mother and guests.

Bearing oranges in their hands like precious gifts, they headed back toward the great hall, laughing and chatting as though they had not witnessed a family contretemps.

"Have you ever considered expanding this glasshouse and selling the oranges?" Miss Irving fell into step beside Whittaker and laughed. "I know—I have the soul of a tradesman."

"Then so do I, for all my noble heritage."

"The French do call us a nation of shopkeepers, and we are nothing compared to the Americans. Have you ever met one? All they talk about is profits."

"I met one at Cambridge who was possibly the most godly man I have ever known. He spoke about his faith more than his income, which, I believe, was considerable."

"And that is just as tedious. I mean to say, of course I attend church, but who wishes to talk about one's feelings for God?" Miss Irving lifted the orange to her nose. "What a heavenly scent."

But not a heavenly minded lady. So of course he could not wed her. What had he been thinking? Not of God's will for a Christian man to seek a Christian wife. He had been ignoring his faith of late, angry for what had been taken from him, blaming God, and turning away instead of toward Him.

"I have heard," he said to be polite, "some say these are the golden apples of mythology."

"Yes, wasn't some maiden distracted by them along a race so she would lose?"

"Atalanta. She was not supposed to marry, yet she was distracted by golden apples and lost the race, so her suitor won her hand, but it never turned out well for them." Remembering the rest of the myth was not proper for polite company, he stopped.

Miss Irving laughed. "The moral of the story is, do not be distracted by golden apples." She pushed open the door to the great hall and joined the others.

"Or just gold," Whittaker murmured.

Of course God would not wish for him to marry for money alone. He had promised to provide, and He would.

Provide for one's needs, though, not necessarily a wife. As the men who had forced him into his current mission had pointed out, he had heirs to the title. He did not necessarily need a wife.

Seeing Cassandra with Mama at the far end of the room, though, he knew he wanted one, and which one. Forget heiresses. He was going to win her back, God willing.

He walked up behind the ladies in time to hear Mama say in a low voice, "He has lost his reason if he thinks to dangle after that heiress."

"I should think she is a wise choice. She is quite beautiful and has nice manners."

Lady Whittaker sniffed.

"She has been very kind to Honore," Cassandra continued.

Mama frowned. "It would be wise from a fiscal perspective, yes, but not . . . Marriages based on financial needs met in exchange for a title are unwise. I know they are as common as fleas on dogs, but they rarely turn out happily."

A stark reminder of how his mother had managed her own unhappy marriage—with infidelity, come to haunt him thirty years later.

"My father would agree with you," Cassandra said.

"I know he would. Your father and I—ah, Whittaker, have you not heard that eavesdroppers hear nothing good of themselves?"

"Yes, I have, and I apologize for listening. Where is Miss Honore?"

"In her room weeping her heart out." Cassandra glanced around at the company refreshing themselves with the oranges and an assortment of sweet biscuits and tea or lemonade. She lowered her voice. "Your friend Major Crawford should know better at his age."

"I expect he does." Whittaker glared across the room at the officer engaged in dialogue with Sorrells. "Is Miss Honore all right—other than being mortified by being caught?"

"She is well enough," Cassandra said. "He was doing no more than kissing her rather . . . er . . . intensely."

For a heartbeat their eyes met, held, flashed a memory or a hundred between them. Then Whittaker's gaze dropped to her lips, and she blushed, mumbled an excuse, and limped away to join Major Crawford and Sorrells under the guise of fetching a cup of tea.

"That was nowhere near subtle, my son." Mama rapped his knuckles with her fan.

Whittaker kept watching Cassandra, her face suddenly aglow, her hands gesturing to accompany her words. "No doubt she is talking of her infernal balloons. If she loved me half so well as she did those machines, she would never once believe we are not supposed to be together."

"Then love them with her."

"I cannot. The idea of going up in one makes me ill. And they are dangerous."

"But the more you try to stop her, the more she wants to do it. Bainbridge is a strict father who gave his daughters so little freedom to think for themselves, they have all rebelled. And when you tell her not to do something, you sound just like her father."

"He has always allowed Cassandra to pursue her studies," Whittaker pointed out.

"Because she sneaked around, stealing books from his library to do so."

"How do you know?"

"He told me, with a bit of pride, I do believe." Mama smiled. "The more he told her not to do it, the more she did."

"Not an admirable trait." Whittaker smiled, his heart soft. "Perhaps her only dishonorable trait."

"And one that has kept her alive since August, or do you not realize how close to death she was?"

"They would not let me see her or tell me anything, at her request."

"Of course she requested it. She did not want you to see her emaciated and ill. And you meekly went away."

"I never—"

But he had. She'd told him to go and he had not stayed to fight.

"Was I supposed to fight my way into her bedchamber?" he asked in self-defense.

"At the least, you could have written her every day. But you take no for an answer because you have always been the best and most obedient of sons, never going beyond anything you think we expect of you." Mama spoke with a blend of gentle reproach and affection.

Whittaker glanced at Cassandra again, now deep in conversation with Sorrells. "Not always, Mama. I have been—"

Mrs. Dunstan headed their way.

"We must talk soon, I think," he said hastily. "I want to tell you something. You and Cassandra."

But not that night. He had to meet with the rebels again in less than an hour. He would need all of that time to return to his other persona and get to the tavern.

"I must take my leave now," he said.

Quickly he bade good night to his mother's guests, then slipped away. In three quarters of an hour, he was up the oak tree and into the first-floor chamber, the second man to arrive.

"Geoff, so glad to see you," Jimmy greeted him. "I was gonna look you up after t'meeting, but since t'others aren't here yet, now's as good a time as any."

"Good enough for what?" Whittaker propped one shoulder against the window frame, where he could watch the movements of the other man and anyone approaching at the same time but still appear relaxed.

"How we can get out of this gang." Jimmy approached slowly, hands in front of him, a signal of his noncombative intentions. "I'll help you find out who the ringleader is if you do me a favor."

The man sounded sincere, but Whittaker did not wish to step into a trap. He shrugged. "Maybe I should go along with Rob and Hugh. After all, the French got rid of their king and queen through riots and rebellion."

"And found themselves with Napoleon Bonaparte. Do we want that in England? Surely you're not suggesting treason, getting rid of the king—or regent now, I s'pose."

"No, but the loom owners have taken note. Some changes have occurred."

"Not many for the good. Fewer looms may mean higher prices, but it also means more men out of work, which means more for the mill owners to choose from and lower wages. We won't make ourselves heard thatta way."

"So you're more intelligent than the rest of th—us." Hearing a footfall crunch below, Whittaker leaned a bit toward the window.

Jimmy grabbed his sleeve and pulled him back. "So are you, so stop pretending," he whispered in a rush. "You know this is stupid and will probably get us all killed with a gun or a rope. Or a knife between our shoulder blades."

Whittaker's skin crawled. No time for further discussion as to what Jimmy's favor might be. The oak tree rustled, and Whittaker and Jimmy moved to the table. By the time Rob and Hugh arrived in quick succession, Whittaker and Jimmy discussed nothing more interesting than which local inn or tavern made the best pork pie.

The other men debated where to make their next move. When asked his opinion, Whittaker simply glared at them through the scanty light and shrugged. "I have no opinions other than those you've already heard."

"Then it's the Melton mills again," Rob said. "Just one change. We won't go at midnight like we a'ways does. We go at dawn. The guards'll be tired by then and think they got through another peaceful night."

Having stood guard, Whittaker knew this was sound advice and started to push back his chair, ready to leave. He wanted some sleep himself.

"Can't go at dawn," Hugh broke in. "Those fools with the balloon are going up in the morning. They might spot something."

Whittaker's hands froze on the edge of the table.

"Then stop 'em," Rob said and stood. "I'm for my bed for a bit."

Whittaker gripped the table so hard he expected the pine to crack.

"You coming, Geoff?" Jimmy asked.

"Yeah, sure I am." Whittaker made himself release the table, rise, go to the window. "Feeling a bit fatigued is all."

"Ain't we all." Jimmy yawned. "I'm for my bed too."

"Sounds fine."

"I'll walk with you a bit," Jimmy said. "Keeps us all safe to stick together in pairs or more, eh?"

"Yes, that it does." In thinking of how to warn Cassandra in time, Whittaker forgot to disguise his aristocratic accent.

They reached the road and strode along in silence until certain they were out of earshot of the other men. Then they remained silent until they reached the slit in the hedge, where Jimmy stopped before slipping through the gap first.

Whittaker was frowning as he followed. "You've followed me before."

"I was paid to." Jimmy grinned.

"By whom?" Whittaker wished his knife were at his waist instead of in his boot. He braced himself for a blow, Jimmy's hand darting for a blade, a pistol.

"Some lordship who said to keep you safe."

Bainbridge? No other "lordship" would care what happened to him. Not that Bainbridge cared. Yet what other nobleman knew of Whittaker's involvement with the rebels?

"No lordship cares about my welfare."

"This one does. Says he wants you with us rebels, but you can't get hurt."

Whittaker curled his upper lip. "You have done a poor job of it."

"I know. That's why I warned you about Rob or Hugh knowing about you. Maybe the both of 'em. You keep slipping away and I can't watch after you, and I won't get my pay if you're killed. So I have to stop you from slipping off." Jimmy's fist flashed toward Whittaker's jaw.

Whittaker ducked, leaped away, then kicked Jimmy in the middle.

"Unfair fighting," Jimmy gasped out as he folded.

Whittaker smashed his fist into Jimmy's jaw. "You will not stop me from going to save her."

"You . . . dead man." Jimmy's eyes rolled up, and he slumped to the ground. Whittaker dragged him beneath the hedgerow for his protection, then raced across the field.

Regardless of—no, because of—Jimmy's warning, he must risk whatever necessary to reach Cassandra in time to stop her from going up in the balloon.

27

Before the first bird commenced its morning song, Cassandra sprang from bed and began to dress in the gown she had commissioned with fastenings up the front—not fashionable for a lady but practical for her. Her ankle was healed so much she was tempted to don her half boots, then decided against it. She could not again risk her barely healed scar rubbing into an open sore.

Wearing her sturdiest leather slippers, she slipped through the orangery and out of the house. Memory of Whittaker saying someone had followed him into the parkland gave her pause at the inner gate. But the person had followed him, not her. She was safe away from him, he claimed, though why made little to no sense. Then again, nothing about Geoffrey Giles, Earl of Whittaker, made any sense these days—his odd comings and goings, his peculiar clothes, the fact that someone wanted him dead at all. He was the kindest, most generous man she knew. She could not work out how he had made enemies.

Cassandra had made, if not an enemy, at least an adversary. One who had kept her awake until well past midnight, who begged, pleaded, and finally walked into her bedroom and slammed the door when Cassandra remained adamant.

"I will write to Father about your behavior—again," Cassandra had persisted in telling Honore. "To enjoy a flirtation is one matter. To slip away during a party and commence kissing a gentleman like that in a private place is quite another. And if you think it will force Father's hand to allow you to wed Major Crawford, you are quite mistaken. On the contrary, he is more likely to forbid an alliance with a man who gives you no more respect than to treat you that way."

"He did not forbid your marriage to Whittaker when he knew." Honore pouted, as she had all evening.

Cassandra gave her sister a twisted smile. "But he did. He told Whittaker to go away after my accident because—because of how we behaved in the carriage before I . . . fell out into the fire."

"You also told Whittaker to go away."

"Of course I did. Would a man want to marry a woman with my scars? But I did not know about Father at the time."

"Because you two engaged in a bit of kissing?" Honore shook her head. "I think not."

"Yes, well, um . . ." Cassandra turned away, but not before her cheeks had begun to heat.

Honore gasped. "Cassandra, you . . . !"

"Not that," Cassandra hastened to clarify. "But . . . we were wrong and now I am scarred as a reminder of my sin."

"But that has nothing to do with forgiveness and repentance." Honore sounded more panicked than placatory. "Surely God would never do such a thing."

"He allowed it to happen. I was already poor wife material for Whittaker, preferring balloons and books to balls and dinner parties."

"I think that is all nonsense. And I will have Major Crawford. He is not at all like Mr. Frobisher."

"We shall let Father be the judge of that. You are still a minor."

And so the battle raged until Honore simply stomped away and slammed her door.

Cassandra wrote Father a letter suggesting he have a care for his youngest daughter's courtship by a military man:

> *She has been indiscreet, you must know. And you need not concern yourself with me. You may trust me to remain on my best behavior despite Whittaker being here after all. He accepts that our betrothal is ended.*

Then she slept for no more than an hour or two, woke, and headed for the rendezvous with Mr. Kent and Mr. Sorrells. They were enthusiastic about her flying on her own, both having taken solo flights and extolling the virtues of being alone in the heavens.

"Nothing is better," Mr. Sorrells had said the night before. "One feels so close to God."

Once she exited the second gate, she spotted the balloon, filling nicely, rising up against a gray predawn sky with the merest hint of brightness along the eastern horizon to assure her no rain should be forthcoming. As she arrived halfway across the field, she noticed the strength of the wind and the slant of the balloon. Not too high for floating through the heavens, but the tilt of the balloon indicated they would drift in the wrong direction.

"Do you still want to go?" Mr. Sorrells greeted her. "We think you should be safe enough, as you can set down long before you reach the water, but if you're uncomfortable, we understand."

"I'll go." Mr. Kent chuckled. "Maybe I can cross the Irish Sea."

"Or the Atlantic." Cassandra smiled and shook her head. "No, I still want to go. It will be a good opportunity for me to test the sails."

"True." Mr. Sorrells looked a bit dubious. "If nothing else, they should slow your progress."

"We will follow on horseback as best we can." Mr. Kent gestured toward a pair of horses tethered a hundred feet from the fire fueling the balloon.

"In the event you find yourself in difficulty," Mr. Sorrells added.

A common practice. Many persons followed balloon flights on horseback, jumping over walls and streams to keep the flying machine in sight. Thinking of her two friends below warmed Cassandra. She experienced no anxiety about her flight and took comfort in knowing she would not be completely alone.

Pulse beginning to race like the wind, she approached the wooden box they had set beside the tethered basket. "Then let there be no more delay."

"Let me lend you a hand." Mr. Sorrells held out both his hands.

Cassandra took one to give her stability as she stepped onto the box. She needed the other hand to manage her skirt and petticoats. From there, climbing into the basket proved easier than mounting a horse. Inside, she found a flask of water and half a dozen apples, a hunk of soft cheese, and a loaf of bread.

"I thought you might get hungry," Mr. Kent admitted, "if you make this a long flight. I know I did the last time I went up. It's all that fresh air."

"You are so thoughtful." Cassandra leaned over the side of the basket to offer him her best smile. "I had no breakfast, and I rather like the idea of having it a mile off the ground."

"We'll get the ropes then." Mr. Sorrells strode to one end of the balloon and loosed the first rope.

Mr. Kent went to the diagonal corner. The basket began to bob and sway with the inflated balloon tugging upward, its filling of hot air anxious to lift up and up.

"This is glorious!" Cassandra cried out and lifted her arms. "If we cannot create wings for men to fly themselves, then this is the next best way to go into the air. It is positively—"

Hoofbeats thundered across the field at a speed too fast for the lack of light in the sky and the roughness of the terrain. "Cassandra, do not go!" a shout carried on the wind. "Do not—"

"Quick," Cassandra said, doubting she was strong enough to unhook the ropes herself now that the balloon was rising. "Loose the other ropes."

But neither Mr. Sorrells nor Mr. Kent did so. They stood watching the approaching rider.

"Cassandra, come out of there." Geoffrey Lord Whittaker reined in a dozen feet away and flung himself from the saddle.

"Now," Cassandra commanded.

Perhaps her voice held authority. Perhaps they simply did not want their morning's enjoyment spoiled by someone who did not appreciate their balloon travel experiments. Whatever the reason, Mr. Kent and Mr. Sorrells sprang into action, unfastening the last two ropes. The balloon began to rise.

"Cassandra, you cannot." Whittaker sounded desperate. In the torchlight, his face gleamed pale, tense.

"I cannot stop it." Cassandra started to lean toward him,

realized she was not rising all that quickly and he might still manage to pull her from the basket. "It truly is safe, Whittaker. Never you—"

"But it is not. Cass—" With a noise rather like a growl, Whittaker leaped onto the box she had used, grabbed the edge of the rising basket, and half-dragged, half-rolled himself over the edge. "How do we get this to land again?"

"We do not." Cassandra glared at Whittaker, her tone hard. "You are here for the duration of the journey."

"But you do not understand." Breath coming in gasps, Whittaker scrambled to his feet and caught hold of Cassandra's shoulders. "It is dangerous today. After the other morning, I've learned some things. I warned you that you were in danger."

"While with you." She smiled at the glorious expanse of the sky arching around her. "Alone, or rather, with my aeronaut friends, I am perfectly secure."

"But you are not. Jimmy, one of the Luddite weavers—oh my." His eyes went out of focus. His face turned green. "We're off the ground," he said in a strangled voice.

Cassandra glanced at the diminishing figures on the ground, growing blurry to her even with her spectacles on. "About two hundred feet. No more than that, I expect."

"Two hundred? Two—"

"Standing is better in a balloon, but kneel if you are going to be sick, preferably over the edge."

He sat. He lowered his head to his knees. "I dislike looking over the gallery into the great hall. That is only twenty feet. Two hundred . . ."

Cassandra resisted the urge to kneel beside him and offer comfort. "You got in of your own free will."

He raised his head, perspiration beading his brow and upper lip. "I thought you would land it again."

"Because you ordered me to? I am your mother's guest, not yours. And, as you admitted yourself, our betrothal is most definitely over; therefore, you have no control over my actions."

"I do if I am trying to save your life."

"The risk I take coming up in a balloon is my risk to bear."

"No, you do not understand." He rose, shaking visibly, and grasped the edge of the basket behind him. "Cassandra, this is more than you simply going up in a balloon. I learned a few hours ago that the rebels intend to stop you from flying today so you do not see their activities this morning."

"Stuff and nonsense." Cassandra brushed past him to inspect the apparatus that kept the balloon afloat.

Just enough fire burned in the brazier to heat the vitriol and iron shavings in a glass beaker suspended above the flames. Heated, the iron and acid produced hydrogen. From the beaker's mouth, a canvas tube coated in wax led up to the balloon to carry the hydrogen gas and give them buoyancy—all a marvel of chemistry and physical science, the newest joys in Cassandra's life.

All seemed well. The balloon and basket continued to rise, swooping upward on a current of air. To the east, what had been a band of bright light now shone as the first rays of a pink and gold sunrise. To the west, the sea sparkled like a dark diamond shot with fire.

"Look." Cassandra pointed to the east. "Besides the fact that we are already a quarter mile off the ground and out of range to all save military guns, making stopping us nigh on impossible, is it not worth being up here?"

Whittaker barely glanced at the sun. "Cassandra, I have no

idea how they plan to stop this flight, but they do. I heard the plans with my own ears and would have been here sooner had I not been delayed by . . . I am such a fool."

He looked so distraught, so shaken and pale, Cassandra could no longer maintain her air of indifference or her true anger for his interference. "You are not and never have been a fool, Geoffrey. Unless it is getting into this balloon when you hate to be off the ground." She tried to smile at him. "But as long as I am sensible, we are in no danger. Mr. Kent and Mr. Sorrells are following our progress on horseback. You might be able to see them on the ground. You know I cannot see that far away, which is a disadvantage for me." She touched the metal frames of her spectacles. "But I know they will be there, so no one—"

"Be quiet and listen to me," Whittaker snapped. He took a deep breath and added, "Please. I would have tried to stop this flight even with someone else aboard. I do not know enough about these contraptions to know what the rebels can do to stop you, but they intend to because of the other morning."

Cassandra wrapped her shawl more tightly around her. "They who? What are you talking about?"

"The trouble I am in. Blackmail. Luddites." He released the side of the basket long enough to shove his hand through his hair, then paused, his hand on his head. "Are we not moving?"

"Quite quickly, I expect. Perhaps as much as fifteen miles per hour. It's a bit too fast for the horses to keep up with us. Why?"

"I feel no wind."

"That is because we are traveling with it, not going faster or slower than it. If you look down, you will have a better idea."

Whittaker shuddered. "No, thank you. I'd rather not shame myself by shooting the cat in front of you. I have done enough to shame myself, but apparently it runs in my blood."

"What are you saying, Geoffrey? Truly, I have heard that sometimes being up high in the air can make a man a bit mad, but we have not gone nearly that far off the ground. That is up miles and miles and—"

"Stop." He was looking greenish-white again. "I have to tell you this. Will we be here awhile?"

"That depends on the wind. If—" She changed her mind before she said that she would set them down before they reached the sea itself. She did not wish to humiliate him by making his fear of high places cause him to be sick over the side. He seemed shamed enough already.

"I think," she said, "you had better tell me everything if you want me to set this balloon down before we have been up more than a quarter hour."

"Yes, but—eh." He turned his head away from her, must have caught a glimpse of the earth far below, and closed his eyes. "I cannot think up here. How can you like this?"

"Be still a moment and stop thinking about how high up we are."

He took a long, deep breath and kept his eyes closed. First his hands loosened on the basket edge enough that the knuckles did not gleam white through his skin. Then his jaw relaxed, the knot of muscles in the corner smoothing out. Finally he opened his eyes and looked at her. "I have never seen you more beautiful than you look right now with the sun shining on your face."

"I have my spectacles on. I must resemble some kind of insect with the sun shining on the lenses." She snatched them off and the world beyond the basket grew blurry.

Whittaker smiled. "I told you six months ago I find them charming. I still mean it. Cassandra, when will you believe me when I tell you I find you beautiful?"

When she stopped loving him so much she wanted to believe him. When she knew he understood the worst of her scars and did not look repulsed even at the mention of them.

"When you are honest with me about everything else," she said.

"I intend to be." He glanced down at the small basket of food at his feet. "I expect one advantage of being up here is that no one will interrupt us—so long as we are safe. That is, if the soldiers in Manchester took action after I rode there to tell them."

"We are safe right now." Though a glance up at the balloon told her they needed either more of the iron shavings inside the beaker, a new coating of sealant, or a better formula, as the balloon was losing too much air and their elevation was dropping more than she liked.

She turned her back on Whittaker and applied the bellows to the brazier. Fire licked at the coals. The vitriol bubbled and the balloon expanded again. Up they climbed, first a little jerk as the balloon tugged on the basket, then the glorious sensation of floating, like gliding on a quiet pond, only better because one was not fighting against the folds of a bathing dress to stay afloat.

She faced Whittaker and caught a gleam of admiration on his face. "You are so unsure of yourself in Society but completely at home up here."

"Yes, it is why I am not an appropriate countess for you. I am a bluestocking at best. It will do nothing to advance you as a member of Parliament."

"You know I have no political ambitions, Cassandra. I go because my title obliges me to. I listen to the speeches. I vote for what I think is right. It is my duty as a nobleman. Beyond that, I want a wife and family. But if I am right, I am not going to live long enough to enjoy either."

"Yes." Cassandra found her knuckles white against the dark wood of the basket. No longer could she avoid being his confidant. "We are quite safe here now, but why did you think someone wanted to stop the balloon? Why did someone throw a knife at you?"

"Or shoot me?" His smile was tight, the dimple nowhere in sight. "It started six months ago. You ended our betrothal because you thought then we were not following God's will for our lives."

"And you quite happily walked away without a fight."

"I learned that one of my weaving mills had been destroyed by the Luddites. I had to find out about the damage and set repairs in motion. The riots have been senseless and harming no one save for the weavers themselves."

"And owners like you who were losing money."

"Yes, it was a financial blow." He glanced away. A shudder ran through him, and he returned his focus to her face. "Do we have to be quite so high?"

"No, but it is more peaceful up this high. One cannot hear a thing from the ground, and if you fear someone may shoot at us or something, the higher we are, the safer we are."

She wanted to be higher, high enough to see the Pennines, but the balloon was not cooperating this morning. Perhaps one of the men had mixed the vitriol incorrectly and the gas inside the balloon was not quite light enough.

"Safe a thousand feet or more off the ground?" Whittaker snorted. "Ah, Cassandra, you may consider yourself a blue-stocking, but you are not a tediously dull one. Never once have I found your company tedious."

"Thank you, I think, but return to your story. You assessed the damage to your mill."

"Yes, and grew angry enough to disguise myself as a weaver and join the rioters to learn who was behind it."

"You never—" Her stomach dropped as though the balloon had lost all its air and plummeted them toward earth. "Geoff— Whit—did you want to kill yourself?"

"No, I wanted to find a peaceful way to end the riots." He speared his fingers through his hair, still long and shaggy like a man without the means to—

"The hair!" she cried. "You are doing it again."

"Yes, but not by my free will. Last spring was enough of a taste of the violence for me. I escaped detection but managed to give the Army the names of two of the ringleaders and see them brought to justice for killing loom owners."

"You, my quiet, bookish fian—I mean—" She stumbled to a halt. He was her nothing, then or now.

But he smiled. This time the dimple showed. "I was taught how to shoot and use a sword, you know."

"Yes, but that is spying. I should think you too honest to want to participate in a deceptive act of espionage."

"But not so honest . . ." He shook his head, and his shaggy hair lifted on a downdraft.

Frowning, Cassandra turned back to the balloon to blow more air into the bag. It seemed to be losing the gas far more quickly than it should. But she could see nothing wrong except that her formula for sealing the silk was imperfect.

"Is, um, something amiss?" Whittaker sounded a bit strangled.

"No." Cassandra turned back to him with a bright smile and noted his white knuckles again. "The gas inside the balloon needs to stay warm and lighter than the air outside to keep us aloft, so I need to feed it from time to time, as it leaks out."

"I thought that is what that foul-smelling substance was for."

"It was, and I am still perfecting the formula. So do go on." His tale-telling distracted him from their height, which was increasing now, enough that she thought she could indeed see the Pennines to the east and an expanse of the Irish Sea to the west. "You played spy, then came back south and convinced me I should wed you. The riots seemed to quiet down up here in the north."

"But have only quieted. They are not over."

"No." Feeling as sick as he had looked once he realized they were hundreds of feet off the ground, she said, "Someone has learned who you are and wants to kill you for it."

"It is far worse than that, Cassandra." His gaze slipped past her. "Are you planning to sail us to Ireland?"

"Not today. Now continue."

"I would rather continue on the ground."

"I think perhaps we are safer up here if someone is trying to harm you."

"No one would expect me up here. But I get all out of order." He took a long, shuddering breath, loud in the stillness of being aloft, and continued to look past her rather than at her. "Your father did not withdraw his approval of our marriage because he thought I dishonored you and would therefore not be a good husband to you."

"I know." Cassandra rubbed at her right thigh. "He blamed you for my—my scars that make me unmarriageable to any man for a dowry no larger than mine. I would have to be an heiress like Regina—"

"Stubble it," Whittaker barked. "A man who truly loves you will have no care about scars."

"And you care." She made it a statement, not a question.

He had looked as sick upon learning about her scars as he did upon leaving the ground. Well, she had accepted the end of their future together, had she not?

She gazed at him with her spectacles on, a rarity, took in his strong silhouette against the rising sun, and understood why she had rejected God at the same time she ensured the betrothal would not continue—guilt, plain and simple. Regardless of punishment from God or whatever the cause of her physical suffering, she had not for a moment repented of her behavior with this handsome, kind, intelligent man. Looking at him now stirred up memories and thoughts she knew to be wrong, and the knowledge burdened her with guilt. In no way could they begin a marriage with guilt weighing her down.

And him too. His unwillingness to look directly at her spoke volumes about his regret over their past. No wonder he cringed at the mention of her scars. They were forever a reminder of their improper behavior with one another. Yet knowing she had lost him forever was no reason for not repenting, for rejecting the truth of God's will for her life and His grace. His will was perfect. If God did not want her married to Geoffrey Giles, Earl of Whittaker, then He had a better plan for her life. She knew that. She had believed it in the spring, and then Whittaker came back only to have her behave abominably once again, against all her moral understanding, because she was too sure she knew what was right for herself and did not truly trust that God did.

"I understand," she added. "It is all right."

"No, Cassandra, you do not understand." He took a step toward her. The basket swayed a little, and he halted, paling again. "I am going to sit down if I may."

"Yes, but the view is better standing."

He smiled tightly. "I know." He seated himself cross-legged on the bottom of the basket and still gripped the side with one hand. "A bit better. Now, what was I saying? Yes, you do not understand about your father and me, and—and he—" He took a long, deep breath, then let it and the words out in a rush. "He knew about my mother, that my elder brother was not my father's son, and that I have proven I have too much of her temperament of disloyalty and dishonor, and with your tendency to rebellion, I should not wed you."

"What did you say? No, no"—she waved her hand in the air—"do not repeat it. I heard you. I simply mean—" Her legs wobbled, and she sank to her knees before him, the brazier a soft hiss behind her, the balloon a bulbous shadow above, and the glorious open sky a blue and gold canopy around them. They might have been the last two people left in the world. "Your mother committed . . . against your father, and because we were . . . indiscreet, my father withdrew his consent to our marriage? I thought he blamed you for my accident."

"He does. I led you astray because I have my mother's—"

"That is preposterous." She grasped the sides of the basket to keep herself from the foolishness of springing to her feet and probably stomping her foot right through the floor of the car. "I was just as complicit. I encouraged you. I have done everything others did not wish me to do since I was at least out of my cradle, if not sooner. I am the one with the rebellious heart, and you are the one bearing the shame."

She never before admitted the truth of her rebellion, and she saw it for what it was now—the author of her pain, her isolation, her losses.

"You are not to blame, Geoffrey. Not for any of this. How could my father, knowing me, believe such a thing of you?"

"I am not without guilt, my dearest one." He brushed a strand of hair from her cheek, then held it, stroking it between his thumb and forefinger. "We both lost our sense of right and wrong to some extent after I became the earl. We were angry with God for tossing us into a future neither of us wanted, instead of accepting it as God's will for our lives and learning how He could use us."

"And the consequences are of our own making." Cassandra bowed her head as though she could see through her skirt and petticoats to the marks on her legs. "I have been blaming God and my father has blamed you, and—"

"Used his knowledge about my mother to blackmail me into joining the rioters again."

"He is blackmailing you into danger like that?" That plummeting feeling punched her middle again.

No, they were sinking, far too quickly. She glanced up to see the balloon dimpling from air loss.

"Wait a moment." She kept her voice calm. "I have to fill up with more air."

She scrambled to her feet and applied the bellows to the brazier. Flames licked at the coals, raising the temperature. The vitriol bubbled, sending its light gas hissing up the tube to the balloon.

But the creases in the balloon did not diminish fast enough. The basket continued to sink toward the ground. Air continued to hiss . . . hiss . . .

Hiss too loudly.

Cassandra tilted her head back and squinted at the balloon. She saw nothing wrong.

"Geoffrey," she asked through stiff lips, "will you look at the balloon and tell me if you see anything odd?"

He stood close behind her, one hand warm and strong on her shoulder. "What am I looking for?"

"A tear," she admitted, though her throat was almost too dry for speech. "I believe we have a tear and the balloon is losing more air than it is getting."

28

Whittaker glanced from Cassandra's stricken countenance to the ground to the balloon that did look less turgid than earlier. The earth was not precisely rushing toward them, but it appeared far closer than it had the last time he had looked, when it had barely been visible. Anything greater than ten feet off the ground was too high for him.

Another wave of vertigo washed over him, and he closed his eyes. "Can it be repaired?"

"It will have to be." Cassandra still spoke in that voice of icy calm. "We are going to crash onto the ground if we lose too much air too quickly."

"What can I do?"

"Toss out ballast to make us lighter. One or two bags of sand, I think, for now." She suddenly sounded far too cheerful. "And I will climb up and wrap my shawl around the tear in the tubing."

"The tear?" Whittaker looked her in the eye.

She offered him a half-smile. "You had not reached the part about someone destroying the balloon, had you? Was it because I warned you about the assassination attempt?"

"That was not the excuse, but yes, I think as much. I will finish if—when we get out of this alive." He stood and gazed up at the balloon, a colorful sphere above them. "But how will you reach the tubing?"

"I thought to stand on the edge of the basket."

"You will do no such thing. If you slip—no, I will never let—" He stopped, and despite the sinking sensation in his middle and feeling that his head was lighter than his body, he laughed. "Perhaps I can reach it. I am taller than you by at least a head."

"But I know what I am doing." She reached for one of the ropes tethering the balloon to the car in which they stood. "If you hold on to me . . ."

"You will still be too short to reach it."

She cast a frown from him to the balloon above. "We need a ladder. Yes, that will do." She grew animated, reaching past him and drawing a knife from the basket of provisions in the rear of the car. "If I cut the mooring lines from the sides, we can tie them around the tether ropes and make a ladder like rigging on a ship. I should have thought of this sooner. It should be a regular part of the balloon's configuration for such incidents. This surely cannot be the first time a balloon has needed repairs in flight."

"But you cannot climb it."

Foolish thing to say. The fastest way to get Cassandra to do something was to tell her she could not. Yet she would respond to logic.

"Cassandra, your skirts. The fire. Unless we douse the coals."

She shifted her gaze from him to the fire to her plain but long gown, and paled. "If we douse the fire, we have no means of filling the balloon with hydrogen again."

"But can we not let out the air slowly for landing?" Even as he asked the question, Whittaker looked down and noticed what lay beneath.

At their current level of elevation, they had caught a strong breeze sweeping them out over the sea. Waves swelled and sparkled, creamy white at their tops. Not a calm sea. A sea rough enough to swamp the little balloon basket in minutes.

"How—" He swallowed. "How did that happen so fast?"

"Different wind currents and velocities at different heights." Cassandra leaned over the side of the car and came up with a length of rope. "If you take that end, I will get this one." She handed him the length of light hemp.

He took it and began to secure it to the mooring line.

"There," she said, "it is high enough not to catch my skirt ablaze."

If she did not slip. Too few inches lay between her standing on that makeshift ladder rung and the brazier.

"You need another step too," he pointed out. "It will still be too low for you."

"We have four mooring lines."

"Yes, but—" His stomach rolled at the thought of what he was about to say, let alone the offer or the action. He swallowed against the sourness of apprehension in his throat. "I will do it."

"You?" Her eyes widened. "You—you have no idea what to do."

"I have been repairing looms for two years. My brain wraps itself well around mechanical devices. This cannot be all that different, can it?"

"No, but you—that is, it—"

He smiled and touched his fingertip to her lips. "You are trying to spare my pride."

"Or your life."

"I would rather spare yours."

"But if you fall—" She yanked off her spectacles and scrubbed at her eyes. "I love you."

"I know." He kissed her lightly, quickly. "And you should know that I love you too."

She shoved her spectacles back on and handed him her shawl in response. "Have a care."

"I will."

If nothing else, he could not slip and fall to his death, simply to have time to persuade her that he still loved her, regardless of her scars, regardless of her lack of dowry now, regardless of any harsh words between them.

Mouth dry, heart racing, he grasped one of the mooring lines and hoisted himself onto the line they had stretched across the basket. The line dipped. The basket tilted.

"Brace a foot on either side," Cassandra commanded. "Now."

For a heartbeat, he could not move. The basket tilted more.

"Geoffrey." She laid her hand on his back.

He dared not glance back and down but knew her conformation well enough to guess that she must be standing far too close to the brazier than was safe in order to reach him. The knowledge yanked him from his paralysis and he shifted his feet.

"Step back, Cassandra," he said as calmly as he could manage. "I truly am all right now."

Her hand left him. Cold touched him where it had been. Heat flooded the rest of him, heat from the fire below and the tubing in front of him. Hot air wafted into his face. Dizziness and sickness washed through him like a draft of poison. He turned his face for cooler, fresher air, and all he saw was sea and sky—blue, green, gray, and foaming streaks of white.

Swallowing hard, he looped one arm around the mooring rope for balance and began to twist the silk shawl around and around the slit in the tubing.

"Knot it tightly," Cassandra directed him from the basket.

"It will impede airflow into the balloon but will also keep it from escaping."

The sound of her low, smooth voice soothed him, calmed him, and he completed his task. No more hot air wafted into his face. Only the cool, sweet draft from the sea.

"Come down slowly," she continued. "Hold on to the mooring lines and bring this foot first." She curved her hand around his booted ankle. "Step back toward me."

Slowly, hesitating every time the basket tilted, he lowered himself to the relative solidity of the floor. His knees demanded that he keep lowering himself until he sat, but then Cassandra wrapped her arms around him and rested her head against his back. Her trembling shuddered through him, shaking off his fear and filling him with peace.

"We are stronger together," he said.

She released him. "We will drown together if I do not get gas back into that balloon."

She now sounded as calm as he felt. More so. She sounded brisk and efficient. Her action proved the truth of her tone. She slipped past him and began to feed the fire. Within moments, the balloon began to lose its crumpled appearance. The sea retreated, flattened with distance. The sky grew broader, more vast.

"Are we not high enough?" Whittaker asked.

"I hope we can catch a current leading back toward land. We are not all that far out."

Whittaker dared to look. She was right. The line of the shore seemed to grow closer at an amazing speed. "Will we set down once we are over land?"

"Yes, if the terrain is flat and we need not fear landing on top of a village." She turned toward him. "I have the sails on the sides, but they have proven to be inadequate for direction so far. I was going to experiment today, but this happened." She gestured to the makeshift patch on the tubing. "It will not hold for long, so I will set you down on terra firma as soon as possible."

He smiled down at her. "Will you still love me on terra firma?"

"I only said that to encourage you." She turned her face away. "I may have realized that I brought my own disasters upon myself, and it does not change the fact that they happened."

"Or my mother's illicit behavior."

"Do you think I care about that?"

"Do you think I care about your scars?"

"I know your mother and her goodness, her faith. You have not seen my scars."

Nor could he outside the bounds of matrimony.

"And someone still wants me dead and is willing to hurt you in the bargain." He looked at the approaching land, at Cassandra, at the sea. He listened to the quiet, the peace of floating through the firmament, and released his grip on the side of the basket so he could cup her face in his hands. "If nothing has changed between us once we reach the ground, I think I want to stay up here all day."

"Geoff—Whittaker, we—"

He kissed her. "I prefer Geoffrey. Not the usual address for an earl but what you called me when we were friends."

"We cannot be friends. You must marry—"

He kissed her again, longer, more insistently. She clung to him for a moment, then drew away. "Who wants to kill you, my lord?"

The question, coupled with the most formal of addresses, knocked him back to earth despite being a mile above it. He grasped the sides of the balloon's car and stared at the colorful ball of silk overhead, shining in the morning sunlight like a day-time moon. "I have spent the last six weeks trying to persuade the Luddites that breaking up looms is hurting them more than the owners. But I have no solutions as to how to fix the problem of low wages, nor any way to stop the mechanization that is putting many of them out of work, except perhaps if they emigrate to America, though they cannot do that now with this war on.

"So they continue to riot and destroy, and my job is to inform one man about the Luddites' plans for attack on mills and other loom locations. He is also the one man who knew about your balloon flight thwarting an attempt on my life the other morning. When one of the rebels said he was going to stop the balloon from going up this morning so no one in it could identify any of the rioters if it sailed over the next target, I knew who wants me dead."

"Major Crawford." Cassandra said the name with the same surety Whittaker felt about the answer himself.

He nodded. "I knew it would not be you and doubted Sorrells capable of anything that would harm you."

"No, he is too enamored with my aeronautic skills. But the major could not have known I was going up, and certainly not you."

"Of course he knew you were going up. You were quite openly enthusiastic yesterday afternoon."

"Oh." She pressed her hand to her lips. "Then why did that man give himself away? But of course. We were supposed to be dead. Or I was."

"And me too, but the man who was supposed to kill me, Jimmy, was in truth working for your father to watch out for me."

Cassandra started. "My father?"

"He wanted my help with the rebels, but not me dead."

"And this Jimmy?" Cassandra glanced up, then down.

Whittaker stared straight ahead. "I am hopeful your father will pay him, and he—Jimmy—will get his family away from here. I only told the soldiers about Rob and Hugh. And Crawford. But the soldiers were disinclined to believe that of a fellow officer."

"I am afraid," Cassandra said slowly, "they may have to." She turned toward the brazier, lifted a jug of water, and doused the coals.

Steam billowed around them. Air began to hiss from the balloon. The car sank through the air with the glide of a bird riding the currents, currents that began pushing them toward the sea the lower they dropped.

"Open the sail on the left," she directed, her voice too tight. Too even. "It will slow our outward progress, if nothing else."

Whittaker did as she bade, working the parasol-type contraption on the seaward side.

It did indeed slow their seaward progress. For a moment, they hovered, suspended in space, then the makeshift repair on the tubing came loose. Her shawl fluttered to the earth, and they began to descend with too much speed.

"Open the other sail," Cassandra barked. "Now."

Whittaker did so. With a jolt, their downward progress slowed. The ground drifted toward them, a brown and gold field like a carpet scattered with grayish-white ants running in circles, bumping into one another, scattering, then bunching up again. The ants became cat-sized, then dog-sized, and finally resolved into sheep. Their panicked baas rose in a discordant chorus.

"Hold on," Cassandra directed. "We will bounce a bit."

They bounced. The basket touched the dried grass, sprang at

316

least twenty feet into the air again, dropped. Each time, more air hissed from the balloon until the trajectory of their upward flings grew shorter and shorter. Then the balloon collapsed.

"Hold on tightly," Cassandra cried. "We are going to—"

The basket tipped over, tossing Cassandra and Whittaker onto the dirt, driving air from his lungs hard enough to stun him. Vaguely, he heard glass tinkle, knew to move because . . . because . . .

"The acid!" Whittaker scrambled to his feet.

Cassandra sprawled on the grass, wheezing and trying to push herself up with her hands. Whittaker caught her around the waist and hoisted her over his shoulder seconds before the vitriol from the broken beaker pooled and smoked where she had been lying.

"And you wonder why I think this is too dangerous." He turned so she could see what had happened.

She pushed against him. "I would be all right if your friends had not wanted to stop anyone from observing their violence."

"They are not my friends. I would not be involved if your father had not been complicit in forcing me into this to spare my mother's reputation and family honor."

"Your mother is the godliest woman I know. If people cannot believe in salvation from past sins after meeting her, even knowing the truth, then they are no one worth knowing." She pushed against him. "Now let me down."

He set her feet on the ground but kept his arms around her. Her glasses had fallen off somewhere, and her eyes were wide and dark, her lips parted and trembling.

"You just accused my father of being in collusion with a—a traitor." Tears hovered on her lashes, then spilled down her cheeks. "And I fear my balloon is ruined. And—"

"Shh." He brushed the tears off her cheeks with his fingertips. "I think your father has been duped by someone with an impeccable military record and good family. And as for your balloon being ruined—"

She sniffed. "You think it is just as well."

"I want you safe and whole, is all." Even before the words left his lips, he knew they were the last thing he should say. "I mean, Cassandra—"

She pulled away from him and turned away. "I hear horses. My friends are likely coming." She shot him a glare. "They accidentally saw my scars and did not mind in the least."

"Cassandra, I do not care—"

The riders were upon them, three of them, but not Kent, Sorrells, and another person. Miss Honore, Miss Irving, and Major Crawford perched atop their mounts.

And the latter two held pistols.

29

"We saw the balloon coming down." Honore spoke in a rush, her words tumbling over one another in her haste. "Miss Irving and Major Crawford suggested we ride this way and see if it was you. And see, it is." She let out a high, hysterical laugh.

"Is something wrong, Honore?" Cassandra squinted at her sister, wishing her spectacles did not lie back in the wreckage of the balloon. "You know I can scarcely see half a dozen feet in front of my face without my spectacles. It is one reason why I am not very good at—"

Whittaker's hand clamped hard on her wrist, halting her words, as he murmured, "Crawford and Miss Irving have pistols." Aloud, he asked, "How may we assist you?" In contrast to Honore, his voice was calm, his face relaxed and void of emotion.

"Pistols?" Cassandra wanted to join her sister in hysterical giggles. "And you thought me being up in a balloon was dangerous."

"We have come to take you home, of course," Miss Irving said.

"Miss Honore wishes to go home now, and I do believe Lady Whittaker is expecting us," the major added. "I left her bound and gagged in her bedchamber."

"You would not dare." Only an infinitesimal tightening of his hand on Cassandra's wrist shouted of his reaction to the news of his mother. "I know we have less staff than is usual, and someone will find her."

"She has given orders not to be disturbed," Major Crawford said, "and all the bellpulls have been cut." His voice hardened. "Again. Yours should have stayed that way, Miss Bainbridge. Who would think that a lordling and his groom could make repairs?"

"Why?" Cassandra glanced toward the balloon car behind her, trying to catch the glint of metal and glass that might signify her spectacles. Plenty of glass sparkled in the sunlight—the wax-coated glass from the vitriol beaker.

"To make you uncomfortable." Miss Irving sounded bored. Her horse shifted. "May we be on our way? We must not keep the horses standing."

"Especially not with the sheep so distressed." Whittaker's tone matched hers. "They did not think much of our descent into their midst. But then, neither did I."

"I th-think it would have made me ill t-to bounce like that," Honore stammered. "Indeed, I feel quite ill now."

"Cast up your accounts elsewhere, my dear," Miss Irving said. "Lord Whittaker, do come take my reins. You shall lead my horse back to the Hall, as I will be holding the pistol on Miss Honore."

"And you, Miss Bainbridge," the major added, "shall ride with your sister so I can manage you both."

"I think not," Cassandra said. Whittaker's hand on her arm proved a steadying force, like ballast keeping a balloon car stable in changing wind currents. The calmness of his voice helped too. She matched his tone. "Of course, if you truly intended to make me uncomfortable here, forcing me atop a horse right now, especially pillion, would certainly be successful. Though I cannot imagine why you would wish to make me uncomfortable here."

"Because you are here." Miss Irving moved her horse two steps closer, close enough for Cassandra to see the gleam of sunlight on the barrel of her pistol. "You were supposed to be in London still recovering from those burns."

"Or dead," Major Crawford added.

"Dead?" she repeated. Whittaker removed his hand from Cassandra's arm and her body went cold. "Why would you want me dead?"

Honore let out one of her high-pitched giggles, and the sheep baaed in protest. "Is that not rich? I thought he should court Regina to make you jealous, and she—she—" Her voice broke on a sob.

Cassandra took a step toward her. Her right ankle screamed in a protest of pain, and she sank to her knees.

"Get up," Major Crawford commanded.

"I cannot." Shooting pain up her right leg was making her ill.

"Then help her, my lord," Miss Irving suggested, a sneer to her voice. "Since she is so precious to you."

Whittaker did not move. "That is hardly the truth of it, is it, Crawford? Miss Irving is too beautiful and rich to resort to killing off her rivals. Not," he added, "that she was ever a contender for my countess."

Miss Irving emitted a throaty noise like a growl. "I would be if—"

"Stubble it, Reggie." Major Crawford remained as even-tempered as Whittaker.

Cassandra wanted to set up a chorus of shrieks to release

the tension building inside her. But with a flock of sheep not a hundred feet away and already distraught, she had no idea what might happen. Did sheep stampede? They were not all that large, and yet enough of them could knock her flat, trample her with their little hooves.

She grabbed Whittaker's arm and hauled herself to her feet.

"Of course Regina's desire to be a countess is not the reason Miss Bainbridge cannot survive this day either," Major Crawford was saying. "You would have to stay alive for her to wed you. And although I am happy to grant my niece a number of favors, keeping you alive is not one of them."

Honore shrieked, and her horse shied.

Cassandra swallowed her own gasp of horror and tried to judge where everyone sat or stood, tried to think, to plan.

If sheep did stampede . . .

"You would have given in to Whittaker's pursuit," Miss Irving declared. "But it was hopeless. I saw how that wind blew straightaway. Even scarring you for life, Miss Bainbridge, has not kept Whittaker away from you."

"Even scarring me for—" Cassandra's breath strangled in her throat.

"The assault on my carriage and fire were no accident." If he grew any more tense, Whittaker would snap like an overwound watch spring. "I guessed as much after everything that has happened since."

"An accident would have been so much more convenient." The major's saddle leather creaked. "Then her ladyship could be found dead by her own hand, such a sad tale of her losing her sons so young." His voice hardened, roughened. "Nothing more than she deserves after what she did to my half brother."

"I do not understand all this," Honore sobbed. "Cassandra,

explain. They will not even tell me why she has a different surname, let alone why they hate you all so."

"Not now." Cassandra took a long, slow breath to keep herself calm.

Beside her, Whittaker did not move so much as a muscle.

"I see you guessed," Major Crawford said.

"I guessed." Whittaker grabbed Cassandra's arm and flung her aside. "Go!"

She landed on her right leg again and screamed, but she went—straight for the sheep. A pistol blasted. Honore shrieked and kept shrieking, and the sheep began to run right, left, straight, alongside Cassandra. Sobbing with the agony in her ankle, she grasped a woolly neck and held on to this unlikely guide as they charged through the sea of baaing, stinking mutton.

Another pistol blasted. Someone cried out. An inhuman wail. Not Honore. Not Whittaker.

"Please, God, not one of them. Pl—" She smacked into a fence.

Hooves thundered around her, behind her, in front of her. She clung to the fence, gasping, certain she had lost her reason.

"I say, Miss Bainbridge," Roger Kent said, "what are you doing in this pasture?"

"Help them." Cassandra waved behind her. "Irving . . . Crawford . . . Kill . . ." Her knees buckled.

Kent and Sorrells galloped off. Ne'er-do-wells though many might think them, neither was a slow-top. Country born and bred, both would be traveling with at least a horse pistol in their saddles. They would help.

If it was not too late.

Slowly, dragging her right leg to keep as much weight off it as possible, Cassandra made her way back to the sheep. After a decade of cursing the need for spectacles, she longed for them now. She could see no faces from across the pasture, did not know friend from foe, and could not hear voices over the sheep's vibrato calls. Neither could she remain where she was out of harm's way.

Pushing woolly bodies aside, she made her way closer to the far end of the pasture. The splash of color from the balloon's silk shone against the brown grass like a jewel. Beyond it, the motion had ceased, grown silent save for sobbing.

"Honore?" she called.

"Here I am." She flung herself against Cassandra and clung, shaking but not sobbing.

Yet the weeping continued. Miss Irving crying softly yet harshly.

"Her uncle is dead," Honore said. "Whittaker—I am going to be sick." She stumbled away.

"Not on the balloon!" Mr. Kent cried. "Females."

Ignoring the last remark, Cassandra left Honore to him and found Mr. Sorrells and Whittaker standing over two figures on the grass.

Whittaker wrapped his arm around her waist and drew her near. "My clever, clever lady. Who else would think of using sheep to take down a murderer?"

"Is he . . . dead?" Cassandra asked.

"Yes," Whittaker responded. "We . . . struggled for his second pistol. It is a dueling pistol, not a cavalry pistol. Hair trigger . . ." He shuddered. "It should not have happened."

"It could have been you," Cassandra whispered.

"I'll ride for the constable," Mr. Sorrells offered. "And the coroner."

"I have to stay here." Whittaker tightened his hold on

Cassandra. "Kent can take you home. Tell Mama—Mama, how could I forget? Sorrells, will you go home with them and—and ensure she is all right? You have more sense than Kent."

"Of course, but don't you want to go?"

"I cannot." Whittaker glanced at the major and shuddered. "The constable and coroner will want to question me."

"And me," Miss Irving said between gulps for air. "I will tell them how he was murdered."

"And they will believe a peer of the realm before a—" Cassandra bit her tongue. "You."

"The circumstances speak for themselves," Whittaker said. "I will come home as soon as I can, but send for me immediately if Mama—if she needs help." He pressed his cheek to hers for a moment. "I am sorry."

"For what?" she asked, but he was already focused on Miss Irving, drawing her away from the major's body.

"Come with me, Miss Bainbridge." Mr. Sorrells held out his arm. "I think we can get you onto a horse without too much discomfort."

"My discomfort does not matter. I wish to stay."

But of course she could not. Someone needed to free Lady Whittaker. Honore was weeping now too, and Lady Whittaker needed to know what had happened. And if Cassandra stood on her right foot any longer, she feared she would faint.

"Just a sprain," she said aloud. "It will heal in a few days."

"I'll carry you." Before she could protest, Mr. Sorrells picked her up and carried her to one of the horses.

He was such a good man, a kind man, that she wished she could have loved him. But she felt nothing despite the intimacy of their contact. Surely that was not right between a husband and wife either. And what did they share beyond their aeronautic interests? Nothing came to mind. Unlike her friendship with Whittaker, based on their love of learning, classical literature, engineering, the faith they had once made an integral part of their lives—until they let the passion between them rule.

He was so calm now, so passionless, talking to Miss Irving, the words too quiet for Cassandra to catch, the tone of gentle kindness pouring across the meadow like sunshine. Yet it touched Cassandra, warmed her from twenty feet away.

"Can you lift me up?" she asked Mr. Sorrells. "I doubt I can manage a sidesaddle."

"You can ride pillion behind Miss Honore. It won't be comfortable, but the ride isn't long."

It was not. In less than a quarter hour, they trotted the horses up the drive of Whittaker Hall. Cassandra slid to the ground the instant Honore reined in, remembering to land on her left foot. Without waiting for Mr. Kent's arm to aid her, she limped toward the front door.

It burst open and Lady Whittaker flew out. For the first time since they had arrived at the Hall, her ladyship's hair was unkempt, her gown torn, and her countenance less than serene. She wrapped her arms around Cassandra and squeezed. "Thank God you are all right. And my son. Please tell me Geoffrey is well."

"As well as he can be." Cassandra blinked back a sudden rush of tears. "The major is dead."

"It was simply awful," Honore wailed, then sprang up the steps and wrapped one arm around Cassandra and the other around Lady Whittaker.

For several moments, while the groom led away the horses and a handful of servants watched from the doorway, the three ladies clung to one another. Finally Lady Whittaker drew back, dashed her sleeve across her eyes, and tucked her arm through

Cassandra's. "You look terrible, and I will not apologize for saying so. What have you done to yourself this time?"

"Wrecked my balloon, probably took a year's growth of life off a flock of sheep, and consequently helped save several lives."

"You are not amusing!" Honore cried. "I have made a fool of myself over a man."

"We all have, my child." Lady Whittaker reached out and drew Honore to her. "One learns better for the next time."

"I do not seem to." Honore began hiccupping with the force of her sobs and ran toward her room.

"I forgot about the incident last spring," Lady Whittaker said. "Poor child. But what about you? You are favoring your right foot. It is not your wound again, is it?"

"No, a sprain, I think. Cold cloths to wrap it in and warm water for washing will set me to rights."

"And hot tea." Lady Whittaker glanced at the servants. "Hot water and tea for both ladies, cold cloths for Miss Bainbridge, and the lavender drops for Miss Honore."

The maids curtsied and nodded and scampered for the rear of the house.

"Come to your room, child," Lady Whittaker said and led the way.

"May I ask how you got free? I mean, if you do not wish to discuss it, I understand, but the major said—"

"He left me tied up and gagged? Yes, he did, the blackguard. And the language he used. My ears are still burning." Though her tone was light, the hand she raised to her ear shook. "He wanted me to watch him kill my son. But my servants grew suspicious and came to see if I was all right when they heard nothing from me for more than two hours. He must have thought he would be back sooner."

"He never doubted he would be back." Cassandra covered her face with her hands. "And now poor Geoffrey has had to—to—" She gulped down her desire to wail and continued to her room. "Who was Miss Irving? Do you know? Is she not a cousin of Laurence and William's?"

"Yes, she is their cousin through the marriage of her mother to their mother's brother. A second marriage for Regina's mother. Ralph Irving. Regina took his name. The Irvings, the Crawfords, the Gileses—we were all friends once." Her voice grew quieter and quieter as she gave the explanation.

"I am sorry." Cassandra stumbled into her bedchamber and over to the chaise. "You need not talk about this."

"Yes, I must." Lady Whittaker bowed her head and clasped her hands before her as though she were praying. "You all deserve an explanation considering how you suffered because of me."

30

Whittaker reached home three hours later. The sun was beginning to set and the Hall was dark save for lights in either wing. Scarcely able to place one foot in front of the other, he climbed straight to his chamber and found Mama waiting for him. She said nothing but clasped his hands and stared at him as though needing to memorize his features.

"I am all right." He freed himself. "If anyone can be after seeing a man die that way." He shoved his fingers through his hair. "And having a constable, a coroner, and a magistrate question me for hours."

"Surely they do not think you—Honore and Cassandra have told me . . . what happened." She looked away. "I gave them no explanations. I will now that you are home. You and Cassandra. Honore was so distraught I gave her a small dose of laudanum, and she is sleeping now. But Cassandra—"

"She is well? She was limping badly."

"A sprain, nothing more. It will heal in days, but I am concerned about her soul and her heart. They are badly bruised."

"I cannot heal either for her. I have tried to protect her and failed."

"You have not failed, my son. She is home safely, is she not?"

"Yes, thank the Lord for that." He managed a smile that quickly faded. He rested his hand on Mama's shoulder. "And you? You are safe? He did not hurt you overmuch?"

"No, bruises, that is all."

Whittaker studied her for a moment, his lovely, gentle mother, who had brought him up to love and trust in God and showed it in her deeds and speech every day. Other than a mark on one cheek that would heal without a trace and redness around her wrists, she looked the same as ever—each hair in place, her gown without a wrinkle, her countenance serene. Despite what he had known for weeks, he still could not believe the truth of it.

"Where is Regina Irving?" Mama asked.

"Regina Crawford Irving—that is her true name, is it not? She is in the village gaol. There will be an inquest on the major tomorrow."

"No trouble for you, I trust?"

"No, except—" He sighed. "They want to know why a respected military officer and beautiful heiress would hate us so. I am afraid . . . in part, he is going to win even in his death and your reputation will be destroyed. I have been trying to protect it for six weeks and failed at that too."

Mama paled. "You know?"

"It is how Crawford blackmailed me into getting myself involved with the rebels again. He threatened to expose your . . . indiscretion. It was how he could hopefully manage my death and have it not attached to him at all."

"Why did you not tell me? Oh, Geoffrey." Mama covered her face with her hands. "I knew something was wrong with your comings and goings and your hair all shaggy and you refusing to cut it. But I never guessed . . ." Her shoulders shook. "You should have told me. I would have stood in the pulpit at church and confessed to the world rather than have you endanger your life. You are far more important to me than a past that has long since been forgiven."

"I was protecting your reputation, your standing in the county. The government is desperate to bring these rioters down, and—"

Mama grasped his shoulders and shook him. "My dear boy, you cannot protect the world from itself. Everyone chooses his own path and whether or not he allows the Lord to direct him."

"I realize that now." He felt like he was in the plummeting balloon. "I tried to stop Cassandra from flying today and nearly got her killed. I tried to stop Crawford, and he was killed. Cassandra and I tried to protect ourselves from—" He looked away.

Mama released him. "Would you like some time to rest? You look worn to a thread."

"I would like to change my clothes and talk to you some more. And Cassandra, if she will."

"I will have hot water sent up to you at once. Come down to Cassandra's room when you are ready. I will have some food for you there. We will talk then."

"I am not hungry."

But the thought of seeing Cassandra left him hollow with the need to see for himself that she was not permanently harmed, that she did not wish to pack her bags and be rid of the Giles family forever.

"You will eat," Mama said, then left him.

As he washed and changed into clothes not splattered in mud and Major Crawford's blood, Whittaker thought of a hundred things he could say to Cassandra. None seemed appropriate.

What would the Lord have?

Mama had said that everyone chose whether or not to let God direct his path. Whittaker had done so, then rebelled when God took him on a journey he did not like. Yet eventually, a small part of the world would be better off for him owning the mills, now that he had been inside the gang of the few Luddites remaining and understood how they thought and what they needed. For all he mourned the waste of his brother's life and the passing of the earldom to himself, the younger son, the tenant farmers had suffered under John's management. Or mismanagement, to be more accurate. And Cassandra?

He paused with his hand on the door latch and bowed his head. "Lord, I cannot change her heart or heal her from what she has suffered. I can't change the past, but I can let You direct my future."

Knowing he could very well end up with a future without the lady he loved, he descended to the great hall and crossed to Cassandra's wing.

She and Mama sat in the Bainbridge daughters' sitting room with a fire blazing and enough candles burning to light the great hall. Cassandra's feet rested on another chair, and she clutched a cup of tea as though it kept her anchored.

She glanced up at his entrance and offered him a tentative smile. "After a decade of hating to wear them, I now wish I had not lost my spectacles. Father said I had to pay for them myself if I lost or broke another pair, and that is going to limit my ability to use my pin money to pay for repairs on the balloon."

"You truly want to go up again after today?" He moved to her side and gazed down at her. "You are either brave or stupid, and I know the latter is untrue."

"Where would England be if Mr. Columbus had not dared cross the Atlantic? Was he brave or stupid?"

"I think he was greedy."

"Perhaps I am too," she said.

He knew he was—greedy for more of her smile, her time, her life.

But Mama sat waiting with a steaming teapot poised.

"Do sit down, Geoffrey." She poured the tea, added a drop of milk as he liked it, and held up the cup. "Mr. Kent and Mr. Sorrells have already arranged to bring the balloon back here. It is now in the shearing shed until the silk is cleaned and resealed and the tubing replaced. And yes, Cassandra told me how you climbed onto that rope to save yourselves." The cup rattled on its saucer. "That was brave of you."

"I am not a good swimmer." He took the cup, and with the only other seat a settee across the room, he settled on the hearth beside Cassandra's chair. "Are you well, my dear? Your ankle does not pain you overmuch?"

"Geoffrey, you should not speak of a lady's ankles," Mama scolded.

"I am well enough." Cassandra looked over his head.

Silence fell save for the hiss of the coals on the fire and the clink of china cups against their saucers.

Then Mama drew in her breath with the faintest of shudders. "When Geoffrey wrote me that he had met you and adored you at once, Cassandra, I encouraged him to court you. I did not think a Bainbridge would have a large dowry, though the money would have been good, but I did not want him to think he should marry for anything less than what he wanted so long as she was a lady who loved the Lord. Many people believe love matches are ruining England's best families, but I think it is more the other way around, as my own marriage was not a love match." She grimaced. "It was not even a liking match. We scarcely knew one another, but Rupert Giles, the seventh earl of Whittaker, needed money, and my brother had a great deal of it he was willing to spend to elevate me from the middle class into the nobility."

"You agreed to the match, though." Whittaker feared he sounded accusatory, but Mama simply nodded.

"I agreed. I was seventeen and did not care for the suitors I had—other mill owners, most of whom were more than twice my age. And your father was handsome and young. But he disliked me on sight and left for the continent soon after our wedding."

"So strange that he seemed to like you when I was growing up," Whittaker said.

"He did. After you were born, things changed between us. But I am getting ahead of myself." Mama set her cup aside and picked up a book. She thumbed the pages without looking at it as she continued. "As I said, he went to the continent soon after we were wed. He sent me to stay with your grandmother and his younger brother. Your uncle had two friends, Ralph Irving and Lucian Crawford. I was forever in their company, and—and Lucian and I became too close."

She closed the book, set it aside, and folded her hands in her lap. She lifted her head, but her gaze was fixed somewhere far beyond Whittaker and Cassandra. "When—when I knew I was *enceinte*, I wrote your father and confessed. I had some notion that Lucian and I would run off to America together, but he ran off and married the first female who would accept his proposal."

"Aunt Giles's younger sister?" Whittaker asked.

"Yes." Mama sighed. "But they had no children for many years until Regina came along. Lucian . . . died shortly after that, and his wife married Mr. Irving, who was happy to give his stepdaughter his name and, apparently, his fortune."

"But how could Mr. Crawford marry someone else so

quickly?" Cassandra pressed a hand to her cheek. "I suppose I am being indelicate to ask, but you were his love and all."

Mama gave Cassandra a sad smile. "It is all indelicate and wrong, yes, but forgiven if not forgotten. As to why Lucian married so quickly, I believe he feared your father would challenge him to a duel, but Rupert did not care enough for me for that. He wrote that he would accept the child as his and pray it was a girl."

"But it was a boy—his heir if he did not denounce you," Whittaker concluded.

"It was a boy." Mama gripped the arms of her chair. "Your father came home and we tried to find something to like about one another. I went to the vicar for advice, and he told me something I knew but had not really applied to myself—how no sin is too great for the Lord to forgive if repented of. I was certainly repentant and turned my heart over to the Lord. Your father never did, unless it was at the end, when the wasting sickness made speaking too difficult for him to say one way or the other, but he must have seen the change in me. I like to think I became less selfish, more giving of love without receiving it. He never said. He simply started treating me as a wife, and you came along, Whittaker.

"I cannot say we ever loved one another, but we did form a friendship of sorts, and everything went well for several years until, quite by accident, we encountered Lucian while we were in Bath seeking a cure for your father's illness. He never said a word." Tears began to trickle down her cheeks. "He simply looked at John, then you, and walked away. I learned later—" She drew out her handkerchief and wiped at her eyes. "I learned later that he rode to Bristol that night and signed aboard a ship bound for America."

"Madness," Whittaker murmured.

"Grief." Cassandra was silently weeping herself.

Whittaker reached up and took her hand in his. "He must have died if Miss Irving's mother married again."

"The ship went down in a storm before it was in the Atlantic." Mama blinked hard. "We will never know what drove him to do something so irresponsible as to leave his wife and daughter behind like that."

"Grief," Cassandra said again.

"Yes, grief." Mama crushed her handkerchief in her hand. "It might have destroyed me too, if I did not have the strength of knowing that God no longer condemned my behavior. Never did I guess that all these years later Lucian's younger half brother would try to steal my son from me. Can the two of you ever forgive me?"

Whittaker and Cassandra leaned toward her, their hands outstretched.

"If God has, how can we do less?" Whittaker said.

"You are not to blame for their actions," Cassandra added.

"There are those who will blame me." Mama clasped their hands in hers. "But if neither of you do, I am well." She stood and gazed down at them. "And if you can forgive me for being the cause of you two nearly dying, it is time you forgive yourselves for your past."

Whittaker's ears felt hot, and Cassandra's face turned the same delicate pink as her gown.

Mama smiled. "Yes, I know about you two. Lord Bainbridge told me when he last wrote." She strode to the door. "He warned me never to let the two of you be alone together, but I think that is precisely what you need right now. I will be across the hall in the library." She opened the door. "What I

336

did, breaking my marriage vows, was terribly wrong. A hundred years ago or so, I would have been executed for it if my husband chose. But never think there is anything wrong with your passion for one another in the right bounds." She smiled. "Like marriage."

The door clicked shut behind her.

Neither of them moved. Neither of them spoke. They did not look at one another. Then the coals shifted on the hearth and they jumped.

"Cassandra."

"Geoffrey."

They looked at one another then and laughed, though there was an edge to the sound.

"Ladies first." Whittaker knelt in front of her chair. "Can you forgive me for how I behaved toward you?"

"I never blamed you. I blame myself. It is all part of my rebellion against God." Her gaze wavered but she did not break eye contact. "I have done everything I knew my earthly father would not like since I was sixteen. Then, when you inherited the title and I did not wish to be a countess, I blamed God and rebelled there too."

"Are you saying—"

"No, let me finish or I may forget something." She rested her hand on the arm of the chair a fraction of an inch from his. "Even my ballooning was a rebellion. Yes, aeronautics fascinates me, but I knew you and Father and everyone would disapprove. You and Father would hate an alliance between me and Mr. Sorrells too."

"And so would you. He's a fine man, but you—well, I should not say so."

"I feel nothing for him, no. You are right." She touched his hand. "But in the balloon today, when you were repairing the tubing, I realized how my rebellion hurt you—and me."

"And us together." He leaned forward and kissed her. At the brief contact of their lips, Guy Fawkes fireworks exploded inside him, and he drew back. "Are you going to keep rebelling and tell me you do not still love me?"

"You know I love you."

"Then you will marry me?"

"I—" She sank her teeth into her lower lip.

Footfalls pattered down the corridor, and someone knocked on the door across the passage. "You have a caller, milady."

Whittaker groaned. "Not now."

"You had best go," Cassandra said.

"I think not." He clasped her hand between both of his. "Cassandra, we have both been wrong in our actions. But God has forgiven us, and surely you cannot continue to believe He wants us apart because of them."

"No, not because of that, because—you cannot wish to wed someone who looks like I do."

"I think you are beautiful. I always have."

"No." She gave her head a vigorous shake. "I do not mean my face. I mean my—my scars. You do not want that when you—if we—in a wife."

"I do if they are part of you."

"You do not know how bad they are. Honore was sick the first time she saw them."

"Honore is sick far too often."

"Well, true." Cassandra gave him a half-smile. "But even Lydia was sickened."

"I promise not to be sick or turn pale when I have the privilege of seeing your . . . um . . . them."

"This is not amusing." Her eyes grew suspiciously bright. "You turned pale when I simply told you how bad they are."

"If so, it was guilt, not the idea of how they look." He raised her hand to his cheek. "But we were not responsible for that fire. Crawford was."

"Yes, but it does not change the consequences. They will forever remind you of him."

"They will forever remind me of God's saving grace."

"Well, perhaps." She blinked and a tear slid down her cheek.

He caught it on his fingertip. "Cassandra, how can you think I would mind your scars when you do not in the least mind my mother's past?"

"But her past brought her to her knees before the Lord."

"And your scars have brought us both to our knees before Him. Cassandra, I love you with all your imperfections."

"I cannot risk you being repulsed after we have spoken vows."

"Then—" No, he could not. He would not even suggest such a thing now.

But, as had so often happened between them, she knew what he was thinking, for she freed her hand from his and grasped her skirt. "Now tell me you do not want to run from this." And she yanked her skirt and petticoats up above her knees.

His throat closed. His eyes burned. What pain she must have suffered, his strong, brave, and stubborn lady. The scars marred her pretty skin, but he knew of but one way to convince her he was not repulsed.

He bowed his head and kissed the scar on her right knee. Then he raised his head and smiled at her. "Cassandra Bainbridge, I still want to marry you."

"I should say so," her father said from the doorway.

Cassandra gasped and shoved her skirt down.

339

Whittaker stood and rested his hand on her shoulder, facing Lord Bainbridge and his mother in the doorway. "I never stopped wanting to marry her, my lord."

"And now I can scarcely say no." Bainbridge strode into the room and glowered down at Cassandra. "I thought we raised you better than to behave like this."

"You would not buy a horse without inspecting it first, would you, Father?" Her gaze clashed with her father's.

Whittaker squeezed her shoulder, a gentle reminder to be respectful.

She smiled. "But of course I could not marry him without your blessing even if I am one and twenty."

Bainbridge cleared his throat. "I appreciate you honoring me that much. I thought the only way to get you to wed the boy was to forbid it."

"Get me to . . . forbid . . ." Cassandra spluttered to a halt, then took a breath. "I am sorry I have been that poor a daughter."

"Just make a better wife." Bainbridge touched her cheek. "He is blessed to have you."

"I am," Whittaker agreed. "Thank you for helping to mold her into the lady she is."

"Yes, ahem, well—" Bainbridge coughed. "I think she has done well for herself. Unlike her elder sister, who did not get it right until the second time."

"I think I will never get it right." Hair hanging in a golden shawl around her shoulders, Honore stumbled into the sitting room, rubbing her eyes. "Papa, I made a fool of myself again. I am hopeless."

Bainbridge's face softened. "No, child, you are not hopeless. You will learn."

"I think not." She shook her head. "I want you to choose my husband for me."

"No, you do not," Mama said.

"I am happy to," Bainbridge said. "We have a new neighbor in Devon I have taken a liking to."

"Truly?" Honore's eyes grew bright. "Is he young? Is he handsome?"

"You will meet him when we all go home for Christmas," Bainbridge said.

"About Christmas," Whittaker interjected before he lost Bainbridge's attention. "I would like us to wed before Advent and not have to wait until after Epiphany. That is less than three weeks away."

Bainbridge arched his brows. "You expect to wait that long? I was thinking how close the Scottish border is. You could be wed at Gretna Green tomorrow if you are willing."

Whittaker stared at him. The man was serious.

"I think Cassandra deserves better than an elopement," Whittaker said.

"I already have better." Cassandra reached up and covered his hand where it rested on her shoulder. "Gretna Green sounds perfect."

"And here I thought I would be the one to elope one day," Honore said.

Acknowledgments

In no way can a few words here express my thanks to all of the people who assisted me in getting through this novel—the cyber hugs, prayers, and phone calls encouraging me while my life felt like chaos. Gina, Patty, Debbie Lynne, Carrie—you're my four musketeers. Thanks to Deb Kinnard too, for making me stick to my daily word count.

Since the Regency is such a special time period with details and mores that readers expect the author to get right, I cannot leave out those who helped me with everything from geography, to research materials regarding the Luddite rebellion, to just the right phrase to sound authentic, especially Nancy Mayer and Jo Ann Ferguson.

And a special thanks to the ladies in the ACFW historical writers group, who described how riding in a balloon feels, as I could never work a trip of my own into my schedule. I will, though.

Google Books—the public domain books—have been an invaluable resource for this era, from the medical controversy over how to treat burns, to the discussion of formulas for keeping air from seeping out of balloons, to the description of the air tube coming out of a balloon and the aeronaut having to fix it in flight. Of course, similar things must happen to my heroine.

Thank you to my agent, Tamela Hancock Murray of the Steve Laube Agency, for not letting me give up on writing a Christian Regency romance.

Last, and never least, thank you to my patient, thorough, and all-around wonderful editors at Revell. Vicki and Jessica, you challenge me to keep improving as a writer.

Laurie Alice Eakes used to lie in bed as a child telling herself stories so she didn't wake anyone else up. Sometimes she shared her stories with others, so when she decided to be a writer, she surprised no one. *Family Guardian*, her first book, won the National Readers Choice Award for Best Regency in 2007.

In the past three years, she has sold six books to Revell, five of which are set during the Regency time period; five books to Barbour Publishing; and two novellas to Barbour Publishing and one to Revell. Seven of her books have been picked up by Thorndike Press for large-print publication, and *Lady in the Mist*, her first book with Revell, was chosen for hardcover publication by Crossings Book Club.

Laurie Alice teaches online writing courses and enjoys a speaking ministry that takes her from the Gulf Coast to the East Coast. She lives in Texas with her husband, two dogs, and two cats and is learning how to make tamales.

Meet *Laurie Alice Eakes* at

www.LaurieAliceEakes.com

• • •

Laurie Alice Eakes

LaurieAEakes

"An adventure that will leave readers breathless."

—Louise M. Gouge, award-winning author of
At the Captain's Command

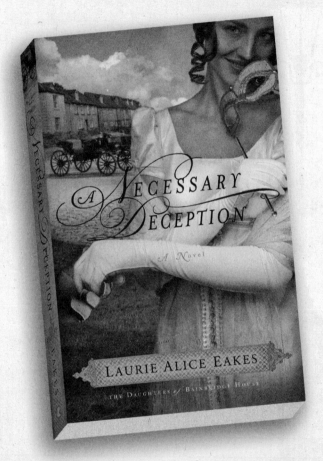

Laurie Alice Eakes whisks readers through the drawing rooms of London amid the sound of rustling gowns on this exciting quest to let the past stay in the past and let love guide the future.

 Revell
a division of Baker Publishing Group
www.RevellBooks.com

Available Wherever Books Are Sold
Also Available in Ebook Format

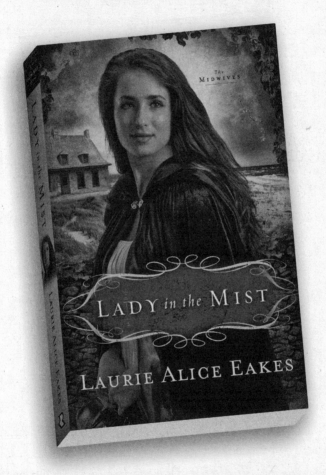

"Make room for this one on your 'keepers' shelf!"

—Loree Lough, author of *From Ashes to Honor*

Heart's Safe Passage is a stirring tale of love, intrigue, and adventure on the high seas. Readers will feel the salt spray and the rolling waves as they journey with Laurie Alice Eakes's vivid characters on the treacherous path toward redemption.